**AL... ...AGO.
MY HUSBAND, THE EARL OF DAVENPORT,
RECEIVED WORD OF HIS DEMISE
FROM AN AGENT IN HIS EMPLOY."**

The towering man lifted his hands as if to say, *Yet here I am*.

Daphne studied him with the intensity of a horologist examining a rare timepiece. He bore her examination without blinking, exhibiting none of the nervousness one would expect of an imposter claiming to be somebody he was not.

In fact, he took a step closer, allowing her to see he was older than she'd first believed—closer to forty than thirty—but no less attractive for it. Deep lines radiated from the corner of his green eye and his guinea-gold hair was heavily dusted with silver at the temples. He was currently smiling, but the determined set of his jaw showed him to be a man accustomed to having his own way, and the deep grooves bracketing his lips were evidence he enjoyed getting it.

This man was tall—remarkably so—golden, and devastatingly attractive. Not even almost two decades, brutal scarring, and the black patch over his eye could obscure the truth. He was, without a doubt, Hugh Redvers, her dead husband's true heir: a man everyone had believed dead for almost twenty years.

A man Daphne had robbed of title, lands, and fortune.

Also by Minerva Spencer

Dangerous

Published by Kensington Publishing Corporation

Barbarous

Minerva Spencer

ZEBRA BOOKS
KENSINGTON PUBLISHING CORP.
http://www.kensingtonbooks.com

ZEBRA BOOKS are published by

Kensington Publishing Corp.
119 West 40th Street
New York, NY 10018

All Kensington titles, imprints, and distributed lines are available at special quantity discounts for bulk purchases for sales promotion, premiums, fund-raising, educational, or institutional use.

Special book excerpts or customized printings can also be created to fit specific needs. For details, write or phone the office of the Kensington Sales Manager: Attn.: Sales Department. Kensington Publishing Corp., 119 West 40th Street, New York, NY 10018. Phone: 1-800-221-2647.

Zebra and the Z logo Reg. U.S. Pat. & TM Off.

First Printing: November 2018
ISBN-13: 978-1-4201-4721-6
ISBN-10: 1-4201-4721-8

eISBN-13: 978-1-4201-4724-7
eISBN-10: 1-4201-4724-2

10 9 8 7 6 5 4 3 2 1

Printed in the United States of America

For my mom, the coolest mom ever

Chapter One

Sussex, England, early 1811

Daphne's head rang louder, but less joyously, than the twelve bells of St. Paul's—perhaps head-butting Cousin Malcolm in the face had not been the best decision?

The thought had barely entered her head when agonizing pain drove it out again. Black spots danced in front of her eyes and she clutched at the rough wood of the ancient tree stump to steady herself, blinking away tears to clear her vision. When she touched her throbbing forehead, her fingers came away with blood: hers or Malcolm's or both. She looked from her bloody hand to the man across the small glade. Malcolm lay sprawled amidst the wreckage of the picnic lunch she'd been unpacking when he accosted her.

Her cousin had aged greatly in the decade since she'd last seen him. His brown hair, once thick and lustrous, had thinned and lost its shine and his bloated body was a far cry from the slim, elegant dandy who'd briefly—but disastrously—held her future in his hands. Eight years separated Daphne and the man who'd once been her legal guardian, and every one of them was etched onto his thirty-five-year-old face; a face now wreathed in pain and fury.

Malcolm scrambled into a seated position and shot her a murderous glare before tearing off his cravat and lifting it to his hemorrhaging nose.

Daphne smiled; a bloody, ringing forehead was a small price to pay for Malcolm's obvious suffering. She squinted to get a better look at his face but his puffy, bloodshot eyes shifted and blurred.

Her glasses! Daphne touched the bridge of her nose and bit back a groan; he must have knocked off her spectacles during their struggle.

Angling her body to keep Malcolm in view, she lowered herself into a crouch and began patting the shaggy grass around her feet, praying neither of them had stepped on them. The glasses were special, made with a split in the lenses to accommodate her poor vision. They were also the last gift from her husband before his death. If she lost them, it would be like losing even more of Thomas. It would be—

"Well, well, well, what have we here?" a deep voice boomed.

Daphne squawked like a startled hen and tipped forward onto her hands and knees, her eyes flickering over the surrounding foliage for the voice's owner. A shadow emerged from between two towering wych elms and shifted into the recognizable shape of a man on a horse; a huge man on an enormous horse.

His features became clearer—and more remarkable— with every step. The massive shire was at least seventeen-and-a-half hands, and the man astride it matched his mount in both size and magnificence.

Daphne knew she was gawking, but she couldn't stop. His sun-bronzed skin and golden hair were an exotic surprise against the pallid gray of the spring sky. But it was the black eye-patch that covered his left eye and the savage scar that disappeared beneath it that were truly arresting. He lacked only a battered tricorn and cutlass between his teeth to be every maiden's fantasy of a handsome pirate. Was he lost on his way to a masquerade ball?

Daphne blinked at the foolish notion and her thoughts—usually as well-regimented as Wellington's soldiers—broke and ran when the stranger looked down at her with his single green eye.

"Lady Davenport?" His appearance was exotic but he spoke like an English gentleman. "Are you quite all right, my lady?"

"Yes, but—" she began, and then noticed his attention had become stuck at the level of her chest. She looked down and gasped. Her coat was ripped open from neck to waist, exposing a mortifying amount of chemise, stays, and flesh. Daphne hastily pinched the torn garment closed with her fingers and forced herself to look up again. But the stranger had turned to Malcolm and was staring at him as if he'd forgotten all about her.

He slid gracefully from his huge horse, as if it were no bigger than a pony, and took a step toward Malcolm, raising an ornate gold quizzing glass. His dark blond eyebrows inched up his forehead as he examined the bedraggled, bleeding man.

Only the distant tweeting of birds broke the tense silence, which stretched and stretched and—

"*Ramsay?*" Malcolm's voice was muffled by the bloody cravat and he lowered the ruined garment, his mouth agape.

Daphne looked from her cousin to the stranger and squinted—as if that might sharpen her hearing as well as her vision.

Ramsay? The only Ramsay she'd ever heard of was her husband's deceased nephew and heir, Hugh Redvers—who'd held the title Baron Ramsay. She shook her head at the bizarre thought; her idiot cousin had to be wrong. Hugh Redvers was dead—long dead.

The giant ignored Malcolm's question, lines of distaste

etching his striking profile as he studied the smaller man. For his part, Malcolm raised the crumpled cravat higher and higher as he endured the silent scrutiny, until only his slitted eyes glittered above the bloody cloth.

Daphne recognized her cousin's malevolent gaze and shivered. After all, she'd been on the receiving end of that same look more often than she cared to remember when she'd been his ward. She turned to the stranger to gauge *his* reaction to her cousin's threatening stare, only to encounter a grossly magnified green eye, the color somewhere between an emerald and peridot. Daphne swallowed, suddenly able to comprehend Malcolm's mortification. This must be what an insect felt like beneath a magnifying lens. She began to shrink away but stopped; she was no insect and *he* was a trespasser. She threw back her shoulders—keeping one hand on her torn coat—and shot him a bold, if blurry, glare.

His lips curved and he lowered his vile glass, took a step forward, and extended a hand the size of a serving platter.

Daphne frowned at his huge, gloved hand; but it was either accept his help or struggle to her feet without it. She placed her hand in his and he lifted her as if she were a feather rather than a woman of five feet ten inches. He did not release her when she was standing. Instead, he bowed over her captive hand and kissed the naked skin with lips that were warm and soft. Astoundingly soft, and yet the rest of him looked so very . . . hard.

"I beg your pardon for not introducing myself right away, Lady Davenport." He nodded toward her cousin but did not take his eye from her. "Sir Malcolm has the right of it. I am Hugh Redvers, Baron Ramsay." His oh-so-soft lips curved into a smile. "Your long-lost nephew."

Daphne shook her head and blurted. "How can that be?"

His eye glinted with amusement. "Well, the earl was my father's oldest brother and the earl's first wife—my Aunt

Eloisa—died, and then the earl married *you*, which would make—"

He was *mocking* her. She drew herself up to her full height and fixed him with an arctic stare. "I am well aware of family genealogy, *sir*. I *meant*, it is not possible you are alive."

He appeared to enjoy that asinine comment even more.

Daphne ignored the mortification that flooded her body at her foolish words. "Hugh Redvers died almost twenty years ago. My husband, the Earl of Davenport, received word of his demise from an agent in his employ."

The towering man lifted his hands at his sides as if to say, *Yet here I am*.

Daphne studied him with the intensity of a horologist examining a rare timepiece. He bore her examination without blinking, exhibiting none of the nervousness one would expect of an imposter claiming to be her nephew.

In fact, he took a step closer, allowing her to see he was older than she'd first believed—closer to forty than thirty—but no less attractive for it. Deep lines radiated from the corner of his green eye and his guinea-gold hair was heavily dusted with silver at the temples. He was currently smiling but the determined set of his jaw showed him to be a man accustomed to having his own way, and the deep grooves bracketing his smiling lips were evidence he enjoyed getting it.

The white scar that almost bisected his face began at his left temple, disappeared beneath the black patch, and reemerged to continue over the bridge of his nose and end at his jaw.

Daphne compared the scarred but still handsome man standing before her against the memories of her ten-year-old self—the memories of an infatuated girl who had idolized her dashing, handsome neighbor and had mourned deeply at the news of his death.

This man was tall—remarkably so—golden, and devastatingly attractive. Not even almost two decades, brutal scarring, and the black patch over his eye could obscure the truth. He was, without a doubt, Hugh Redvers, her dead husband's true heir: a man everyone had believed dead for almost twenty years.

A man Daphne had robbed of title, lands, and fortune.

She opened her mouth to say—to say what?

"My lady?"

She swung around to find Caswell, her groom, standing at the head of the narrow path, his eyes bouncing like cricket balls from Daphne to the towering stranger to the local squire dripping blood on their picnic blanket.

Before she could answer him, her elder son's voice rang out behind the groom.

"I am *not* telling a bouncer, Richard. The fish was enormous—far bigger than that minnow you caught." Lucien sounded aggrieved. "If only I hadn't slipped and dropped the pole."

Richard, Lucien's younger twin by twelve minutes, had only one word for his brother's claim. "Bosh."

Lucien had to turn sideways to squeeze around the frozen, staring groom. "I say, Caswell, what—" And then he, too, stopped in his tracks, his mouth forming an O of surprise. Richard came around Caswell's other side, and he and his brother stared, their identical brows wrinkled with confusion.

Because they were healthy, bloodthirsty young males, the first thing to snag their attention was the man with the crimson neckcloth. Then they turned to look at the one-eyed giant beside their mother. That sight, while interesting, couldn't hold a candle to Hugh Redvers's awe-inspiring horse, which was grazing not far behind him.

All other thoughts vacated their heads and they moved toward the enormous horse as if pulled by a string. Ramsay watched their rapt progress toward his horse with open amusement. He said something in a language Daphne believed to be Arabic and the animal sauntered forward, extended one foreleg toward the twins, and bowed low over it before returning to a standing position and regarding the two small boys with a haughty equine stare.

"He's smashing, sir!" Lucien said to the man he'd unknowingly robbed of title, land, and money.

Daphne briefly closed her eyes. *Can this really be happening?*

"May we pet him, sir?" Lucien asked, jarring her from her misery.

"You may," Redvers said. "Just don't stand behind him, he's got a kick that will send you to Newcastle."

The boys grinned, as if such warnings of grievous bodily harm made the prospect of touching the great horse even more appealing.

"His name is Pasha."

Malcolm cleared his throat and all heads swung in his direction. His chest was puffed out like a pigeon's and he resembled an overgrown, pudgy schoolboy who'd been soundly thrashed and was desperate to salvage some dignity.

"Just what the bloody hell is going on here, Ramsay?"

"*Language*, Hastings." Ramsay's single eye narrowed until it was barely a slit. "You know, I was wondering the same thing myself." The words were quiet but there was a chill in the air as he contemplated the other man.

Malcolm lifted his bloody cravat. "What, this? This is nothing." He shrugged. "My horse is rather skittish and something startled him."

Ramsay turned to look at the placid creature cropping grass a few feet away and then back to Malcolm, his eyebrows arched.

"I kept my seat, of course, but I took a rather nasty

knock." Malcolm glanced at the carnage on the picnic blanket. "Terribly sorry about your picnic, Coz." He cut Daphne a sneering look before turning back to Ramsay.

The men stared at one another for a long, charged moment before Malcolm muttered something unintelligible, led his horse to the nearest stump, and hoisted himself into the saddle, his feet flailing as he sought his stirrups.

When he was secure on his mount, if not in his pride, he swept the small group with hate-filled eyes, his glare lingering longest on Daphne. She read the threat in them clearly: he was not finished with her, nor would he forgive or forget what had transpired between them today. He kicked his horse with unnecessary viciousness and thundered away. An awkward silence hovered in the small clearing as the sound of horse hooves faded.

"Quite an appalling seat, I'd say," Lucien observed.

Her son's coolly damning indictment of Malcolm's equestrian skills drew a bellow of laughter from the one-eyed stranger.

Not a stranger; he is the Earl of Davenport.

Daphne shivered, and not because it was cold. For a moment she was paralyzed by the enormity of what was happening—by the overwhelming impossibility of it all. She took a deep breath and held it until her lungs burned, the sensation bringing her back to herself. She was a woman of science and reason, not a frightened schoolgirl. Submitting to hysteria in the face of facts was not her way—at least not for long. She exhaled, expelling the mindless terror along with the air. She did that several more times, until her heartbeat slowed, and then she stared at the very-much-alive man before her.

His return from the dead was . . . well, Daphne had no words to describe the unexpected event. But she did not need to find the correct words right now; she could find them later—when Hugh Redvers was not standing right in front of her.

"I'm famished, Mama. May we eat?"

Lucien's question was so mundane it added to the sense of unreality. The whole affair was like some kind of farce—a three-act play lampooning English manners, the first act having taken place offstage over a decade earlier.

An uncharacteristic bubble of hysterical laughter tickled the back of her throat like an unpleasant vintage of champagne, and it took her several attempts to swallow it down. Daphne told herself a bit of hysteria was justified—first Malcolm and his threats and now *this—this*—well, whatever this was.

Still, collapsing into a quivering heap would not help anyone, least of all her sons. Daphne glanced from Lucien and Richard's expectant expressions to Ramsay's interested one. *Food? At a time like this? When a man had returned from the dead? When—*

"What happened to the hamper, Mama?" Lucien's brown and gold eyes, so like his father's, flickered over the rumpled blanket and scattered contents.

Ramsay looked every bit as curious as her son, but, she suspected, for entirely different reasons.

Daphne forced her mouth into a smile. "Eating our luncheon sounds like an excellent idea, Lucien." Why shouldn't they eat? Indeed, what else should she do? Blurt out the truth to Ramsay in front of her sons and servant? Yes, food first. Explanations and confessions later—much later.

And about Ramsay . . .

"You must join us, Lord Ramsay."

He inclined his head, clearly willing to play his part in the farce. "It would be my pleasure." He gestured to the trampled food and crockery. "May I be of assistance?"

Before Daphne could answer, Lucien made a noise of

shocked delight and pointed to Ramsay's gloved left hand—
a hand missing its third finger.

"I say! What happened to your finger?" Lucien had to tilt
his head so far back to meet the giant's gaze he was in
danger of tipping over backwards. "And your eye?" he added
for good measure.

Heat flooded Daphne's face. "Lucien!"

His head whipped around. "Yes, Mama?" he asked, all
wide-eyed innocence.

"Any more questions like that and you will ride back to
Lessing Hall inside that empty hamper."

Lucien shot a worried glance at the picnic basket, his
shoulders sagging with relief when he realized his mother's
threat was a physical impossibility. He gave the towering
lord a sheepish look. "I'm sorry I was rude, sir."

Ramsay smiled. "I'm sure there will be ample time later
to regale you with tales of all my missing parts. But for now,
perhaps we might give your mama a few moments while
Pasha demonstrates some of his other tricks?" He turned his
back to give Daphne some much-needed privacy and she
almost wept at the small show of kindness.

She turned to Caswell—who'd been watching and cata-
loguing the incident, no doubt to regale the servants' hall
with the story over dinner. "Please see what can be salvaged,
Caswell."

"Very good, my lady."

Daphne located her flattened hat beneath a large earthen-
ware flagon of tea and used a hat pin to fasten her jacket
closed. Her spectacles were not far from her hat, their lenses
intact but the delicate nosepiece twisted. She carefully unbent
the soft gold until the glasses rested on her nose, albeit un-
evenly. Next she went to work on her hair, which had come un-
moored during the struggle and now spiraled in all directions.
She finger-combed the waist-length wheat-colored tangle,
twisted it into a knot, and secured it with her few remaining

hairpins. Once she had done all she could, she went to assist Caswell.

Cook had included enough bread, fruit, roast fowl, Scotch eggs, cured ham, biscuits, tarts, and cream cakes to feed a dozen hungry men, and only a few items had been ruined during the struggle.

Daphne took a plate, piled it high with food and handed it to her groom, who hesitated.

"Don't be foolish, Caswell, there is plenty of food for all of us."

His face reddened but he took the plate and bobbed his head. "Thank you, my lady."

Daphne knew her egalitarian behavior—a relic of being raised by her coal-heiress mother—still shocked the Lessing Hall servants, even after a decade. But really, why should the man stand around while food spoiled?

She prepared four more plates and within a short time they were all settled on the blanket with food.

Daphne had no appetite.

Instead, she crumbled a piece of Cook's excellent bread into increasingly tiny pieces while her sons peppered Ramsay with endless questions about his horse.

She had questions of her own and they pushed their way into her mind like hungry weasels invading a henhouse. The most pressing question of all was how much Ramsay had heard before he'd interrupted her undignified fracas with Malcolm.

Had he heard Malcolm's threats? The blackmailing? The accusations about the twins?

For years she'd been haunted by nightmares that someone would eventually learn of her lies and expose her to public shame and ridicule. But *never* had she expected to face the man her deception had wronged the most.

Daphne studied that man from beneath lowered lashes.

She'd been a girl when Hugh Redvers disappeared, but—like every other female between eight and eighty—she'd been bewitched by the Earl of Davenport's wild, handsome heir. The young lord had not only looked like a Greek god, he had always had a kind word and ready smile, even for a gangly, shy, and bespectacled neighbor girl ten years his junior.

He laughed at something one of the boys said and the sound pulled Daphne from her trance, making her realize she'd been leaning toward him, like a moth hovering too close to a flame.

Daphne shook her head at the fanciful thought and resumed her examination. She had to admit that time—some of it harsh if his *missing pieces* were anything to go by—had made him even more attractive. She wrenched her eyes away from his face and catalogued the rest of him.

He was dressed in the manner of an English country gentleman, but there was a subtle foreignness to the cut of his garments. His forest-green riding coat was sculpted to his broad back and shoulders and his waistcoat was a pale green that matched his remaining eye far too closely to be an accident. As for the supple buckskins which encased several leagues of leg? Well, the less said on that subject the better. Daphne was still contemplating that skintight garment when Lucien's insistent voice interrupted her ill-mannered ogling.

"Is that not correct, Mama?" Lucien's tone let her know this wasn't the first time he'd asked the question.

"Hmmm?" Daphne looked from her son's dogged expression to Hugh Redvers's grinning one, and her face heated like a schoolgirl's, an unfortunate habit that showed no sign of abating with age. The dreadful man *knew* she had just subjected him to a ruthless, thorough, and intimate physical inspection; and he'd *enjoyed* it.

Daphne ignored his smirk and addressed her son. "Is what not correct, Lucien?"

"Papa promised that Richard and I could have our hunters when we turned ten. And that is only in a few months," he reminded her, as if Daphne might have forgotten the day she gave birth to her only children. Lucien nudged his silent sibling and Richard nodded in support of his elder twin. Daphne sighed; the vexatious subject of hunters came up at least once a day.

"We can speak about this later, Lucien." Oh, and they would, they would; her son was relentless.

She looked from Lucien's stubborn face to the baron's smiling one and decided it was past time she took control of the conversation.

"Have you only recently returned to England, my lord?" It was an asinine question, but, really, what question wouldn't be at this point?

Ramsay's smile grew, as if he could hear her thoughts. "Come, we are family—you must call me Hugh."

"Family?" Lucien repeated, forgetting—at least for the moment—the matter of hunters. "Are you a cousin, like our cousin John Redvers?" Lucien frowned, "Although he is dead, now."

Ramsay laughed. "I certainly hope I am nothing like Cousin John Redvers—dead or alive."

Daphne hoped so, too. John Redvers had been a weasel-faced drunkard whose only achievement in life was the remarkable speed with which he had dissipated his inheritance.

When Hugh Redvers had been declared dead all those years ago, it had been John—his feckless younger cousin— who'd become the Earl of Davenport's next heir. John had been one of the reasons—if not *the* reason—the earl had re-married in his seventies.

Another reason had been that the orphaned daughter of

the earl's closest friend had been seventeen, two months' pregnant, and desperately in need of a husband.

"Mama?"

Daphne realized Lucien was still waiting for her to explain his kinship with the magnificent newcomer.

"Baron Ramsay is your papa's eldest nephew. The one we'd all believed lost at sea so long ago." Daphne cut him an accusatory look, but Ramsay appeared not to notice—or care—if his smile was anything to go by. Indeed, his handsome face wore the same expression of lazy amusement it had since the moment he'd entered the clearing. The only time he had not appeared pleased had been when he looked at, or spoke to, Malcolm.

"Papa told us about you, my lord," Richard, her usually quiet and reserved son, said. "He said you were a better hand with a sword than anyone he'd ever seen." Richard's reverent tone implied that praise from his beloved papa was high praise indeed.

Ramsay's smile faded and his full lips parted; for a change, nothing came out. It was as if the possibility of a compliment from Daphne's late husband—a man with whom Hugh Redvers's disagreements had been legendary—had robbed him of speech.

This breach in his confident façade made Daphne feel considerably less flustered, which was what she'd been feeling from the moment he'd entered the clearing and caught her crawling around in the grass with her coat gaping open. She had looked a bloody, ragged mess while he'd sat on his fairy-tale horse with his good-looking face and big, gorgeous body and . . . Well, suffice it to say, she could not help enjoying his discomposure, no matter how petty that might be.

"I am gratified to hear your papa had at least a few fond memories of me." Ramsay's tone was light, but Daphne heard the tension beneath it. He looked from one twin to the other and smiled. "I must admit I'm pleased to discover two such fine cousins."

The boys flushed with pleasure.

Ramsay's green eye slid from the boys to Daphne. "Two fine cousins *and* an aunt."

While Daphne might have no experience with handsome, virile men below the age of seventy, even she could see the sort of man he was: a dangerous one. At least to women like her—serious, unsophisticated matrons; women who could be of no possible interest to him.

Whatever he saw on her face brought back his piratical smile and twenty years disappeared in an instant. Daphne was once again an awkward little girl afflicted with an enormous case of hero worship. It was beyond maddening; it was humiliating.

She pulled her gaze from his mesmerizing person, her face so hot that steam was probably rising from her head, and noticed everyone's plate except hers was empty; she latched on to that excuse like a sailor clutching his last pint.

"We must be getting back," she said, getting to her feet. She ignored the disappointed noises both boys made, brushing crumbs from the crumpled, grass-stained skirt of her habit, looking anywhere but at Hugh Redvers. She needed to put some distance between herself and the man—even if it was only a few feet.

While Daphne repacked the hamper, Caswell and Ramsay helped the twins re-saddle their ponies. When they'd finished their respective tasks and were ready to mount, Ramsay tossed Lucien into the saddle with an ease that left the boy breathless with laughter. Richard had already led his mount toward a tree stump, so Ramsay turned to Daphne.

"Auntie?" His single green eye contained enough wickedness for six eyes and she scowled up at him, hating that being called *auntie* made her blush. After all, Daphne *was* his aunt, although she was over a decade younger and there was no blood relationship. So why—

Two huge hands slid around her waist and lifted her into the saddle, expending as much effort as an average man might use to hang a picture. Daphne was just as breathless as Lucien—but mercifully did *not* giggle—when Ramsay handed her the reins. And then winked at her.

Heat bloomed in her chest and she opened her mouth. He smiled up at her, his eyebrows raised, and she realized he was expecting—indeed, *anticipating*—some scandalized response from her. She closed her mouth.

He chuckled and turned to his horse. He grasped the pommel of his saddle with his left hand and then swung his six-and-a-half-foot body onto the massive shire in a motion so easy and graceful, Daphne couldn't be sure she had actually witnessed it.

Her sons cooed and murmured in awe. "Can you show us how to do that, Cousin Hugh?"

Ramsay had to look down at least two feet to meet Lucien's eyes. "Of course. But you'd need to keep your pony a bit longer—I couldn't teach you to mount a hunter, at least not yet."

Both boys appeared to absorb that information, their identical faces serious and thoughtful—and more than halfway convinced.

The baron didn't smile when he looked at her, but Daphne could feel his smug amusement at having quashed the tedious subject of hunters so easily.

She ignored him. "Lead on, Caswell."

The groom put Richard in front of him and Lucien behind before heading out of the clearing.

"After you, Lady Davenport," Ramsay said when Daphne tried to maneuver her horse into the rear. His voice was a sensual purr even though his words sounded innocent enough.

Daphne shook her head but didn't bother to argue. The winking, the sly looks, what did they mean? Was he flirting with her?

Surely not.

Still, never having engaged in such frivolity herself, Daphne was hardly adept at recognizing flirtation. Not that she had ever *wanted* to flirt. Even if she'd had the inclination to indulge in such a vapid activity, she had never had the opportunity. She'd been seventeen when she married the Earl of Davenport. And before that? Her hand tightened on the reins. Well, before her marriage there had only been Malcolm.

Her mare's ears twitched at the tension in her body and Daphne forced herself to relax. She would think about Malcolm and his demands later. Right now she had her hands full with the man behind her.

It didn't matter if he was flirting with her or not. Daphne might be woefully inexperienced when it came to the opposite sex, but even she knew better than to engage in flirtatious banter with a man who'd been a hardened rake at the tender age of twenty. Flirtation was probably as natural as breathing to the odiously attractive man.

Daphne would just have to ignore any lures he cast toward her—and he'd lose his charming smile and friendly twinkle when she eventually confessed the truth to him.

She shuddered at the thought of that particular conversation. Just how could she return what was legally his without destroying her sons' lives in the process? How?

She was still brooding on the calamitous subject when her horse crested the rise and a fantastical scene drove all other thoughts from her mind.

Chapter Two

"Good Lord," Daphne murmured, not sure where to look first. It was like a scene from *The Arabian Nights' Entertainments*.

The entire front lawn and at least half of the tree-lined drive that curved in front of Lessing Hall were obscured by people, animals, and possessions. There were mountains of trunks and luggage, heavy brass-strapped chests portending treasure, massive oaken casks, roll upon roll of colorful carpets, elegant furniture, exotic animals, and equally exotic men of every size and nationality and description.

It was a blinding visual cacophony.

Daphne rode to the edge of the mayhem and stopped beside Caswell, who was staring in openmouthed amazement. The groom was holding the reins of her sons' ponies and Lucien and Richard were nowhere to be seen.

Daphne was surveying the colorful mélange for signs of her children when a remarkable-looking man with honey-colored skin and eyes like molten gold sauntered up to them. He was not just breathtakingly handsome, he was also half-dressed. He wore only obscenely tight buckskin breeches, glossy polished boots, and a worn leather vest that exposed arms rippling with muscles and acres of golden skin. He was leading two dogs that looked as if they'd been packed in a box and then hastily taken out full of wrinkles. A huge red parrot with a beak larger than Daphne's fist rode on one shoulder. The man's unnerving gold gaze brazenly roamed the length of her body and then flickered away and over her shoulder.

Daphne couldn't decide if she was insulted or amused by his obvious dismissal of her person.

Ramsay reined in beside her and heaved a gusty sigh. "Martín, would you please find a shirt and coat and then put them on." It was not a question.

The younger man's sinfully lush lips pulled into a mocking smile, exposing white, even teeth that added to his perfection. "*Oui, Capitain.*" He did not move.

"Now, Martín."

He chuckled and rejoined the circus behind him, not moving with any particular haste.

Ramsay dismounted and came to help her down. "I apologize for Martín; he's rather a force of nature. He and the others will not be here long. I've taken rooms at the Pig and Whistle, but I'm afraid they do not have space to accommodate all my possessions. I recalled my uncle kept several large barns for storing his tenant farmers' harvest and hoped I could impose upon you just until I determine my plans."

His request jarred Daphne out of her speechless contemplation of the spectacular sight before her. The irony of the *real* Earl of Davenport taking rooms at an inn and asking if he could store his belongings on his own property sent a hot wave of shame surging through her body.

"You must stay at Lessing Hall, Lord Ramsay." She was pleased with her cool, level tone. "As you pointed out, we are family. It would be ridiculous for you to lodge at the Pig and Whistle." He raised his eyebrows and Daphne hurried on. "There is ample room at Lessing Hall for dozens more servants, and the stables are nearly empty since the earl's death. This was your home before, Lord Ramsay, and so it should be now." Her heart thudded in her ears as she waited for his response.

It was a long moment before he nodded, his piercing gaze and warm, caressing smile once again reducing her to the status of awkward adolescent. "I am grateful for your hospitality, my lady. If you are not—"

"Is that a monkey?" she blurted, pushing up her spectacles.

Ramsay chuckled. "Yes, that is a monkey, although you had better refer to him as Mr. Boswell when you are within his hearing—if you wish to remain on his good side." He gave her a mocking bow and sauntered into the fray.

Daphne was still gawking at the awe-inspiring display when what could only be the screech of a monkey—Mr. Boswell, she mentally corrected—came from behind a tower of casks and was followed by the equally simian shrieks of her children.

Daphne was already headed toward the sound when Mr. Boswell shot out from behind the casks, scrambled over a mountain of burnished copper chests, and streaked past Daphne carrying something large and shiny in one small hand. Hot on his heels were the boys, laughing so hard they could hardly run. Bringing up the rear was a slight man wearing a turban. Humans and monkey flew past her, looped back around, and then disappeared behind a wall of neatly stacked crates.

Daphne edged around a massive collection of wooden barrels, carefully picking her way toward where Lord Ramsay stood conversing with several men.

He gave her a rueful smile and gestured to a beautiful gold chain in his hand. "Mr. Boswell is vexed with me and has taken my quizzing glass to demonstrate his displeasure."

Daphne could not find it in her to mourn the loss of his wretched glass. She stood on her toes and peered over the mountains of baggage, looking for some sign of the boys.

"Is that creature safe?"

"Mr. Boswell? He has never bitten anyone who was not intent on doing him harm."

Daphne turned to stare at him.

He raised one big hand and gave her a reassuring smile. "You needn't worry, he won't hurt them."

One of his men laughed and Ramsay scowled and fired off a volley in French, the words far too rapid—and colorful—for Daphne to translate them. The men dispersed quicker than a puff of smoke, leaving Daphne alone with him.

"Ah!" Ramsay pointed toward a towering stack of trunks. "There, you see? Here they come, all safe and sound with Kemal."

Kemal was the soberly attired man wearing the turban. Mr. Boswell was perched on his shoulder and the boys followed behind, their adoring eyes fastened on the small animal.

"Mr. Boswell feels deep remorse, my lord." Kemal handed Hugh his quizzing glass and turned to glare at the monkey until the diminutive creature removed its hat and executed a formal bow in Ramsay's direction.

Daphne bit back a smile. The little beast was turning his tiny felt hat round and round in his hands with downcast eyes in a convincing show of contrition.

Ramsay frowned at the monkey before commencing to fumble with the chain and quizzing glass. Humans and monkey observed with interest as Ramsay's huge fingers struggled with the delicate chain and clasp.

Daphne watched as long as she could bear it before stepping forward and taking both items from his unresisting hands and squinting down at them. The chain wasn't broken but the clasp was bent. Fortunately the metal was soft and she was able to gently tug it straight, until the tiny hinge opened and closed smoothly. Once she was satisfied with her work, she slid the glass onto the chain, closed the clasp, and gestured for Ramsay to lean forward.

Only when his golden head was inches from her face did Daphne realize how brash her actions had been. But it was too late to retract the offer so she lifted the chain over his bowed head, needing to stand on her toes to accomplish the task. The deed took only seconds, but it brought her close enough to catch a whiff of his scent: an intoxicating blend of sun-warmed skin, fine wool, and something sharp and tangy she could not identify. Her first impulse was to bury her nose in his crisp, shiny locks and inhale until she could place the scent that eluded her.

Thankfully she did not yield to that impulse.

Instead, she dropped the chain and stepped back, her heart pounding frantically at her brief brush with sensual madness.

She cleared her throat and avoided his disconcerting green eye. "I will go find my housekeeper, Mrs. Turner. She will arrange accommodations for both you and your servants and determine the most convenient place for you to store your possessions."

Daphne turned without waiting for his answer—or, God forbid—his questions.

Hugh studied the departing figure of his young aunt, enjoying the slight sway of her hips beneath the heavy train of her habit. He was, quite frankly, stunned by his uncle's widow. Oh, he'd known the old man had married a girl more than fifty years his junior—but he hadn't expected *this*. Hugh had possessed only vague recollections of the little neighbor girl he'd left behind seventeen years ago. But this woman? This tall, lithe, cool, perfectly sculpted, self-contained creature? Hugh shook his head; both at her and at his immediate, and unfortunate, reaction to her. She was bloody gorgeous.

He watched until she disappeared up the steps of Lessing Hall and then he reconstructed her in his mind's eye, but without any clothing—a specialty of his. He smiled at the mental picture, which was more than a little gratifying. But even more enticing than her beautiful face and slim body had been the haughty, appraising intelligence he'd seen in her frosty blue eyes. Hugh knew it was juvenile, but he'd always had a weakness for women who appeared immune to his charm; charm that, he'd been told more often than was good for him, was not inconsiderable.

And then there was the way she'd looked up at him when he rode into that clearing. Hugh grinned. Even crawling about on her hands and knees with her hair half down, she'd been in possession of her wits—or at least she'd managed to *look* like she was.

Beautiful, smart, aloof, *and* doughty! Could there be a more intriguing combination?

Hugh pushed back his hat and scratched the scar at his temple, his smile fading as he thought back to that clearing. Just what the devil had *that* been about? He certainly did not believe Malcolm Hastings's ridiculous story. What had the two of them been up to? Hugh would have given a great deal to have come upon the fracas even a minute earlier. Not that she hadn't handled the matter herself, if Hastings's bloody nose was anything to go by.

Good Lord, she had looked fierce! The furious light in her eyes when she'd shifted her angry blue glare from Hastings to Hugh had gone straight to his groin.

Hugh paused to consider his body's reaction. Just what *was* it about self-possessed, haughty, furious women he found so arousing? He shrugged and chalked it up to his fascination with danger in general; and dangerous women in particular.

She is the mother of your dead uncle's children. The rogue thought thrust itself among the more lusty ones crowding his head, but Hugh brushed it aside. So what if she'd been married to Thomas? It wasn't as if he was lusting after either of his *real* blood-aunts. That thought—meant to be reassuring, instead conjured up visions of his batty Aunt Amelia and terrifyingly militant Aunt Letitia. Hugh shivered.

She was Thomas's lover. This thought was harder to ignore and clanged loudly as it slammed down, caging his libidinous fantasies like an iron-toothed portcullis.

"Blast and damn," Hugh muttered. Since when had his conscience developed into such a loud, nosy, and *insistent* presence—especially when it came to his *amores?*

She bore Thomas's children.

The unsettling image of his uncle and young wife—as invasive as the proverbial serpent in the original garden—slithered into his brain and swallowed up his randy imaginings entirely. The enticing naked image he'd constructed with such care disappeared as quickly as a seaman's self-control in a whorehouse. Hugh recoiled from the unwelcome image that replaced it: that of his ancient uncle bedding the spirited, nubile creature who had just left him.

Hugh closed his eyes against the horrifying image, but the damage had already been done; never had his ardor been so thoroughly extinguished.

But that wasn't enough for the pitiless voice in his head. *You have come back to pay your debt—not create a new one. You must do your duty and return to your* real *business.*

Ah yes, his real business. Well, he was here now, so there was no point in thinking about the places he wasn't, or about the things he wasn't doing.

Hugh shoved away the hectoring inner voice and turned his attention to the motley band of sailors overrunning Lessing Hall's manicured lawn.

Part of him thoroughly enjoyed the spectacle—especially when he considered how the sight would have outraged the old earl. His stiff, proper uncle had been a starched-up man who had feared a vulgar display more than a public shaming in a stockade.

But another part of Hugh—the small part that was forever English, no matter how much he would never belong here—wanted to protect this delicate place from the turbulence of the outside world. From men like *him*.

The verdant park, the elegant sprawl of bricks that comprised Lessing Hall, the somnolent air which hung over it all—it was a cool oasis of tranquility and calm. Standing in this peaceful slice of green, a person could forget that a short distance away men like Napoléon Bonaparte were tearing apart the world with violence and greed.

That was Hugh's world; not this one.

He had just turned twenty when his uncle banished him from Lessing Hall in shame seventeen years ago. Seventeen years; a lifetime.

He now had more in common with the human flotsam and jetsam he'd deposited on this pristine lawn than he'd ever had with his uncle or anyone else in England. Hugh's memories of the late earl were pale recollections, but he knew his uncle would have been scandalized by the man Hugh had become—a man hardly more civilized than the Barbary corsairs who had captured, enslaved, and brutalized him all those years ago.

Thomas Redvers would have been horrified to learn his heir hadn't just found a place in the savage hierarchy of the Mediterranean; he had killed, fought, and clawed his way to the top, until he dominated it.

It would have embarrassed the old earl to learn Hugh was One-Eyed Standish, the mysterious captain of the *Batavia's Ghost,* a man variously known as the King's Privateer, the King of the Pirates, and other, far less flattering epithets. A man who had captured more corsair vessels and sunk more French ships than any other in His Majesty's navy.

That's who Hugh was—not an earl, not an English gentleman. He hadn't belonged here when he was twenty, and he certainly didn't belong here now—he never should have returned.

"Spilt milk, you fool," he muttered. "You *are* here." He glanced around for his two young cousins, hoping they'd not been compromised by Mr. Boswell's unsavory sense of humor.

Kemal stood not far away with the twins, who were gawking at the parrot Hugh's sailors had christened the Great Sou'wester. The vile bird was screeching multilingual imprecations, encouraged in his bad behavior by the boys' laughter. Hugh shook his head, grateful the Sou'wester spoke very few words of English.

Satisfied the boys were nowhere near loaded weapons or animals dangerous to more than their vocabulary, Hugh looked about for Will Standish, the man responsible for dragging him back to England after seventeen years.

His uncle's sandy-haired stable master stood near a precariously leaning tower of crates, shooting scandalized looks at Hugh's second mate, Martín. In spite of Hugh's direct order, the younger man still had not donned a shirt and coat. Hugh rolled his eyes. That was just what he needed right now, a brawl between his incorrigible second mate and his prudish ex-servant.

Not that he'd ever viewed Will as just a servant, of course. Will was the only son of the old Earl of Davenport's steward and just a few months younger than Hugh. Will's father had been an educated man who'd raised his son to take over his position—a destiny Will fought tooth and nail. It hadn't surprised Hugh to learn his old friend had taken the position of stable master, which was what he'd always wanted, rather than steward.

Hugh and Will had been raised like brothers, regardless

of the social gulf between them. But after Hugh went away to Eton and Will began to study stewardship with his father, their relationship had subtly shifted. By the time Hugh was sent down from Oxford in disgrace, they were no longer close. Even so, when the earl banished Hugh to the Continent, he engaged Will to accompany Hugh in the capacity of manservant. And probably Hugh's minder, as Will had always been the more responsible and levelheaded of the two.

And it had been Will who'd been begging him to come back ever since.

Yet today—when Hugh had ridden up the driveway to Lessing Hall for the first time in almost two decades—Will had greeted him with a coolly appraising look more suited to a stranger.

Hugh's eyes narrowed; Will was still wearing that same irritating expression now. Apparently his erstwhile friend had spent the intervening years mastering the art of looking superior and impassive. Well, Hugh supposed it was better than spending seventeen years fighting, killing, and carousing in the brothels of the world. He dropped his quizzing glass and strode toward the men.

"Martín," he barked in his captain's voice, "Clothing!"

The young Frenchman turned slowly and gave Hugh an insolent stare before strolling off.

Hugh turned to his friend. "William."

Will crossed his arms. "Aye, my lord."

Something in the man's bland tone made Hugh's temperature rise and he had to struggle to keep a civil tongue. "The letters." It was not a question.

"I have them, my lord." Will's mouth settled into a prim, judgmental line as he extracted two ragged pieces of paper from his waistcoat.

Hugh unfolded them. Both were brief and written in the jerky hand of a person who did not write often.

The first one read:

*I no the old erl liked and trusted you, will standish.
So Im giving you fare warning. Get ladee daffnee
away from lessing hall befor her and the boys take
harm. They are in teribell danger. Her lif wont be
worth living if she stays.*

The second one read:

*I wont tell you agin, will standish. Her lady ship is in
danger wors than deth! Take her away somewere
very, very far. Her and the boys. Bad, bad things will
hapen. This is yur last warning.*

Hugh's head buzzed and he gaped at the other man, waving the notes in the air. "*This? This* is all you have?" He realized his voice had climbed an octave or two and he took a deep breath and brought it back into the normal range. "I've come running halfway round the globe for . . . *this*."

Will drew himself up even straighter—something Hugh hadn't believed possible. "I've only done what you bade me, sir. I believed the letters were explicit and threatening." He gave Hugh a self-righteous glare that would have done a saint proud. "Perhaps I may have erred on the side of caution, but I used my best judgment, *my lord*. Lord Davenport was very good to both me and my sister—especially after her troubles. I would do anything for his lady wife and sons."

Hugh ignored Will's sanctimonious tone and focused on what his friend was saying, swallowing his desire to bluster and rant. After all, Hugh had been the one to put his trust in Will once he had decided to *remain dead* to his family all those years ago.

It had taken Hugh a few years after escaping captivity to realize he didn't really wish to sever all connections with the country of his birth.

So he'd reestablished contact with Will Standish, asking

him to occasionally apprise him of matters at home but to keep his survival a secret. Will had sent him perhaps two dozen letters over the years, each and every one begging Hugh to allow him to tell the earl he was alive. Each and every time Hugh had refused—especially since he'd had no intention of returning to England or assuming the earldom. It was Hugh's belief he had caused the earl nothing but grief and the old man was better off believing him dead and moving on with his life. Even so, Will had continued to beg him to return in each letter until . . .

Hugh snorted; what a fool he was! Will hadn't needed to beg him to return in his last letter because he'd finally gotten what he wanted.

Will returned Hugh's searching look with a glare of hostile insolence no friend *or* well-behaved servant would employ. Hugh sighed; the man had always been obstinate, opinionated, and headstrong. The only time Hugh had ever prevailed in an argument with him was when Will had been so shot through with fever he'd been delirious.

Did it count as a victory if the person you were arguing with was almost unconscious?

Hugh pushed away the pointless thought. "You purposely misled me about the magnitude of the threat to Lady Davenport, didn't you?"

Will's jaw worked, but he said nothing.

Hugh let out a string of curse words that made the other man flinch. "Your message made it sound as though Lady Davenport and my young cousins were in imminent physical danger—as if the whole damn lot of them were characters in a Sussex version of *The Castle of Otranto*." He held up the scraps of paper. "Why didn't you take the letters to her?"

Will shifted from foot to foot, his eyes dropping to the grass. The only parts of his face still visible—his forehead and the tips of his ears—were scarlet.

Hugh exhaled. "I see." And he did. Will had seen a

chance to get Hugh back on English soil and he'd pounced on the pretext—no matter how flimsy.

He knew he should have felt flattered his oldest friend wished him to return so badly—but he wasn't. Instead, his jaw ached with the effort of not yelling.

"You purposely deceived me to get me back here, didn't you? Did you ever think about what my return from the dead would mean to the woman you were claiming to protect?"

Will didn't move or speak.

Hugh threw up his hands. "Well, as of today, *I'm* her biggest bloody problem. My presence in her well-ordered life will be far more detrimental to her peace of mind than a few anonymous notes." Hugh didn't even bother to mention the biggest threat the other man had unleashed on the poor widow: Hugh. An unprincipled, immoral dog who would lust after his own uncle's widow and do everything in his power to have her.

Hugh closed his eyes and took a few deep breaths before opening them again and charting a new course.

"Can you *imagine* the scandal the news of my return will unleash on her household?"

Will looked up at last, his expression mulish. "*You* told me to send for you if I thought you were needed here—by either his lordship or anyone else in your family. I truly believe Lady Davenport and her sons are in danger— *some* kind of danger—so I wrote to you. My lord." The last two words were a grudging afterthought.

Hugh massaged his scarred temple, which throbbed in times of aggravation. Times like now. Aside from his instant fascination with his widowed aunt, the brouhaha his sudden reappearance would stir up was enough to make Hugh weep. Just wait until the rest of his family learned he was back; just wait until his Aunt Letitia learned he was back. *Good God in Heaven.* The woman was more frightening than a ship full of armed corsairs.

Hugh closed his eyes and tried to block out the scene. Was it too late to run back to the harbor, jump on his ship, and disappear again?

Chapter Three

Daphne's maid began speaking before the door had even closed.

"Why has he come back here after all this time? Why did he wait until *now* to return—until *after* Lord Davenport died?" Rowena demanded, pacing and wringing her hands so hard Daphne could hear the joints popping from across the room. She didn't pretend to misunderstand whom Rowena meant.

Daphne wondered the same thing herself, of course, but saw no point in admitting it.

"I can hardly put such a question to him, Rowena. Besides, why shouldn't he come back to Lessing Hall? It was always his home. It is still his home. It is we who are trespassers here, as you well know." Not to mention thieves and liars, she could have added. "In any case, his reasons do not alter the fact that he has returned and—"

"Do you know the name of his ship?"

Daphne blinked at the rude interruption, staring hard at the smaller woman's reflection in the mirror as she came forward to remove her habit.

"I beg your pardon?" Rowena had been her mother's maid and Daphne had always treated her more like an aunt or older sister, but that did not mean she would tolerate such a hostile cross-examination.

"Do you know the name of his *ship*, my lady?"

"The name of his ship? Why would I know which ship he returned on?" Daphne yanked out her hat pin and snatched the hat from her head before spinning to face Rowena rather than argue with her reflection in the mirror. "Why are you asking these strange questions?"

"Because his ship is the *Batavia's Ghost* and *he* is its captain."

Daphne stared at her servant as she tried to make sense of her words. She could not have heard her correctly. "*Batavia's Ghost*?"

"Yes."

"But that is—"

Rowena nodded grimly. "Aye, *Batavia's Ghost* is One-Eyed Standish's ship."

Daphne laughed. "You have been terribly misinformed. Just because Lord Ramsay has only one eye does not—"

"They are speaking of nothing else in the servants' hall."

"I'm not sure you should—"

Rowena grabbed Daphne's arm, her hand like a small iron claw. "One-eyed Standish and Hugh Redvers are the same man. He is the King's Privateer, my lady."

Daphne only stared.

Her silence seemed to enflame the older woman, whose dark eyes burned like a zealot's. "The man is a monster— that's why Lord Davenport sent him away all those years ago. And now he will be seventeen years to the worse. There is no telling what mischief he will make. No good can come of his return, my lady. He will learn the truth about the boys and he will ruin everything we have worked so hard for." The older woman's chest was rising and falling in shallow, rapid gasps and spittle flew from her mouth. "You cannot let him

stay at Lessing Hall—you *cannot*. He must leave—anywhere
but here. He is—"

"Stop it, Rowena!"

The hatred on the older woman's face made Daphne's
flesh crawl and she yanked her arm away from her grasp.
"What is wrong with you? Do you think I could steal everything that is his and then deny him shelter under his own
roof? *Of course* he must stay here and *of course* I will tell
him the truth. I simply need some time to find the best way
to approach it all." These last words were more for herself
than her servant.

Rowena grabbed Daphne again when she tried to turn
away. "You do not understand. You were only a girl when
Hugh Redvers left. He was a hellion—the very Devil himself—good for nothing but gambling, fighting, and whoring.
He did wicked, *wicked* things—unspeakable things that got
him sent away from that fancy school. Things that went far
beyond boyish misadventures—he was bad . . . *evil*. As soon
as he came back to Lessing Hall in disgrace, he killed one
of the earl's horses and got Meg Standish with child and
abandoned her."

Daphne gaped.

"Aye, you can look at me that way, but it is true—Meg
and more than a few others. The countryside is littered with
his blond, green-eyed bastards. And now he is the Devil with
decades of experience—" She squinted at Daphne's riding
coat. "My God! There are two buttons missing and—Is this
blood?" Her voice leaped at least two octaves and her dark
brown eyes flickered up and down Daphne's person, finally
seeing her.

"It is not my blood; it is Malcolm's," Daphne said absently,
stunned by Rowena's tirade.

The flush that had colored Rowena's cheeks drained from
her thin face. "Malcolm? What happened? Did he—"

Daphne grabbed her shoulders. "Rowena, stop. You cannot

behave this way every time Malcolm's name is mentioned or you will most certainly expose me."

"What happened, my lady?" she persisted.

"Malcolm approached me when the boys and Caswell went down to the stream. He tried to . . . engage me."

Rowena sucked in a breath. "He must have been watching for you. Watching the house and waiting. He's probably been waiting for his chance ever since the earl died."

"We can't know that," Daphne protested, although she suspected Rowena spoke the truth.

"Did he hurt you?"

"No, I hurt him. I . . . hit him." Daphne's face warmed with a combination of embarrassment and pride at the memory of his bleeding face.

"You hit him?"

Daphne turned to the mirror so the overwrought woman might finish the task of undressing her. "Yes, I hit him in the face with my forehead. I might have broken his nose—that is where the blood is from. And then Lord Ramsay showed up and Malcolm departed." Daphne left it at that. After all, what good would it do to tell her hysterical servant about the blackmail demands Malcolm had made *before* she broke his nose?

She shuddered to imagine Rowena's response if the older woman learned Malcolm threatened to disclose he was the real father of her children if she did not agree to marry him. Or that he would give Daphne time to think about it but the delay would cost her £1,000.

Most especially, she could not tell Rowena how Malcolm had grabbed her, telling her he was going to give Lucien and Richard a little brother or sister to ensure Daphne made the right decision. Daphne's reflection smiled grimly back at her; that's when she'd head-butted him. Breaking his nose hadn't made up for the last time Malcolm had touched her, but then, what could ever do that?

She met Rowena's gaze in the glass.

The older woman's face was rigid with terror. "I can guess why Malcolm was there, but why was Hugh Redvers looking for you? What on earth does he want, my lady—what? Why has he returned after all these years?"

Daphne couldn't blame her servant for putting the question into words. Why *had* he returned after an absence of almost two decades? More importantly, what had he seen and heard today?

By the time Hugh was able to seek refuge in his chambers, Kemal was already there, fussing with Hugh's clothing and muttering to himself about imperfections visible only to himself. Kemal might have come to valeting late in life, but he'd taken to his position with a vengeance.

Mr. Boswell was moving around inside his wooden house, which was a perfect miniature of Hugh's house in Shanghai. Horace and Horatia, the two shar-pei pups, were nestled together on a large velvet cushion.

Only the Great Sou'wester registered Hugh's entrance. *"Abandon ship! Abandon ship!"* The bird followed the order with maniacal laughter.

"I should have left that vile bird on the *Ghost*," Hugh muttered.

Kemal ignored the comment and began a minute inspection of Hugh's clothing while it was still on his person.

"Kemal—" Hugh began, too fatigued to tolerate the man's obsessive ministrations.

Kemal dropped his hands. "I will shave you while your bath is filled, Captain."

"Excellent." Hugh thought back on the day as Kemal pulled off his boots.

The excitement the *Batavia's Ghost* had generated when it approached the harbor would have been comical had it not almost led to its sinking by the local constabulary, a nervous and rather inexperienced group inclined to fire first and ask questions later. The excisemen who minded this part of the coastline had never before encountered such a famous vessel and had remained skeptical even after viewing the *Ghost*'s letter of marque. It had taken Hugh's impressive collection of endorsements to convince them, one such letter written and signed by Admiral Nelson himself.

It had been the admiral who'd convinced Hugh to pursue a career as a privateer.

Hugh had been engaged in a spot of smuggling the first time he'd encountered Nelson's ship, the *Agamemnon*, fleeing a French squadron. Recognizing a countryman in distress, Hugh had distracted the lead French vessel with his cannon before turning tail and barely escaping the skirmish himself. His actions had been enough to allow Nelson to escape and fight another day.

A few months later Hugh had met Nelson in Tunis, where the story of Hugh's escape preceded Hugh like a sirocco.

Nelson had shown his gratitude with documents to ease Hugh's way in difficult situations and also to assist him in acquiring his letter of marque for the *Ghost*. The famous admiral was the first to thank him—and also the one who would christen Hugh the King's Privateer—but over the years many other members of the British Navy, from humble seamen to the head of the navy, had come to appreciate the *Batavia's Ghost* and its one-eyed captain.

Hugh slipped into one of his gaudier robes, an emerald-green and gold affair that had been a gift from his mistress in New Orleans. He pulled off his eye patch and tossed it onto the dressing room table, taking a seat in front of the glass while Kemal prepared to shave him.

He sighed as he studied his battered and scarred reflection; he looked old—and he felt even older. Light glinted off the razor as Kemal stropped it, reminding Hugh of another, equally sharp blade that had cleaved his eye neatly in half fifteen years ago. Only the fact that his eyes had been open when the blade fell had saved the eyelid; a blessing he hadn't appreciated until sometime later. Hugh knew he should count his blessings that all he'd lost was one eye, but he still felt rage when he looked at the scar: rage at the men who'd done this to him. Hugh had killed five of those men, but the last one—the worst one—was still living and breathing when so many far better men were not. The scar ached at the thought, just like it always did; just like it would until Hugh put an end to it all.

But that would need to wait. First he would have to look into the matter of Will's threatening letters.

A lovely face floated into his mind. The countess's distant, untouchable beauty and eminently touchable body would have been hard enough to resist. But the severe looks she'd given him whenever he teased her had guaranteed his interest.

"Captain?"

Hugh blinked and looked in the mirror. Kemal had finished shaving him while he'd fantasized about his nubile young aunt.

He stood, shrugged off his robe, and went to the gray-and-white marble bathing chamber, where steaming water awaited. Joints popped and muscles ached as he lowered himself into the extra-long tub, a vessel which had been constructed for Hugh's grandfather, a man who'd been even taller than Hugh. He lay back and let his mind drift as he soaked, guiding his thoughts away from his alluring aunt back to this past journey.

Hugh had been on his way to England in response to Will's letter when he'd received an urgent message from a woman he hadn't spoken to since before his escape from Sultan Babba Hassan.

The woman had been a girl the last time Hugh saw her—

only fourteen when she'd been given to the sultan by Faisal Barbarossa, the notorious corsair captain who'd captured her, Hugh, and dozens of others. Even now the memory of that day was agony. The girl had cried as if her heart were breaking as they dragged her away. Foolishly, Hugh had gone after her and Barbarossa's men had grabbed him and whipped him bloody for his useless efforts.

Hugh had put her from his mind over the next two years, afraid he'd go mad if he thought about her life in the sultan's harem—only a stone's throw from where he labored every day under the overseer's lash. But he had never forgotten her and had risked everything to send her a message when he planned his escape. She had never replied.

Until now. Somehow she had managed to survive seventeen years in the sultan's palace. But it appeared her luck had finally run out and she was in terrible danger. The message had been emphatic: Hugh must come to Oran immediately.

Had it not been for Will Standish's urgency, Hugh would have gone to Oran himself. But Will's missive had been almost frantic, so Hugh had deposited three of his best men in Gran Canaria with instructions to hire the next ship headed for the Mediterranean. Once they reached Oran, the men were to find the woman and her son and keep them safe until the *Batavia's Ghost* returned for them.

Hugh soaped the mass of scars that ran up his left arm and across his chest while he considered his ship's next journey—a journey that would have to take place without Hugh. Now that he'd returned to England he might as well stay and get to the bottom of the threatening letters. He had already taken steps to have the *Ghost* ready to leave quickly— perhaps even on tomorrow's tide, with his first mate at the helm. Hugh wanted to send the *Ghost* on its way before word of his return reached the ears of newspapermen and turned Eastbourne into a circus. He grimaced. *That* powder keg would explode sooner rather than later and Hugh would need to be here to put out the flames when it did.

Hugh considered the two letters Will had shown him. As of right now, the first and only person on his list of suspects was Malcolm Hastings. Hugh didn't know if Hastings was the source of the letters, the reason for the warning letters, or another threat altogether, but he would certainly find out.

He lowered his torso into the tub and sluiced away the soap. He didn't like sending the *Ghost* into danger without him, but he also couldn't dismiss Will's concerns out of hand and leave Lessing Hall without looking into the matter.

Hugh snorted. Not that he could stay in good conscience, either; at least not if he had to fight his urges to bed the beautiful widow every step of the way.

Chapter Four

Daphne spent the remainder of the day seeing to the myriad housekeeping matters Hugh's arrival engendered. As a result, she returned to her chambers with less than an hour to rest, wash, and change for dinner.

She was certain the gown Rowena had selected for the evening was the most unattractive item of clothing in her wardrobe—perhaps in existence. Daphne had always allowed her maid to choose her clothing because such matters were of no concern to her. But even Daphne, with her utter lack of fashion knowledge, could see the drab gray dress was spectacularly ugly.

For a moment she considered reminding her maid she was out of mourning and ordering her to select another gown. Ultimately, however, she decided she was in no mood to engage in a second argument with her emotional servant.

Besides, it annoyed her that she was even entertaining thoughts of dresses. She'd always despised frivolous matters such as clothing and fashion.

It annoyed her still more that the reason behind her sudden interest in clothing—all six-and-a-half feet of him— was a man who would never notice a tall, matronly, and bespectacled woman like herself.

And it *especially* annoyed her that her body's response to his potent masculinity had been so immediate and almost overwhelming.

She told herself that women far more sophisticated than she probably wouldn't remain unaffected in such a man's presence. But that didn't help her humor.

It wasn't just his gorgeous exterior—which was bad enough—it was the confidence, danger, and sheer animal magnetism he exuded.

And then there was the fact he was One-Eyed Standish.

Daphne rolled her eyes; he was a *pirate,* for pity's sake. And not just any pirate, he was *the* pirate. Well, if one were to be precise—and precision was a characteristic Daphne valued highly—the man was not in truth a *pirate* but a privateer. A pirate with the King's blessing, in other words. The very same man all of Britain referred to as the King's Privateer.

It was beyond fantastic that her very proper husband's nephew would turn out to be none other than One-Eyed Standish, the scourge of corsairs and French sailors everywhere. What would Thomas have said about his nephew's return? What would he have thought about his normally prosaic young wife's immediate attraction to a man who was a consummate rake and scoundrel? Daphne had to smile at the thought. Thomas had possessed a finely honed sense of the absurd—as did Hugh Redvers, although he took no pains to hide it as her staid, elderly husband had done.

One thing Daphne knew for certain was that close proximity to Hugh—living in the same house with him—would lead to danger. And most likely humiliation.

But what else could she do? Disclose the truth about her sons at the dinner table tonight and leave before morning? And go where? How would they live? Would she have to tuck the twins away in the decaying house in Yorkshire—the only piece of property she truly owned?

She had her jointure, so there would be enough money to

scratch out a humble existence. But what kind of life would her sons have in the aftermath of such scandal? And what if Hugh Redvers was the kind of man who wanted retribution?

Sickness and fear roiled in her stomach and she pressed her hands against her midriff. Hugh Redvers had gone without what was his for years—surely Daphne could take a little time to consider how best to broach the matter? To make plans?

Malcolm's bloody face drifted through her mind and she closed her eyes. *Malcolm.* She had forgotten about him and his threats. Good God. How long did she have, with Malcolm nipping at her heels like an ill-tempered lapdog?

Daphne brooded on the matter while Rowena fussed with her hair, attempting to conceal the scratch and goose egg on her forehead. Daphne had almost come to blows with her fractious maid when Rowena had discovered the injury.

"You must get in bed immediately, Miss Daphne."

"I will do no such thing, Rowena."

"Indeed, you must. I will make a poultice and you will—"

"I will not argue with you," she'd said, her voice cold enough to freeze water. But of course that had not been the end of it and Daphne *had* argued for half an hour more.

How could she possibly lie in bed with a smelly concoction on her head while Hugh Redvers was at large? She was far too restless to keep to her bed, even if she had felt like it.

She stared at Rowena's deft hands as the maid tamed her unruly blond curls, her mind on Hugh Redvers and the evening ahead. How she wished she'd asked Thomas more about his long-lost heir when she'd had the chance. But the subject had always been a painful one for her husband and she knew Thomas blamed himself for sending Hugh to the Continent all those years ago.

A familiar tightness built in Daphne's chest at the thought of her beloved husband, friend, and mentor. Thomas had been good to her in so many ways—from the moment he'd offered her the protection of his name to all the years that

followed. He had been especially good to her children—
whom he had always called *theirs*.

"They are the best sons a man could wish for, Daphne.
And you, my dear," Thomas had said on his deathbed, "are
the daughter I always wished I'd had. While I'm sorry
you've been forced into a marriage of convenience rather
than enjoying the union of love you deserve, I'm honored to
have been of use to you."

Daphne had stayed with Thomas day and night after the
riding accident that had left him paralyzed and broken. She'd
been unable to envision a life without his safe, caring presence.
Without his love.

"I only wish your mother could have lived to see the
beautiful, strong woman you've become, Daphne. She would
have been so proud." The earl's eyes had been clouded and
distant, and she knew it was her mother, Althea—Thomas's
dearest friend—that he was seeing rather than Daphne.

"You are still a young woman, Daphne, and it is my dearest
wish that you finally find happiness after I'm gone."

"I *have* been happy with you, Thomas."

His pain-filled smile had been gentle. "I want you to find
love—love like I once had."

Tears welled in Daphne's eyes as she remembered those
words—among his last.

Rowena squinted at Daphne's reflection, her hands pausing in their work. "Are you ill, my lady?"

She shook her head and brushed away her tears with the
back of her hand. "I feel fine. I would like to wear the jet
tonight, Rowena."

Her maid frowned before taking the magnificent jet
necklace—yet another gift from Thomas—from its box and
fastening it around Daphne's neck.

Daphne nodded at her reflection and stood, allowing
Rowena to drape a rather ugly gray shawl over her shoulders
before turning to leave.

Her step was light and she realized she was looking forward to dinner in spite of all her worries. After Thomas's death the evening meal had been an uncertain event as only Daphne and her sister-in-law Amelia remained at Lessing Hall. To say Amelia was absentminded was to do the absentminded a great disservice. Amelia either forgot dinner altogether or misjudged the time and showed up hours late, or even early. When she did manage to arrive on time, her mind was someplace else. And when she *was* mentally present she could not be heard over the deafening barking of her dozen pugs, which followed her everywhere, including the dining room. Eating with somebody who was physically and mentally present would be a novel experience.

Hugh was already in the dining room when Daphne arrived.

Daphne's husband had been a big man, but he'd been over seventy when they'd married and his formidable frame had been diminished by time. Hugh Redvers was in his prime and the rough-hewn old hall with its massive wooden furniture and huge cast-iron chandeliers was a perfect backdrop for his powerful presence.

Daphne could imagine Hugh Redvers drinking and carousing with his thanes after a day killing off Norman invaders. Aromatic rushes would cover the floor and dogs and women would circle the periphery of the heavy trestle table as the men plotted over tankards of mead, their eyes fierce with memories of the day's violence. An entire ox would be turning on a spit in the gargantuan fireplace and—

"Auntie?" Hugh's handsome face was bent towards hers. "Is aught amiss?"

She blinked rapidly, the image of him in rough leathers and flowing hair dissipating. "No, I am fine."

His single eye flickered over her unflattering dress, his expression showing nothing of what he made of the hideous garment. He, by contrast, was exquisite, piratical perfection in his evening clothes. His tailcoat of black superfine made his broad shoulders appear positively gargantuan while his simply arranged neckcloth separated his attractive face from a chest as expansive as a cricket pitch.

Black satin breeches molded themselves lovingly to the flexing thews and sinews of his thighs, and thin white stockings sheathed muscular calves to stunning advantage. The only color in his ensemble was his waistcoat, which was a green so dark as to be almost black.

His raiment was civilized, but Hugh Redvers was mischief on legs—gorgeous legs—and his proper attire did nothing to tame him. He emanated power, danger, and a barbarous disregard for social strictures and mores. He was the kind of man who did whatever he wished, not caring whether or not his behavior conformed to the dictates of polite society.

Something about the gleam in his eye made Daphne want to run and hide. She stifled the foolish urge and turned to look at the portrait he had been studying when she entered. It was a full-length painting of his Aunt Eloisa, Thomas Redvers's first wife. Daphne wondered if he found it odd that a giant portrait of Thomas's first wife hung in their dining room.

"You don't mind dining under the imperious scrutiny of your predecessor?" he asked, echoing her thoughts in a way that sent ripples of worry down her spine.

Daphne pushed up her spectacles and moistened her lower lip, which was unaccountably dry. "Do you think she appears imperious? I believe she looks rather sanguine."

He bent low and leaned close to her, as if to view the portrait from her angle. Heat surged up the right side of Daphne's body and she inched away, praying he would not notice the evasive move.

"No," he finally said. "She is definitely imperious and rather judgmental, too. When I was a boy I always felt she was looking down on me in complete agreement with my uncle when it came to my various infractions. Of which there were many."

"I have no problem believing that."

His lips pulled into a wicked smile. "You are looking at me with such stern disapproval—very much like a schoolmistress confronted with a naughty boy. I think you would like to discipline me? Perhaps make me write out some improving verse a hundred times?" He held out his huge hands. "Or maybe rap my knuckles with a ruler?"

Daphne knew she was as red as a lobster. "I assure you I was thinking nothing of the sort."

"Oh? What were you thinking?" She pursed her lips and he chuckled. "Have you been listening to tales about me, Auntie? Has somebody been maligning my character?"

Daphne could not believe he expected an answer to those questions. She looked at the three place settings, wondering how long she should hold dinner for her sister-in-law.

The baron noticed her quick glance. "I see my aunt Amelia is characteristically late."

"I'm afraid she doesn't always recall mealtimes these days."

"Not just these days." He followed Daphne to the table and waved away the footman, seating her himself. "Aunt Amelia often drifted in, complete with pug army, midway through a meal, after the meal, several hours before a meal. On one memorable occasion she interrupted the gentlemen in the middle of cigars and port."

Daphne didn't need to imagine the scene; her absent-minded sister-in-law had done the same thing on one of the few occasions she and Thomas had entertained. It had driven Daphne's normally calm husband to distraction.

"I would have thought your return after nearly two decades would have brought her to the table on time," Daphne said. Surely not even a woman as scatterbrained as Amelia

Redvers could fail to notice her nephew's return from the dead?

Hugh laughed. "On the contrary, I encountered her in the gallery earlier today and she gave no indication that she had even noticed my absence. I confess it quite took me down several notches."

"I expect there are still several notches beneath those."

He gave one of his disconcerting bellows of laughter. "Touché, my dear auntie! I'm flattered you noticed my . . . notches."

Predictably, Daphne's face heated at his innuendo. "Your use of that word will only serve to stir ignorant speculation."

"Notches?"

The corner of her mouth began to twitch upward but she ruthlessly pulled it back down.

"The word *auntie*, Lord Ramsay, as you well know. I do not like to think of you going about the country reminding all and sundry of our ridiculous relationship."

He leaned toward her. "What activity *do* you like to think of me doing?"

Daphne coughed to cover the traitorous laugh that broke out of her. She *absolutely* refused to encourage him. Instead, she narrowed her eyes in a manner she generally reserved for quelling her rambunctious sons.

"You may use my Christian name, which is Daphne."

"Your wish is my command . . . Daphne." His warm tone and sensual lips made her name sound like some type of scandalous foreign undergarment.

She frowned and gestured for her butler to begin serving. Six footmen flowed into the massive room and laid out the first course under the direction of Gates's gimlet eye.

"Thank you, Gates," Daphne said after enough food to feed a small village was laid out on the table. "Lord Ramsay and I will serve ourselves."

"Very good, my lady," Gates murmured, giving no sign he thought her request unorthodox.

It *was* unorthodox, but Daphne wanted to talk to her new *nephew* without an audience of sharp-eyed and sharp-eared servants. After all, it was entirely possible she might have to address the subject of Malcolm. If so, she didn't mean to share the distasteful conversation with the entire neighborhood.

They helped themselves to the various dishes and the room was silent but for the sound of cutlery on china.

When it became clear he had no intention of voluntarily satisfying her curiosity, she laid down her fork and knife and turned to him.

"And by which name shall I call you—Lord Ramsay or Captain Standish?" If she thought to unsettle him with her knowledge, she was mistaken. Instead, he sat back in his chair, as indolent and relaxed as a pasha surveying his domain.

"You are correct . . . Daphne, I have been known as One-Eyed Standish for quite some time now." He raised his glass in the gesture of a toast. "But I daresay we must bid farewell to that name for as long as I am back in the civilized world." His mocking tone conveyed his opinion of said world. And just what did *that* mean? *For as long as he was back.* Was he going somewhere? Before Daphne could ask, he continued.

"As I said earlier today, we are family—you must call me Hugh."

Daphne returned his lazily amused smile with one of her own. If he wished to lean on their tenuous relationship, far be it from her to ignore such an opportunity.

"Very well, *Hugh*, as we are family, perhaps you would enlighten me as to where you've been these past two decades? I believe I deserve to know as much, since your sudden return from the dead means our lives will be the main topic of conversation in every hamlet, town, and city in Great Britain before the week is out—if not already."

Rather than looking chastened, he grinned. "Why, what an excellent idea, *Daphne*." It was not the answer she'd expected. But then, he wasn't finished yet. "As we *are* family I suppose it is within both our rights to demand an intimate personal history of one another." He leaned toward her. "I must admit I am just as curious about *your* past as you are about mine."

Daphne swallowed. Well. That had been rather ill-conceived and foolish of her, hadn't it? She might as well just blurt out her entire, humiliating tale now and spare herself the future agony. Instead she clamped her jaws shut. Tightly.

He took a drink of wine. "If you don't think it ungentlemanly, I can go first?"

She nodded, no longer trusting herself to speak.

"Let us hope I can slake your curiosity while neither boring you insensible nor exposing you to subjects unsuitable for a woman's delicate ears," he mocked.

Daphne burned to lash out, but refused to give him the satisfaction. He was a devil, and she would do well not to wander so eagerly and foolishly into his traps.

He held his glass to the light, admiring the ruby color. "I'm sure you've heard my uncle and I did not part on the best of terms." It was not a question. "I'd been sent down from Oxford for engaging in a duel and for . . ." He paused and then waved the glass enough to send the liquid sloshing. "Well, it does not signify what else. Nobody was harmed, at least not seriously." His lips curved into a smile that matched his black patch, savage scar, and hard green eye.

Daphne was positive that even her hair blushed at what he left unspoken.

"That wasn't the first time I'd been a very bad boy, or even the tenth. My uncle and I had been butting heads since my first summer back from Eton, where I'd learned from some of the older boys just how much fun it was to misbehave.

The earl had endured my wild ways much longer than he should have—certainly longer than *I* would have in his place." He shrugged. "In any event, he was away from Lessing Hall when I came home under a cloud of shame. While awaiting his return I took out one of his prize hunters while I was quite drunk and rode recklessly. The horse had to be put down." His roguish smile drained away. "After that debacle the earl decided I should remove myself from England until I learned self-restraint. This was when France was rife with problems for people of our station so we— William Standish was to accompany me to keep me out of trouble—decided to sail to Italy after a brief stop in Gibraltar.

"Not long after we departed Gibraltar, a storm sent our ship off course and we hit an obstruction." He dismissed the disaster that had altered the course of his life with a casual shrug. "William and I were on deck staring down the storm, as foolish young men will." His eye was vague as he sifted through the past. "We were very lucky. Most of those belowdecks perished. We helped fill the first two lifeboats with women and children and were waiting for the next boat when the ship pitched and we were thrown over the side."

Daphne realized her fork had been paused midway to her mouth for quite some time and lowered it to her plate, too fascinated to eat.

"William's leg was crushed between two large pieces of debris and it was all we could do to keep him afloat. Thankfully, the storm relented sometime before morning and we were able to secure some larger pieces of wreckage and form a raft of sorts. I lashed William to the raft but the loss of blood had rendered him unconscious and created another problem." He refilled his glass and met her eyes. "Sharks. Although nothing in size to the sharks I later saw off Africa, these beasts were nonetheless anxiety-provoking.

"I cannot say how long we struggled to stay on our barely floating collection of rubbish while I repelled hungry sharks.

What I can say is I was overjoyed when I spotted a mast in the distance." He fixed her with a humorless smile. "My joy quickly turned to something else as the ship drew closer. I'm sure you are aware of the Barbary corsairs?"

Daphne nodded. Who hadn't heard of the brutal pirates who'd roamed the Mediterranean and raided with impunity for hundreds of years?

Hugh absently stroked the side of his face, his fingers tracing the scar. "Their practice was to ransom anyone of value. Will's injury would have meant certain death if they'd known he was a mere servant, so we contrived to exchange identities." He snapped his fingers and the sudden noise made Daphne jump. "In the blink of an eye I became Hugh Standish, humble servant to Baron Ramsay, heir to the ridiculously wealthy Earl of Davenport."

Not for a second did Daphne believe *they* had contrived anything. If Will Standish had been unconscious at the time, as Hugh indicated, the decision would have been Hugh's alone. Something occurred to her and she opened her mouth, but then closed it, not wanting to interrupt his fascinating story.

But he'd seen her and he leaned toward her, his gaze uncomfortably intense. "Yes, my dear? You have a question?"

"It just occurred to me—your title. It is not one of Thomas's."

His eyelid lowered and he leaned back, once again relaxed, as if she'd not asked the question he was expecting. "It is a title I inherited through my mother—one of the few that pass through a female when there is no immediate male heir. Unfortunately the name was all that was left of the ancient but impoverished barony. The lands and manor that ran with the title were gone even before my mother's generation." He shrugged. "I am the last of her line and the title will die with me. To be honest, I had all but forgotten I was Ramsay until Hastings brought it up today." His gaze sharpened. "About that—"

"I'm sorry, my lord—for interrupting your story. Please, do go on."

Amusement glinted in his eye, but he didn't pursue the subject of Malcolm. "The corsairs released Will with the understanding he would arrange for both our ransoms. It was unusual for them to release a prisoner before they had money in hand, but they knew he would die without proper care and then they would receive nothing."

He stood and replenished Daphne's wine goblet. "You are not hungry, Daphne?"

"Your story is much more interesting than food."

"I am gratified to please you," he murmured, making the innocent statement sound improper.

"We were not the only captives on the ship. The pirates had collected others as they roamed and raided, and the ship was full to capacity as we headed back to their home port of Oran." His eye narrowed until there was only a sliver of green. "This particular band of corsairs operated at the pleasure of Sultan Babba Hassan, whose palace was on the outskirts of Oran. They would stop in Oran, pay their tribute to the sultan, and sell whatever slaves they did not want, in the market." He gave her a wry smile. "I was one of the lucky ones and did not have to undergo the humiliations of the slave market after we disembarked. However, I had managed to attract the captain's attention by behaving . . . well, *unwisely* during the journey, and I did so again when we reached shore." He waved his three-fingered hand as if dismissing a fly. "The ship's captain, Faisal Barbarossa, gave me into the care of Sultan Babba Hassan, for whom I was expected to labor until such time as the ransom money arrived."

Daphne was still considering the best way to ask what he'd done to earn the captain's ire when he continued.

"It does not matter what I did to make the Barbarossa so unhappy. Unfortunately, I also managed to make the sultan unhappy. Babba Hassan only spoke directly to me one time, some months later—after my uncle's agent had come to Oran with ransom money for both Will and me." His amiable smile hardened into an expression that made her shiver. "The sultan relished telling me that he'd never planned to ransom me—not for any amount of money—and that he had informed my uncle's agent that I'd died."

Daphne made a soft sound of horror and he cut her a look of gentle amusement.

"Do not despair, my dear Daphne. The story has a happy ending, at least for me. You see I eventually escaped, and when I did, I took Faisal Barbarossa's ship with me—right after I cut off his head." His posture was relaxed and his glass dangled loosely from his fingers, but Daphne's blood ran cold. For the first time since meeting him, Daphne glimpsed beyond the amiable smile he wore like a mask and saw what that corsair captain must have realized just before he lost his head: Hugh Redvers was danger distilled into human form.

Danger smiled and leaned toward her. "No doubt you've heard about the exploits of the *Batavia's Ghost* over the years that followed, but that is a story for another day." He set his glass on the table, his eye as green and hard as an emerald. "Now, I believe it is *my* turn to ask a few questions."

Chapter Five

Hugh would have wagered his remaining eye that a look of terror flashed across Daphne's face at his words, but the expression was gone far too quickly to be certain. Now what the devil might he ask that would terrify her?

He began with a subject that was fairly burning a hole through him. "I admit I am curious as to how you came to marry my uncle. That must be quite a story. Won't you share it with me . . . Daphne?"

"But . . . you haven't told me why you stayed away for so long—and left everyone believing you were dead or—"

"No, I haven't."

Her mouth opened and Hugh stared at that plump lower lip of hers, imagining it beneath his. Instead of speaking, she took a deep drink from her glass and then set it on the table. Hugh refilled it.

"Do you recall my mother?"

He blinked. "Your mother?" Hugh searched his memory, but the only image he unearthed was one of his uncle's greenhouse. "She had an interest in orchids, didn't she?"

"Yes, she was obsessed with them—it was through orchids that my mother met Thomas and through their shared passion that I came to know him."

The sound of his uncle's Christian name on her lips caused uncomfortable sensations in his gut and reminded him, with brutal clarity, that his uncle had been a *man* and this woman had been his *lover*. She had borne his children—children who were Hugh's blood relatives.

Jealousy was so foreign to Hugh that he wasn't even sure it *was* jealousy bubbling inside him like acid. Whatever the emotion, it was damned unpleasant.

He took a drink of wine but it tasted like bile. "You did not share my uncle's interest in orchids?" he asked roughly.

"No, it was his vast library that drew us together."

Hugh could only stare.

"Lessing Hall was my escape in those days, and I enjoyed many wonderful afternoons in the library reading or discussing books with the earl." Her fond smile turned arch. "Unlike many men, your uncle found pleasure in my thirst for knowledge, even if it was political philosophy instead of orchids." Her expression became challenging. "After we married, Thomas urged me to submit one of my papers to the Philosophical Society."

Hugh's brain was whirring like a stripped gear. *Books?*

She frowned at his silence, her blond brows lowering. "You find that offensive? A woman studying philosophy?"

Hugh shook his head. "It makes no odds to me if a woman studies shipbuilding or millinery," he assured her. "It is your, er, shared passion for *books* I find fascinating."

Her pupils narrowed, making her eyes appear even bluer. For a moment he thought she might throw something at him. He had not meant to offend her, but did people really marry one another—more to the point—did girls of seventeen marry men of seventy because of a mutual love of books? Rather than make matters more clear, her explanation made the union seem even more perplexing; so perplexing that Hugh refused to believe it.

He stared at her and she glared back, a red stain creeping

up her neck. Hugh wasn't sure that was a sign of guilt or anything nefarious; the woman had the most delicately blushing skin he'd ever seen and colored at the drop of a hat.

Hugh changed the subject. "You had no desire for a larger family?" He knew his question was offensive by society's standards and wouldn't have been surprised if she put him in his place. Instead, she answered.

"More children would have been welcome, but Thomas was satisfied with two sons—" She stopped, her smooth brow furrowing. "Not that they supplanted you in his memory, of course."

Hugh had to laugh. "Pray do not think to spare my feelings, my lady. I know better than anyone what my uncle's opinion of me was and how much I did to earn it. The earl took me in—an orphan of three when my parents died—and raised me as his son after his own wife and son died in childbirth. Instead of showing any gratitude, I was wild and ungovernable. I did nothing to repay his kindness." *Which is why I am here* now, *trying to protect his widow without bedding her*, he could have added, but kept to himself.

She regarded him steadily through her distorting lenses, her thoughtful examination making him rather edgy, a feeling he had very little experience with.

Hugh shrugged away the unwonted sensation. "I have always believed my death must have been liberating for him."

She did not hasten to reassure him otherwise and he liked her all the better for it.

"I cannot speak to that, but I do know your death changed him and caused him to open his doors—and his heart—to a young girl who had few connections, nobody to aid her in finding a husband, and very little interest in seeking one if she had." She gave him a direct look. "I will speak frankly, my lord. The life my mother and I had at Whitton Park was most unpleasant. My stepfather, Sir Walter, had long ago dissipated the fortune my mother brought to the marriage.

Sir Walter also made it no secret that he despised both my mother and her heritage." Her full lips twisted into a bitter smile. "He would never let her forget he had only stooped to marry a coal heiress because he needed money." She shrugged. "It only became worse after his death. Because my stepfather had no son—yet another crime for which he blamed my mother—his nephew Malcolm inherited and became our sole source of support. My mother had nothing and I would not come into my small inheritance until I was twenty-one." A log in the huge fireplace popped and sparked and Daphne started, swallowing hard before continuing.

"Living under Malcolm's dominion was uncomfortable enough while my mother still lived, but when she died . . ." She stared at him, her blue eyes bleak. "Well, it was not a pleasant development and, at the age of seventeen, four years seemed like an eternity to wait for an inheritance."

So, his uncle had rescued a damsel in distress. Hugh knew her predicament must be all too common: a young woman of gentle birth forced into marriage. But had there really been nobody else but her seventy-year-old neighbor? Hugh refused to believe it. Thomas Redvers had been a wealthy, powerful man and his sister, Lady Letitia Thorne-hill, was one of the *ton*'s most influential leaders, a woman whose hobby was arranging marriages. Surely the earl and his sister could have found Daphne a more suitable spouse?

"You recall your cousin John?"

The question pulled Hugh from his musing and he grimaced and nodded.

"John gambled away his own father's estate and lands in less than five years. You must be aware of how many people depended on the Earl of Davenport, my lord. Thomas could not risk their fate to a man like John. He needed an heir." Not surprisingly, her cheeks were now a dark crimson, but her gaze was steady and unashamed.

Hugh couldn't help feeling there was more to this story

than she was telling, but he couldn't say why. Instead of pressing her on her marriage, he pursued a different, but equally interesting, subject.

"If I may ask, what is your relationship with your cousin Malcolm? It seemed from the scene I interrupted that there is very little love between you?"

Or, maybe too much love?

The thought shot through his mind like a stray ball from a musket. Was it possible the incident he'd observed had been the result of fury born of love rather than hate?

But the flash of revulsion that spasmed across her face at Malcolm Hastings's name convinced Hugh otherwise. Her full lips tightened until they were a thin pink line.

"Malcolm and I are not on polite terms."

Hugh smiled at the understatement.

"My cousin is laboring under the misapprehension that I need male guidance now that I am widowed." She cleared her throat and fiddled with the spoon beside her plate. "*His* guidance, to be precise."

Again, Hugh felt she was holding something back. "And he did not want to take no for your answer?"

"He did not." She studied her half-filled glass of wine for a moment before looking up. "Likely my reaction was too violent by half."

Hugh believed she was very proud of her reaction, and probably had every right to be.

"Perhaps I should tell him *no* in a way he might accept?" Hugh offered.

The same expression of near terror flickered across her face and her hand fluttered like a frantic bird before she lowered it to her lap. "No, please, that won't be necessary. I daresay he understands me now. I beg you will not bestir yourself on the matter."

Hugh was on the point of asking whether this was the first time Hastings had bothered her when Aunt Amelia and her dogs burst into the room, accompanied by the butler and three footmen. After many years' service, Gates was familiar with Lady Amelia's habits and quickly surrounded her with dishes of food, dispatching footmen for anything else she required.

Amelia had been a fixture at the Hall since Hugh was a boy. He could not recall a time when she'd not been surrounded by her pack of exuberant, deafening dogs.

"Good evening Hugh, Daphne," Amelia said in her ringing voice, a necessity if she was to be heard over the commotion. She commenced to spoon soup into her mouth, either not realizing or caring she was the only one eating.

"I am pleased to see you have returned, Hugh. How long will you be staying with us this time?" She took a piece of food from one of the many plates before her and threw it to the barking animals, a feeble attempt to quiet them, which failed spectacularly. In addition to mad barking, the room was now filled with the sounds of snarling, and scrabbling toenails, as the animals competed for the scrap.

"I'm flattered you noted my absence, Aunt," Hugh bellowed.

Irony was wasted on his Aunt Amelia. "Klemp tells me you've brought two unusual dogs with you." Klemp was Lady Amelia's aged maid, a woman as shrewd as her mistress was vague.

"I have brought two shar-pei, a breed particularly prized for their intelligence and loyalty."

Lady Amelia sniffed. "I do hope they will not vex my pugs. It is only lately that Riot has learned to respect their delicate nerves." She put her unfinished soup on the floor next to her chair and the din was deafening.

"Riot?" Hugh shouted.

His aunt ignored him.

"Riot was your uncle's wedding gift to me," Daphne explained, clearly skilled at pitching her voice to be heard above barking pugs without having to yell. "He is quite old now but still has the disconcerting habit of giving cry at any moment, a characteristic which made him unpopular on the hunt."

Hugh could not have heard her correctly. "I'm sorry. Did you say my uncle gave you a *dog*?"

Daphne cut him a cool look—that superior, aloof stare that sent blood rushing south. What would she say if she knew how much that look aroused and enticed, rather than repressed, him? Could she be teasing him on purpose? Hugh doubted it; she did not strike him as a woman who was interested in flirtation.

"I agree that Riot is a most dreadful hound," Amelia said, although Daphne had said nothing of the sort. She continued in her stentorian voice, "His distracting howling upsets the pugs. They are very sensitive, you know." Hugh looked down at her sensitive pets, which had run out of food and were now querulously barking and nipping at one another.

Heedless of the racket occurring beneath her, Lady Amelia continued. "I cannot think what was in Thomas's head to give you such an unsuitable beast. If he'd only asked *me*, I should have advised him to acquire a pug for you."

A look of unholy amusement flashed across Daphne's face but disappeared in half an instant.

Hugh stared, transfixed.

She noticed his rude ogling and raised her eyebrows. "Yes?"

"I don't wish to belabor the matter, but back to the dog. My uncle thought you would appreciate a baying *hound* as a lapdog?"

"I teased him about Riot shortly before we were wed and he nursed a grudge on that score."

Hugh's eyes bulged. "You *teased* my uncle?"

She frowned but didn't answer.

Hugh was too stunned to pursue the topic. This playful

version of the grim, humorless Earl of Davenport bore no resemblance to the cold, emotionless man whose only interests
had been mourning his dead wife, breeding his bloody orchids,
and trying to bend his nephew to his will.

Daphne turned to discuss some matter with Lady Amelia,
and Hugh studied her while he tried to absorb what she had
said. So, his uncle had finally left behind his mourning to
rescue the young girl, had he? Well, she possessed attrac-
tions enough to lure any man, even one as dour as his uncle.
In fact, she was downright bewitching. One moment she
appeared sophisticated and comfortable with the running of
a formidable household like Lessing Hall, the next she was
blushing at some innocuous comment he'd made.

She is your uncle's widow, his suddenly ubiquitous conscience chided.

Oh, shut the hell up! Hugh refilled his own wineglass and
gave himself up to brooding.

The remainder of the meal passed noisily, and only the
most basic conversation was possible with the din of Lady
Amelia's dogs waxing and waning depending on how much
food she distributed.

"Shall we retire and leave you to your port?" Daphne
asked when his aunt finished feeding her meal to the pugs
and the dishes had been removed.

"I have no desire to converse with myself over a glass of
port in this vast cavern of a room." With only his annoying
thoughts for company. "I noticed a rather nice piano in the
music room. Do you play?"

"Yes, I do play."

"Will you play for me, *my lady*?" Hugh knew he should
stop provoking her blushes but he couldn't resist.

"If you wish."

He grinned at her quelling tone. "Excellent, it has been too long since I have enjoyed any music. Will you join us?" he asked his aunt.

Lady Amelia lowered her lobster fork, which she'd been using to clear an obstruction from between her teeth. "The pugs find loud noises excessively disturbing. I do hope you will close the music room door. I will bid you good evening." Without another word, she stood and sailed from the room, barking dogs in tow.

"Thank God for that," Hugh muttered after the door had shut behind her. He extended his arm to Daphne. "Is she your only company here at the Hall?" he asked as they walked to the music room, which was in the shortest wing of the E-shaped building.

"I would not call her company," Daphne began, and then stopped. "That did not come out the way I intended."

Hugh laughed. "I thought you showed remarkable restraint. What the devil was my uncle about, leaving you here with nobody for company but Aunt Amelia and her ill-behaved pugs? Do you not have any family or friends who could offer you some companionship in this great pile?" He opened the door to the music room and followed her inside.

She did not answer his question immediately. Hugh hadn't known her long, but he could already see she did not speak rashly or foolishly—yet another thing about her that was attractive. So, too, the sweet rounded curve of her jaw, which he had been staring at over dinner and had an overwhelming desire to kiss. Or lick. Or bite. Or—

Hugh sighed. He was not looking forward to curbing his rampaging lust—nor did he suspect he would be any good at it. His impulsive behavior had been one of the many characteristics that had irritated and disappointed his uncle.

Hugh had to admit it often got him into trouble, but it had also saved his life on more than one occasion.

"My mother was my only relation and I'm afraid my stepfather's behavior mitigated against developing any friendships." She shrugged, lifting the piano lid. "I am as much—if not more—to blame as Thomas for the lack of entertaining." Color began building yet again in her cheeks. "Most of our neighbors were not comfortable with our marriage, as much as they tried to hide it."

Hugh could imagine. "What about my family? We were never terribly close, but my aunt and cousins did occasionally visit."

"Thomas said Amelia was enough for him to bear and too much interaction with Lady Letitia was fatiguing, so he rarely issued invitations to Lessing Hall."

Hugh laughed. "I can't argue with him there."

She seated herself on the piano bench. "We went to London on occasion, but I am not inclined to fashionable pursuits and I prefer to spend my time with my sons, reading, or seeing to estate matters. My days feel very full to me." She looked up. "Have you any preference in music?"

"I count Herr Beethoven as my favorite, but I will leave the choice to you."

She riffled through the pile of sheet music until she found what she wanted.

"Shall I turn for you, my lady?"

"Please."

The piece she chose was of recent vintage, *Sonata quasi una fantasia,* and her playing was superb. Hugh wasn't surprised; she struck him as the type of person who would approach every activity or pursuit with intelligence and dedication.

He took the opportunity of standing so near to study her. Even up close she was flawless, with creamy skin and blond curls that set off her pale blue eyes to perfection. Her lower lip was deliciously full, a sensual counterpoint to her prim upper lip and aloof gaze. She was tall, willowy, and sylph-like and even the monstrous garment that swathed her from toes to neck could not hide her beautiful body. But she'd spoken the truth when she said she was not fashionable. Her spectacles, gravity, and natural dignity did not lend themselves to giggling, mincing, and frivolity. But while her exterior was that of a beautiful, untouchable ice queen, she burned as she played, her lithe hands plying the keys with erotic mastery that made his body hum with desire just watching. Watching and wanting those hands on his body.

Tendrils of her luxuriant hair had come loose as she played. Some spiraled wildly, glinting pale gold in the light, some lay damply against the exposed skin of her throat. Each time Hugh turned a page, he bent lower than necessary, breathing her in, inhaling her. She smelled clean, unper-fumed with anything but the vague scent of soap. Never had Hugh realized just how heady another human's natural scent could be.

By the time the final notes came to a crashing conclusion, Hugh ached with the effort of holding his body in check. The cavernous music room was silent but felt crowded and small, the atmosphere heavy with a maelstrom of emotions he had no interest in examining.

Her arms trembled with the mere physicality of the past moments and a slight shudder passed through her, as if she'd just come out of a trance. She followed his hand—which rested on the piano—up to his face and blinked, surprised to find she wasn't alone.

Hugh gazed into her heavily lidded eyes and was astounded by the violence of his need to touch her—embrace her. Instead, he took a small step back, even that much a struggle.

"You are magnificent," he said, his voice hoarse. He took her hand and held it for an indecently long time while he drank her in. "I thank you for an enjoyable evening, Daphne.

However, I believe the fatigue of a very long day has caught up with me," he lied, kissing her fingers in a way he knew to be scandalous.

His treacherous brain hurled compelling reasons to stay, complete with graphic imagery. Most of the images were variations on a common theme: Hugh lifting Daphne's dreadful gown and mounting her like a depraved animal. He looked from her parted lips to her questioning eyes and released her, dropping a necessarily stiff bow before striding toward the door.

Hugh cursed in several languages as he made his way toward the wing that held the family quarters, his mind still back in the music room. It was no wonder his uncle had decided to wed again after so many years. The simmering sensuality in her was enough to animate a block of wood. But could she have loved the earl? Or had she married him for a title and security? Hugh could not believe that was the answer, but neither could he imagine her going to Thomas Redvers's bed, no matter how much she might love his library.

Not that any of that mattered. What mattered was this situation had all the makings of a disaster. He'd been near her less than one damned day and was already well down the path to obsession. Hugh had no experience when it came to denying his passion; he had no experience when it came to denying himself *anything*. Denial had no part in his life. He'd spent every moment since escaping Babba Hassan's prison living his life to the fullest—a vow he'd made all those years ago. And that vow had been especially true when it came to the fair sex. Hugh loved women, adored them, and he pursued his sensual appreciation as often and as vigorously as possible.

He had subdued his urges tonight, but he would not continue to be so lucky. Even if his obsession led to something more than recriminations and heartache—which was not likely if his past relationships were anything to go by—a union between an aunt and nephew was considered beyond the pale in England, even without any blood relationship.

"Blast and damn." Here he was again, tangled and tied and twisted by society's expectations and his own warring desires; the very reason he'd fled England to begin with! The situation was a bloody powder keg, and his pitiable lack of self-control was an open flame to a very short fuse.

Kemal was waiting in Hugh's chambers, his mouth already open before he'd even shut the door.

"Please, not tonight, Kemal," Hugh said, stopping his servant before he could get started. "Unless it is an emergency, we'll talk about it tomorrow."

The older man grunted. "There is no emergency." He undressed Hugh in silence before helping him into his favorite robe.

"You must be tired," Hugh said, all but pushing Kemal out the door when he began fussing with Hugh's evening clothing. "You can leave that," he ordered, gently removing his coat from Kemal's hands. "Get some rest, good night." Hugh closed the door behind his servant with a decisive *click*. The only person he wanted in his room tonight was Daphne. And what he wanted with her didn't involve clothing.

He poured a stiff brandy and stretched out on the bed, balancing the cut-glass tumbler on his chest, watching it rise and fall as he considered the cool enigma he'd left in the music room. It wasn't that he was vain—his lips twitched into a smile; well, perhaps he was a *little* vain—but women generally threw themselves into his bed. Thus far Daphne did not appear to view him as anything other than an inconvenience, which enflamed his interest more than all the lace negligees or come-hither stares in existence.

An image of her face rose up in his mind—the way she

had looked at dinner, when she'd so fleetingly exhibited that tiny flash of humor.

Hugh shook his head and drained half his glass in one gulp.

He knew the signs. When tiny looks—or looks of any kind, for that matter—piqued his interest, things were going to become uncomfortable. He had always reveled in his obsessions, pursuing them with ruthless single-mindedness, not stopping until he was satiated. Sometimes that took a night; sometimes it took a year.

Hugh massaged his pounding temples and rose from the bed to refill his glass. He set the drink down, removed his eye patch, and tossed it onto his dressing table. Looking at his scarred face and blind eye in the mirror sobered him and reminded him who he was. He was a killer, not an English gentleman. He was a man who lived for vengeance and justice and had done so for fifteen years—and would continue to do so until justice had been served, even if that took the rest of his life. Hugh groaned as his overactive imagination suggested appealing scenarios. He had come here for one simple purpose: to *protect* her, not to debauch her or embroil her in a scandalous liaison.

Tomorrow he would speak to William and they would make every effort to get to the bottom of the threats. And after the matter was settled Hugh would remove himself from this country and from his uncle's distracting young widow and go back to the only thing he knew: revenge.

Daphne ran her hands over the keys as she considered Hugh's abrupt departure. No doubt he'd found the evening an agonizing bore and couldn't wait to get away. Her fingers wandered back to the *Presto agitato*, the intensity of the piece feeding her already unsettled mood.

He was the kind of man who would be accustomed to

sparkling conversation with beautiful, sophisticated women. His appetites would be prodigious in that department and women would flock to him.

According to Rowena, his amorous adventures had always been legion; why should that be any different now? Surely he would soon relocate to London, where opportunities for such activities were so much greater. And just why had he come back to Lessing Hall?

Daphne realized she was pounding the keys with unnecessary violence and stopped. She lowered the protective cover and rose from the bench, going to the large mirror across from the piano.

The face that looked back at her was familiar and bland. Aside from her hair, which she acknowledged to be attractive, she could discern nothing remarkable. Her eyes, although large, were a shallow, pale blue, the color made even more insipid when paired with pale skin and light hair. She could not see without the aid of glasses and she was unfashionably tall, just as her mother had been. In fact, other than her deceased husband—and now his nephew—she couldn't think of a man who did not have to look up at her.

No, she thought, as she looked at her milk-and-water reflection, there was nothing about her appearance to excite any ardor.

The same could not be said of Hugh Redvers. He'd only just arrived and already she was falling under his spell. She should be appalled at her desire; after all, he was Thomas's nephew. But her attraction to Hugh Redvers did not disturb her—at least not for moral reasons. But for just about every other reason? She shook her head; just thinking about untangling this mess was painful.

How could she give Hugh back what was his without disclosing the truth not only to him, but the world? And what was the legality of such a situation? Daphne shuddered at the thought of consulting a solicitor. And if—*when*—she told him the truth, how could she convince him she had not duped the earl into marrying her? Would he ever believe staid and proper Thomas had conceived of such an immoral deception? Why would he? Nobody would believe it.

If only she had some proof.

Daphne snorted. "If wishes were horses, then poor men would ride."

Chapter Six

It was not yet daybreak when the sound of a loudly whispered argument outside Hugh's bedroom door woke him. He rubbed the sand from his eyes and pushed himself out of bed, shrugging into his robe before tying the patch over his eye. He found Lucien and Richard seated at the foot of his door, each in possession of some fine metal soldiers.

Lucien grinned up at him. "Cousin Hugh, you're awake! Mama said we were not to bother you until you'd woken up."

At which point they were to bother him at will, Hugh supposed. He peered down at the armies assembled at his feet. "Are you lads having a battle?"

"The Battle of the Douro and—"

"Mr. Philbin calls it the Second Battle of Porto," Richard corrected.

Lucien rolled his eyes. "That's because he's a *curate* and he *has* to be stodgy." He cut Hugh a quick glance. "Isn't that right, sir?"

"Which side are you?" Hugh asked, dodging the issue of stodgy curates altogether.

"I am Wellington and Richard is Soult." Lucien sounded smug at being on the winning side. Probably not for the first time, Hugh guessed.

Richard appeared unperturbed at being assigned the role of the unfortunate Soult. Hugh wouldn't be surprised to learn the quiet twin had a trick or two hidden up his sleeve for his more gregarious brother.

"Is it true, Cousin Hugh?"

"Hmm? Is what true, Cousin Lucien?"

"Caswell said your ship is the *Batavia's Ghost*? That is the ship that saved the *Agamemnon*. She's also taken more vessels under letter of marque than *any* other." He bit his lip and squirmed. "If that is your ship, then—"

"You are Captain One-Eyed Standish," Richard said with cool certitude. At that moment he looked exactly like his mother—other than his eye color.

"You are correct, Richard, that is my ship."

"One-Eyed Standish," Lucien breathed, savoring the words as if they were a magical talisman.

Hugh chuckled. "But you must continue to call me Hugh, Cousins."

They did not seem to hear him and hero worship blazed in their eyes. Hugh shook his head. *Bloody hell.*

Lucien was the first to recover. "Rowena says the *Ghost* is anchored off Eastbourne."

"That is true."

"Sometimes Papa would take us into Eastbourne to see the ships. You can watch them from the Pig and Whistle. They have splendid lemonade," he added helpfully.

"Is that so? I am partial to lemonade." Hugh paused, as if something had just struck him. "Would you care to come and inspect my ship today and perhaps have some lemonade afterwards?"

"Yes, please!" The boys leapt up, soldiers forgotten at their feet.

"Lucien, Richard." The admonishment came from behind Hugh and he turned. "I told you not to pester Lord Ramsay and—" She stopped in mid-scold, her eyes dropping from

Hugh's face to the V of his silk banyan, a garment designed for comfort rather than concealment. As if on cue, a treacherous red stain began its painstaking journey up her neck. She was wearing another atrocious gown, this one a dreary gray the texture of tree bark.

Hugh decided he liked her eyes on his body. "Good morning, Daphne." He also decided he liked saying her name first thing in the morning.

Her eyes jerked up, and she blinked, as if surprised to find a head connected to his body. Her rigid posture and flushed countenance gave away her unease but her expression was as cool and rippleless as a frozen pond.

"Lucien, Richard, please gather your soldiers, it is time for your breakfast."

"But, Mama—"

Daphne raised her eyebrows and Lucien heaved a pained sigh but began collecting his toys, muttering beneath his breath.

She looked anywhere but at Hugh, her compressed lips and stern expression only making him harder. He crossed his arms and leaned back against the door frame, the movement causing his robe to open wider. "I've offered to take the boys to see my ship today."

Her eyes flickered up at the statement and became stuck on his chest.

She cleared her throat. "That is very kind of you."

Hugh grinned at the almost imperceptible tremor in her voice. "I would welcome your company, if you have the time."

"Perhaps. We can discuss the matter at breakfast." She looked away. "Once you've had time to put on some clothes."

Hugh laughed at her chiding tone, the same one she'd used on the boys.

She ignored him and hustled the boys down the hall.

* * *

Daphne shepherded the twins toward the schoolroom, cursing herself for a bumbling and blushing ninny in the face of nothing more than a naked male chest. Well, and he'd not been wearing a nightshirt beneath his ridiculous silk robe, either. What kind of man wore such outrageous, sensual clothing?

Daphne shook her head, irritated by the stray thought.

Besides, it hadn't been the robe so much as what was beneath it. She might be ignorant when it came to sexual relations between men and women, but she understood the biology of male arousal. The man was outrageous to be standing about in broad daylight like a stallion in rut. And she was an idiot to have reacted like a slack-jawed chit.

Daphne pushed away the memory of his monstrously tented robe, instead recalling his offer to take the boys with him today. She felt an unpleasant smile curve her lips. The arrogant and mostly naked man might know how to fluster gauche countrywomen, but he had no idea what an outing with two enthusiastic young boys entailed.

Her smile grew at the image of the imperturbable rake after a day spent with Lucien and Richard, running amok and unchecked. It would be no less than he deserved if she allowed him to take the lively twins with nobody but himself to curb their behavior. Indeed, that was what she should have done—left him with them.

Instead, she had simpered. Simpered! *How very kind of you. We can discuss it at breakfast,* she mimicked under her breath.

Well, it could have been far worse. Her first impulse when she'd seen his bare chest had been to flee in terror. Instead, she'd stood like a post, torn between her fear his robe would open wider and the desperate desire that it might. Thankfully, that portion of hallway was dimly lighted so at least he hadn't been able to see her wretched blush.

Daphne cringed at the memory of the brief exchange. She

was a respectable widow, not a girl in her first Season. It was time she learned to behave like one.

Hugh, Daphne, the boys, Kemal, *and* Rowena departed for Hugh's ship shortly after breakfast. Daphne could not decide whether Rowena had come along to watch her, Hugh, or the boys.

For his part, Hugh looked as amiable as ever and seemed to notice nothing amiss, focusing his attention on the boys rather than Rowena's raptor-like stare. He fielded their non-stop questions with an easy competence that made it seem as if he'd been doing nothing but raising boys all his life.

Rowena sat across from Hugh and stared, unblinking and harsh-faced, like some pagan totem—as if she suspected he might produce a cutlass from his impeccably tailored coat and kill them all where they sat.

There was no mistaking which ship belonged to the feared privateer One-Eyed Standish. *Batavia's Ghost* was not only the largest ship at anchor, she was also the most exotic and dangerous looking—just like her owner.

When they boarded the *Batavia's Ghost,* her crew stood in a long row along the railing, as if for inspection. Daphne realized she was about to be introduced to sixty of the most intimidating men she'd ever met.

The boys walked slowly down the line and shook the hand—or hook, in one memorable instance—of each sailor, almost paralyzed with joy to be meeting the most famous band of privateers in the world.

Daphne nodded and smiled, entranced at the number of missing eyes, ears, and other body parts. But it was the last man in line who made the biggest impression, mainly because he was just that: the biggest. He was even taller than Hugh and probably weighed more than three men. His long, glossy black hair was pulled back into a knot held with a beaded leather clasp. He wore a heavy silver ring in his nose, silver cuffs on his wrists, and a wide band of the same metal around a bicep the diameter of the boys' waists. The only garment on his upper body was a vest made of some type of fur, the animal's head still attached. He wore fringed buckskin trousers and his enormous feet were encased in leather slippers.

"This is Two Canoes," Hugh said. "He was named thus because even as a child he was of prodigious size and needed two canoes to transport him."

Daphne smiled at the gargantuan man, who pointedly turned away, an expression of withering disdain on his hawklike features.

Hugh took her arm and leaned close as he led her toward his cabin, leaving Rowena to guide the boys.

"You must remember that Two Canoes, like most of my men—" He paused and then corrected, "Well, with the exception of Martín, perhaps—has spent very little time, er, socializing with women."

Daphne gave him a skeptical look. They were sailors—wasn't that what sailors did? Womanize?

Hugh shook his head, as if she had spoken out loud. "Every one of these men has, at one time in his life, been a slave—some of them were even born into slavery. Two Canoes was taken from his village in America by English sailors when barely more than a lad and then captured by corsairs not long after that."

A wave of shame washed away her suspicion. "Oh. I am sorry, I didn't know."

"How could you?" He continued without waiting for an answer. "In any case, I am sure Two Canoes does not intend any insult. Among his people, women and men occupy quite different and separate spheres. Theirs is a society with sophisticated rules regarding hierarchy and rigid roles for each sex." Daphne swore there was a hint of approval in his voice.

"Even their meals are eaten apart and their courtship and mating rituals are very different from English customs."

Words like *sex* and *mating* conjured unwanted images in Daphne's mind, ensuring that her face was the color of a poppy by the time they went from the dim light of the corridor into the well-lighted captain's quarters.

She risked a glance at Hugh and was greeted by another of his wicked smiles. He chuckled at whatever he saw on her face and her foot itched to kick him. Oh, the man was such a wretched tease!

"Why do I feel like Two Canoes is not the only man on this ship to hold such antiquated beliefs when it comes to the sexes?" She turned her back on his laughter.

Hugh showed the boys his luxurious cabin, a well-conceived space that held many fascinating objects—foremost of those being a very large bed covered with a rich dark green velvet counterpane and a multitude of cushions. Daphne tried not to imagine what the handsome pirate did in such a bed.

The boys were particularly curious about a shadowbox containing a variety of shark teeth.

"Those are large, but this one is in a class by itself." Hugh showed them the single fob on his watch. The tooth was set in gold with a large ruby at the top.

"This is the tooth of a great white shark we encountered on a journey around the Cape of Good Hope. We'd hooked a rather large rockfish and its ascent attracted the great white. We finally brought the monster on board, and, believing it to be subdued, we approached too closely. I am lucky only to have lost this." He pulled the glove from his left hand and held it up for their inspection. His nails were clean and impeccably manicured, but it was a hand that had seen its share of work. His third finger was missing and deep cuts extended into the fingers on either side. "When we opened the beast's stomach we found a rather impressive ruby necklace.

We took our trophies, had several excellent meals, and nursed our battle scars from the encounter." He grinned down at the marveling twins. "So there, Cousins, is the story of the missing finger."

"Did it hurt?" Lucien asked.

"Like the dickens."

Richard shot Daphne a glance. "Is that how you lost your eye, too?"

Hugh chuckled. "No, the shark had to be satisfied with a finger. Now, shall we inspect the rest of the ship while your mother and Rowena rest here for a few moments? Two Canoes and Martín told me they would show you how to load a cannon."

The prospect of roaming the ship without female oversight drove thoughts of Hugh's missing eye from her sons' minds and they began to pull him from the room.

"Please excuse us, ladies," Hugh begged as the door closed behind them.

Rowena sniffed, her expression pinched. "What an unsavory-looking lot that was."

"I believe sailors are often colorful men." Daphne studied the small collection of books in the built-in bookshelf.

"Sailors?" Rowena snorted. "Pirates is more like."

"Mmmm." Daphne was not in the mood to argue. Hugh had books by Swift, Pope, Defoe, Smollett, and Paine. There were also a few Daphne had heard of, but not read. And there was one title, *Fanny Hill*, by John Cleland which was new to her. She took the volume from the shelf, opened it at random and read a few sentences. And then she reread the passage and slammed the book shut. Good Lord! Blood thudded in her ears and she swallowed, staring down at the book as if it were a dangerous animal. She foolishly glanced around; there was only Rowena, and she was busy with her eternal mending. Daphne opened the book again, this time to a different page. She didn't have to read very many words before she closed it again, clasping it tightly to her chest, as if it might somehow get away. Thomas's library contained thousands of books; it was one of the most respected libraries in the south of England. But it contained nothing like this. Nothing.

Daphne stared down at the book's innocuous calfskin binding, her mind churning. She wanted it. Badly. She could not recall a time she'd experienced such gut-wrenching covetousness. Her hands seemed to assume minds of their own and, before she knew it, she'd opened her reticule and tucked the slim volume inside. There! Yet another thing she had stolen from Hugh Redvers.

She ignored the hot guilt rolling through her body and looked at the shelf; the gap between books was conspicuous, so she grabbed another volume to make the single gap less glaring and dropped into a chair.

Rowena looked up from her needlework and squinted. "Is aught amiss, my lady?"

"I beg your pardon?"

"Your cheeks have become quite red."

"A trifle warm." Daphne fanned herself with the book, her mind on the volume in her reticule. She had just *stolen* something, a book—a thing she valued above all other possessions. She stared at the door to the cabin, her heart still pounding. There was time to put it back. She reached for her reticule, but then stopped. Even from her brief look she could see the book contained valuable information. When had she ever rejected an opportunity to learn? And just a quick glimpse had been most enlightening. Not to mention . . . disturbing. Perhaps this book could help her understand some things. Things she could ask no one else— things a woman her age *would* know if she'd had a real marriage. Besides, she wasn't *stealing* it so much as borrowing it without Hugh's permission.

She imagined his expression if she were to ask to borrow it and shuddered; he would tease her to madness.

A searing flare of anger blazed in her chest; she was a widow—a mother of two and a woman of twenty-eight, and yet she was utterly ignorant and inexperienced when it came to sexual relations. It was ridiculous. She opened the book still in her hands—something of Pope's, she noted absently—too agitated to read it.

Really, it was insupportable! How was she supposed to live with these tumultuous feelings he caused inside her on an hourly basis? How was she supposed to tend to her children, manage a vast estate, and pursue her philosophical work if she could think of nothing but . . . *him*?

Daphne didn't fool herself that reading this stolen book would solve any problems. Likely it would just cause more. No, the only solution to Hugh Redvers was to get away from him, or for him to leave. But she could not eject him from his own house. She would have to be the one to leave.

She was staring blindly at the book in her hands when the thought popped into her head: Why not go to London? She had planned to go after her mourning ended. The boys required a full-time tutor and she needed . . . well, she couldn't think of what she needed just now, but she was sure she must need *something*.

Yes, London. She would get away from Hugh's distracting presence just long enough to decide how to go about confessing the truth to him—to get her ducks in a row for the day when she must take her sons and leave.

Daphne sagged with relief at having made a decision—any decision. She was about to reshelf the Pope book when the door opened. Hugh stopped near the bookshelf and bent to pick up yet another book, one she must have knocked to the floor in her frenzy.

He held it up. "Did you want this, my lady?"

"It must have fallen when I pulled out this one." Daphne shoved the Pope volume at him and he re-shelved both books. The vacancy on the shelf seemed to glow more brightly than a beacon, but Hugh did not appear to notice.

"Lucien and Richard have inspected my ship to their satisfaction and are starving, having not eaten for almost three hours. If it is all right with you, my lady, Kemal will escort you to the Pig and Whistle while I exchange a few words with my first mate, Mr. Delacroix."

Daphne was ridiculously relieved to leave Hugh's cabin, where all she could think about was the book she'd stolen and what Hugh did in the large bed that took up half the room.

Hugh watched as Kemal led Daphne and the children toward the old inn. She had certainly seemed flustered about something. He pushed the thought aside and turned to the grizzled Frenchman, the only other man still alive to have escaped Babba Hassan's prison.

"We'll be ready to leave on the next tide, Captain. Or should I call you 'my lord' or is it 'Your Grace'?" Delacroix's weather-beaten face was as unreadable as ever but his dark eyes glinted with amusement.

Hugh scowled. No doubt his crew was greatly entertained to learn their captain was actually an English aristocrat. "Very droll. You know who you will be collecting, my friend, and I beg you to be very cautious. She is not without enemies, as you are well aware."

"Aye, Captain," Delacroix said with no change of expression to indicate his true feelings on the matter, which were, most likely, that Hugh was an insane man to risk his ship for one of Sultan Babba Hassan's wives.

"Do not risk your lives. No heroics—do you understand?"

"Aye, Captain."

"I am sorry to send you off after so little shore leave."

Delacroix shrugged. "It is better that the crew—myself included—do not linger in this sleepy English town. There are no whores, no decent wine or food, and no amusing entertainments. The citizenry is hostile and too many days spent here would result in one of us doing something foolish and ending up dangling from a gibbet."

"I daresay you are correct." Hugh knew there was no point reminding Delacroix of the danger involved in venturing so close to Oran. They'd been together since both of them were breaking boulders on the outskirts of the sultan's palace, each believing that was how they'd end their days. Instead he said, "I want you to take Martín with you. God knows I don't need him running amok here."

Delacroix gave him a lazy smile. "I'll keep him out of trouble."

Hugh did not doubt that for a minute. Delacroix was one of the few men able to control the young, arrogant New Orleanian.

Hugh extended his hand and Delacroix grasped his forearm. "Until you return, my friend."

"Aye, Captain." Delacroix smiled sardonically up at his captain before shooting a meaningful glance toward the Pig and Whistle. "I wish you fair winds and calm waters, Captain." His knowing look gave Hugh a moment of surprised embarrassment.

"You rogue," Hugh said, chuckling as he turned away. He could only hope Delacroix recognized the signs of Hugh's obsession because the two men knew each other so well. He hated to think his interest in Daphne was so obvious to *everyone* around him.

Daphne had just finished ordering tea when Hugh entered the private parlor at the Pig and Whistle. He took a seat across from her, a boy on each side, and submitted with patience to their relentless grilling: Where was the *Batavia's Ghost* bound? When was it leaving? What was it doing?

He responded to their questions, but Daphne couldn't help thinking some of his answers were rather vague.

When there was a lull in the conversation, Daphne saw her chance.

"I, too, have a trip in mind—although not as exotic as Mr. Delacroix's. I've decided it is past time we went to London."

"London?" Lucien and Richard exclaimed together.

"London?" Hugh echoed, sounding remarkably like his putative cousins.

"But, Mama, why are we leaving just when Cousin Hugh has come home?"

Hugh's honey-blond brows arched like silent echoes of Lucien's question, and Daphne had the urge to throttle her eldest son.

"Cannot Cousin Hugh come with us, Mama?" Richard asked.

Daphne stared at her usually reticent son, a boy who often went entire days without speaking, until Daphne had to tease information out of him, just to make sure his voice still worked.

"Lord Ramsay likely has many important matters to see to now that he's come back from—" She paused, but he just looked at her, expectant. "Well, now that he is back."

The boys appeared to be struggling to absorb this new

development and Daphne couldn't blame them. She sounded like a dunce.

Only Hugh wore his customary smile, as if he knew she was trying to run and hide.

"It just so happens I had an idea to visit London myself, Richard. I'm sure we will see each other in town," Hugh added, his words easing their crestfallen expressions even though both boys still stared at her.

"We shan't leave for London immediately." Nobody spoke and Daphne sighed, defeated. "Certainly not before the end of the month."

The twins looked relieved, but Hugh's smile grew larger, as if he couldn't wait to hear what she had to say next.

Naturally she didn't want to disappoint.

"Now that you've returned to England, perhaps you might take some interest in your uncle's estates." Daphne bit her tongue; she'd meant to introduce the subject in a subtle fashion, not hurl it at his head like a brick. The room was silent but for the muted voices of inn customers in the adjacent taproom. She glanced around the table: Rowena scowled, the boys tilted their heads, and Hugh cocked an eyebrow.

"It would allow me to spend more time on my studies," she explained.

Hugh's second eyebrow joined the first.

"It is not only Lessing Hall I must see to, but all the other properties. All five of them." *Must* she sound so desperate? "Randall is an excellent steward but he is stretched rather thin. He has already requested some assistance. Naturally I would spend time familiarizing you with Lessing Hall's operations. It would be a great help," she repeated when he appeared to have gone mute. "Particularly if I decide to spend some of the year in London. Or elsewhere." She clamped her jaws tightly together to stop the flow of blather.

A crease had formed between his eyes and his expression

was very different from his usual teasing look. "I am your servant, ma'am."

Daphne shut her mouth and vowed to keep it shut for at least the rest of the afternoon. First she'd made plans to get away from the distracting man, and then she'd offered to spend more time with him showing him the workings of the estate.

Who knew what she'd say if she kept talking?

Chapter Seven

Hugh's presence was not as disruptive as Daphne had initially feared. She spent part of each morning with Hugh and Randall—her overworked steward—who was overjoyed at the prospect of some assistance. The unseasonably warm spring weather disappeared as suddenly as it had come, keeping the three of them inside and studying the daunting bookwork for the properties while they waited for a break in the wretched weather to inspect the estate.

Randall's presence kept Hugh from being a dreadful tease—for the most part—and also prevented Daphne from behaving like a besotted fool. For the most part.

Their afternoons were spent separately, Hugh managing his business—which seemed to involve a great deal of correspondence—and Daphne working on her most recent paper and taking care of the usual household tasks.

The evenings still presented something of a danger in terms of spending too much time with him, but Lady Amelia had suddenly decided to put in an appearance every evening, and Hugh did not again request Daphne's presence in the music room.

They saw each other so infrequently that Daphne almost wondered if he was avoiding her just as much as she was him.

As a result, the days fell into a comfortable pattern, until the third week after Hugh's arrival, when blue sky began peeking through the clouds, heralding a change in more than just the weather.

It was noon and Daphne was in the smallest sitting room, where she'd come to work on her paper. Instead of drafting her conclusion, however, she was rereading *The Critique of Pure Reason*. The beautiful logic in the book was a balm to her fevered brain and she was deep in thought when something disturbed her and she looked up to find Hugh leaning against the door.

"Oh!"

"I'm sorry to startle you. I knocked several times, but there was no answer." His arms were crossed over his chest, as if to barricade the door with his big body. He was frowning. "I must say I am *severely* disappointed."

Daphne's heart froze and her mind skittered like a frightened rodent.

Good Lord! Had he found out? Had—

He grinned at whatever it was he saw on her face and a wave of near-crippling relief—mingled with annoyance—rose in her throat and she closed her book with a snap.

"Disappointed, my lord? At what? Seeing a woman reading a book?"

"Well, there is that." He pushed off the door and commenced to prowl, inspecting random items in a distracting fashion that made her entire body tense before finally stopping in front of the settee on which she was seated. He reached down and gently prodded the book she was clutching, cocking his head until he could read the title.

"Hmm." His expressive eyebrows shot up. "A little light reading?"

Daphne clutched the book more tightly and fixed him with the haughtiest look she could muster. "Yes, well, I'm afraid I've already dashed through this month's issue of *The Lady's Magazine*."

His sensual lips curved and smile lines bracketed his beautiful mouth.

"Have you indeed?" His warm, knowing look caused disparate parts of her body to tingle and heat.

She heaved a sigh of irritation to cover the disconcerting reactions. "Is there something I may help you with, my lord, or did you come to discuss ladies' fashions?"

He lowered himself onto the settee beside her, his body ludicrously large on the tiny piece of furniture. When he shifted his hips to insinuate himself into a more comfortable position, the action brought his warm hardness closer to her. Daphne considered inching away but there was no place left to inch—no place that wasn't filled by Hugh Redvers.

Amusement glinted in his green eye. "My dearest Lady Davenport," he drawled, the honorific sounding even more intimate on his lips than her Christian name, "I should dearly love to discuss the latest fashions in hemlines with you. Or"—his smile shifted and became sly—"even German philosophy."

Daphne could only stare; his recognition of Kant was so unexpected, so . . . *erotic*, the thumping in her heart dropped lower. She squirmed and her hip brushed his. A bolt of lightning shot from the point of contact and she sprang to her feet. He rose with her, making her escape only temporary as he towered over her, favoring her with a solicitous look while taking her hand. The feel of his warm, slightly roughened skin against her own caused her throat to constrict to the diameter of a pea.

"I apologize if my reference to ladies' garments was . . . inappropriate." His contrite expression was belied by the smoldering gleam in his eye and his fingers slid beneath her palm and brushed the thin, sensitive underside of her wrist.

Daphne snatched away her hand and used it to smooth her skirts, swallowing convulsively before clearing her throat. "I have business to attend to. I've been shirking my duties." She hated how breathy and foolish she sounded, and glared up at him, as if her condition was his fault. Which it was.

"Shirking?"

Daphne ignored his invitation to banter. "You needed something from me?"

"Yes, I do need something from you." He loomed over her, standing closer than politeness allowed.

Daphne waited. And waited. "Well, what is it?" she finally snapped, irked that he'd driven her to ask.

The corners of his mouth curled up and charming crinkles appeared at the corner of his eye. Oh, he was such a pest! Why did she keep rising to the bait he dangled? She crossed her arms over her chest and waited. She would not say another word. Not one more word.

"I just encountered Randall. He was looking for you."

"Yes?"

"He was rather frantic. He has been called away on family business." He waved a huge hand dismissively. "Something about a daughter and a child and so on."

"His eldest daughter is close to her confinement."

"I believe that was it. In any case, that means he will not be able to join us on our inspection of the Dower House." He smiled slowly. "I'm afraid we shall have to do that together. Alone."

Her heart stuttered. "If you'd care to postpone, we could—"

"I would not."

Daphne filled her lungs and then slowly exhaled. An entire morning spent with him. Alone. She compressed her lips and nodded. "Very well." She waited. "Was that all?"

"No, I also wanted to ask why you abandoned me in the library."

"The library?" she repeated stupidly.

"Yes, you know—the room with all the books? You've emptied out that charming desk. Have I driven you away by some action of mine?"

Daphne's mind raced. She could not tell him the truth— that she could no more concentrate on a book in Hugh's presence than she could cartwheel to London. No, she could not say that. So she lied.

"I thought you might wish for some privacy."

His eyebrows shot up. "Did you? And is that what you did when my uncle was alive—work in this room?" He glanced around the cramped, poorly lit room with an expression of distaste.

"No. I worked in the library."

"But now you have abandoned the library so that I might have it all to myself?"

Frustration joined the host of other emotions roiling in her bosom. Why could he not leave her be? What was he getting at and why was he here?

"I have done so out of consideration for *you*. Courtesy," she added, in case he didn't know what consideration meant.

It was vexatious to be pressed on the issue, especially since the truth was so humiliating. That she'd fled the library because concentration was impossible with him nearby; that all she could think about when he was in the same room was his face, his body, and his teasing looks; and, most of all, that the urge to do with him the things she'd read in his wicked, wicked book was overpowering.

She gritted her teeth; that horrid, blasted book she wished she'd never seen but could not stop reading. And rereading.

Daphne realized he was quiet and glanced up. He was smiling, as if he could see inside her head—all the naked images of his person crammed in there, and how they cavorted with naked images of *her* person, and—

"Considerate?" he repeated. "I find it very *inconsiderate*, Daphne. It would please me if you did not abandon either your desk or the library or any other part of Lessing Hall because of me. I assure you, my dearest auntie, I will quell my unease at seeing a woman surrounded by so many books— or—horrors!—reading one." His words were light, but his expression was not. "If you continue to evacuate rooms when I enter them, I can only think you wish me away from Lessing Hall."

"No," Daphne blurted. "That is, I should be very happy to continue working in the library."

"I'm pleased to hear it. Do you need help moving your things?"

"Thank you, no. There is not much here."

Hugh smiled and bowed, leaving the room without another word.

Daphne collapsed on the settee with a ragged sigh. Lord. Now she had no excuse to avoid him. Each day it was more and more of a struggle not to grill him on his past— especially when the newspapers seemed to speak of nothing else. But she knew what opening such a door would do, and she had no interest in sharing the details of her own past. No, they were in a state of détente and prying would upset that delicate balance.

Weeks had gone by and she was no closer to telling him the truth than she had been that first day in the glade. If anything, she was farther away. Enforced time with him had only made her realize how much she liked the man who inhabited that gorgeous body. Behind his lazy amusement and teasing manner was a keen intellect and fascinating person. He was also a kind and gentle man who spent part of every day with her sons, who viewed him as a god.

It had taken every bit of self-control Daphne could muster to avoid following him around like a puppy—just to be near him. And now she was committed to a morning ride with him to the Dower House? A half day with him? *Alone?*

She closed her eyes and prayed for rain.

Hugh smiled as he closed the door to the dark little room where he'd found his beautiful young aunt hiding; as if she could hide from him.

He thought of the book she'd been clutching and his smile grew into a grin. The things the woman read must be bloody well incomprehensible to all but a few minds in the entire country. Not only that, but it appeared she read them in their original languages. He'd seen her many language books, which filled several rows in his uncle's vast library. Not just French and Italian—subjects deemed proper for the delicate intellect of a woman—but German, Greek, Latin, and even Dutch.

"Bloody hell," he said under his breath as he strode toward the Great Hall, his mind stuck on the woman behind him instead of the task in front of him. He shouldn't tease her—it wasn't only ill-mannered, it was dangerous; dangerous to his peace of mind.

Hugh gave a bitter bark of laughter. What peace? Every day he wanted her more.

When he'd realized she'd removed her possessions from the library, a room she loved, he'd been relieved. And then unhappy. And finally furious. Relieved she'd removed temptation, unhappy he could no longer sit and watch her while he pretended to read, and furious his presence had driven her from a room in her own house.

He scrubbed a hand roughly through his hair, wishing he could remove his head and shake out its contents, which seemed to be mostly useless rubbish these days, anyhow. He'd promised himself he would leave her alone and be grateful she'd begun avoiding him. At least one of them was showing good sense. That intention had lasted all of a day. He *couldn't* leave it alone; he couldn't leave *her* alone. What was it about her? And what the hell was she hiding? Because it had taken him only hours in her company to know she was hiding *something*—and whatever it was, she burned with guilt over it.

Not that it was any of his business. He should let her get away to London, but he'd taken every opportunity to put a spoke in her wheel. It would be better for all involved if she left, particularly if the anonymous letters were correct and she was unsafe here. Especially since there'd been another letter last night.

Thinking about the most recent missive made him glare fiercely just as he passed through the foyer, where a footman loitered near the front door.

"Find William Standish and bring him to the library," he ordered, forgetting he was not on the deck of his ship.

The man shot away like an arrow from a bow and Hugh felt a pang he'd spoken so harshly. After all, it wasn't the poor sod's fault Hugh was in the throes of adolescent infatuation at the age of seven and thirty. He glanced at the enormous longcase clock just inside the library and saw it was a quarter past two; the perfect time for a brandy. He poured two fingers of rich amber liquid into a glass—added a third for good measure—and went to look at Daphne's language library, as if he might know its owner better if he looked at the books closely enough.

He shuddered at the fatuous thought. Good Lord, he was an idiot!

Was this cursed attraction to her punishment for his past behavior? As if he'd enjoyed too many years of carefree whoring, and some vile cosmic force had taken note of his erstwhile happy, pleasure-seeking, and ultimately selfish existence and decided it was time to extract payment? Payment in the form of sexual frustration, a feeling he couldn't recall ever experiencing until now. And, by God, a feeling he did not like in the least.

An image of Daphne came unbidden to his mind, her slim, graceful body, her cool sapphire eyes, and those plump lips he couldn't stop imagining beneath his. He stared at the desk before him and visualized her on it, his hands lifting her skirts and stroking her long legs all the way up. He would take her slowly, exploring her most private places with a deliberation calculated to drive that remote look from her face. He'd tease her with fingers, hands, lips, and tongue until those aloof blue eyes melted and she begged to be put out of her misery. And then he'd fill her so deeply she'd not know where her body ended and his—

"You summoned me, sir?"

Hugh yelped and spun around. "Good God, man! Must you creep about so soundlessly?" His high-pitched voice was bad enough—but his erect rod—proclaiming his tortured state for all and sundry to see—was beyond infuriating.

Will wore his signature superior smirk. "I apologize if I startled you, my lord."

"Sit."

Hugh dropped into the chair behind the massive desk and gripped the arms while his hammering heart slowed. He stared at the smooth surface in front of him. The desk was a work of art and Hugh would always think of it as his uncle's possession—just like everything else in the blasted place.

Just like his widow.

"Damn and blast," he groaned. He was so bloody hard it hurt.

"My lord?"

Hugh threw back his drink and adjusted his pounding

erection before leaning back in his chair and scowling at the other man. "I want to know every last detail about this letter."

The superior look slid from Will's face. "I found it last night—just before I left for home. I've asked anyone who might have been near where the note was left, but nobody saw anything and nobody unusual was here either yesterday or for two days prior." He pinched the narrow bridge of his nose. "It was on the floor in the tack room, I've no idea how long it might have been there." He shrugged. "I'm sorry, my lord, but I'm afraid I've exhausted my sources of information."

"Sources? Which sources are those?"

Will's pale face reddened. "Perhaps *sources* is the wrong word. Other than the servants here, I did speak to one of the weavers who works with my sister, and she has a cousin who is a cook-maid—" His voice petered out as Hugh's eyebrows went up and up and up. He expelled a noisy mouthful of air. "The truth is I've no idea how to go on with this, my lord. The note could have come at any time, from anyone."

"What about the man you know from Tunbridge Wells? The runner or whatever he is, has he turned up anything?"

"He said the situation over at Whitton Park is tense as the servants have not been paid in some time, but other than that . . ." Will shrugged. "He is doing all he can, but he has discovered nothing linking anyone to either the letters or her ladyship."

"Is there anyone else we could use?"

"Not anyone I would trust. I daresay you wouldn't want any word of this to get out."

"No, I wouldn't." Hugh drummed the desk with the three fingers of his left hand. Should he tell Daphne about the notes? Was it possible she might be aware of what was going on? He dismissed the thought. Why worry her when they weren't even certain there was a problem? He was beginning to think it was all a prank, some disgruntled ex-servant stirring the pot. After all, what bloody danger could she be in at Lessing Hall? It made no sense.

"We'll give your man a few more days. I am hesitant to go prancing about asking questions myself about such a sensitive matter. I'm afraid my interest would not go unnoticed." That was a bloody understatement. Word of Hugh's return had spread like proverbial wildfire. Every paper Hugh read was full of his exploits, both real and imagined. Anytime he went into Eastbourne, he could feel the weight of hundreds of eyes; he didn't even want to think about how bad it would be in London. Already he'd hired five men from the village to patrol the property and they'd tossed a dozen newspapermen from the estate. Who knew how many others lurked undetected? No, he'd not be able to look into a damned thing without drawing a crowd.

Hugh plucked the quill from its holder and absently smoothed the barb. "I want to get someone into Whitton Park. That is all we have at present—Lady Davenport's enmity with Hastings."

Will nodded. "I agree. Unfortunately, your uncle severed all connections with Hastings when he and Lady Davenport married. We have almost no contact with Whitton Park— neither its master *nor* servants."

"That in itself is rather unusual in such a small community, is it not?" Hugh met Will's pale blue eyes. "Do you know the source of the disagreement between my uncle and Hastings?"

"I have no clue, my lord. Your uncle went to Whitton Park with some regularity when her ladyship's mother was still alive."

"Ah yes, the orchid connection," Hugh said, his lips twisting.

Will gave him an odd look before speaking. "I have

always assumed the earl stopped paying visits because of Lady Hastings's death, but perhaps it was because of something Hastings did? The man is generally known to be a disreputable character, and you know how your uncle was about such things."

Yes, Hugh did know. His uncle had been a bulwark of respectability, a stickler for proper behavior; he would have wanted nothing to do with a man like Malcolm Hastings. Or a man like Hugh.

"The late earl was not the only person in the neighborhood who did not welcome Hastings's company, although he did take things one step further by making sure there was no overlap in staff, except Rowena Claxton, who was with Lady Davenport at Whitton."

Hugh smiled at the mention of Daphne's hostile maid. Lord, but that woman disliked him! She was old enough to remember what he'd been like as a lad. No doubt she worried—

"Do you think it might be one of Hastings's servants sending the messages?" Will asked, breaking into his thoughts.

Hugh thought about the scrap he'd interrupted that first day. Perhaps that was the danger the notes warned about— that Hastings was trying to force Daphne into marriage. But Hugh couldn't see it. His advances were obnoxious, but he could hardly *force* her to marry him.

Hugh shrugged. "I don't know, but I want you to ask your man to try and get somebody inside. Perhaps Hastings is seeking to hire a new servant or some such. Tell him to make it a priority. In the meantime, make sure Lady Davenport never leaves the house alone."

"She usually takes Caswell and he is well able to protect her against Hastings."

Hugh snorted. "She's already proven herself more than capable of dispatching that rogue."

Will unbent enough to chuckle, but Hugh could not join him.

Yes, she might be able to protect herself from Hastings, but who would protect her from Hugh?

Chapter Eight

God ignored Daphne's prayers, and three days later the morning dawned clear and warm, an almost unprecedented English spring day. As planned, Daphne and Hugh met after breakfast and rode out to inspect the Dower House.

The old house was a ramshackle monstrosity to the west of Lessing Hall, just beyond the boundaries of its well-manicured park. As they rode down the overgrown drive, Daphne realized it had been over a year since she'd last been near the old house—not since before Thomas had been injured.

"My goodness, the roses are in a poor state," she said, as Hugh helped her dismount and tethered their horses to a post near the long, rose-covered walk.

"They're not the only thing that wants tending." Hugh frowned as his eye drifted over the wild lawn and overgrown shrubbery. "I remember coming here as a young boy." He ducked low under the rose arbor to avoid long tendrils that snagged at his head. "My great aunts Matilda and Mary lived here for many years. They were spinster sisters of my grandfather. I was terrified of them when I was little and hated it when my uncle made me visit. I was certain they were a pair of skinny witches who cooked and ate children."

He gave her a lopsided grin that made her knees weak. "I was a rude little scrod." They climbed the moss-covered steps and Hugh knocked on the chipped, peeling door. "Who lives here now?"

"Only old Kenwick," Daphne said absently, her side on fire where his arm brushed against her habit. Would this horrid, embarrassing infatuation never go away?

"Kenwick?" Hugh paused in his brutal pounding on the door to look at her. "Truly? The man was older than dirt when I was a boy. What the devil is he doing living here?"

Daphne hoped the old butler was too deaf to hear Hugh's none-too-flattering description of him.

"Thomas offered him a cozy cottage with a servant to tend to him, but Kenwick insisted on staying in the Dower House and doing what he could to keep things in order. Which doesn't look like much," she admitted, squinting through the dirty sidelight beside the door.

Hugh grunted and resumed his savage knocking. "Kenwick must be even deafer than he used to be. He cannot live here all alone?" His accusatory look made her defensive.

"A girl comes and does his cooking and cleaning. He is not the most . . ." Daphne was still searching for a polite word to describe the crotchety old caretaker when the door creaked open and a very old man stood in the doorway. He resembled a scrawny bird that had been stripped of its feathers and then dressed with extreme care in an outfit a butler might have worn three-quarters of a century earlier.

He peered up at them down the length of his beaklike nose. "Who is making that infernal racket?" His voice was thin and querulous and his joints creaked audibly as he tilted his head and squinted at Hugh.

"Kenwick, you old rascal," Hugh bellowed. "Don't you recognize me?" He gave the wizened old man a broad grin.

Kenwick merely blinked under the onslaught.

Hugh laughed. "I thought you should never forget my

face after that thrashing you administered when I knocked a cricket ball through the breakfast room window."

The old man's jaw unhinged. "Master Hugh?" His bony old hand clutched at the door frame for support.

"None other," Hugh shouted. He peered over the ancient butler's head into the room beyond. "I say, Kenwick, must we keep Lady Davenport out here on the stoop while we reminisce? It's deuced rude to treat her ladyship like a dunning agent."

"Er, yes, Master . . . that is . . . my lord." Kenwick glanced from Hugh to Daphne in some confusion before he remembered himself enough to totter backward into the hall and open the door wider. Hugh's massive body dwarfed the modest entry hall and his golden head grazed the low chandelier, which was festooned with dusty cobwebs.

"Follow me, my lord, my lady." The old man crept with glacial speed toward the small first-floor drawing room and flung open the door, nearly toppling over in the process. The room beyond was dark and dank with heavy velvet drapes pulled tight to protect its contents. Kenwick inched toward the drapes and gave them an ineffectual tug, an action which sent clouds of dust billowing but only moved the fabric an inch and admitted a sliver of light. He stared at the uncooperative window covering, a mildly offended expression on his face before he dropped his hands to his sides and turned.

"Would you like some tea, my lord?" He spoke in the loud voice that only the very hard of hearing—or Hugh—employed, swaying gently from side to side with the effort of keeping himself upright.

Hugh let out a bark of laughter, unable to hide his amusement at the horrifying vision of the antiquated man lugging a loaded tea tray across the house.

"We don't want tea, Kenwick. We've come to look at the place." Hugh gently laid one enormous hand on the old man's shoulder. "Don't disturb whatever it is you're doing, we're just going to have a look about."

"A look about?" Kenwick yelled. "Well, you needn't have disturbed me for that, Master Hugh! Mind you don't break anything," he admonished before turning to leave. "I've not finished my tea. It'll be cold now." He inched toward the door, complaining to himself as he heaved it open and then slammed it shut.

Hugh pivoted on his heel to stare at her. "Bloody hell! You should be grateful he hasn't burnt the place to the ground with himself in it."

Daphne grimaced. "I hadn't realized he was so . . . old."

Hugh grunted and strode over to the largest bank of windows, taking a heavy drape in each hand and yanking the two open to let some light into the room. The action revealed an enormous water stain that ran from the middle of the window frame all the way up to the ceiling.

"Goodness," Daphne murmured, feeling guiltier by the minute. After all, she had been the one Thomas had left in charge of such matters.

Hugh stared at the spot where the wall met the ceiling. "We had better look upstairs."

They made their way up the dark, narrow staircase, smelling the problem long before they saw it. The room directly above the drawing room had a window that must have broken some time ago.

Hugh took a few steps into the room and stopped. "We should go no closer." He pointed toward a window that was covered with a tattered, rotten curtain. "Look at that stain—it runs all the way up under that bed. I daresay half the room is rotted through. This will be no small project to fix," he concluded, looking from the soggy mess back to her.

Daphne was very conscious of his body beside her, as well as the fact they were alone—not to mention her guilt that her neglect was the reason this problem had festered.

She turned away from him, struggling with the unwanted emotions. She'd taken no more than a few steps when the floor sagged beneath her and she lurched forward. Hugh's arm lashed out and jerked her back.

He grabbed her shoulders and roughly swung her around to face him. "Just what the devil do you think you are doing? You could have broken your neck. I just told you the floor was unstable." His green eye sparked with anger and his full lips had thinned to nothing.

Daphne wrenched herself away and turned to look where she'd just been standing, preparing to accuse him of exaggerating. But what she saw made her gasp; the place where she'd just stepped was now a gaping hole. She bit her lower lip. Again she felt his hand on her shoulder; this time his touch was gentle as he turned her.

Daphne felt like a fool, and she didn't like the foreign emotion. She could not make herself look any higher than his chest, but he took her chin with his gloved fingers and tilted her face up.

His handsome features were taut and intense, but no longer angry. "Daphne—" He stopped and shook his head. Daphne stared into his emerald eye, mesmerized by the gold shards that glinted in the green, like slivers of sunlight through a forest canopy. His fingers tightened and his disconcerting gaze traveled from her eyes to her mouth and then back.

He gave a low groan of frustration. "Oh, bloody hell," he muttered, just before his mouth crushed hers.

Daphne closed her eyes.

Finally. The word echoed so loudly inside her head that, for a moment, she feared she'd spoken out loud.

If she had, Hugh did not appear to notice.

He slid one big gloved hand around her nape and drew her close, making her feel as fragile as the stem of a flower. His mouth was hot and demanding; demanding things that

Daphne desperately wanted to give, but didn't know how. He must have sensed her tension and turmoil because his lips instantly turned soft and teasing.

"Daphne," he whispered, brushing his lips back and forth, trailing small, gentle kisses over her mouth, again and again, not limiting himself to her tightly pursed lips, but roaming over her chin, cheeks, and even her jaw before nibbling her lower lip.

Daphne realized she was standing on her toes, pressing her face against his, unable to get close enough.

His lips curved into a smile against hers. "Mmmm, you taste so sweet."

Daphne shuddered and grabbed onto his body to steady herself as his gentle sucking set off colorful explosions behind her eyelids. The tautly bunched muscles of his upper body were hard and hot beneath the smooth wool of his coat and her hands traveled the broad expanse of his shoulders toward his neck, lightly grazing his cravat before she pushed her fingers into his thick, surprisingly wiry curls.

He growled and inched even closer, releasing her lip and then pushing at the seam of her mouth with his tongue, as if he was trying to . . . enter her.

Daphne inhaled sharply and the room shifted beneath her feet as he took her face in both hands and tilted her, stroking into her . . . tasting her . . . *licking* her.

She had read about kissing and had imagined how it might feel; but her brain—her powerful reasoning ability—had, for once, utterly failed her as he came deeper inside her with each velvet stroke of his tongue.

The few poor, pitiful shreds of reason she'd been clinging to blew away like dandelion fluff in a high wind.

He consumed her, the hot, persistent invasion of his wickedly skilled tongue turning her boneless. She was vaguely aware that one of his hands was moving south, lightly tracing the side of her breast and following the curve of her waist, finally coming to rest on her hip. Daphne tightened her grip on his hair and pulled him close, opening herself as she molded her body to his.

Skill. That's what it is, nothing but skill. The pragmatic voice that ruled her waking hours sliced through her passion like a razor, leaving it torn and tattered. *He is using his skills on you, Daphne. Just as he has used them on countless others.*

No, this is different! she insisted. *This is perfect. . . as if it were meant to be. I feel—*

You feel exactly like Meg Standish must have felt right before she opened her legs to him.

The words were like a bucket of ice water on her enflamed brain, instantly dousing her roaring ardor.

"No," she muttered against his mouth.

"Daphne?" His wicked tongue paused its distracting labor and his soft, hot lips came to rest against her ear, "Is aught amiss?" His breath was a warm teasing feather on her sensitive skin. He felt so good; so . . . *right.* Her hands acted on their own, sliding up his lapels and settling on his shoulders. She pulled him down and down and—

He will despise you when he learns the truth.

Daphne jerked as if she'd been struck by a whip, staggering away from him.

"Daphne?"

She turned away from his heavy-lidded stare, her heart thumping against her ribs hard enough to hurt. What had she done? How could she do such a thing, given the secret between them?

She laid her forehead against the cool wood-paneled wall and sucked in a breath, holding it. Unwilling to face the mortifying vision that threatened to swamp her: that of a gauche country bumpkin desperate for Hugh's caresses. She was just one more woman in a long line of easy conquests that stretched back decades. And even if he really cared for her now, he soon wouldn't.

Blame for herself and, irrationally, for him, swirled together inside her, the emotional chaos welling up in her throat. She swallowed and blinked back the tears that threatened to unravel the last of her composure, reminding herself that she'd had the willpower to stop him—and herself. The realization spread through her, leaving strength in its wake. She filled her lungs to bursting and began the long, uphill journey toward her wits and dignity.

When she turned, he was waiting for her, confusion writ large on his handsome face. "Daphne, I—"

She raised a hand. "No. Don't apologize, my lord." Her voice was cold and steady. "I could have stepped away, but I did not. We are both complicit in our behavior. All I ask is that you never mention this unfortunate incident, which I have already put from my mind."

He waited a long time to answer. "As you wish," he finally said, taking the hand she'd raised and pressing a light kiss into her palm, his breath hot through the thin kid glove.

The simple action set fire to her insides and she clenched her jaws against the wave of lust, anger, and . . . loss that surged through her body. Her hard-earned dignity gave way to self-preservation and she broke away from him and clattered down the stairs, ignoring his calls, not caring if he followed.

Hugh reached Pasha in time to see Daphne disappear down the drive. How she'd managed to mount her horse in such a hurry was a mystery to him. He leaned against the old rose arbor and tried to find a more comfortable position for his still-hard cock. There wasn't one.

He shoved back his hat and scratched at his scar. What the devil had just happened? She was upset with him, there was no denying that, but he couldn't help feeling it wasn't that simple.

Hugh knew he deserved her anger for instigating the kiss and allowing his hands to wander. She had spent her life in this small community and had no doubt suddenly come to her senses, realizing their behavior far exceeded the bounds of the acceptable nephew/aunt relationship—no matter how tenuous that bond felt in their case.

He couldn't blame her. There would be plenty of people who'd be horrified by his actions—*their* actions. Yet somehow he didn't believe that was the reason for her reaction—at least not entirely. She had been so receptive at first, all but launching herself into his arms when he kissed her. And then something had happened to cool her ardor in an instant. But what?

Hugh squinted at the weed-choked drive as he considered their kiss. As arousing as it had been to finally lay his mouth on hers, there had been something in her response that had been . . . tentative, as if she'd never kissed a man before.

Hugh shook his head; that was impossible—she had children. Almost as soon as the thought entered his head, Hugh realized how asinine it was. Plenty of men took their wives under cover of darkness, viewing sex as a furtive, dirty activity to be used only for procreation. Had his uncle—

The revolting image of the earl taking his young wife's innocence without even a kiss or caress slammed into him, wiping every other thought from his head. His erection—which had been as hard as a pike only seconds before—was gone in a heartbeat. Perhaps forever.

Hugh tried to shake the distasteful thoughts from his head but could not. Why was he surprised the poor woman had never been kissed—she'd been only seventeen when she'd married the earl.

There were scads of men, both young and old, who took their pleasure from their wives and didn't bother with their partners' needs. Indeed, many men appeared to believe wives were some peculiar subset of women—unlike mistresses or whores—who had no physical needs beyond food and shelter and clothing.

Hugh chewed the inside of his cheek. Was that what had happened to Daphne? Had she given her virginity to a man who'd not even kissed her?

Hugh could not bear the pictures his brain created. He shook his head hard enough to leave him dizzy, but still he could not rid his mind of disturbing images and thoughts.

Hugh knew her inexperience and everything it implied should have killed his desire for her—or at least warned him off. But it hadn't. No, unfortunately for both of them, he wanted her just as badly as ever.

Chapter Nine

The episode in the Dower House should have sent Daphne running for London like a scalded cat. But of course it didn't. Especially not after Hugh showed up to dinner that evening and behaved as if nothing untoward had happened—exactly as she had asked. Instead of pleasing her, his behavior incensed her.

Daphne dug in her heels and followed his lead. They chatted about estate affairs, the weather, crops, the current state of affairs in Europe—everything but the hulking matter between them. She even forced herself to spend an hour in the library after dinner, pretending to work on her paper but really eyeing him furtively and fuming. She refused to show him how much the brief interlude had upset her when it clearly meant less than nothing to him.

Daphne might be a naïve, ignorant, woefully inexperienced ninny when it came to men, but she knew what had happened. He'd been amusing himself with her because there was nobody else at hand. A woman would have to be a self-destructive idiot to invest any meaning in his behavior. And Daphne was not a stupid woman. At least not under normal circumstances.

But her common sense had gone begging where he was concerned and it was up to her to get it back. The first step was to behave as if the episode had never occurred.

Daphne was still trying to figure out how to do that the following morning, when something happened to wipe all thoughts of her recent humiliation from her mind.

She was on her way to breakfast when Gates intercepted her with a letter on a salver.

"This came for you late last night, my lady. I'm afraid I did not see it until just now."

Daphne recognized Malcolm's handwriting even though she'd not seen it in over ten years. She no more wanted to pick up the white square of parchment than she wanted to put her hands in a viper's nest, but . . .

She took the letter. "Thank you, Gates." She turned around and headed toward the library, no longer hungry. Once inside, she ripped the letter open while leaning against the door.

I have not forgotten our little chat in the woods, even if you have. If I don't have £1,000 in my account by the end of the week, I will come to see you personally. And I will have my proof with me. After I visit your newly returned nephew—who will no doubt be thrilled by what I have to show him—I will visit every one of your other relatives. And then, perhaps, I will go to the newspapers. I know exposing you will do nothing to forward my plan, but I will not hesitate to make your life a misery if you do not give me what I want. I know your mourning period is over and I would like to have our wedding take place soon. See how considerate I can be about observing all the proper conventions? Don't make me show you how inconsiderate I can become.

She dropped her head back against the door with a soft thud. There was nothing new in this letter—she still didn't know what "proof" Malcolm had about the twins, but she doubted his threat was a hollow one. Whatever proof he had found, he must have either recently discovered it or he'd bided his time and waited for years—until Thomas could no longer protect her—to use it. Daphne could not imagine her impatient, reckless cousin waiting weeks—not to mention years—for anything, especially not something that would involve her humiliation. So, what was it Malcolm had recently learned? And from whom?

She pushed aside her pointless musing and went to her desk, staring at the parchment and quills that lay scattered across the glossy mahogany surface.

You must tell Hugh the truth. The invasive thought wrapped itself around her as tightly as the arms of a lover—just as it did every night before she went to bed and every morning when she woke in its embrace.

But each and every time she thought about telling Hugh the children were Malcolm's, the same thought stopped her: He would never believe the earl had known. He would believe Daphne had passed off her bastards on an elderly widower—a moral, upstanding man who never would have agreed to such a deception.

She could see Hugh's disgust and loathing in her mind's eye. And it would be the same with his family members, servants, neighbors—anyone who learned the truth. Her sons would face those horrified, judging expressions and their lives would be ones of shame, isolation, and penury. All three of them would become social outcasts.

Daphne simply could not do that to them—not until she had to. And she did not have to . . . yet.

She looked down at the letter crumpled on the desk, and fury joined fear and humiliation. Why pay £1,000 to hide a secret she was going to have to confess, anyway? And the money she would pay was simply more money she would owe Hugh. What was she waiting for that she would even consider paying such an amount?

The answer to that was pitifully simple and foolish: Time. She needed as much time as she could get before she ruined her sons' lives.

Wishing for more time was an irrational desire, but wasn't she entitled to make just *one* irrational decision in her life? When had she ever done so in the past? Never! Not after Malcolm attacked her and not after she'd learned she was to have a child. She had wanted to run and run and run like a hunted animal. Instead, she had behaved with bloodless pragmatism and had married a man almost six decades older than she.

Tears welled in her eyes at the thought of Thomas and she angrily brushed them away. It wasn't as if she hadn't loved Thomas and been grateful for everything he'd done. He had been so good to her, treating her like the father she'd never had. But the truth was Malcolm had robbed her. With a single act of vicious violence he had made her a mother, but Daphne had never had a chance to be a lover or a wife. She hadn't even thought of such things before Hugh—and if she had, she certainly hadn't felt as if she had missed them. Until now.

Oh, she knew her foolish, pathetic, ridiculous, *scandalous* feelings for Hugh would not lead to love and marriage, but at least she felt *alive* and like a woman. Daphne's face burned at the shameful admission—even to herself.

She needed a little more time, and this was the only way to get it.

She glared down at the hateful letter. Malcolm had been an inveterate gambler even before he'd reached his majority. He must have gambled away whatever came to him from his brief marriage to a young heiress from the Midlands, a downtrodden-looking woman Daphne had seen in Eastbourne a few times.

Nausea rose in her at the mere *thought* of being Malcolm's wife. How could he be so stupid as to believe she would allow herself to be blackmailed into marriage with a man who'd raped her?

Daphne loved her sons and would not change what had happened, even if she could—how could she, if it meant losing them? But that did not mean she didn't bear Malcolm hatred enough to reduce him to a pile of smoking cinders. The only positive thought she had for him was that he'd knocked her unconscious before defiling her; at least she had no horrid memories to give her nightmares—not that he hadn't mocked and taunted her afterward.

A cracking noise made her jump and she looked down to see she'd snapped the quill in half. Daphne frowned; there was no point in becoming emotional about it after all these years. She was a grown woman—not a scared girl of seventeen. She had choices now. They weren't *good* choices, but at least she was no longer powerless and destitute.

She stared at the ink and paper before her, hating what she was about to do. Giving in to a blackmailer might not be wise, but it was a small price to pay for more time—even a little more time.

Daphne picked up another quill from her desk.

Daphne halted in the doorway to the breakfast room. Hugh was seated at the table, eating. He usually ate in his room.

He looked up from his newspaper and stood, his lips curving into a warm, welcoming smile. "Good morning, my dear." He wore a dark green coat, buckskin breeches, and top boots that shone like black glass; he looked every inch the country gentleman. Well, except for the savage scar, eye patch, and wicked glint in his eye.

"Good morning." She smoothed her already smooth gray skirt. "Some tea and toast, please," she said to the hovering footman before taking the seat Hugh had pulled out for her—the chair closest to him.

"May I serve you something from the sideboard, my lady?"

"No, thank you." It would be all she could do to choke down tea and toast.

He resumed his seat and Daphne watched with morbid fascination as he commenced to eat his breakfast: a sirloin, two slabs of ham, a mountain of eggs, several thick, crusty pieces of bread, a steaming cup of inky black coffee, and a pewter tankard of ale.

He grinned at her stunned expression. "I need some energy. I'm off to Tunbridge Wells today."

"Will you be *sprinting* there?"

He chuckled. "Have you any commissions for me while I'm in town?"

Daphne thought about the transfer instructions she'd just written, authorizing the draught for Malcolm. Well, it would save her a trip.

"Could you drop off a letter with my banker? I use Barings, and a gentleman named Pickard sees to my business."

He finished chewing a mouthful of food and washed it down with some ale. "It would be my pleasure. Is there nothing else? Do you need any ribbons? Some lace? Colorful baubles? Perhaps the latest German philosophical tome?"

Daphne ignored his jesting. "Gates informed me two newspapermen were discovered hiding in the dairy."

The humor drained from his face. "Ah, yes, that. I apologize."

"It is hardly your fault. Even so, I shouldn't like any of them to approach the boys."

"Neither would I. I've already engaged men from East-bourne but will hire several more to patrol the property until the furor dies down." He refilled his tankard from a pitcher. "There is another thing."

"Yes?"

"I daresay you might have noticed there's been a rather daunting amount of post for me?"

That was an understatement. It seemed every aristocrat in Britain had sent a missive in the past weeks. His formidable aunt, Lady Letitia, had sent several. Daphne could only imagine what Hugh's stern, terrifying aunt had said—several times.

She allowed herself a slight smile. "Oh, has there? I hadn't noticed."

He snorted. "Very droll. In any case, I'm having a devil of a time keeping scads of family from converging on Lessing Hall and—"

"Oh, please—don't keep them away on *my* account. I'm sure the boys would enjoy seeing family. Especially their Aunt Letitia, whom they've not seen since their christening. Also, a number of neighbors have called. On you, not on me. It is *your* duty to respond."

"In *any case*," he repeated, "I've only managed to delay my Aunt Letitia by promising to make haste to London. I shall be glad to accompany you to Town if you are willing to delay your departure until the *Ghost* returns."

Daphne ignored the leaping and fluttering in her chest and said coolly, "When would that be?" Not that it mattered, as she'd done nothing about arranging her own plans.

"Unfortunately, it will be almost a month."

A month! A month! She would have him here for another month!

"I will see if it fits with my plans."

He winked at her. "Well, that's all a man can ask, isn't it?"

Daphne looked down at the toast she'd been holding halfway to her mouth for the past minute and bit it. Hard.

The meal continued in silence until Hugh pushed away

from the table and leaned back in his chair, patting his flat midriff with one massive hand. "Poor Pasha! I'm afraid I shall need a ladder to mount him after this meal."

Daphne pulled her eyes from the taut, narrow waist of his coat to the empty plates in front of him. "You are an insatiable eater."

He stretched his immaculately booted legs while regarding her through a half-closed eye. "I am insatiable in many ways."

The small bite of toast she'd taken expanded to the size of a loaf and she masticated laboriously before swallowing.

"What business have you in town?" She was impressed by how cool she sounded when he continued to look at her in such a manner.

"I, too, have some banking. It's damned inconvenient hauling around trunks filled with pieces of eight." Daphne's eyes widened and Hugh laughed. "My dear Daphne, you really must not believe everything I say. I am actually well-acquainted with bank draughts."

A new fantasy filled her mind, this one involving her teacup and his beautiful head.

He smiled, blissfully unaware of her violent thoughts. "Will tells me I can find some decent livestock and perhaps even a suitable rig in Tunbridge." He took another drink of ale and casually dragged the back of his massive hand across his mouth.

Daphne's cup clattered against her saucer.

"Oh, I beg your pardon," he said when he saw her shocked expression. He plucked up his napkin and dabbed it lightly over his mocking smile, making Daphne realize his lapse in table manners had been deliberate. She shook her head; he seemed unable to resist provoking a rise from her and she seemed unable to resist obliging him.

He tossed his napkin onto the table before standing, his lithe movements giving no sign he'd just consumed enough food for three men. "I should be off if I am going to be back by dinner. I shall see you this evening, Daphne."

She waited until after he'd left the room before going to the window, which overlooked the front drive. In a few moments he descended the steps wearing a coat with a dozen capes and a tall beaver hat. He joined Kemal, who stood with the horses, and pulled on his gloves while exchanging a few words with the much smaller man.

They were preparing to mount when William Standish and his sister Meg approached in a gig. Hugh tossed his hat and whip to Kemal before striding toward Meg and sweeping her into an embrace that lifted her off the ground.

Bitter yearning clawed at her as Hugh swung the tiny woman around, both of them laughing. He gave her a kiss on the mouth and the two chatted in the manner of old friends. Had they been lovers, too? Was Rowena correct in believing Hugh was the father of this woman's child—a beautiful blond-haired boy of sixteen or seventeen. A boy Daphne knew had no acknowledged father?

She glanced at William, who stood off to one side, watching the interaction between his sister and former master with an impassive expression. After a few minutes Hugh lifted the petite woman into the gig and waved as she drove away. And then he turned and smiled directly at Daphne, raising his crop to his hat in a mocking salute.

Daphne jerked back from the window and then felt like a fool. "Horrible man," she muttered under her breath. After watching them disappear down the drive, she returned to the table. But her tea had grown cold and she had lost what little appetite she'd had.

Daphne received a letter from Randall a few days later. He'd written from his daughter's house in West Riding—not far from one of the Earl of Davenport's properties—to say he would inspect the northern estate while he was in the area. That meant he would not be back for the planned inspection of Elm Cottage.

Daphne would have postponed the outing another few weeks, but a young couple was waiting for its repairs before they could marry. Besides, she could hardly put off all her dealings with Hugh until Randall's return. There were a dozen other tenant cottages that needed attention, not to mention a pressing drainage issue with the home farm.

Elm Cottage was on the border of the property that marched with Malcolm's, and Daphne hadn't been near the little farmstead since well before Thomas died. She arrived at the stables a few minutes early to find both Pasha and Carmel already saddled but nobody about. She'd just decided to step outside to look for Hugh when Rowena emerged from the tack room.

She saw Daphne and started. "I didn't know you were going riding, my lady. I should have been there to help you dress."

Daphne didn't bother reminding the older woman she'd told her about the ride a mere two hours earlier.

"What are you doing down here, Rowena?"

"I had a recipe for Will Standish to bring to his sister." Her eyes moved to something over Daphne's shoulder and narrowed.

Hugh stood in the doorway behind her. "I'm sorry I'm late, Daphne." He smiled at Rowena. "Ah, good afternoon, Miss Claxton."

Rowena made a grunting sound. "I'd best be getting back," she said to Daphne. "You be careful, my lady."

Hugh watched her go with a rueful smile. "Was it something I said?"

Daphne could think of no acceptable excuse for her servant's rude behavior. "Shall we be off, my lord?"

The day was another brilliant, sunny masterpiece with a sky the color of a robin's egg. Daphne kept up a running commentary on the various schemes and plans she and Randall had formed for a few of the properties they passed, only pausing when they approached the cottage where William Standish lived with his nephew and sister.

The blond man was out pruning one of the fruit trees in his small orchard and Daphne prepared to rein in. Will saw them and paused in his work, but Hugh merely waved and did not stop.

How curious.

Daphne couldn't help herself. "You mentioned on your first evening home that you and William Standish had once been quite close?"

"Yes, Will and I are the same age and Meg only a year younger. The three of us roamed the estate like a pack of young hounds. Their father was the earl's steward for many years, a position I know he wanted Will to one day assume."

"Yes, Thomas offered him the position more than once, but Mr. Standish declined it."

"Will loved working with horses too much to be steward. It was a bone of contention between him and his father." He gave her a wry smile. "We are not as close as we once were. I'm afraid he's been angry with me since I sent him back to England all those years ago."

"Angry? Whatever for?"

"He believes I robbed him of a grand adventure when we switched identities and I sent him back in my place."

"But you saved his *life*."

"Most likely."

"Surely he must be grateful for that."

Hugh cut her a sideways look. "Must he?"

"Of course, he is not a foolish man."

"Not foolish, but wistful, perhaps. I daresay reading the exploits of One-Eyed Standish in the newspapers all these years has caused its share of heartburn. He believes it could have been *he* who lived the life of a carefree, swashbuckling privateer."

Daphne had no response for that; men were certainly odd creatures.

"The truth is the sultan's men would have killed him before we even reached Oran rather than doctor him. A slave who could not work was not worth anything."

"A slave? But I thought you said you avoided being sent to the slave markets?"

He smiled, but there was no humor in it. "My dearest Daphne, I might not have been sold at market, but what else did you suppose I was to the sultan?" He did not wait for an answer. "In a way, Will is right to envy me. I've seen wondrous things in my life. A mountain exploding fire in the middle of the ocean, the Great Wall of China at dawn, a flock of coral-colored birds so vast the sky itself was pink." He shrugged. "I robbed William of those things. But I also robbed him of rowing under the lash of a brutal overseer, of watching friends die from beatings, starvation, cruelty, or neglect, of quarrying stone under the merciless Saharan sun until you could hear your own brain boiling—" He stopped and laughed bitterly. "But what a bore I am."

Daphne wanted to grab his arm and shake him, to force him to share the wonders—and even the horrors—of his fascinating life.

But a lifetime of reticence won out and all she could say was, "You are not boring me, Hugh."

His gaze flickered over her at her rare use of his Christian name—as if he heard something else beneath her words—and he continued. "Rather than covet my life, William should have lived his own to the fullest. That is the most important lesson I have learned in almost four decades. Life is fleeting and precious and a man"—he cut her a glance—"or a woman, must seize every opportunity to enjoy it. Never take even one day for granted." His smile turned self-deprecating.

"There you have it, Daphne, the profound philosophy of Hugh Redvers—a man whose careers include hellion, slave, and privateer."

"And what career is it that you are pursuing now?" She could see her question surprised him, but he recovered quickly.

"Oh, I am on a holiday."

"A holiday?"

"Yes. I have not returned to stay, only to make a certain peace with my past." His mouth turned down at the corners and he stared grimly ahead. "I should have done so when my uncle was still alive, I know that, but I was weak-willed and could not make myself come back."

Daphne did not believe for an instant that was the reason he'd stayed away. "Will you depart on the *Ghost* when it returns?"

"Hmm?" he asked, turning away from whatever thoughts seemed to be obsessing him.

"You will leave England soon?"

His teasing smile told her his brief moment of confidence was at an end. "Why, Daphne, are you trying to be rid of me—already?"

He spent the rest of the short ride teasing and flirting with her; speaking lots of words, but saying nothing.

It took them a little over an hour to fully inspect the small cottage and two outbuildings. They were returning to their horses when the sound of angry voices could be heard coming from the small stand of trees behind the cottage.

Hugh held a finger to his pursed lips and motioned for her to stay by the horses. Daphne nodded and he moved quickly, and surprisingly quietly, disappearing behind the corner of the house. A few seconds later there was a female shriek followed by the low rumble of Hugh's voice. And then nothing. She'd just decided to investigate when two people came around the corner, Hugh right behind them.

"Fowler?" Daphne recalled a moment too late that her former maid had married the man behind her, Owen Blake. Daphne had been surprised and not a little hurt when Fowler had decided to stay at Whitton Park to wed Blake all those years ago. She knew most people believed the rather homely Mary Fowler was fortunate to snare the handsome footman, but Daphne had never trusted the preening Blake. She'd also suspected him of carrying tales to Malcolm.

She hadn't seen either of the Blakes up close since leaving that wretched house ten years ago; neither had aged well. Mary's skin was a yellowish gray and a fine webbing of telling red veins spread over her nose and cheeks. Her husband's once-handsome face was florid and jowly, the whites of his eyes bloodshot. Both servants stood with the tense posture of people who'd been interrupted in the middle of something embarrassing.

Daphne looked from face to face. "Is aught amiss?"

Hugh shrugged, staring at the other two.

Mary Blake dropped a wobbly curtsy. "There's nothing amiss, my lady. We were looking for Blake's hound, Sprite. I'm afraid I left the door to the shed open and she got away."

Daphne could hear the lie in her words. "Lord Ramsay and I have been here over an hour and have not seen her."

Blake's eyes swept Daphne in a bold and unfriendly manner. "I'm sure the bitch will make her way home when she is hungry enough." He turned to his wife. "We'd best be getting back to Whitton Park. My lord." He nodded at Hugh and took his wife's arm. Mary Blake shot Daphne an apologetic look over her shoulder as her husband all but dragged her away.

"What in heaven's name was that all about?" Daphne asked after they'd disappeared.

Hugh lifted her into the saddle and handed her the reins.

"They were arguing quite heatedly when I came upon them, but I could not make out the substance of the disagreement. I collect they must live just beyond that stand of trees?"

"Yes, their cottage is one of the larger ones on Malcolm's estate."

"I do not believe they were arguing about a dog." He shrugged and glanced around. "If I remember correctly, there should be a shortcut that leads to a rather pleasant meadow." He shot her a challenging look. "Do you care for a gallop?"

Daphne could see the notion of besting her on horseback amused him. "You must mean the South Meadow? Yes, there is a rather nice path just ahead." She pointed over his shoulder and when he turned to look, she snapped her reins and Carmel bolted toward the real path.

Delighted laughter echoed behind her. "She plays us foul, Pasha!"

Daphne grinned as she reined in to guide Carmel down the twisty path through the section of woods. The trail was seldom used these days and branches clawed at her hair and habit. The sound of hooves and shouted curses behind her told her the low-hanging branches were even harder on the huge man and his big horse.

Sunlight bathed the path ahead of her and she leaned low and gave the frisky mare her head, exploding from the woods into the meadow.

Daphne had ridden this stretch of land hundreds of times and knew it like the back of her hand. Even so, she expected the magnificent Pasha to overtake her much smaller Carmel any moment. But Hugh had still not caught up with her when she reached the rise at the other end of the bowl-shaped meadow. She reined in, expecting him to fly past and surprise her. But when she swung Carmel around and swept the meadow, all she saw was Pasha, prancing near the trailhead into the woods. Riderless.

"Good God!" She drove Carmel back down the hill, her pace beyond reckless. Hugh's body lay crumpled in the grass a short distance from his saddle. Daphne slid gracelessly to the ground before Carmel had even stopped and dropped to her knees, lowering her cheek against his nose and mouth, holding her own breath to listen. A puff of warm air grazed her skin and she choked back a sob and kissed him hard on the mouth, weak with relief.

Naturally he chose that moment to open his single eye. His lips moved.

"What was that?" Daphne leaned closer.

"The lengths to which a man must go for a kiss," he whispered and then laughed, the action sending a spasm of pain across his face. "Blast!" He squeezed his eye shut and that was when Daphne noticed his head rested on a rock, and there was a smear of red on it.

Cold fear slithered down her spine. "Hugh, can you move your hands and feet?"

He opened his eye and shifted his legs and arms, wincing.

Crippling relief replaced fear; thank God he was not paralyzed as Thomas had been after his fall.

She met his puzzled gaze. "You hit your head. Hold still while I check." She pulled off her gloves and tossed them aside before sliding her fingers into his hair. There was a sizeable goose egg oozing blood, but not heavily.

"Where else do you feel pain?"

He lifted a hand to shield his eye from the sun and then quickly lowered it. "It feels like I have broken my collarbone, something I've done before." He gave her his standard teasing smile, but it was shadowed by pain. "It is also bloody uncomfortable when I breathe."

That sounded like broken or bruised ribs.

"We need to get you back to the house, and I think a carriage would be the best thing."

His face wore an expression she'd never seen before:

embarrassment. He nodded. "While it crushes my masculine pride to agree with you, I doubt I could mount Pasha at this point."

"I'm going to fetch your saddle and put it under your head so you are more comfortable."

His saddle lay not far from where Pasha was calmly cropping grass.

She lifted it and swept a hand beneath it to flip the girth-cinch on top and keep it from dragging. That's when she noticed it was only half as long as normal. She peered at it and saw the tightly woven strap was torn: the tear straight and without ragged edges. Almost as if it had been . . . cut. Her body froze while her mind raced. This wasn't an accident, this wasn't—

Movement in her peripheral vision reminded her of the man who lay injured and waiting, and she swallowed her worry, hefted the saddle higher and carried it toward him. He watched in silence as she removed her riding coat, folded it into a square, and slid both saddle and coat beneath his neck, adjusting them until some of the tension seemed to drain from his body.

"Better?" she asked, her hand stroking the damp hair from his forehead before she knew what she was doing.

His wicked smile had returned. "Much better, thank you."

"If your skull is concussed you should not sleep—try to keep your eyes open. Count sheep or doubloons or . . . or women to keep awake."

His white teeth flashed. "I'll count Daphnes."

Daphne had to swallow down her heart, which had leapt into her throat yet again. "I will be back as soon as I can." She began to push herself up.

He caught her hand, his single pupil large. "Be careful, Daphne."

A chill shot up her spine at both his eye and his words but

then she realized he could not possibly know about the cut girth—at least not yet.

Daphne nodded and roughly squeezed his hand. "Stay awake."

She caught Carmel's bridle, used an old tree stump as a mounting block, and headed for Lessing Hall as if the Devil himself were on her heels.

Chapter Ten

The carriage journey to Lessing Hall took no more than a half hour, but Hugh's face was gray and the lines of pain around his eyes and mouth were deeply etched by the time it was over.

Daphne left him in Kemal's capable hands and hastened to her room, where she changed out of her habit by herself rather than ringing for help. The process took longer but she needed time alone to compose herself, to think about the cut girth. And most of all, to pray Hugh Redvers had not taken any permanent harm.

Garbed in a dress of somber dark gray, she headed downstairs three-quarters of an hour later.

Gates met her in the Great Hall. "Doctor Nichols arrived not long after you did, my lady."

"That was very fast."

"It was fortunate he was home at the time." Gates opened the door to the Yellow Drawing Room and followed her inside. "Would you like me to have tea sent in, my lady?"

"Yes, but wait until the doctor is finished and send him in. Did he say how long he would be?"

"He was just—"

A knock interrupted whatever he was going to say and

the door opened to expose Doctor Nichols with his scuffed black bag.

"Thank you for coming so quickly, Doctor." Daphne smiled at the older man, pushing away the memories his kind, weathered face unfortunately evoked—memories of Thomas slowly wasting away in his sickbed.

He regarded her through keen, gray eyes and bowed. "I am sorry I am once again needed, my lady."

"Will you stay for tea?"

"Tea would be lovely."

Gates left and Daphne gestured to one of the comfortable, overstuffed chairs.

"How is Lord Ramsay?"

"His lordship has at least two cracked ribs and a few more that are bruised," he began in his abrupt way. "He also has a broken collarbone and a badly bruised muscle in one leg. Those injuries can only be treated with time and rest. My biggest concern is his head. He is showing no signs of concussion but there is a sizeable lump and I would like to keep him under observation for forty-eight hours."

Daphne nodded. "Of course."

"I want to keep watch for any forgetfulness, confusion, slurred speech, or a persistent, severe headache. If you notice any of those symptoms, send for me at once." He hesitated. "He is rather a determined man and I fear he might not stay abed."

Daphne thought of Kemal's serious, intelligent—and equally determined—eyes and smiled. "I believe his manservant will be of some help in that regard."

"Yes, I spoke to him already—a most sensible gentleman."

The door opened and a servant entered with the tea; Gates must have anticipated her orders to have had it ready so quickly.

She dismissed the maid and turned to the heaped tray, allowing the tea to steep a moment longer while she prepared a plate. The doctor's eyes widened at the selection of pastries and sandwiches she handed him.

"Ah, you are too kind, my lady." He ate a small sandwich in two bites and then smiled sheepishly. "I'm afraid I've been too busy for breakfast or tea today." He accepted the cup of tea and gulped down a steaming mouthful, eating a lemon tart before sighing, an expression of contentment on his worn features.

"I gave him a mild sedative—which I would not have done if I'd been terribly worried about a concussion—only because I believe it might keep him in his bed and he needs rest more than anything. His ribs are bound and should be tightened periodically. Aside from that"—he shrugged—"time and rest." He sipped his tea before continuing. "Keeping him under observation might seem unusual when I'm not overly worried about concussion, but I saw signs of prior head trauma—rather severe." He fiddled nervously with the handle of his teacup. "I'll be frank, my lady. Lord Ramsay has been exposed to extremely brutal treatment."

Daphne's cup and saucer rattled as she set it down and the doctor glanced away, swallowing loudly. "He has . . . well, he has a great number of scars. Some of them—" He broke off, his cheeks puffing out as he noisily expelled a mouthful of air. "I would go so far as to say he's been tortured."

The room was silent but for the ticking of the gaudy ormolu clock on the mantelpiece.

Daphne struggled for something intelligent to say, but all she could manage was, "Torture?"

His kind eyes were bleak. "In addition to evidence of several skull fractures, there are dozens—maybe even hundreds—of scars on his chest, back, and arms—" Again he stopped, and then nodded abruptly. "Yes, it is my professional opinion he was tortured."

They sat in silence.

It was the doctor who finally broke the spell when he set

down his empty cup and saucer and cleared his throat. "I hate to eat and bolt away, but Kitty Fenwick is in the straw and it's her first child."

Daphne nodded absently, still reeling.

The doctor heaved himself to his feet. "I'll be back to-morrow morning if I have no word from you in the interim. I can see myself out, Lady Davenport." He retrieved his bag and quietly left the room.

Daphne had been a fool to think life as a slave would leave no scars, but should she have guessed he'd been tortured? She'd assumed the scar across his face was the result of one of the many sword battles she'd imagined him engaging in. She recalled the cut girth and closed her eyes, a sick feeling blooming and blossoming inside her. Will Standish would have seen the girth by now and Daphne already knew what he would say: somebody had cut it—somebody had wanted to hurt Hugh. If the girth had broken only seconds earlier—while he'd been tearing through the trees . . .

Daphne told herself not to borrow more trouble. She needed to focus on what *had* happened and why. Hugh Redvers had been gone from England almost two decades; who could possibly gain from his death?

Daphne could think of no one.

No one except herself and her sons.

Kemal was in the dressing room when Daphne entered the Rose Room—a bedroom her husband had occupied for the six months before his death. She fought down the thick, noxious fog of emotions the room elicited and turned her attention to its current occupant.

Hugh's sleeping body dwarfed the enormous four-poster bed. He was breathing deeply and regularly, his torso bare but for a stark white bandage. The patch that covered his eye had been removed and she saw the eyelid was undamaged, the skin above and below pulled by a thin white line. She shuddered when she realized his eye had been open at the time of his injury; he would have witnessed whatever had delivered such a punishing cut.

Her gaze slid from his eye to the white scars that criss-crossed his massive shoulders and chest. The doctor had spoken the truth: they were too numerous to count.

She reached out to touch the raised lines that were only partially hidden by the golden hair, her mind unable to absorb what she was seeing. Who or what had done this to him—how could any human survive so much pain?

Only when she saw the tears on his bandage did she realize she was crying. She looked up to find Kemal standing across from her, his face an unreadable mask. She lifted the blankets higher, covering the terrible secrets carved into his skin, and then gestured toward the dressing room. She shut the door so they might speak without waking their patient.

"Doctor Nichols told me Lord Ramsay had prior head injuries?"

"That was before I was with him, my lady."

Daphne wanted to prod and pry, but she suspected this man was too loyal to speak about his captain.

"The doctor wants somebody with him at all times. You take the first watch and I will relieve you at midnight."

"I am capable of staying awake for many hours, my lady. I do not require any assistance."

She smiled at him. "There are two of us to share nursing duties, Kemal. There is no reason for either of us to become exhausted."

He bowed his head. "As you wish, my lady."

Daphne left Kemal to his duties and went to the school-room, where the boys were anxiously waiting for her.

"Mama, what happened?" Lucien demanded, his fore-head wrinkled with worry.

Daphne turned to Rowena, who often spent time with the

boys to give their somewhat elderly nurse relief from her boisterous charges.

"I will speak to the boys in private," Daphne said, leading her sons toward the battered table where generations of Redverses had done their schoolwork—or not.

She waited until the boys were seated. "Lord Ramsay had an accident while riding Pasha. He is doing well and resting in the Rose Room."

The silence was ominous and Daphne looked from one pair of identical brown eyes to the other. "Come, I know you must have questions."

Richard shoved back his chair hard enough to knock it over, his eyes blazing. "Is he going to die—just like Papa?"

Daphne took his hand and pulled him toward her. "Of course not, sweetheart!" She squeezed his small, rough fingers. "He has a broken collarbone and a few bruised ribs. It is nothing at all like Papa's injuries." She could not tell them about the possible danger to his head.

Richard's expression turned mulish. "Papa fell from his horse and you put him in the Rose Room and he *died*."

Her son's logic was infallible.

Daphne drew both boys close, one in each arm. She spoke into Richard's curly blond hair. "Yes, that is true, Richard, but your papa's injury was much more severe and he was not as young and healthy as your cousin Hugh. He is only in the Rose Room because it is the nicest room on the main floor." She kissed the top of his head. "It is only a room, Richard."

"May we see him?" Richard said, squirming away to look at her.

"He is resting now and will sleep through tonight. It is possible you might visit him tomorrow or perhaps the next day." Richard continued to look skeptical, his expression so like hers, it caught her by surprise.

"Why would Hugh fall, Mama?" Lucien sounded amazed his idol could have such an accident.

"It happens to even the best riders. I have taken falls and so will you. Come," she said, taking advantage of the moment of calm introspection to herd them toward the washbasins and the hated before-dinner ritual.

When she left them an hour later, they were still subdued, but at least they were chattering to each other.

Rowena was waiting in a chair in the hallway. "How is he?" she asked, putting aside her needlework.

"He is sleeping."

"Will this delay the trip to London, my lady?"

Daphne frowned. "How could you even ask such a thing, Rowena? Of course we will not leave him here while we jaunt off to London." Honestly, sometimes Daphne wondered if the woman wasn't unhinged.

"Yes, of course." Rowena looked down at her hands, which she was lacing and unlacing. "For how long, my lady?"

Daphne glared at her bowed head, sorely tempted to give in to her fear, anxiety, and anger and deliver a thorough dressing down. But she held back; Rowena was old and set in her ways and she had taken Hugh in dislike—a thing she'd done often enough in the past. What good would scolding her do?

"I refuse to justify that question with an answer," she finally said. "Doctor Nichols wants to keep him resting for at least two days. I shall watch him tonight. You may sit with him tomorrow, if you care to be helpful." She turned to leave, but Rowena's voice stopped her.

"I should sit with him tonight, my lady. It would be more proper," she said, managing to sound nervous and adamant at the same time.

Daphne spun around. "Proper? To care for him when he is sick?" She strode back toward her. "Rowena, are you not sensible of what we owe this man?" She didn't wait for an answer. "You can relieve Kemal tomorrow afternoon and that is an end to it."

She marched away without waiting for an answer, deliberately putting Rowena and her phobia of Hugh out of her mind. To own the truth, Daphne was more than a little worried about her *own* state of mind since Hugh Redvers's arrival. And now there was this—somebody trying to hurt or kill him?

She wanted to barricade herself in the library and never come out again.

Daphne woke just before midnight. She'd slept, but only lightly, anxious about spending the night in Hugh's bedroom even though he would be sound asleep. She considered her sleeping cap for a long moment and then removed it. After tidying her hair she put on her periwinkle-blue dressing gown, the most flattering garment in her entire wardrobe. This would be the first time she wore clothing around him that was not gray or black and he would be asleep. Daphne was ashamed to admit to such vanity, but there it was. She tied the eight ribbons that closed the gown and picked up the book she'd been reading to the boys at bedtime.

Kemal was waiting for her and stepped into the hall to give her a brief report.

"He slept without waking but had a fitful period after which I tightened his bandages." He gave her a speculative look. "You may leave such tasks until the morning, if you wish, my lady."

Daphne was amused by his concern for her tender female sensibilities. "Get some rest, Kemal. I will take good care of your captain."

Kemal bowed deeply and padded away down the hall.

Hugh had a bit more color than earlier and a slight sheen of perspiration glistened on his forehead. He did not stir when Daphne seated herself beside the bed and adjusted the brace of candles to keep it from shining on his face.

She wasn't sure how long she'd been reading when he began moving restlessly and mumbling. She leaned closer to listen, but the words were too garbled. She was just about to return to her reading when he flung himself onto his side and then cried out as he rolled onto his injured ribs.

Daphne tried to roll him onto his back, but it was like trying to move a fallen oak tree. She exerted more pressure on his shoulder and his other hand shot out and grabbed her wrist, yanking her toward him.

His eyes were wide open, both of them. "I'll see you dead before I let you lay a hand on me again," he hissed, his grip as brutal as a snare.

"Hugh, it is Daphne," she whispered as he tightened his grasp.

He stared up at her with mismatched eyes, one a blazing emerald green, one a cool, mossy gray, as if it had been leeched of color.

"Please, you must lie back, Hugh." She grabbed his arm with her free hand and used her body to press him back, careful to avoid his ribs and collarbone.

"You lying bastard! You killed them—all of them!" The words were filled with a soul-wrenching agony and he thrashed wildly, pulling her onto his ribs. He yelped and released her, falling back onto the bed and shielding his chest with both arms, his eyes squeezed shut.

Just as suddenly as he'd erupted, he became still, his breaths coming in shallow, ragged bursts. Sweat ran down his temples in rivers.

Daphne wet a cloth in the basin of cool water and sponged his brow; he radiated heat like a banked fire. With her free hand, she stroked the fine silver-gold strands at his temples, a motion that seemed to soothe him. After a few minutes his breathing slowed, and he wasn't perspiring so heavily. She continued to smooth his damp hair, feathering the fine lines around his eyes and tracing the deep groove that ran from the side of his nose to his mouth. His face was a study in contrasts, his angular chiseled jaw softened by full lips and long blond lashes that fanned his sun-bronzed skin. His nose was as straight as a knife's edge, the white notch in the bridge the only flaw.

The urge to press her lips against his—to taste him again, to dip into the heat and the softness of his mouth—made her thighs tighten in a way that sent powerful spirals of pleasure straight to her sex. She forced herself to look away from his tempting mouth. Not that the sight of his scarred, muscular shoulders lessened her desire to touch him.

His arms were crossed protectively over his chest, his biceps bulging and his right hand bunched into a fist. She gently loosened the fingers, massaging his taut, striated forearm until the muscles relaxed. Once his hand was open she put her own against it, palm to palm.

Thomas had been a tall man, only a few inches shorter than Hugh, but his hands had been those of an aristocrat: white and elegant and unmarked, hands accustomed to doing nothing more strenuous than holding the reins of a horse and tending orchids.

Hugh's fingernails were neatly squared and smooth, but the hand against hers was not that of a man of leisure. It was massive, its scars, enlarged knuckles, and the thick muscles of his fingers and wrist silent evidence he'd known punishing work. His forearms were brawny but well-defined, leading to heavily muscled biceps that were as bronzed as his face, making her realize he must go without a shirt on occasion. She swallowed at the thought, the sight of all this masculine power lying within her reach making her giddy and aroused as she recalled the last time his big hands had been on her body.

She laid his arm at his side, her palms sweating, her

hands shaking. She needed to get away from him—away from who she became when his body touched hers. After a lifetime of rational thought and behavior, why had she suddenly developed such a capacity for self-destruction and foolishness?

She glanced up and gasped: he was watching her, both eyes open, his face a mask of feverish intensity. Moving faster than she would have thought possible for a man in his condition, his hand shot behind her neck and he pulled her down, his lips crushing hers before she could make a sound.

His arm was like a vise, holding her motionless while his hot mouth sealed over hers. This was not like the last kiss, when he'd gentled her. This time he pushed into her without hesitation, thrusting without invitation and showing no restraint. Daphne opened beneath the onslaught and he held her in an unbreakable embrace.

Instead of feeling caught or bound by his touch, his hold freed her and she surrendered to the silken heat of him, their mouths engaging in a challenging, sensual joust she had relived a thousand times over. This time she did what she'd been too scared to do before. She tilted her head and seized the offensive, stroking deep into his mouth and mimicking his actions, exploring him without reserve, her body shaking with . . . something.

He made a deep sound of pleasure and his hand slid down her neck, grazing the taut column of her throat before drifting over her shoulder and settling between her arm and rib cage, where he stroked up and down the side of her breast, a butterfly touch that followed the contours of her body and became firmer with each pass.

His tongue wrapped around hers and they engaged in an erotic dance as he taught her newer, more exciting moves. His hand caressed her side again, this time boldly curving around her breast, his thumb grazing her nipple through the fine silk of her dressing gown, moving in circles over the taut, sensitive tip, over and over.

She gasped and pulled away and he nudged her chin, tilting her head back to get at the sensitive underside of her jaw, nuzzling and sucking and biting his way down, and then back up to her lips.

Daphne opened her eyes and looked straight into his. Up close the injured eye was fascinating, bisected cleanly, a pale gray ring that surrounded a pupil that appeared to be frozen open, so large it seemed to swallow her whole. She wanted to dive deeply until she found him—the man who lived behind the easy laughter, the smooth, lazy charm, the skilled lovemaking.

He pulled her closer and the arm she'd been using to support her body slipped and she dropped onto his chest.

"Aiyee!" He thrust her away like a burning coal, pressing his body into the bed to get away. Daphne jerked back and pushed up her heavily fogged spectacles.

"I'm so sorry, Hugh!" She shifted her weight and Hugh hissed in a breath.

"Daphne, perhaps you should return to your chair." He was cradling his chest, his expression apprehensive.

His words scalded her. "Oh. Yes, of course." She leapt to her feet and dropped clumsily into her chair, commencing to fuss with her rumpled gown, too miserable to even think— a first in her adult life.

"Daphne?"

She twitched her skirt straight and retied one of the ribbons.

"Daphne, look at me, sweetheart."

She looked up at the warmth in his voice and the endearment.

He smiled, and there was both amusement and pain in the expression. "I apologize for sending you away, but I'm afraid I can't exercise any restraint if you remain within reach." He gestured to the bedding that covered him, now tented around his hips.

Daphne's brain took a moment to absorb what her eyes were seeing.

"Oh!" She looked away, lust, mortification, and curiosity swirling inside her. "It is I who should be apologizing for waking you." She directed her words toward the bedpost.

"Yes, you should."

Her head whipped around.

He was grinning. "There, I knew that would get you to look at me rather than the furniture." He laughed and then winced. "Damnation, that smarts!" He clutched his side and took several shallow breaths. "Wicked woman, stop trying to beat me up or make me laugh. Tell me, what you are doing here at this hour? Dressed as you are." His one eye did the work of two as it roamed her body, smoldering. The sheet around his waist jumped in her peripheral vision.

Her mouth went dry at the primitive desire on his face and she yanked her eyes away. How could he discompose her with only a look? She stared at the patterned carpet and did what she always did when she needed to focus her attention and gain control of her thoughts: she conjugated Latin.

Amo, amas, amat—

"Daphne?"

amamus, amatis, amant.

"Do I need to ring for Kemal to get an answer?"

She looked up at the threat. "Doctor Nichols wants to keep you under observation for a while."

"What the devil for?" He didn't wait for an answer. "Where is Kemal? Surely he should be here *observing* me?"

"He *has* been observing you, for the greater part of the day and evening. As much as watching you snore is a delight to him, I insisted he get some sleep."

Hugh raised his eyebrows at her tart tone and then frowned, his left hand going to his temple. A hard, cold look

slid across his face and transformed him into someone
else—someone terrifying.

"Where is my eye patch?" His voice held a chill menace
she'd not heard since that day in the clearing, with Malcolm.

"I do not know—it was not on you when I arrived."

"Will you find it for me, please?" His mismatched eyes
skewered her as if she were a thief he'd interrupted riffling
his luggage.

"Of course I will bring it to you," she said with deliberate
calm, rising from her chair and going to his dressing room
on shaking legs. Once she was beyond his sight, she leaned
against a tall cupboard and caught her breath. What in heaven's
name was *that* all about? He'd gone from teasing lover to
gelid stranger in a heartbeat. Who *was* this man?

Daphne stared into the small mirror atop the bureau, forcing her pulse to slow and schooling her face into neutral
lines before picking up the leather patch and returning to the
other room.

"Here." She tossed the small scrap of leather onto his
chest and turned away.

"Thank you, Daphne," he said a moment later.

She turned and found him smiling up at her, as sunny as
ever.

"May I have a glass of water, please?"

Daphne hesitated. Had she imagined the personality
change? It had happened so quickly it—

"I apologize for my rudeness." His expression was honestly repentant, without his characteristic amusement.

She nodded, more than a little shaken. It didn't startle her
that he would apologize; he did not seem like the kind of
man who would find it difficult to admit when he was wrong.
What startled her was his ability to shift moods in an instant.
He appeared so amiable now—but was that amiability just
a mask?

She brought him a glass of water.

"Thank you. I'm afraid I'm overly sensitive. I do not care to expose my deformity to the world in general."

"I am not the world in general." For once it wasn't an effort to give him a cool look.

"You are correct, Daphne. As usual," he added, his expression far too meek for her to believe. "It has been so long since I've had a ministering angel that I've forgotten—" His gorgeous face distorted with a huge yawn. "I beg your pardon! I'm not sure what has come over me."

"Doctor Nichols gave you a sedative earlier. He wanted you to rest. You should get some sleep."

"What if I'm not tired?" She raised her eyebrows and he chuckled. "All right, I'm a little tired." He looked down at the white strips of cloth around his chest and his smile grew. "I think my bandage needs to be tightened."

She snorted and picked up her book, determined to ignore him whether he slept or not.

"Daphne?"

She turned a page.

"Daaaaaaphneeeee . . ."

The laugh broke out of her before she could stop it and she looked up. "What?"

"Won't you read to me? Please?" His brilliant green eye was half-closed and he appeared sleepy, an overgrown boy playing at being a pirate, complete with eye patch. He looked . . . adorable.

Daphne huffed out a disgusted sigh. She would read to him—or sing an aria or declaim a Shakespearean soliloquy—anything to put him to sleep.

As it turned out, he was fast asleep before she'd read five minutes. Once he was breathing deeply, she closed the book and slumped in her chair, exhausted. He looked even more beautiful asleep than he did awake, and considerably less alarming. His hair was tousled and the tanned skin of his face and neck glinted with golden growth.

Daphne was completely, utterly, foolishly infatuated; there was no use trying to deny it. She should have been outraged both times he'd touched her. Instead, she was shattered that he'd stopped. Her hands twitched to stroke his face, neck, and all the parts of him she could imagine but had never seen. She drank in the sensual curve of his full lower lip, remembering how he'd felt and tasted—how his mouth was soft and firm at the same time. And his upper lip, much more chiseled but every bit as skillful and teasing.

Raw, demanding want pulsed through her body and she dropped her head back and closed her eyes. What was she to *do*? Did this type of thing simply need to run its course— like a fever or infectious disease?

Her mind drifted back to the book she kept hidden in her bedside table. At least now she knew something about what occurred between men and women. She had read the entire book, several parts more than once. The story in *Fanny Hill* was rubbish, but the graphic descriptions provided information beyond price.

The analytical part of her mind, which she'd formerly believed the largest, was fascinated by the variety of physical acts possible between a man and a woman. The other part of her mind, a part she'd never known existed before Hugh arrived, thrilled at her new knowledge of human bodies and what they could do with one another.

Daphne was shocked and excited by how merely reading about lovemaking could cause such physical reactions. Her newfound knowledge of what men and women did in private made her regard men—Hugh in particular—in an entirely new light. She imagined him doing to her those things she'd read about. Would she look at every attractive man she met with this new curiosity? Was that how men regarded *her*?

What a fascinating new world she had discovered, and it had existed beside the regular one all along. How glad she was none of that world had been contaminated by Malcolm and what he'd done to her on that long ago afternoon. She now understood *what* he had done, but was more confused than ever why a man would want to do such things with an unconscious woman. She was also more determined than ever to keep him away from every part of her life.

Daphne sighed, too tired to think of Malcolm right now. Instead she pondered the man sleeping on the bed; Hugh was far more than a lighthearted rake. Tonight his mood had gone from carnal to cold in an instant. She should not be surprised to find dark currents beneath his genial façade. How could there not be after such a past—after he'd suffered such terrible physical abuse?

Daphne swallowed. How would he react when she confessed what she'd done? Which expression would he wear then?

And then the memory of the cut girth came crashing down on her.

"Oh God." The words slipped from between her frozen lips. Will Standish would see the saddle soon—if he hadn't already. He would know what it meant and he would wonder who had done such a thing and why. And then he would tell Hugh, and Hugh would have those same questions.

Questions that had only one answer, as far as Daphne knew: her.

Chapter Eleven

Hugh woke to sunlight streaming through a small gap in the heavy drapes and blinked away the swirling dust motes. A quick survey of the room showed only Kemal, sitting beside the window, plying his needle on a garment.

Memories of last night flooded his mind and Hugh closed his eyes, recalling his inability to restrain himself. It was neither the sleeping draught nor a concussion that had made him grab her. He'd woken from a troubled sleep and found Daphne wearing an expression of tenderness he had never expected to see—at least not directed at him.

"You are awake, my lord."

Hugh opened his eyes. Kemal had approached in his silent way and studied Hugh from the foot of the bed.

"Yes, I am awake," Hugh agreed, grimacing as he levered himself into a sitting position so that he would not be looking up at people, something he was most unaccustomed to. Kemal arranged the cushions and bedding so that Hugh was soon comfortably placed to take a cup of tea and some fresh bread and butter Kemal seemed to have conjured from thin air.

"What is the diagnosis, Kemal?" Hugh asked as he inhaled the fragrant bergamot tea, Kemal's own blend.

"We are looking for forgetfulness, disorientation, or nausea."

"Who are you? Where am I? I believe I may vomit," Hugh said lightly, smiling and raising the cup to his lips.

"Quite so, my lord." Kemal nodded, reaffirming Hugh's belief the man was entirely without a sense of humor and more interested in straightening bedclothes than engaging in conversation with his patient.

He missed Daphne.

"How long am I expected to endure such observation?"

"Two days, my lord."

Hugh snorted and took a bite of warm bread and melting butter. "Not bloody likely," he said thickly. He hadn't rested that long when his face had been sliced in half. Even with the promise of Daphne's company, Hugh could not submit to forty-eight hours of bed rest. He grinned: unless Daphne was actually in bed *with* him.

"Is there anything better than hot bread and butter?" Hugh asked, helping himself to another slice.

Kemal merely raised his eyebrows at Hugh's rhetorical question.

Hugh sipped his tea and thought about yesterday, trying to recall how he'd fallen off his horse—which he'd not done since he was a boy. The last thing he remembered was flying off Pasha, his feet still in the stirrups. He frowned. That couldn't be right.

He drained the rest of his rapidly cooling tea and popped the last of the bread into his mouth. He needed to get dressed and speak to William. And then he needed to speak with Gates about something. He blinked his eyes, his lids heavy. . . why did he feel so bloody tired? He raised the teacup and then realized he was no longer holding it.

"Wha—?"

Kemal was pulling the blankets up around him.

"Kemal?"

"Yes, my lord?"

Hugh opened his mouth. And then forgot what he wanted to ask.

Kemal leaned so close the pores on his nose were alarmingly huge.

Hugh tried to shy away but his body was too heavy to move. "Uhh—"

"You need to rest, my lord."

Hugh stared at one particularly stout hair, mesmerized. "No, I—" Kemal's nose wavered and grew and Hugh couldn't seem to blink it back into shape. "Ahh, I am going to take a quick nap. Don't let me sleep past a half hour."

"No, my lord." His normally serious servant was smiling and his voice came from very far away.

The next time Hugh woke, Kemal was reading at his bedside.

"Good morning, my lord," he said, his gaze flicking up and then back to the book in his lap.

Morning? Hugh lifted his arm to push back his hair and gasped at the pain.

"Bloody he—" A huge yawn came over him, which also caused pain. And his head felt as though it had been stuffed with cotton wool and then beaten with a plank.

He stared accusingly at the other man. "You put a sleeping draught in my tea, didn't you?"

"Yes, my lord."

"Hell and damnation!" Hugh winced and lowered his voice. "You are *never* to drug me again, do you understand?" he demanded, sounding weak and peevish.

"Yes, my lord. No more drugs," Kemal agreed, his eyes back on his book—as if Hugh were *boring* him.

Hugh scowled. "What the devil are you reading?"

Kemal held up *Gulliver's Travels* but didn't stop reading.

So, Daphne had been here last night and Hugh had missed her visit, thanks to Kemal and his blasted sleeping draught.

"Put down that goddamned book, fetch my robe, and ring for a bath! I'm getting out of this bloody bed." He glared to let his servant know the matter was not up for debate.

Kemal bit back a smile as he went to arrange for his grumbling employer's bath. He had witnessed his captain injured many times over the years, but never had he seen the big man submit with such grace to nursing as he had these past few days.

His smile grew into a smirk; of course Kemal had seen that he slept through much of it. Lady Davenport had reported this morning that the captain had passed a night of uninterrupted sleep.

Kemal liked the countess very much. Together they had nursed the fractious privateer with very little fuss. Although Kemal would rather have attended the captain himself, he'd realized the pretty, bespectacled woman was most interested in observing the baron—especially when it came to things the English doctor had *not* asked them to look for.

Kemal chuckled as he laid out the shaving items. He'd been with One-Eyed Standish for a decade and a half—ever since Standish had escaped Sultan Babba Hassan. He had seen the man pursue—and be pursued—by many women. Some of those women had almost brought the big man to heel and some had merely made fools of themselves: like the Italian duchess they'd rescued from a corsair ship. The fiery noblewoman had been furious at the captain when he deposited her back with her family without offering for her hand. She had shocked her proud brothers and amused the entire crew of the *Batavia's Ghost* by throwing articles of clothing, shoes, and even a fish from a nearby vendor's cart at the captain's head as he made his escape.

Yes, many women had set snares for the King's Privateer. And they had all failed. But Kemal was beginning to think the baron might have finally met his match in this quiet, serious beauty.

He chuckled and shook his head. He only wished Delacroix were here to share in such a fine joke and he cursed himself—yet again—that he'd not thought to wager with the first mate before he departed. It would have been a good opportunity to take money from the sage Frenchman who'd relieved Kemal of so much gold over the years.

Thoughts of Delacroix and the *Batavia's Ghost* sobered him. A big part of Kemal's heart had wanted to leave with the ship when it sailed from Eastbourne. He had not been away from the ship for this long in years. Captain Standish had understood Kemal's yearning.

"You may go with the *Ghost* if you wish, Kemal. I would never ask you to stay on land."

The captain had offered to retain another valet so that Kemal might go back to the sea, his only mistress—an unforgiving one who'd long ago brought Kemal to his knees.

Kemal had been torn by the offer, but, in the end, he knew his place was with the privateer he'd served so long. If not for One-Eyed Standish, Kemal would have spent the remainder of his days chained to an oar on Faisal Barbarossa's ship, doomed to live and die in only a foot of space.

Yes, that would have been Kemal's fate. He had no wealthy family to ransom him. Indeed, he didn't even have any family to return to since corsairs had kidnapped every person in his small village when he was a boy of eleven. He had spent another nine years on the Barbarossa's ship before One-Eyed Standish beheaded the vicious corsair captain and commandeered his vessel.

The crew of the *Batavia's Ghost* was Kemal's family

now—and the only family he needed. Yes, it had been his lucky day when the baron entered his life.

It had also been a bloody day, and the first time Kemal watched One-Eyed Standish fall under the sway of his demons and become one himself.

Kemal knew firsthand the stories men told about the fearsome privateer—that Standish had fought as many as seven men at one time and vanquished them—were no exaggeration. He'd seen days when the captain's demons would not be sated with any amount of blood; when his hatred of slavers and those who purchased slaves was so fierce he killed everyone in his path, even those who might have surrendered.

Although One-Eyed Standish was greatly feared and had never been an easy man to understand, he had always been a favorite with his crew. No captain worked harder beside his men or divided the spoils more fairly. Still, those who had served him long enough caught a glimpse into the dark heart of the man and knew he was driven by something brutal and fearsome. Nobody who'd seen him plying his sword could fail to recognize the rage within him. Kemal had seen more than one man throw down his weapon when faced with the mere prospect of facing the maddened giant.

He knew something terrible had happened to Captain Standish when he'd been the sultan's slave. Something so terrible that even killing the Barbarossa—the man who'd captured him—had not banished the captain's demons. In the fifteen years that followed his escape, the captain had pursued the men who'd betrayed him with a singlemindedness that crossed the border into obsession. Kemal knew only one man remained on the captain's list—Emile Calitain.

The *Batavia's Ghost* had pursued Calitain for fifteen years, but Kemal had never even seen the man. He knew the infamous slaver had once been the captain's closest friend and had betrayed him.

Delacroix, who had been with Standish since escaping from the sultan's prison, had once told Kemal he thought killing Emile Calitain would release the captain from the demons who possessed him.

Delacroix knew Standish better than anyone, so perhaps he was correct. But Kemal did not think killing another man would be the answer. No, Kemal had hopes this cool, tranquil woman and this peaceful place might be the cure for whatever ailed the driven giant.

Doctor Nichols arrived not long after Hugh finished his bath. He gave Hugh a brief examination and declared him fit to resume non-strenuous activities. Hugh wasted no time taking advantage of his liberation. He'd just finished dressing, even allowing Kemal to tie his cravat since he couldn't lift his arms high enough, when somebody pounded on his door like a madman.

"Go see what that is all about," Hugh said, fastening the remaining buttons on his waistcoat and wincing.

When Kemal opened the door, two small bodies hurtled into the room, leaving Rowena Claxton standing stiffly in the doorway.

"Hugh! Hugh! Hugh!" The yells were muffled by Hugh's coat as both boys clung to him for all they were worth, unaware of the agony they were inflicting on his ribs and leg, not to mention the damage they were doing to his clothing.

"Cousins!" The word tore from his throat with a yelp and Hugh was glad he was able to yell something that wasn't an expletive.

"Mama wouldn't let us see you," Richard said, by this time as distinct and recognizable to Hugh as if he did not share identical features with his brother. Hugh was amazed by how different two people could be even though they were mirror images of each other. "She said you were asleep all that time."

"She said you fell off Pasha," Lucien added, his voice edged with a disbelief Hugh found flattering.

"Well," Hugh said, gently disentangling them from his bruised and tender torso, "I'm afraid it is true. Pasha is disgusted and refuses to allow me on his back until I can prove myself worthy."

Richard glared at his brother. "Lucien should not have mentioned it. Mama says even the best riders take a spill. Even Papa fell from his horse," he added. Hugh knew that in Richard's eyes this settled the matter.

"Yes, that is true," Hugh admitted. He wanted to deal carefully with the twins' godlike image of the late earl. "Your father was perhaps the best horseman I ever saw," Hugh said, speaking the truth.

Richard flushed, his rosy skin causing him to look the very image of his mother, but for his brown eyes.

The sound of a throat being cleared made Hugh look up.

"Lucien, Richard. You've seen Lord Ramsay and now we should return to the schoolroom." Rowena refused to look at Hugh.

"Nonsense," Hugh said, taking childish pleasure in contradicting the old crone. "The boys are welcome to relax in my chambers while I finish getting ready. I will see they return to the schoolroom after they've passed along any news I've missed while lounging in bed."

"The curate will be here for their lessons at the half hour, my lord."

Hugh could see she was burning to defy him but didn't dare. "I'll have them back before then."

She dropped a perfunctory curtsy and turned on her heel.

Hugh smiled down at the boys. "I know Mr. Boswell felt your absence keenly these past days." Hugh knew the opposite was true but couldn't see why the odious little beast shouldn't endure a proper mauling, just as he had.

Mr. Boswell emerged from his boudoir at the sound of his name and stretched with majestic languidness. He gave the boys one of his most disdainful looks while putting on his fez, taking his time adjusting the red felt hat in the small mirror that hung beside the door.

The twins loved the display and surrounded the monkey, peering into his house, opening and closing the cunningly designed doors and windows under Mr. Boswell's gimlet eye.

Hugh turned to find Kemal holding up a coat.

He grimaced. "I suppose I must." He gritted his teeth as Kemal helped him into the garment and then tied his left arm in a sling he'd made from one of Hugh's old coats.

Hugh grinned. "Very fashionable, Kemal."

Kemal gave Hugh a slight smile before handing him his signet ring and ruby fob.

Hugh turned to the boys. "Shall we take a quick trip to the stables and assure ourselves Pasha has taken no harm from my ham-handed treatment?"

"Huzzah!" Lucien yelled.

They arrived in the stables to find Will speaking with a groom.

"My lord." The smaller man gave Hugh a genuinely pleased smile—the first one since he'd returned home. So, all he'd needed to do to regain William's friendship was crack a few bones and rattle his wits.

"We have come to see Pasha. He is well, I hope?"

"Aye, my lord, fit as a fiddle." Will led them past a dozen stalls to reach Pasha's. The massive horse was lolling against the far side and chewing a mouthful of hay in a desultory fashion. Hugh clucked his tongue and Pasha ambled over. Hugh smoothed his muzzle, giving him words of praise before he spoke the command that meant he should remain still.

"You may enter and pet him," Hugh told the boys.

He turned to Will but kept the twins in view. "Well? Out with it, I can see something is bothering you."

Will's jaw worked as if he were chewing a mouthful of rocks. "Has Lady Davenport told you about your saddle?"

"My saddle? No."

"Somebody cut your girth."

Hugh gaped. "I beg your pardon?"

"Aye, somebody tampered with it." Will kept an eye on the boys while Hugh studied him.

"Somebody?" Hugh repeated. "Who in God's name would do such a thing?"

Will shrugged.

"Who noticed it first?"

"I did, after we brought you back."

Hugh chewed his lip. Had Daphne seen it? After all, she'd carried the saddle over to him. She was an experienced horsewoman, but perhaps she'd been too shaken at the time.

"When could this have happened?"

"Your saddle was in the tack room with all the rest; anyone could have tampered with it. It could have happened anytime—even before this last ride—and only broken after some use."

Hugh recalled the day of the accident, his mind running through the events of that morning until he came upon one that stood out.

"What is the name of Lady Davenport's former lady's maid—the one still at Whitton Park?"

Will's blond brows shot up. "You mean Fowler—or Mrs. Blake, rather?"

"Yes, that's the one. We came across her and her husband, a surly sort, just outside Elm Cottage. They were arguing behind the building. I suppose they could have tampered with my saddle when we were in the cottage."

"But why would they?"

Hugh shrugged. "What if the two of them were doing something on behalf of Malcolm Hastings?"

"You mean perhaps they thought to sabotage Lady Davenport's horse and made a mistake?"

Hugh snorted. "Only a true idiot could mistake Pasha for Lady Davenport's mount." Hugh paused. "Unless they tampered with both?"

Will shook his head. "I already checked. Nothing wrong with her saddle or any of the others."

Hugh stared at the boys without really seeing them. "I give up," he admitted, shaking his head. "Why the devil would Hastings—or his servants—want me injured or dead? What could he possibly stand to gain?"

"Didn't you thrash him once—at the public day, after your second year away at school?"

Hugh shifted his sling and winced. "Good Lord," he said, sifting through his memories. "Did I?"

Will nodded. "It was when we found him back behind the stables with the old vicar's daughter—she was crying."

Hugh squinted for a long moment and then shook his head. "Bloody hell! I'd forgotten all about that. What a memory you've got." He raised his eyebrows at Will. "Old Vicar Hawthorne's daughter, the one with the—"

Will chuckled. "Aye, that's the one. You asked her why she was crying and she said Hastings had tried to kiss her."

"Lord—that was *ages* ago. We were just boys—perhaps thirteen—it's ludicrous."

"You humiliated him in front of several others."

Hugh shook his head. "No, that would be too foolish— even for Hastings."

"Who else could it be?"

"I have no idea." Hugh scratched the scar where it disappeared into his hairline. "I can only think it has something to do with the threatening letters. I don't suppose there has been any luck on that?"

"I meant to tell you, I spoke with the agent the day of your injury. He says Hastings is not hiring. In fact, it appears he's been letting servants go, quite a few of them."

"He's skint?"

Will nodded. "Aye, dodging dunning agents."

"That doesn't surprise me. Well, if he's not hiring, then we'll need to find another way to get somebody into the house. I've been thinking Martín may be the answer."

Will blinked. "Your second mate? Why? What could he do?"

"When I first met him, he was working in a brothel in New Orleans. Women flock to him like crows to corn."

William blanched at the word *brothel*; perhaps Hugh should have claimed he'd met Martín in a church or tending to lepers?

"And how do you propose to utilize his *skills*?" Will's mouth was a flat, disapproving line.

"He'll need to meet a wench on the Whitton staff. Any wench."

"It sounds like releasing a fox into the henhouse."

Hugh shrugged. "It's not my henhouse. Besides, it's far better to have Martín working his way through Whitton Park than Lessing Hall. We'll be doing Lady Davenport a good turn if we can divert his energies." He glanced at his friend's outraged expression and bit back a grin. "Or perhaps you would like to try charming one of the ladies?"

Will gave him a withering look. "Your ship won't return for months—what should we do in the meantime?"

"At this time of year the winds are propitious and I'm expecting the *Ghost* anytime during these next few weeks. For the time being we will just be extra watchful—we now know to check saddles, carriages—anything and everything. And see to it neither she nor the boys set foot beyond the front door without somebody watching."

Will nodded grudgingly, his thoughts obviously stuck on Martín.

The boys were still stroking the long-suffering Pasha, who cut Hugh a look of equine martyrdom.

"All right, Cousins, your tutor awaits." Hugh turned back to Will. "For the time being just have your agent keep a round-the-clock watch on Hastings. When Martín returns I will place him in your hands to use as you see fit." Hugh paused. "Please believe me when I say you will not be the only one who has to suffer his disrespectful behavior." It was difficult not to laugh at the image of prudish Will dealing with the amoral golden-eyed Lothario. "I feel it's only fair to warn you—" He stopped, as if he'd changed his mind.

"Warn me about what, my lord?"

"Well, you'd be wise to keep any woman you fancy out of Martín's path. I doubt there's a female alive who could resist him."

Will gave a snort of disgust, his mouth pursed with disapproval.

Hugh threw back his head and laughed, and was immediately punished for his teasing by an agonizing pain in his ribs.

Chapter Twelve

Daphne was hunched over her desk with J. F. Fries's *Neue oder anthropologische Kritik der Vernunft* and a German dictionary open before her. She'd hoped to finish a first draft of her paper before she left for London. She'd published several scholarly articles under an alias, Publius, but hadn't sent anything to the London Philosophical Society since Thomas's death.

As things stood, it did not seem likely she would ever send anything to them again—not unless they wanted a paper on the subject of Hugh Redvers.

Daphne was still staring at the same page she'd been looking at for the past half hour when the door opened and the subject of her irritating ruminations paused in the doorway, so handsome and vibrant her chest felt as though somebody were standing on it.

"Am I disturbing you, my lady?"

Daphne wanted to fling down her quill and shout, *Yes! Of course you are!* and then hurl a book at his head—a *big* book.

Instead she gestured to a chair. "Please, have a seat. How are you feeling this morning?"

He gingerly folded his long body into the wingback chair

across from her desk. "I am sore but otherwise quite well." He lifted one boot as if to lay it on his opposite knee but then winced and lowered it back to the floor. "I never had a chance to thank you for your nursing."

A vision of his mouth on hers and his hand on her breast slammed into her like a tidal wave and her nipples hardened. She hunched her shoulders.

"It is of no account," she said, transferring a pile of papers from one side of the desk to the other. And then moving them back again.

"It is of great account to me, Daphne." He was no longer smiling and Daphne had no idea what his intense, almost harsh, expression meant. And then it was gone and he was once again amiable. "I wanted to thank you and I also have some questions for you."

"Questions?" she repeated shrilly.

"William Standish thinks my accident was not an accident."

Daphne almost wept; for one terrible, endless moment she had feared he'd learned about Malcolm. She realized he was waiting for an answer. "As do I. I believe the girth on your saddle was cut."

"May I ask why you didn't think to mention this to me?"

Was there something odd in his voice? Something *accusing*?

"It did not seem like the proper time when you were bedridden and groggy from laudanum. And I've not had a chance to speak to you since then."

He nodded, apparently satisfied. "Can you think of anyone who might have done this?"

"Why would you think *I* would know anything?"

His smile was oddly gentle. "I don't think that, Daphne. I am only asking."

"No, I cannot think of anyone. Unless . . ."

"Yes?"

Daphne eyed his alert expression. It was too late to turn back now. "May I speak bluntly, my lord?"

"I wish you would."

"Could it be somebody from your past?"

He cocked an eyebrow and Daphne felt the hideous beginnings of a wild blush building, and sighed. "Could it be the brother, father, or . . . husband, of . . . somebody?"

He stared blankly for a moment before throwing his head back and laughing. "Oww!" he yelled, clutching his side, but still laughing. When he'd finished laughing and gasping in pain, he looked up, wiping tears from his eyes. "My dear Daphne, are you trying to kill me? You have outdone even Will Standish in imaginative speculation."

Whatever that meant. Daphne gave him her coolest stare. "I am so pleased to amuse you."

"Do you believe it might be some cuckold with a very long memory? Or perhaps a man I've managed to cuckold in the brief time I've been back?"

She didn't answer and, to her surprise, he did not taunt her any further. Instead, he stretched out in his chair, tipped his head back and stared at the ceiling —as if the answer might be found there. The minutes ticked past and she took the opportunity to graze on his body like some ruminant released into a verdant pasture, her eyes lingering on the front of his snug breeches.

"Hmm."

The sound reminded her there was a man attached to the breeches and she looked up.

He shrugged and then winced. "Nobody comes to mind just now but I shall give it careful thought. Can *you* think of anybody?"

"Me?" Again her voice was sharp. "What would I know of such matters?"

He pushed out his lower lip and tilted his head, his expression one of whimsy. "You introduced the subject. I thought you might have . . . inside knowledge."

Just what was he implying? "I know nothing of your exploits—now *or* then."

He smiled and rose to his feet, his hand moving to cradle his side. "My new curricle will be delivered later today. Perhaps you might care for a drive tomorrow?"

Daphne blinked at the change of subject. "Have you asked Doctor Nichols?"

Hugh came closer, until he was towering over her desk. And her. "I did, but he did not care for a ride. He suggested I ask *you*, instead."

Daphne bit her lip. "You are maddening, my lord."

"So I've been told. Often."

"Are you sure you are healed enough to be tooling about in a carriage?"

"If it will make you feel better, *you* could take the ribbons and squire me about."

"I daresay the sight of a woman handling your cattle would cause you to suffer a relapse." She lifted her shoulders. "If you believe it is wise to racket about in a curricle, then I am willing to trust your judgment."

He gave her an odd, lopsided smile. "Do you, Daphne? Trust my judgment, that is?"

What did he mean? By the time she opened her mouth to ask, he had already turned to leave.

The door closed with a soft *click* and Daphne lowered her head onto her desk. Hugh was looking for a person with reason to harm him. Of course he was. Good God. How she wished she had told the truth before this attempt on his health—or life. How could she possibly tell him now?

To Daphne's relief, Hugh did not again raise the subject of his injury or who might have caused it. Nor did he avoid the subject because he was avoiding *her*. On the contrary, he seemed to seek out her company more than ever, going riding with Daphne and the boys, joining a fishing expedition on one particularly fine day, and even accompanying them into Eastbourne, twice.

Two wonderful, glorious weeks flew by before she knew it. Hugh and Daphne had finished dinner one evening and were preparing to engage in a game of chess when a footman entered the library with a message.

Hugh glanced at the rectangle of parchment on the salver and then at Daphne. "I beg your pardon, my lady, but this is in Delacroix's hand—the *Ghost* has returned." The message must have been brief because he looked up after only a few seconds. "I'm afraid I shall miss my chance to thrash you at chess this evening."

Daphne snorted softly. He was an average chess player, at best, and she had beaten him in every match so far.

He took her hand and raised it to his lips, delivering a lingering kiss along with a lingering look. "I would not run off if I could delegate receipt of this particular package to anyone else."

Daphne hoped he couldn't hear the pounding in her chest. She nodded and tugged her hand away. "I shall take the opportunity to work on the drain problem. I believe I might have found a solution." She regretted her prosaic words the moment they left her mouth.

Hugh laughed. "I look forward to discussing drains—or any other subject you desire—when I return, my dearest Daphne."

Several hours later Daphne was still awake and working in the library. She was so engrossed in calculations and plans, she almost didn't hear the sound of carriage wheels in the courtyard below. She consulted the mahogany longcase clock and saw it was after midnight. It could only be Hugh returning from the ship.

She worked for another quarter hour and then realized she lacked one portion of the drawings, which must still be in Randall's office. Grumbling, she picked up a candlestick and headed to fetch the plans. On her way she noticed a small candelabrum on the console table outside the smallest sitting room—a room nobody ever used.

She opened the door and froze. The only source of light in the room came from the crackling blaze in the fireplace. Hugh sat on a sofa, and he wasn't alone. Pale arms clung tightly to his neck and a woman's face was buried in his cravat. He had his mouth to her ear but looked up at the sound and met Daphne's eyes. For a moment neither of them moved; then the woman turned to see what had disturbed Hugh.

Even in the subdued light Daphne could see her hair was a gorgeous auburn and her enormous eyes were lined with what could only be kohl, a cosmetic aid Daphne had heard about but never seen. The woman was swathed in a black cloak; the only visible parts of her were two delicate arms and tiny feet shod with strange, colorful sandals.

Hugh began to disentangle the woman's arms. "Daphne." He sounded pained rather than guilty at being caught clutching a strange woman in the middle of the night.

Daphne locked eyes with the woman, who no longer looked startled. Instead, her perfect, bow-shaped mouth curved into an expression of regret or shame or—

"Daphne?"

She wrenched her eyes from the beautiful stranger and began backing out the open doorway, looking anywhere but at Hugh's face. "I apologize for interrupting. I did not know anyone was in here. I came this way looking for the rest of the cottage plans. I was working on the drains," she added inanely. "I didn't know anyone was in here," she repeated, searching behind her with one hand for the door handle.

"Daphne, wait." He lunged to his feet, his body angled toward her, one hand outstretched.

Daphne's vision wavered and blurred and her fumbling hand located the handle. As Hugh moved toward her, she stepped back into the hall and pulled the door shut, seizing her heavy skirts in one hand and sprinting, not for the library, but for her chambers. She didn't stop running until she was inside her room. She slammed the door shut and locked it before flinging herself onto her bed, clutching a pillow to her chest, as if for protection. Something warm slithered down her cheek; she squeezed her eyes shut on the hot rush of tears but an image of Hugh with the woman in his arms waited for her behind her eyelids. She dropped her head back against the headboard and stared blindly at the opposite wall. Was this woman the "urgent package" Hugh needed to collect?

Daphne snorted. How like a man to confuse a woman with a package!

And he'd had the nerve—the temerity—the *gall*—to bring her *here,* into *her* home. Daphne bit her lip. Well, it was really his home; not that he knew that, of course. She ground her teeth as the image filled her head, even with her eyes open. She shook her head violently until the picture dissolved in a red haze of pain. The insidious thoughts, however, were not so easily dislodged.

How dare he bring his mistress to Lessing Hall? This was Daphne's home—where her children and Lady Amelia and *she* lived.

She squeezed the pillow until her arms ached. Who was the little redhead? His mistress? Or . . . might she be his *wife*? His wife? The thought was like a slap in the face.

Why not? her cold inner voice demanded.

Daphne hurled the pillow across the room and it struck a bronze statuette on the mantelpiece. The sculpture teetered back and forth several times before crashing to the marble hearth, the resultant *clang* deafening but strangely comforting.

Daphne stared at the still-wobbling statue, horrified. She had never done such a thing in her life. Emotional outbursts of any kind were anathema to her. Even during the worst times—when she'd been living under Malcolm's roof and enduring his constant harassment—she had not given in to her temper. No, not until Hugh arrived had she started feeling this way—behaving this way. Before he'd come along she'd had no trouble sleeping or concentrating and had spent her time raising her children, managing a household—several, in fact—and living a fulfilling life.

And now? Now she spent her days gazing at nothing while thinking of *him,* seeking out opportunities to spend more time with *him*, and—and—

A low, fierce growl slipped from her lips. Just who did he think he was? Some eastern potentate assembling his harem? In *her* home? The word *harem* created images that were far worse than the one of Hugh with the woman in his arms; images of Hugh reclining among silk cushions—his muscular body naked, of course—with kohl-eyed beauties around him, eager to please. He was touching them, his big, gentle hands stroking and exploring while they opened themselves to him and—

The tightness between her thighs made her dizzy and she pressed her knees together, as if such pressure might stop the dreadfully titillating sensations. But it only sent teeth-gritting pleasure surging from her sex to the rest of her body.

"Stop. It."

The sharp words focused her scattered wits. Daphne

inhaled deeply, held a breath, and then slowly released it, an action that had often saved her sanity in the months following Malcolm's attack. In a few moments she was less agitated, if not exactly calm.

The woman's hair had been a fiery copper and her skin milky white. Could she be a European whom Hugh had caused to be dressed like a woman from a harem? It was even possible she was an Englishwoman, perhaps a local prostitute, someone he'd engaged after he'd visited his ship? Daphne groaned, her brain whirling. The only thing she knew for certain was that they'd been holding each other like lovers.

How could she ever have believed there was anything growing between Hugh and herself? He'd merely entertained himself with her because she was the only woman in the vicinity. And she'd been so eager for his attention and so . . . so . . . *easy*.

Anger joined mortification and shock and Daphne could almost feel her heart hardening in her chest. She *hated* him. She'd been an idiot to delay going to London, which she'd only done until she could conceive of a way to tell him the truth, to give him back his inheritance. Then she could take the boys and—

You are lying to yourself, Daphne.

"No." She shook her head and whispered. "No, I'm not." Daphne groaned and closed her eyes.

Yes, she was. And she didn't need her nagging inner voice to tell her that. She hadn't lingered at Lessing Hall for the correct answer to appear in her head—there *was* no correct answer. There was only the unavoidable, unpalatable truth. A truth she would tell him tomorrow. Yes. Tomorrow she would end it all—her blind, foolish infatuation *and* her decade-old deception.

Daphne exhaled, suddenly—and bleakly—calm, now that

she'd made a decision. She should thank him for what he'd done tonight rather than blame him.

Yes, she should thank him and be very, very, very grateful his actions had brought her to her senses before she'd done something inexcusably foolish. Something like fall in love with him.

Chapter Thirteen

Hugh had to bite his tongue to keep from yelling. How the hell was he supposed to explain this to Daphne? He glanced down at the source of his troubles, the silent woman on the settee.

Euphemia Marlington's kohl-blackened eyes were speculative. "You are married, Hugh?" Her voice was low and musical, slightly accented from so many years speaking a language other than English.

"No, I am not married." He shoved his hand through his hair, furious with himself rather than Mia, who'd done nothing wrong.

"She is your concubine?"

"Good Lord." Hugh closed his eye and shook his head. Just wait until this one hit the *ton*.

Other than red hair and green eyes, Mia Marlington bore no resemblance to the girl who'd haunted him for seventeen years. She was as beautiful as any woman he'd ever seen and ten times more devious. Not to mention twice as dangerous as a nest of vipers and more exotic than one of his uncle's rare orchids.

He gave her a tired smile. "English gentlemen don't keep concubines, Mia."

"Tsst!" Her sibilant dismissal and smoldering glance caused Hugh to step away and put his uncle's huge desk between them.

Yes, the girl he'd met all those years ago was gone. In her place was a woman who'd entered a ruthless killer's harem at fourteen, going from adolescent odalisque to mature, beautiful, and wily concubine. Hugh knew what it took just to survive Babba Hassan's cruelty; he couldn't imagine the strength of will she must possess to have actually flourished.

"Well-bred Englishwomen never mention such subjects as concubines in polite conversation, Mia. Nor do they make that hissing noise."

Lady Euphemia, only daughter of the Duke of Carlisle, regarded Hugh with eyes as old as sin.

"Whatever she is to you, she is very angry. You had better make amends or it will not be safe to go to sleep under the same roof with her." A knowing smile curved her lips.

Hugh supposed she knew as much about the nature of man as any woman alive, particularly the bad side. No woman ended up surviving a harem—as Mia had done until recently—unless she was as adept at deadly, Byzantine politics as her lord and master. Just thinking of her life among a group of women all fighting for the survival of their male children made Hugh shudder.

"You will come with me to the house of my father," she ordered before yawning daintily.

Hugh sighed and massaged his temple, which hadn't stopped pounding since meeting the woman he'd risked his men's lives to rescue. Only a few hours in Mia's company made him realize he could not entrust her to anyone else. She was a bloody force of nature.

Delacroix had all but thrown her into Hugh's arms when he'd stepped aboard the *Ghost*.

"She is all yours, Captain. And if you know what is good for you—and your ship and crew—you will remove her immediately." The old sailor had not looked so frazzled since their days under the sultan's lash.

"Is something amiss?"

Delacroix threw up his hands and muttered a very vulgar word in French. "She brought the *Ghost* to the brink of mutiny—dangling her favors before the men, trying to convince one of them to seize the ship and return for her son after we dropped him where he'd asked." He shook his head and made an angry clucking sound. "Thank God the boy left. He was on the verge of dueling with at least three of the crew for dishonoring his mother."

Hugh had been with her for only a few hours and already understood what his haggard first mate had meant.

Right now she was staring at him with open displeasure, but at least she was no longer threatening him with mutilation, which was what she'd done when he had bodily removed her from the *Ghost* and told her, in no uncertain terms, that he was not sending his ship back for her son.

Hugh sighed. He would have to accompany her to her father's; she would need somebody to serve as cultural translator, at least for a few days. Not that even a year would be enough for her to fit into the *ton*.

Hugh pitied the tiny woman. A high-stickler like the duke would tend and care for her, but she would never be accepted by society. No man among the *ton* would take an ex-harem slave as a wife—no matter how much money Carlisle heaped on her.

Hugh had seen it before with reconciliations between long-separated family members. They might cherish the memory of a lost loved one, but the person who came home was not the same one who'd left. How would her family reconcile their memory of an innocent daughter of fourteen with the reality of a woman steeped in sin and treachery?

While Mia's contemporaries had been learning watercolors

and the pianoforte, she had been learning the art of pleasuring a man as if her life depended on it: because it had.

"Hugh? *Hugh!* Are you attending to me?" Mia's imperious voice broke into his thoughts.

"Hmm, what were you saying?"

Her eyes narrowed to dangerous slits but she maintained her temper, no doubt saving the tongue-lashing for later, after she'd forced him to do whatever it was she wanted.

"I wish to go back for Jibril," she said for the hundredth time.

Hugh sighed. "Jibril is almost a man grown and you must allow him to fight for the only birthright he knows. If he fails he can find his own way back here." Privately, Hugh thought that would be disastrous. Mia, at least, had spent her first fourteen years in England. Jibril was the son of a sultan and the product of North Africa; he would never fit in here.

"Come," he said, changing the subject, "we should both get some rest as we will be leaving before first light. I just heard horses—that will be Kemal arriving with your possessions. He will take you to your room, where a hot bath and food await you."

She grudgingly nodded, the gray smudges beneath her green eyes mute testimony to her exhaustion.

Kemal was waiting for them when they entered the hall. "I will put her in the Rose Room, my lord."

"Thank you, Kemal. Good night, Mia. Try to get some rest."

Kemal bowed to the tiny woman and spoke to her in rapid Arabic. She rewarded him with a glorious smile and a stream of Arabic in return.

Hugh went to the library, half hoping to find Daphne. The room was lighted by two dozen candles, and drawings and papers covered her desk, but she was not there.

His shoulders sagged with relief—he was such a coward. But what could he say to make things better? Nothing. He poured three fingers of brandy and put the problem of Daphne aside, turning his thoughts to Delacroix's disturbing news.

The wharf master in Gibraltar said Calitain's ship passed through only two days before—heading west. The scarred Frenchman had sounded both aggrieved and guilty.

You could not have pursued Calitain and *made it to the rendezvous. You did the right thing, my friend.* Hugh had meant what he'd said, but he couldn't help feeling just as frustrated as his first mate. It was poor luck Calitain had returned from wherever he'd been hiding. Hugh had pursued that traitorous bastard around the globe for *years*, only catching sight of him three times. Each time blood had been shed—lots of blood—but never Calitain's.

Hugh looked down and saw his knuckles were white just *thinking* the man's name. Calitain was the turncoat responsible for the death of six of Hugh's closest friends, not to mention the loss of Hugh's eye and a great many other scars on his body and soul. Calitain was the lowest order of criminal and Hugh was burning to go after him. But that was his hatred speaking. To leave now would be to chase his own tail.

Instead he would do the wise thing and send word to the various ports—Hugh had friends everywhere—to keep an eye out for the *Golden Scythe*, Calitain's ship. It didn't surprise Hugh that Calitain had returned to the waters off the Continent, no matter how dangerous they were. Calitain had been involved in the slave trade since he'd quit being a slave himself, and Europeans low in morals and money often financed slave ships, especially since imported slaves now fetched a high price in the American South.

Delacroix would locate Calitain, and then Hugh would deal with him. He smiled grimly at the thought and took a sip of brandy. And then he remembered Daphne.

Hell and damnation! He could not tell her about Mia— at least not yet. After all, it was not his secret to tell. Mia deserved to be the one who decided how and when her story would be revealed.

Which left him with no explanation for Daphne, at least nothing that would keep her from believing him a swine of the lowest order.

Hugh gritted his teeth and took out a sheet of paper. Thank God he'd be miles from Lessing Hall when she read the weak missive.

Daphne was up bright and early the next morning, fueled by cold rage, humiliation, and determination. Like Samson bearding the lion, she marched down to the breakfast room. But when she flung open the door to the cheery, sun-filled room, all she found were Lady Amelia and a dozen pugs.

Daphne stared. The older woman *never* came to breakfast—*ever*. Why, of all mornings, was she here today? How was Daphne supposed to speak to Hugh with Amelia and her dogs in attendance?

The answer was simple: she wasn't. She'd begun to back out of the room quietly—not that anything short of cannon fire could be heard over the pugs—when the old lady glanced up.

Daphne stopped and forced herself to smile. "Good morning, Amelia."

The older woman's usually vague eyes were as sharp as ice picks this morning. She lifted her fork, which had an entire fish impaled on its tines. "Do you know if these are the *only* pilchards Cook keeps? The pugs don't care for these at all."

"I'm afraid I can't answer that." Daphne hesitated and inspiration struck. "Gates would know. I will go and—"

The butler chose that moment to appear, bearing a salver with a letter on it. "Lord Ramsay left this for you, my lady."

Daphne frowned, something heavy and cold settling in her stomach.

"Where have you been, Gates?" Lady Amelia demanded. The butler opened his mouth but Lady Amelia waved her hand, forgetting she still had one of the offending pilchards on her fork. The fish sailed across the breakfast room and collided with a marble bust of some long-dead Redvers before slithering to the floor. The pugs skittered across the polished wood, toenails clicking as they descended, *en masse,* on the fallen pilchard.

Oblivious, Lady Amelia glared at the butler and held up her empty fork. "Who is responsible for this wretched pilchard business?"

Gates wrenched his eyes away from the grease-slicked bust, a slight notch between his eyes, his lips parted.

Daphne took pity on her long-suffering servant. "Please have Cook send in some pilchards."

His gaze slid to the dish full of pilchards on the sideboard.

"*Fresh* pilchards," Daphne clarified. "And a pot of tea, please."

"Right away, my lady."

A place had been set a safe distance from Lady Amelia's chair. Daphne stared at the letter for a moment before opening it.

My Dear Daphne:

By the time you read this I will be gone from Lessing Hall. I apologize for the uncomfortable situation you encountered last night. Unfortunately I cannot say anything further on the matter other than to assure you things are not the way they seem. Please believe me when I say that I will explain everything *when I am at liberty to do so.*

*I hope to be gone no longer than a week—two at
the most—and I look forward to speaking with you
on my return.*

> *Your servant,*
> *Hugh*

She read it again, just to confirm it really said as little as
she thought it did. It did.

"Is that from Hugh?"

Daphne looked up to find Lady Amelia had carried the
chafing dish of bacon to her seat.

"Yes, it is."

Amelia dropped a piece of bacon onto the floor and det-
onated an explosion of barking.

Daphne winced.

"Has he taken those odd *dogs* with him?" the old lady
shouted over the din.

"He did not mention the dogs in his letter."

"Did he say what he was doing with that Marlington
chit?"

Daphne squinted, as if that would somehow help with the
noise. "With *whom*?"

Amelia tossed another piece of bacon onto the floor.
"That redheaded gel who climbed into the coach with him
this morning."

"You saw Hugh leaving?"

Amelia picked up another piece of bacon and Daphne
fought the urge to scream—not that she would be heard
above the dogs.

"Yes, the racket of carriage wheels woke the pugs." Her
silver eyebrows descended into a line as straight as the blade
of a sword. "I hope he does not plan to make a habit of such
uncivil behavior."

More bacon hit the floor and Daphne soldiered onward. "You mentioned a woman, my lady?"

"The girl is his daughter, I would swear to it." She paused in the act of distributing more bacon, a brief, sphinxlike smile curving her lips. "He was sweet on me, you know."

It was all Daphne could do not to snatch the dish of bacon from the old lady's hands and hurl it into the hallway. Instead she swallowed, took a deep breath, and tried again. "I beg your pardon, but *who* was sweet on you?"

"He was Thomas's friend and spent an entire summer here. I'd recognize a Marlington anywhere. Red hair, the whole lot of 'em."

"Marlington?"

"Yes, the Duke of Carlisle. He was sweet on me," she repeated. "But I never liked him after he pulled one of my pugs' tails."

"And you say this woman is his daughter?"

"Must be—that hair, no mistaking it."

A footman entered bearing pilchards, and Lady Amelia looked from her empty dish of bacon to the heap of fish, and frowned. "No, no, no! We've already got plenty of those— what we need is more bacon."

Discussion ensued, but Daphne did not hear it. All she could think of was the woman Hugh had left with.

A duke's daughter?

Daphne told herself she should be grateful for Hugh's departure because it saved her a very painful conversation. She could hardly be faulted for her silence if he wasn't actually *here* to confess to, could she?

Her conscience told her that logic was spurious, but Daphne did not care.

Another thing his absence saved her from was further acts of foolishness. Because that was what she was, a fool.

She cringed every time she thought of her naïve infatuation. But that was all over now. Instead of mooning over the duplicitous rake, she began making plans for her long-delayed trip to London and arranging to have the house in Yorkshire readied for occupancy.

Without Hugh to distract her, she also completed the rough draft of her long-suffering paper in just under a week. She was astonished by how much she'd missed her work and rejoiced at the return of her peace of mind.

It was unfortunate that peace was short-lived.

Unlike Daphne, her sons were devastated by Hugh's abrupt departure, their sorrow mitigated slightly by the discovery that Mr. Boswell and the parrot—*and* the two dogs—had remained behind.

Hugh had taken Kemal with him and left his disconcertingly attractive second mate, Martín, in charge of his animal entourage. Daphne doubted he was the best role model for two young boys, especially after Rowena told her of the seductions and fights his presence had sparked in the servants' quarters. While Daphne did not entirely trust Rowena's judgment on the matter, she had no doubt Martín Bouchard was a consummate ladies' man. The combination of dark honey skin, golden eyes, and sun-bleached hair made him unusual, exotic, and extremely attractive.

He also had a magnificent physique, which he took pains to exhibit. He wore breeches of butter-soft leather—so tight as to be obscene—boots as highly polished as his captain's, and shirts of fine lawn, which he topped with form-fitting waistcoats. His habit of forgoing a coat caused discontent and grumbling among the male staff and starry eyes and heaving breasts among the females.

Hugh had warned her that one must choose one's battles with Bouchard, so Daphne had ignored his inappropriate attire and arrogant attitude.

Until now.

She was in the library selecting the books she would take with her to London when the boys crashed into the room, brandishing swords and engaged in a noisy duel.

"What fine swords—wherever did you get them?" Daphne asked. "Here, let me see one."

Richard stopped jabbing and slashing and handed her the sword, hilt first. It was made from wood but cunningly painted to resemble metal, complete with jeweled hilt.

"These are impressive."

"Uncle Malcolm gave them to us," Lucien said, taking advantage of his brother's unarmed state to prod him in the armpit.

Richard yelped and Daphne's vision wavered. *Malcolm . . .*

She had to steady herself against a nearby bookshelf before handing the weapon back to her son. "Never attack an unarmed man, Lucien." Her voice was raw and edged with hysteria. *The boys had visited Malcolm—their father . . . How? How had this happened?*

She swallowed down her fear. "Where did you see Sir Malcolm?"

"At Whitton Park, Mama, that's where he lives." Lucien sounded amazed his clever mama didn't know such a simple fact. "Martín takes us with him when he sees his friend. She gives us cakes from the kitchen," he added fatuously.

Daphne's first urge was to run down to the stables, find the young idiot, and throttle him.

Nurse came into the room just then. "Ah, here you are. I've been looking *everywhere* for you, young masters. You haven't finished the work the curate left for you."

Daphne waited for the boys to leave before yanking the bellpull, pacing furiously until a servant answered.

"Find Martín Bouchard and send him to the library immediately."

By the time Gates ushered a partially clad Martín into the

library a half hour later, Daphne had walked a rut into the carpet.

Her usually imperturbable butler sported two telltale spots of red on his cheeks.

In fact, Martín was the only one who appeared to be at ease. He wore an expression of amused condescension but not a coat, waistcoat, or neckcloth. His unbuttoned shirt exposed a shocking expanse of muscular brown chest and Daphne felt the dreaded flush heat her face. Just looking at the man made her body taut and tingly and her brain hazy and hot; not even Hugh exuded such raw sexuality.

An insolent smile played around his sensual lips, telling her he was well aware of the effect his body had on women.

"You may go," she told Gates, whose stiff posture radiated a degree of outrage she might have found amusing in other circumstances.

Daphne waited only until the door closed before launching her attack. "You have been taking my sons to Whitton Park?"

She watched in openmouthed astonishment as he lowered himself unbidden into a chair, stretched out his booted legs, and crossed his muscular arms. Once he was comfortable, he gave her a mocking smile along with a careless shrug.

Molten rage erupted inside her and she sprang to her feet, grasping the edges of the desk to stop herself from flying over it. "You will answer my question *now* or you will pack your things and get out *today*."

Wide-eyed terror supplanted his smirk and he shot to his feet, understanding glimmering in his golden eyes as he realized he was dealing with a tigress protecting her cubs. "*Oui*, I mean yes, my lady." He glanced from her face to the door, as if gauging the amount of time he'd need to reach it. "Why?"

"I go to talk to a girl oo work for Aystink. Ay-sting." He stopped and frowned. His jerky and laborious speech reminded

Daphne that Hugh was always nagging the younger man to speak English.

"*Je veux que vous parliez français,*" she ordered.

His muscular shoulders sagged. "Thank you, my lady. My English is not so good," he admitted, answering her in his own language.

"Answer the question," she repeated in French.

"I never left the boys alone. They came with me and my friend to the kitchen and had something to eat, with some coffee." He shuddered to communicate his feelings on English coffee. "I brought her some *real* coffee the second time," he confided, momentarily distracted.

Daphne crossed her arms and he hurried on. "I only went three or four times and we didn't see Aye—" He stopped and grimaced. "Aye—Ayestink." He threw up his hands. "I cannot say that name."

"Hastings, yes, I understand." Daphne forced the words through clenched jaws. "Go on."

"We didn't see him until the third visit. He told me the boys were his nephews." Martín shrugged. "So I thought nothing was wrong, eh? He asked me to return today because he had gifts for them. I did so and he gave them the swords and we all ate some cake—with good coffee this time—and then we left." He raised his brows, his golden eyes hopeful.

"That is all—just the two times?"

"*Oui.*"

Daphne heaved a sigh and sat, motioning for him to do the same. He sat, but his posture remained as tense as a hare's.

Daphne considered what she should say. She couldn't forbid Malcolm to see the boys without generating questions from her sons, but it made her flesh crawl to think of him anywhere near the boys. Getting away from him was yet another good reason to go to London—even sooner, now.

She met Bouchard's nervous gaze and spoke in French.

"My cousin leads a somewhat, er, debauched existence and I don't wish to expose my children to him." That was no more than the truth. "Of course, *you* are welcome to go where you please and see whomever you please." She stared hard at him, hoping he would understand her true feelings on the matter.

He swallowed audibly. "*Oui*, madam."

"I would appreciate it if you said nothing of this to my sons—or to Sir Malcolm."

"*Oui,* madam." He gave her a tentative, respectful, and nervous smile. Daphne would have laughed at how quickly she'd tamed Hugh's notoriously unruly second mate if she wasn't so sick to her stomach.

"You may go." She turned her blank stare to her desk to indicate her dismissal and he left without a sound. Once he was gone, Daphne slumped in her chair, nausea pitching and roiling inside her. She had planned to wait for Hugh's return, to confess face-to-face and be prepared to leave. But now that Malcolm had seen her sons—talked to them? No, now she must speed up her departure. She must leave Lessing Hall without wasting another minute.

Daphne left Lessing Hall three days later. The trip to London with two lively boys was every bit as brutal as Daphne had anticipated. Even stretched over two days, with frequent stops, she was ready to throttle her offspring by the time the well-sprung Davenport coach rolled up in front of the towering town house.

Davenport House had been built after the family's original London residence burned down in the Great Fire of 1666. The seventh Earl of Davenport had not rebuilt in the same location, which had not been far from where Pepys lived. Instead, he'd chosen to build a newer, even bigger mansion not far from Burlington House.

Because he was screamingly wealthy, the seventh earl had employed the master of English Baroque, Christopher Wren, to design his new house: a house complete with a dome, *à la* St. Paul's Cathedral and Castle Howard.

By the time Daphne had settled the boys in their quarters and shared a late meal with them, she was grateful she'd not told her formidable sister-in-law—Thomas's elder sister Lady Letitia—that she'd be arriving until a few days later. That tiny fib would give her three days to become accustomed to the city before hordes of visitors began descending.

She spent most of her first day addressing the myriad domestic matters that awaited her after an absence of four years. Again she ate an early dinner with the boys and got a full night's sleep.

The second day was for entertainment, and she and Rowena took the twins to a marvelous shop which sold kites, marbles, dissected puzzles, and an intricate paper theater for the boys to assemble and manage. Later they spent an enjoyable few hours at Astley's.

The third day they made Hatchards their first stop and Daphne placed an order for two hard-to-find books and purchased several crates of new books for herself and her sons. Next they went for ices and after that a visit to Hyde Park—which was blissfully empty in the hours before the daily strut commenced—to test out the new kites.

They returned to Davenport House to find Kemal in the massive entry hall, surrounded by mountains of luggage and issuing orders, while Ponsby, Daphne's intimidating London butler, stared daggers at the turbaned man. But Kemal had faced bloodthirsty pirates and was unconcerned by the frosty glare of a mere butler.

Kemal gave her a low, graceful bow. "Good afternoon, my lady."

"You have only just arrived?"

"Yes, my lady."

Daphne pulled off her gloves, taking her time and hoping he would elaborate, but it was Lucien who spoke.

"Is Mr. Boswell here?" Both boys were peering at the piles of luggage as if the monkey might be lurking within. "Or is he coming with Cousin Hugh?"

Kemal smiled, clearly amused by the notion of Hugh traveling with the devious monkey. "I am afraid not, Lord Davenport. Lord Ramsay is driving his new curricle and Mr. Boswell does not care for such travel."

Daphne snorted and then composed her features when Kemal turned his calm, speculative gaze on her. She had come to like and respect the man during their brief time nursing Hugh. She also realized his sharp eyes missed very little and she would have sworn he was both aware of, and amused by, her infatuation with his employer.

She ignored his knowing look. "I daresay Cook would like to know if Lord Ramsay will be here for dinner."

"Of course, my lady."

It was not the answer she was hoping for, but Daphne refused to expose either her curiosity or infatuation any further than she already had.

"I will leave you to it." She ushered the boys up the grand blue-and-gold breccia steps that led to her chambers and the schoolroom.

So, he would be here soon—perhaps even tonight. The thought released a swarm of butterflies into her chest and Daphne frowned at her body's treacherous reaction. She squared her shoulders as if she was preparing for battle. Which she was—against herself.

As it turned out, Hugh did not appear for dinner that night.

Daphne rose early the following morning, determined to continue with the second draft of her paper, no matter how little sleep she'd had. Instead, she sat at her desk, stared into space, and assessed her moral dilemma with an energy and enthusiasm she usually reserved for academic conundrums.

You would do better to draft your confession than to consider the morality of the situation, her rigid, relentless conscience nagged.

I will tell him when I tell him. Why should I make haste to ruin my sons' lives when he seems to care only for gallivanting around the country with his lover?

Two wrongs do not make a right.

Daphne snorted. *How profound.*

But her conscience refused to be drawn into a petty argument, so Daphne stared down at the sheaf of foolscap before her without seeing it. She still had no idea what she would say to him about the woman. The best thing she could do— for her pride—was pretend she didn't care. Which she shouldn't. After all, what business was it of hers where he went or whom he went with?

Even the social stigma associated with lusting after her nephew had lost its ability to shock her. Daphne knew she should be ashamed, but instead she found it intriguing that her morality could be so flexible on such a social taboo.

She brushed the quill's feathered edge against her jaw as she considered the fascinating topic of morality and society, her mind racing with possibilities for her next paper.

A knock on the library door interrupted her musings and Daphne looked up to find Ponsby standing in the doorway.

"Lady Letitia and Lady Anne are here, my lady."

Daphne glanced at the clock and saw it was not quite eleven. Only one thing could have brought her sister-in-law to Davenport House so unfashionably early.

"Did Lord Ramsay arrive last night?"

"Yes, my lady—quite late."

Daphne's mouth curved into a grim smile. Hugh's eldest aunt was a society matron who greatly resembled the late earl with her bone-thin height and piercing gray eyes. Unlike Thomas, however, she seemed to lack a softer side.

"I'm sure Lord Ramsay is eager to greet his aunt and cousin. Would you please let him know they have arrived and are waiting?"

Daphne didn't care how late he'd arrived or how tired he was. He could entertain his family—a family he should have approached weeks ago rather than hiding at Lessing Hall. Or cavorting with his mistress.

Lady Anne rose when Daphne entered the Blue Drawing Room.

"It has been too long, Daphne." The pretty brunette held out both hands, her green eyes sparkling. Anne was only a few years younger than Daphne and, although they'd only met twice before, she had enjoyed the brief time they'd spent conversing.

Daphne smiled. "It is very good of you both to call. I am glad to see you again."

Lady Letitia—who'd remained seated in a cobalt-blue velvet wingback chair—harrumphed and pounded her silver-handled cane on the wood floor.

"Yes, yes, this is all well and good, but where is my *nephew*?"

Daphne kissed the old lady on her heavily powdered cheek. "He should be down shortly, ma'am."

"Don't tell me he is a worthless slugabed?"

Before Daphne could answer, the door opened and Hugh entered.

He grinned, looking from face to face, his gaze lingering on Daphne. "What a lovely sight for my poor old eye first thing in the morning!" In spite of a very late night, he looked fresh and unfairly elegant in a dark green coat and fashionable buff pantaloons. His hair was still damp so he must have made haste with his toilet to greet his guests.

Daphne ignored him and rearranged the skirts of her lavender gown.

Anne's jaw sagged. "Hugh?" Her voice was breathy with wonder.

Hugh caught her up in a crushing embrace. "You must be Cousin Melinda's girl—little Anne. You were hardly more than a baby when I last saw you."

"I remember you," the girl said, blushing furiously. Daphne was pleased to see he had the same effect on his blood relations as on her. "How wonderful that you are alive, Hugh."

He laughed. "I couldn't agree more."

Lady Letitia's cane thumped the floor. "Leave the poor gel alone, you rascal!"

Hugh winked at Anne and turned to his aunt, who was glaring up at him with eyes as cold and hard as gunmetal.

"Aunt Letitia, how delightful to see you again." He moved as if to embrace her, but she planted the foot of her cane against his chest.

"Not so hasty, young man. Stand back and turn around, so that I might see you."

His green eye danced as he held out his arms and turned for her, clearly pleased to display his magnificent person.

"That's enough," she snapped when it was clear the order hadn't reduced him to mortification. She dropped her glass but not her glare. "Hugh." The old lady made his name sound like an execration. "You may kiss me." She finally offered up her powdered cheek.

He did, but he also folded her into a gentle embrace. "How good it is to see you, Aunt."

Even thick powder could not hide the rosy tint that spread over her high cheekbones. "Hmmph! You're looking well enough for your age, I suppose."

Hugh grinned. "I would ask after your health, Auntie, but

I can see you are blooming and have not changed even a whit in almost two decades."

She shot him a withering look. "I see time has not dimmed your frivolous nature." Her lips, already thin, became even thinner. "I hope you've enjoyed your dramatic reappearance, boy. I can assure you that I *have not.*"

"I apologize for my lack of sensitivity, Aunt." He dropped his chin but Daphne saw his lips curve.

So did Lady Letitia, and her color flared. "You are a rude, selfish boy who has always taken pleasure in making mischief at the expense of others!"

"I cannot argue with you, Aunt."

His docility only angered her more. "I suppose it would have been too much to ask that you notify the family before you made your public entrance?"

"Again, I cannot argue with you, nor do I wish to. I can only tender my deepest apologies."

Lady Letitia's steely eyes narrowed and she made a rude noise. "Must you tower over me like a great lurch? I shall get a crick in my neck staring up at you."

Hugh dropped to one knee and took her hand. "I hope you shall give me an opportunity to make up for my shamefully *de trop* reappearance, Aunt."

Lady Letitia snatched away her hand. "Fool!" She jabbed her cane at the nearest chair. "Sit!"

Still grinning, Hugh sat and the tension dissipated.

"Well," Anne whispered, lowering herself onto the settee beside Daphne. "I am glad *that* is over. She has been furious for weeks."

They watched for a moment as Hugh and his aunt spoke.

"So," Anne said, turning back to Daphne. "What are your plans now that you are out of mourning?"

Daphne tried to keep one ear on Hugh's conversation with his aunt while answering Anne's many questions, but Hugh and Lady Letitia—normally loud—had chosen to speak in almost inaudible tones. Which made her even more curious.

Daphne and Anne were just making plans to go riding that day when Hugh stood and gave them a rueful smile.

"I hate to dash off, ladies, but I'm afraid I have a prior engagement."

Prior engagement? What prior engagement? He had only just arrived in the middle of the night.

He kissed his aunt's cheek, embraced Anne, and took Daphne's hand. "Please do not set a cover for me this evening. I'm afraid I shall not return until quite late."

Daphne tugged away her hand, disappointment mingling with pain. "I shall notify Cook."

"Hmph," Lady Letitia snorted.

Hugh chuckled at his aunt's nonverbal comment and gave Daphne a conspiring wink.

Lady Letitia waited until the door shut behind him before shaking her head. "That man! What a hornet's nest he has cracked open with his dramatic return." Her words said one thing but the glint in her eyes said she wasn't entirely disappointed. "I've informed my inconsiderate oaf of a nephew you are both in good time to attend the ball I am giving for that idiot John's unfortunate daughter." Her expression became grim. "She's got more hair than wit, and I'm grateful her father died before he could get his hands on her meager dowry." Lady Letitia gave a dismissive *tsk* at Daphne's horrified expression. "Oh, don't give me that prudish look, missy! Thomas must have said that much and more when he faced the dreadful prospect of John as his heir."

Daphne looked away from the other woman's piercing gaze. Did Letitia guess to what lengths the late Earl of Davenport had gone to avoid John Redvers's inheriting? Daphne wouldn't be surprised. She'd always suspected Letitia's astute brain and sharp, prying eyes were a big part of why Thomas kept his family at arm's length after they married.

"It is past a year, is it not?"

Daphne nodded. "Only a little."

The older woman gave her signature snort. "Thomas would not have wished you to go on mourning. You must cast off your blacks." She flicked a dismissive, hawk-like gaze over Daphne's lavender gown. "You must see Madame Thérèse and give her my name. She possesses all the arrogance of her breed, but it is not misplaced. She will know how to dress you."

Daphne murmured the appropriate thanks.

"I would love to accompany you, Daphne."

Daphne smiled at Anne and nodded, not telling her cousin that she hoped to merely send Rowena along with her measurements and dispense entirely with the tedious act of shopping.

Lady Letitia chuckled suddenly. "You've no idea the number of impertinent questions I've endured these past weeks because of my wretched nephew. I look forward to extracting my pound of flesh from his hide in the weeks to come."

"I encouraged him to come to London and pay his respects more than once," Daphne said, happy to heap fuel on the flames of the old lady's wrath.

"Ha! You are not his minder, gel, and he is a man grown." She made a rude *cluck* of disgust. "God knows you have enough on your plate without taking my tiresome nephew in hand. Although I daresay you're quite skilled at managing dolts after ten years of living with Thomas and my fool of a sister." Lady Letitia shifted in her gilt chair, which was too small for her tall, angular frame. "I suppose I *should* ask how my batty sister goes on, but I doubt the answer would be either edifying or interesting, so I shan't." She gave the floor a sharp rap with her cane and heaved herself to her feet. "We must be getting on."

Daphne accompanied the women to their elegant equipage

and waited while Lady Letitia's footman helped her inside. Once the frail-looking old woman was settled she turned to Daphne, an expression of bemusement resting oddly on her sharp features. "I must own I'm not sure I *want* to know the whole of what Hugh has been up to these past twenty years."

Daphne knew exactly what she meant. As she watched her sister-in-law's carriage roll away, she realized the only thing more agonizing than wondering what Hugh Redvers had done during his years abroad was wondering what he'd done for the past fortnight.

Hugh was still smiling when he climbed into the carriage waiting to take him to his club. One would have thought his Aunt Letitia's own four children would have been enough to keep the woman occupied, but his aunt always spared attention—too much, in Hugh's opinion— for her orphaned nephew.

His smile faltered when he thought of his other aunt—a woman whose attention he wanted far too much. Hugh grimaced at the memory of Daphne's frosty expression this morning. She was not pleased with him.

Well, unfortunately—thanks to the Duke of Carlisle— Daphne's displeasure could not be helped, at least not for now. Not surprisingly, the duke had buttonholed Hugh when he'd returned Mia to her family's country estate.

"I would ask you not to speak of my daughter's return to anyone, Lord Ramsay. I will have to admit your part in bringing her back, but I'd ask at least a month before you answer any questions—enough time that I might—" He'd broken off, his pale, freckled skin a fiery red. "Well, enough time for my daughter to get her story straight."

Ha! Enough time for the *duke* to fabricate a story was more like it. But Hugh had given his word and now he must stand by it. So here he was, muzzled on the subject.

Hugh believed the duke was futilely swimming against the tide. There was too much money to be made on such a juicy story for it to remain a secret. Already word of Mia's return had spread like wildfire—even from remote Yorkshire—and tales of the "Duke's Mysterious Daughter" competed with Hugh's name in the scandal sheets.

Hugh gazed out the carriage window at the crowded streets. After almost two weeks of dealing with Mia's stiff, awkward family, he'd looked forward to returning to Lessing Hall—to Daphne—even though he knew their relations would necessarily be uneasy. When he'd returned to Lessing Hall to find Daphne gone, he told himself it was better that way— better for *her* to stay away from him. He had nothing but scandal to offer her. He would find whoever was threatening her and then board the *Ghost* and continue pursuing his wretched life's work.

But then he'd spoken to Martín.

Hugh had been correct in believing Martín was the perfect man to insinuate himself into Whitton Park. Martín's new lady-love—a kitchen maid in Hastings's employ—told him Sir Malcolm had recently come into some money— money he claimed came from Lady Davenport.

Sir Malcolm had also boasted Daphne was to marry him now that her period of mourning was over. The maid hadn't been the only witness to his words; several other servants had heard him make the same claim while he was deep in his cups.

Hastings had stayed at Whitton Park only long enough to pay his grumbling staff their much delayed wages before hying off to some mysterious assignation. The consensus among his employees was that Sir Malcolm's *assignation* most likely involved a gaming table, cards, and a bottle of something expensive in London.

Hugh didn't believe for a moment that Hastings's new-found money was a wedding present from Daphne. But Hugh's gut—a surprisingly reliable organ—told him the wretched little worm probably spoke the truth about the *source* of the money. The scene he'd encountered that first day—Hastings's bloody face, Daphne's disheveled appearance and furious eyes—was burned into his mind's eye. Hastings was holding something over Daphne; Hugh was certain of it, and it maddened the hell out of him that she would not confide in him.

Lord! How he wished—for the hundredth time—he'd arrived in the clearing only a moment earlier that day. He knew he should just confront Daphne, but something about prying secrets from her left a bad taste in his mouth; he wouldn't like somebody digging around in his past.

It pained him greatly that she wouldn't come to him with her problems. He believed she'd been on the brink of confiding in him a dozen times, but any trust he'd built between them would have fled after she'd caught him with Mia in his lap.

"Blast and damn," he muttered to the empty carriage. Hugh was sore, tired, and irritable. He wanted to be lounging in the library with a book and pretending to read while watching Daphne, or escorting her and the boys about London and engaging in foolishness. Unfortunately, Mia stood between them and there wasn't a damned thing he could do to clear the air—yet.

So, here he was, off to look for that idiot Hastings. Well, he might not be able to spend his time with her, but he could protect her. Just the thought of her doling out money to her repulsive cousin made his blood boil.

The best way to find the man would be to visit clubs, and clubs meant gaming and carousing—activities that now left him cold. Hugh heaved a sigh. The days ahead would be beyond taxing. He'd need to spend every waking hour reconnecting with old acquaintances who had long believed him dead, crafting vague responses to endless questions, dodging prying newspapermen—

Hugh groaned. The bloody newspapers! He'd forgotten about the bloody newspapers. He closed his eyes and dropped his head back with a dull *thunk*. The scruffy men who invented and disseminated what passed for news had not been lingering about Davenport House this morning, but he'd eat his hat if they weren't there by the time he returned home tonight.

Hugh yearned for the days when things were simpler, when all he had to worry about were murderous corsairs trying to kill him and the entire French navy trying to sink his ship.

Chapter Fourteen

Daphne froze in the doorway to the breakfast room. There sat Hugh, enjoying one of his gargantuan breakfasts and perusing the paper.

She'd heard him return home often enough these past few weeks—his heavy step passing her door at first light and not leaving his chambers again until dark—but she'd not caught a glimpse of him since that first day.

But here he was, bright-eyed and bushy-tailed.

He got to his feet, his eye sweeping her from head to toe and then from toe to head, his expression flatteringly poleaxed. "Good God, Daphne, you are like a daffodil sprung to life in that shade of yellow. You look spectacular."

Daphne gritted her teeth against the joy that exploded in her chest. "What a surprise, finding you here, my lord."

He grinned at the chill in her voice. "Have you missed me, Daphne?"

"A fresh pot of coffee, please," she said to one of the footmen, and then turned to find Hugh looming over her, a plate clasped in his huge hands and an ingratiating smile curving his lips.

"May I be your servant this morning, my lady?"

She plucked the plate from his fingers. "Please, resume your meal, Lord Ramsay."

He chuckled and she heard the scrape of a chair as she approached the chafing dishes on the breakfront. Her appetite had fled the moment she'd seen him, but she hardly wanted him to know that.

"I am delighted to see you have left off your mourning, Daphne."

She selected one of the smaller slabs of ham and some coddled eggs before taking the place setting farthest from his.

"How are you finding London so far?" he asked, undaunted by her frosty treatment.

"Busy."

"But not all work, I trust?" He sawed off a chunk of very rare beef and Daphne blanched and looked away. *He* had not been losing sleep or been unable to eat worrying about that night at Lessing Hall. "Have you been keeping yourself entertained?"

"I am interviewing tutors, if you should wonder at the volume of young men coming and going from the house," she said, and then wished she had not.

The forkful of beef stopped halfway to his mouth and he grinned. "I am obliged to you for setting my mind at rest. Lord knows what impression I may have put upon such activity otherwise." He popped the beef into his mouth and chewed, his green eye sparkling.

Just what the devil did he mean by that? That young men couldn't possibly be calling on her for any other reason? Daphne realized he was watching her expectantly and reminded herself how much he reveled in baiting her. She could deprive him of that much enjoyment, at least.

He washed down his food with a mouthful of coffee before speaking. "Is this tutor idea something my aunt has cooked up?"

"I hardly need Lady Letitia's advice when it comes to educating my children." She chewed her lip, wishing she could take back her churlish response.

His mouth curved into a slow smile but he said nothing, turning back to his rapidly diminishing breakfast.

The *clink* of cutlery filled the room. Silence was fine with Daphne.

"Have you seen much of my aunt?" Hugh asked.

Daphne studied his face for signs of a trap, but he appeared innocent. Well, as innocent as he could ever look. "Your aunt has taken me on as her pet project." She frowned. "We have been paying calls—every day for weeks—not to mention the usual round of evening entertainments." Her tone made it plain he would know as much if he ever bothered to leave his clubs.

He chortled but did not rise to the bait.

"Between them, your aunt and Anne are contriving to introduce me to every member of the *ton* worth knowing." Daphne did not share with him that she found the activity exhausting and vapid.

Still, it was better than the alternative—which was to get on with telling Hugh the truth, scandalizing the *ton*, and packing her sons off to the wilds of Yorkshire, where they could enjoy a life of shame, isolation, and penny-pinching economy.

Yes, and what about that, Daphne? Just when are you planning on getting around to that?

Daphne had no clever mental response.

"You have my deepest sympathies," Hugh said.

She blinked. "I beg your pardon?"

"Why, Daphne! You are not hanging on my every word?"

"No."

He threw back his head and the breakfast room echoed with his laughter. Daphne told herself not to feel such a sense of achievement for merely making him laugh.

"I was offering you my sympathy for the past few weeks. I know how relentless my aunt can be." He ate the last bite of beef and turned his attention to a slab of ham. "I expect Aunt Letitia to swoop in on me at any moment and take me in hand."

"Is that why you have been hiding at your club?"

He chewed and swallowed before responding. "How astute of you, Daphne."

"Coward."

"And very proud of it."

A laugh slipped out before she could stop it and he cocked one eyebrow in a way that made her vibrate with . . . *something*. She ignored whatever it was and fixed him with a cool stare.

He smiled at her attempt to suppress him. "Don't you have any place to hide, Daphne?"

She took the opportunity of the footman's arrival with fresh coffee to ignore him.

"To own the truth, I'd half expected my aunt to show up at White's or Watier's with that cane of hers and beat me over the head until I accompanied her to Almack's."

Daphne stirred milk into her coffee and enjoyed the mental image of the wizened, bent old lady beating Hugh with her cane.

"I see you like that thought, my lady."

She did not bother to deny the accusation.

"I can only suppose she is biding her time and will pounce on me at this wretched ball of hers."

His suspicion was correct, but Daphne felt no desire to warn him. Hugh would have very little rest once his aunt had him in her clutches. She smiled with grim anticipation at the thought of his formidable aunt attempting to mold the big man to her will. The two would be worthy opponents. For all his apparent amiability, Hugh had a will of iron.

He paused in his demolition of the ham steak. "I am at

liberty today and had it in mind to take the boys to the Tower."

Daphne experienced a strange pang at his words. Luckily she was quick enough to suppress an answering smile. As far as she was concerned, Lord Ramsay could save his charm for his redheaded mistress. Or fiancée. Or concubine. Or—

"Have they already been?"

"I beg your pardon?"

"*Tsk*, *tsk*, my lady, you are demolishing my delicate self-esteem this morning." He laughed at her scowl. "I asked if the boys have already gone to the Tower?"

"Not yet."

"Excellent. Would you care to accompany us, my dear Daphne?"

Her eyes narrowed at both his offer and endearment. He had been avoiding her since coming to London—for *three weeks*—and had disappeared with hardly a word two weeks before that. Did he think she would forget all about the episode at Lessing Hall if he stayed away long enough? Was *that* what he'd been up to?

"I am engaged this afternoon."

"Ahhh."

"But perhaps Rowena could accompany you."

That amused him. "She wouldn't consent to ride in the same vehicle with me unless it was a tumbril, she was a guard, and I was on my way to Madame Guillotine." He shook his head. "No, thank you. I shall take Kemal with me; his boy-wrangling skills are unparalleled." He heaved a sigh and laid down his knife and fork, his plate empty. "By the by, why does your faithful retainer hate me so intensely?"

"She does not hate you," Daphne lied. "Yorkshire folk merely require time to warm up to new acquaintances."

"Hmm. Are you dining at home tonight?"

Daphne blinked at the change of subject. "Yes, I've invited your cousins Melinda and Simon, as well as Anne."

"But not my aunt?"

"She is engaged elsewhere."

He smiled. "Excellent. Please add me to your number."

Daphne stared as he drank the last of his coffee. Just what had inspired this sudden urge for domesticity? Was he tired of gaming, carousing, and his redheaded companion?

"Well," Hugh said, tossing his napkin onto the table and standing. "I had better find Kemal and collect the young monsters." He dropped a mocking bow. "I shall see you this evening, my lady." The door clicked shut behind him.

Go after him, tell him now.

I can't, not when he is going to take the boys out. And tonight—

Excuses, excuses, excuses.

Daphne stared at the uneaten food on her plate, her body as taut and brittle as a dried-up twig.

Tell him.

"I . . . I can't."

"My lady?"

Daphne looked up to find the young footman, William, hovering beside her. "You said something, my lady?"

"I don't need anything more, William, you may leave." She waited until the door closed before shoving away the plate and dropping her head into her hands.

Tell him. The words pulsed in her head with the persistence of a war drum.

I will tell him. I will—

When?

I will tell him after the ball.

There was no answer—derisive, or otherwise—and her shoulders slumped with relief because she knew this time she meant it. Hugh would be relaunched into society, back in the bosom of his family. There could be no more excuse to delay. None.

Daphne could gather up the pieces of her life and escape with what was left.

Hugh dispatched Kemal to fetch the two boys rather than chance encountering Daphne's hatchet-faced protector in the schoolroom. While he waited, he sifted through the remarkable number of invitations he'd received since showing his face at White's. Thus far, he hadn't accepted a single one— he hadn't come to London to attend *ton* functions; he'd come to find Hastings. Not that he'd had any luck.

Instead of assemblies and balls and dinner parties, he'd gone to White's, Boodle's, Brooks's, Watier's and at least two dozen other lesser clubs and hells, looking for the bastard.

Other than a handful of amusing incidents, Hugh's tedious nights of drinking and gambling failed to yield even a groat of news about Hastings. By the end of three weeks Hugh had concluded the wretched sponger really had gone to some *secret assignation*.

In any event, Hugh had had enough. He'd risen early and stayed out late and spent all the time he could stand in clubs, gaming establishments, and brothels. Until he had reliable information that Hastings was in London, Hugh would please himself. And pleasing himself meant seeing Daphne. Hugh was ravenous for her company. He needed to be with her, even if they only engaged in innocuous entertainments like sightseeing, meals, and bickering.

Hugh tossed aside the unopened invitations and went to stare out the window of his private study. He'd moved from his original suite of rooms to one overlooking the street. This location was noisier but he was able to keep an eye on things—specifically the crowds of gawkers and newspapermen that accreted wherever he was. Just as he had at Lessing Hall, he'd needed to hire men to keep the street clear. Ponsby had reported no disturbances in the house or its environs and Hugh wanted to keep it that way.

Hugh's thoughts drifted back to Daphne. The constraint between them was his fault, and it made him want to smash things. He took a deep breath and exhaled slowly; he just needed to be patient. He knew Mia was already attending *ton* functions; with any luck his silence would not have to go on for much longer.

As to what he and Daphne would do once she knew the truth? Well, what *could* they do? It made no difference to him whether they became social outcasts, but he could hardly expect her to feel the same, especially not when she had two young sons.

Hugh groaned. He'd never before experienced the particular brand of emotion he was feeling. Oh, he'd felt something similar on occasion, when he couldn't get a woman out of his mind. But in the past, his obsessions had always been colored by the desire to get a particular woman into his bed. Not that he didn't wish to get Daphne into his bed, because he wished that very much, but that wasn't the entirety of what he wanted from her, or even the most compelling part. He'd enjoyed revisiting Lessing Hall with her and discussing the management of the property. He liked spending time with her sons, who were clever and charming and bursting with life. He liked their evenings together in the library, their chess games, their rides about the property, their—

He exhaled heavily. He wasn't just obsessed with her, he was—

Hugh groaned and shoved a hand through his hair and propped himself up against the window frame, closing his eyes. He was behaving like a heartsick fool—because he *was* a heartsick fool.

He'd wait until this bloody ball was over, then he'd remove himself from Davenport House even if he could not yet leave

England. He would continue his search for Hastings, but at a distance.

"Blast it all!" he cursed, pushing away from the window. It was not his way to be so self-sacrificing and civilized. If she did not have two small children, he would spirit her back to his ship, and make love to her until she agreed to—

The door to his chambers flew open and two small bodies barreled into the room.

"Hugh! Hugh!"

Hugh smiled down at them, his throat oddly tight. Why had he ever believed Daphne would be the only one he missed when he left England behind?

Chapter Fifteen

Daphne woke early; indeed, sleep had eluded her for most of the night. Today was the Thornehill ball, and tomorrow morning she would tell Hugh the truth. And then she would leave—she had already paid for seats on the next mail coach. She would have to arrange for their possessions to be brought to Yorkshire later. If she began packing now, Rowena would cause a fuss. In fact, Daphne feared the older woman's reaction to her news more than her sons'.

Daphne scarcely recalled the house in Yorkshire. She had been to her grandfather's property once, seven years ago, at Thomas's urging when she'd inherited both the house and a moderate competence—the money she and the children would now use to live.

"Your grandfather was a great man, Daphne. There is no shame in deriving one's wealth from hard work and ingenuity, no matter what many in our class might think. Don't let Walter Hastings's bitterness spoil that," Thomas had cautioned her when she'd told him to sell it.

Thomas had been right, of course. The house was all Daphne had left of her coal baron grandfather's fortune— most of which Walter Hastings had wasted. It was drafty, remote, and inhospitable, but it would be far enough from

Lessing Hall and London that she could collect her wits and consider her future.

A knock on her study door pulled her back to the present.

Ponsby entered with a salver bearing a card: Sir Marcus Lawry.

"I do not recall a Sir Marcus Lawry."

"He and the late earl were acquaintances of long standing."

Daphne looked at the stack of correspondence she'd hoped to get sorted today and then sighed.

"Very well. Where is he?"

"In the Yellow Drawing Room, your ladyship."

Daphne walked the short distance to the grand but uncomfortable drawing room, hoping the drafty room would keep the caller from staying too long.

An ancient gentleman wearing a skirted coat and full court wig, complete with powder, greeted her. "Thank you very much for seeing me, Lady Davenport." He made a stiff but courtly bow.

"It is my pleasure. Please be seated, Sir Marcus."

He lowered himself with obvious relief onto one of the miserably hard chairs that littered the room.

"I understand you knew my late husband?"

His huge wig nodded. "We were close friends for many years. Although I did not see Thomas as often these past few years, we did correspond regularly. I saw him whenever he came to London, particularly if he came on a matter for the Society—that would be the Horticultural Society, of course—of which I am also a member. I was very sorry to have missed his funeral. I'm afraid health problems made that journey impossible." Sir Marcus paused for a moment and then reached into the large pocket of his skirted chartreuse coat and extracted a battered leather packet. "I last saw Thomas when he came to London two years ago. I believe you were with him at the time."

"Yes, that was not long before his accident. He delivered a paper during that visit."

Sir Marcus smiled. "I was there to listen—absolutely brilliant, as usual. In any case, I'd committed to dinner at Davenport House but was called away at the last minute. Before I left, Thomas came to see me and gave me a letter." A flush crept up his neck. "He told me the contents of the letter, just in case you should ever need a witness." He laughed suddenly. "I'm not the best choice, you must be thinking. Especially as I could have given Thomas a good eight years!"

So the man was even older than he looked—which was saying something. Daphne swallowed a guilty pang about seeing him in this arctic, cavernous room and not offering him tea.

"When I read in the papers that Lord Ramsay had returned, I decided now was an excellent time to give you this. I have not been in the best of health and I felt I should pass it to you." He struggled to stand up and hand her the packet and Daphne quickly rose and went to him, earning a grateful smile as he sank back into his seat. "Much obliged to you, my lady. You are as kind as you are beautiful." A devilish twinkle sparkled in his cloudy green eyes as he surveyed her with the practiced look of a very old rake.

Daphne couldn't help smiling: here was Hugh in another forty years.

"I will remain here while you read it, in case you have any questions."

"You are very kind. I shall order some tea."

"I would greatly appreciate it. At my age tea is one of the few pleasures I am still able to enjoy," he added wickedly.

They made small talk while the kitchen sent up a tray. After she'd settled her guest with a cup of tea and a large plate of biscuits, Daphne opened the packet. There were two envelopes. She opened the one entitled *To Whom It May Concern* first.

> *I, Thomas Redvers, am writing this letter and swear to the validity of its contents before erstwhile magistrate, Sir Marcus Lawry.*
>
> *Knowing the malicious lengths to which Malcolm Hastings has gone in the past, I am compelled to leave this sworn document as proof against any claims he might make against my wife, Lady Daphne Davenport, or my sons. He has formerly, in order to blackmail money from my wife, threatened to make public spurious claims of patrimony of my two sons, Lucien and Richard Redvers. I, Thomas Lucien Edward Redvers, Earl of Davenport, do swear these children are the issue of my body.*
>
> *Sworn, et cetera,*
> *Thomas Redvers, Earl of Davenport*

Daphne put the letter down and looked up.

The old man was waiting, his expression serious. "Read the second letter, my lady, and then we can talk."

> *Dearest Daphne:*
>
> *I am writing this letter because I believe Malcolm might one day threaten you and our sons, not to mention the Redverses' family honor. If I am correct, the accompanying letter will at least prove I was aware of his spurious claims. If I am wrong, there is no harm done. Sir Marcus is my closest friend— other than you—and he has made arrangements with*

*his solicitor to deliver a copy to you in the event of
his death.*

*There is something else I must confess. My
nephew, Hugh Redvers, is alive and operates as the
privateer One-Eyed Standish.*

Daphne looked up. "He knew about Lord Ramsay."
Lawry nodded. "Yes. For the first few years it was just a
suspicion. But then a friend of his—an admiral who'd come
across Hugh in person—confirmed his suspicions."
Daphne's eyes blurred and she ducked her head, squeezing her eyes shut until she was sure no tears would fall. She
opened them a moment later and forced herself to continue.

*I am sorry I could not bring myself to confide in you.
I'll admit it was partly due to shame; shame that I
had so alienated the affections of my favorite nephew
and heir that he would rather I believe him dead than
come home.*

*I also worried you would not accept the
protection of marriage if you thought you were
depriving Hugh of his inheritance. And, knowing
you, you would have followed your conscience, no
matter the consequences.*

A drop of water hit the page and a folded white handkerchief appeared above the letter.
Daphne took it without looking up. "Thank you."

*I could not have that, Daphne. You must believe me
when I tell you that Hugh never wanted this life for
himself. I knew he would not come back. That left my
nephew John, and . . . well, I could not allow that to
happen. Not only for you, but for the hundreds of
people who rely on me. I have never regretted my*

*decision to marry you. Nor do I regret my two fine
sons.*

> *The letter accompanying this, and the word of Sir
> Marcus, should eliminate any claim Hastings might
> make. The scandal he could create, however, is
> another matter and there is no notary or judge who
> can purge the thoughts from people's minds once the
> seed has been planted. If Hastings ever makes
> demands, you should approach William Standish for
> help. He knows how to reach Hugh. If you ever need
> an ally against Hastings, I believe you could find no
> better man than my nephew. I hope I am wrong in
> my suspicions and I regret I cannot always be here
> to protect you.*

> *My love to you, my adopted daughter.*

> *Thomas*

She folded the paper, smoothing out the wrinkles before
looking up.

"Thomas was a man among men," Sir Marcus said. "I
know you and the boys made his last years very happy ones."

"Thank you."

Even in death Thomas was protecting her and her sons—
not to mention saving her from unspeakable ignomiy. She
thought of Hugh and the proof she could now offer him, and
her heart sang.

Hugh might be upset at her deception, but at least he
would have no reason for disbelief or disgust. Well, at least
not about her marriage. She would never tell him the truth
about Malcolm—that episode was too shameful. Nor did he
have any right to know such an unsavory, personal story. It
would be far better if he believed she'd been a foolish and
promiscuous young girl who'd gotten herself into trouble.

Yes, she thought as the sick, grinding sensation returned to her stomach. Far better.

Hugh and Daphne arrived at Lady Letitia's impressive gray fortress on Grosvenor Square a half hour early, along with the rest of Hugh's family.

Anne seized Daphne's hands and held them out to her sides while she examined her gown, her mouth an O of surprise. "Did *you* choose this gown?"

Daphne laughed at her obvious skepticism.

Anne blushed. "I didn't mean—"

"Yes, you did, and you needn't apologize. To answer your question, I did not. Rowena and Madame Thérèse engaged in fisticuffs and Madame won."

"It is absolutely stunning and *perfect*."

Daphne was not so sure of that, but she had no interest in discussing her clothing. Instead, she chatted with Anne and her parents for a few moments before excusing herself to greet Lady Letitia, who sat in great state on a tapestry-covered wing-back chair, her gouty foot resting on a matching ottoman. She was swathed in puce from head to toes and diamonds the size of hazelnuts festooned her ample bosom and swollen fingers. She was talking to her butler, but waved him away when she saw Daphne approach.

"Ah, Daphne. Come, sit beside me, my dear." She gestured to a chair.

"Good evening, my lady."

The older woman scrutinized her through her ornate quizzing glass. "I suppose that sour-faced maid of yours chose that gown?"

Daphne's gown was midnight-blue silk that was far too low cut and form-hugging for her comfort. Not only that, but she wore only one nearly insubstantial petticoat beneath it.

But it was too late to regret her decision now—even if it was leading to conversations she found more than a little tedious.

"I usually leave all my clothing decisions in Rowena's hands, but this gown was chosen by Madame Thérèse."

Lady Letitia gave a bark of laughter. "Wise decision. I daresay your head is too full of high-flown rubbish to give a tinker's cuss what you wear—just like my brother's head was." She tapped her glass against the upholstered arm of her chair and kept Daphne pinned like an insect with her steely stare. "I dread to think what your life was like with my brother."

Daphne began to protest, but the old woman forestalled her with a loud *tsk tsk*.

"I know he wasn't *cruel* to you, my dear. But he and my sister are like a pair of helpless infants who require tending. I daresay it was *you* who took care of them both. Before you came along, I expected Thomas and Amelia to be wearing bibs and slippers every time I visited Lessing Hall." Something like sadness seeped into her hard gray eyes. "You were good for my brother in many ways. I'm pleased he could return the favor."

Daphne's brow wrinkled. What was the older woman saying?

Lady Letitia waved her hand. "But that is of no consequence now." Her eyes slid to where Hugh stood. "I daresay you needed a whip and spurs to get *him* here tonight."

Surprisingly, Hugh had been ready and waiting with no prodding from anyone. He had also been uncharacteristically subdued and quiet during the brief carriage ride.

"I believe he was eager to come this evening," she lied.

"Hmmph." Lady Letitia's glare intensified the longer her eyes lingered on Hugh, who was talking to his cousin Simon. "I'd as well set my money on fire or toss it out a coach window as expect him to appreciate this ball."

"I cannot imagine he is insensible of the honor you do him."

"Ha! Then you must lack for imagination, missy. Just look at him over there. As happy and carefree as a lark. No thought for how he has disrupted our lives—especially yours—by returning willy-nilly after almost two decades."

Daphne took full advantage of the older woman's order to study Hugh.

He had his hands clasped behind his back and was leaning down to hear something Simon was saying, a ready smile on his gorgeous face. There were miles of muscular calf and thigh encased in stockings and snug black-satin breeches. He wore a green-gold waistcoat beneath his black tailcoat, a color that made his blond hair shine like a newly minted guinea under the blazing chandeliers. It was indecent, really, how godlike he looked talking to his shorter and stockier cousin.

But even in elegant evening clothes—and without the saber and tricorn the broadsheet artists were so fond of depicting him with—he still looked like the King's Pirate rather than a staid English peer.

Daphne turned and met Lady Letitia's too-shrewd gaze. Naturally she blushed as though she were guilty of something.

"I daresay you know a great deal about doltish men, having been married to Thomas. I do not like to speak ill of the dead," Lady Letitia said, preparing to do exactly that, "but my brother was even less cognizant of his surroundings than the rest of his species. Most of the time he went about wishing we were all orchids he could feed manure and keep in the dark."

Daphne bit back a smile. Thomas would have enjoyed setting to rights his sister's confusion of mushrooms and orchids.

Anne came to ask her grandmother a question and the mysterious conversation was over.

* * *

The massive drawing room—its cream walls and black-and-white marble floors obscured by acres of exotic tropical flowers—filled up quickly as the handpicked elite of London society arrived for the exclusive pre-ball dinner. Daphne found herself passed from hand to hand among the crème de la crème of the English aristocracy and knew her sister-in-law was behind it.

She had just disengaged herself from a dizzying conversation with Lady Jersey and Mrs. Benjamin Morton when the red-haired siren Hugh had disappeared with entered the room. Both Lady Letitia and Hugh moved to greet the woman, who was accompanied by a pair of men who could only be relatives, given their distinctive hair color.

Anne appeared beside her. "That is Lady Euphemia Marlington."

So, Lady Amelia had been correct that morning. Well, Daphne was not completely surprised given the sensational stories she'd read about the woman in the broadsheets. Not that she necessarily believed most of them.

"That is her father, the Duke of Carlisle, and her brother, Marquess of Abermarle. They are a handsome family, are they not?"

Daphne could not actually see faces, only three auburn heads. Rowena had all but ripped her spectacles from her face before the ball and Daphne had been too agitated about her impending confession to protest.

"You can't attend a ball wearing *spectacles*, my lady. Not with that dress." The dour woman's militant scowl had made Daphne believe Rowena might wrestle her to the floor if she attempted to leave the house with glasses perched on her nose.

Now she was glad of her poor vision. It was evident from the way Hugh had hastened toward the auburn beauty that he held her in high regard. Had he only waited for her to be restored to her family to pursue their relationship? She turned away to gaze sightlessly on some other cluster of guests, struggling against the despair that pooled in the pit of her stomach.

She felt a light touch on her shoulder and turned, fixing a smile on her face for Anne.

But it was not Anne.

"May I have the honor of taking you in to dinner?" Hugh asked.

Her gaze flickered toward Euphemia Marlington and back to Hugh.

"Why?"

He took her hand and placed it on his arm.

Her entire body thrummed at the feel of his hard, corded heat beneath her parchment-thin glove. Lust twisted inside her, almost driving her to her knees.

"Why?" she repeated.

"You know how I am." His lips curved in a teasing, sensual smile. "I care only about getting my own way."

She removed her hand from his forearm. "You had better escort someone of more consequence."

"There *is* nobody who has more consequence to me than you." A subtle tightening of his facial muscles transformed him from teasing lover into determined predator. "My aunt tells me this ball is partly in my honor. As such I will please myself."

Daphne couldn't see the faces of those around her, but she sensed her hesitation was making the two of them conspicuous. She placed her hand on his arm and he led her to the dining room without speaking. Her eyes widened when she approached the long banquet table, and not only because it groaned beneath more china and silver than she'd ever seen in her life. No, she stared because Lady Letitia had seated her beside Hugh. She didn't need to look at him to know who was responsible. She could *feel* him gloating.

Seated on Hugh's other side, she saw with a plunging sensation in her stomach, was Lady Euphemia.

"Daphne," Hugh said, his voice devoid of its usual humor, "this is Lady Euphemia Marlington. Lady Euphemia, this is the Countess of Davenport."

Both women curtsied and Daphne couldn't help noticing the tiny newcomer's sinuous grace.

"I apologize for my intrusion into your house, Lady Davenport. And also for my . . . hasty departure." She bit her lip and glanced down, her eyes every bit as entrancing without kohl. "I was eager to be reunited with my father and brother after so many years."

What could Daphne possibly say to that? She nodded and smiled. "Welcome back to England."

A look of relief passed over the other woman's face, as if she'd expected Daphne to demand explanations. But, as far as Daphne was concerned, it was Hugh's job to explain, not this stranger's.

She turned to her other dinner companion and found Lady Euphemia's brother, the Marquess of Abermarle. Up close, Daphne could see he was perhaps a few years younger than she. The combination of alabaster skin, light green eyes, and aquiline nose made for a very handsome man. Like his sister, he had dark auburn hair which tumbled in loose, sensuous curls over his smooth, white brow. Here was a man every bit as beautiful as Hugh Redvers—although without the fascinating combination of menace and humor.

A vindictive smile curved her lips as she greeted her handsome companion; it was time the arrogant Lord Ramsay realized he was not the only attractive man in London.

Unfortunately, even the charms of a handsome marquess

could not keep Daphne from trying to listen to what was being said on her other side.

Daphne did not hear much, but the few things she *did* hear were less than lover-like. In fact, it sounded as though Hugh and Lady Euphemia were quarreling—although she didn't know what about since they were speaking Arabic.

When Abermarle's other dinner partner asked him a question, Daphne turned to Hugh, who was waiting for her, a petulant expression marring his handsome features.

Euphemia Marlington was speaking to the elderly gentleman on her other side. Whatever she was saying to him had caused his eyebrows to meet his receding hairline and his face to turn an alarming shade of red.

"Making yet another conquest, my lady?" Hugh's eyes met hers briefly before dropping to her lower than usual décolletage.

Daphne's neck and chest warmed under his inspection. "I cannot say the same for you, my lord." She cast a pointed glance at Euphemia Marlington. "She does not look nearly so besotted with you as she did the last time."

Hugh grinned, as if he found her efforts to give him a setdown piquant or charming.

"Mia knows where my true interests lie." A huge, hot hand landed on her knee and Daphne jumped.

Lord Abermarle turned, a frown marring his perfect forehead. "Is aught amiss, my lady?"

"Pepper," she lied, taking a drink of water to illustrate she was fine before turning back to Hugh.

"Are you deranged?" she hissed between gritted teeth.

"No. Merely aroused." His hand burned through the thin fabric of her dress like molten lava. "And very bored by this dinner."

"If you don't take your hand off my leg, I will stab it with my fork."

He surveyed the array of silverware. "Tell me, my lady, which of these many forks is meant for such a purpose? I'm afraid I've quite forgotten." He removed his hand and Daphne immediately missed it. "At least you've not threatened to head-butt me. I'm rather fond of my nose." He turned so she could view said feature in profile.

Daphne glanced around the table to see if Hugh's shocking behavior had attracted any notice. But the only person who appeared to be looking at them was Lady Letitia, and without her spectacles, Daphne was unable to read the older woman's expression.

"Will you please behave?" she whispered between her smiling lips.

"Behave? Behave like what? A man besotted?"

"Like a gentleman rather than an idiot."

He chortled at that. "What will you give me if I behave?"

"Why should I *give* you anything?"

"I am accustomed to a barter economy."

A soft hiss escaped her before she could stop it. "Why are you doing this to me?"

"Would you rather I did what I really want to be doing to you?" he asked in a voice like velvet.

When she didn't answer, he leaned closer. "Would you like a hint?"

"No."

"I'll give you one, anyway. What I would *rather* be doing involves your body and mine and no clothing. Or forks." He leaned forward in a way that must surely be attracting every eye at the table. "But I think you know very well what I would rather be doing."

"I will scream," she hissed.

Hugh burst out laughing at her empty threat and his distinctive bellow caused conversations up and down the table to stutter.

Daphne wanted to crawl under the table. Instead, she turned back to Abermarle, who was waiting for her.

"I can't help feeling envious that Lord Ramsay is the beneficiary of your wit, my lady."

Daphne somehow doubted the marquess would find being threatened with cutlery and called an idiot as amusing as Hugh had.

"Is Lady Euphemia your only sibling, my lord?" she asked, steering the topic of conversation away from Hugh and the things that made him laugh.

Hugh leaned back in the hideously uncomfortable chair and hid a yawn with the back of his hand. He knew he was behaving badly, but the stifling atmosphere had brought back all the things he hated about England.

And he was ready to throttle Mia for her incessant demands. He didn't doubt she was finding England trying, but returning to Oran would be tantamount to suicide.

He'd finally had to tell her—baldly—to stop her relentless nagging. She hadn't liked that one bit and had given him a look that would scald the bristles off a hog. But at least she had stopped nagging. She was now bothering the poor old bastard on her other side and Hugh watched with amusement as she *bothered* the randy old goat into a state of heightened arousal.

He glanced around the table and snorted; the meal was hardly half over and already he'd alienated both his dinner partners. He found it diverting that he—the guest of honor—was the only person at the table not engaged in conversation.

His attention wandered back to Daphne.

For the last three-quarters of an hour he'd been forced to watch young Abermarle fall head-over-heels for her, and he wanted to reach across Daphne's glazed, stuffed quail and grab the marquess by the neck and squeeze. But even a savage like he knew such an action would be frowned upon—and not just because cross-table interactions were faux pas.

So he put the violent image out of his mind and thought about what he would say to Daphne when he finally got her alone, which had to be soon, before he did something damaging to the next unsuspecting male who had the audacity to look at, speak to, or, God forbid, dance with her.

And that dress she was wearing—good God! It looked as if her demented maid had painted it onto her body. Hugh's first urge upon seeing it tonight had been to throw his coat over her and not uncover her again until they were alone. Preferably in his bed. He couldn't pull his eyes away. Her corset thrust her perfect breasts deliciously high until they were two mesmerizing swells above silk stretched taut and near bursting. Her nipples could not be more than a fraction of an inch below the low neckline. He *swore* he could see them outlined against the silk. The bodice began to expand and expand and he looked up to find Daphne glaring at him through eyes that shot pale blue fire.

Hugh shrugged at her and shifted in his seat, his erect rod jammed against the placket of his breeches. The brutal, persistent ache in his pants made him hate, more than ever, the superficial entertainments those around him favored. Well, at least the females. The men ringing the table would only be interested in cards, drinking, whoring, and horses, and not in that order.

Hugh had already whored his way across the globe, lost interest in playing cards more than a decade ago, and he had a good horse. As for drink? Well, he liked a fine brandy as much as any man, but beyond that . . .

What he wanted was Daphne, and soon.

Would this dinner never end?

He closed his eyes and considered the vortex of emotions that had been churning inside him for weeks. Lust, curiosity, anxiety, and—he suspected—love, not that he could be certain. He had never given any thought to the concept of love before, and perhaps he was mistaken. But whatever emotion he was experiencing, it was a singular sensation that both imprisoned and liberated. He felt . . . *chained* to her; only truly happy when she was near. How could that be? Had he become a slave, yet again? If so, why was he so pleased with his new condition?

He felt movement beside his chair and opened his eyes in time to see a footman deposit a syllabub. Hugh almost leapt to his feet and yelled, *Huzzah!* just as Lucien would. It was about bloody time.

The table broke up soon after that. All Hugh could think about was how long he needed to stay at this wretched affair before he could steal away with Daphne back to Davenport House, where he'd straighten out the situation between them once and for all.

Daphne could not wait to get away from the dinner table. Although she tried to ignore Hugh's fondling and staring, she was certain the entire table must have noticed her distraction—not to mention her arousal. Her treacherous body responded to his least look. Never in her life had she possessed so little control over her own person. She fully expected the crowd to part in horror as she left the dinner table, pointing and whispering at the wanton Countess of Davenport, a woman so depraved she was obsessed with her dead husband's nephew.

Luckily, Hugh could not continue his torment of her—at least not right now. Instead, he stood with his family near the entrance to the ballroom, looking very much like a martyr facing a fiery, agonizing death as he greeted hundreds of guests.

Daphne looked at the shimmering colors, low-cut gowns,

and profusion of jewels on the arriving guests and realized her bodice was no more indecent than most. She'd thought the midnight-blue gauze over a sheath of palest silver had looked simple and elegant when she'd put it on tonight, but now she saw it was almost conspicuously plain.

Her jewels, on the other hand, were unparalleled. The sapphire choker from Thomas was a work of art, row upon row of pale blue fire interspersed with satiny pearls. The only other accessory she wore was a spray of sapphires in her hair, which Rowena had dressed in a simple knot with curls cascading down her back.

Daphne fingered the stones at her throat idly as she looked around the room, her eyes drifting again and again to the tall figure at the ballroom entrance. She recalled the way he'd stared at her during dinner and her nipples tightened. She crossed her arms over her chest and turned away from the receiving line. She needed to think of something else, anything else. Preferably something repellent, guaranteed to keep her rebellious body far from arousal.

"*Sir Malcolm Hastings!*" Lady Letitia's majordomo proclaimed from the head of the stairs.

Chapter Sixteen

Hugh couldn't help laughing. The very man he'd been searching for so diligently in every pesthole, whorehouse, and gambling hell stood directly in front of him, lifting Anne's gloved hand to his mouth.

Hastings's dissipation was etched deeply into his face, but he was still handsome, or at least he would be if his mouth wasn't twisted into such an annoying smirk.

"Hastings, what a surprise. You look much improved from the last time I saw you." Hugh made no effort to keep his own smirk off his face. "I'm pleased to see your nose suffered no permanent damage. I had no idea Lady Letitia enjoyed the privilege of your acquaintance."

Rather than appear chastened by Hugh's not-so-subtle digs, Hastings smiled more widely.

"Unfortunately, I can claim no acquaintance with Lady Letitia. Rather it is your *other* aunt who pressed me to attend when she learned I was in town."

Hugh snorted. What a brazen, bloody lie. Even from across the room Hugh had seen Daphne freeze like a deer at her cousin's name. Hugh stared into the man's unusually light brown eyes as he fought the urge to pick him up and bodily carry him from his aunt's house.

Unusually light brown eyes.

Four other eyes flashed across his mind, and it was like the tumblers in a lock falling into place. *Great bloody hell!* His brain spun drunkenly and rational thought eluded him.

And so did Malcolm Hastings, slipping away into the crowd. Hugh looked to where he'd last seen Daphne; she was no longer there.

Daphne struggled to mask her revulsion as Malcolm swayed toward her, his hateful face oozing smug contempt.

"Hello, sweet cousin," he crooned, taking her by the wrists and holding her arms out to her sides. His eyes roamed over her like a swarm of insects before he leaned in and kissed her moistly on each cheek. "What a proud husband you will make me," he whispered in her ear.

Daphne tugged at her hands but he only released one. "What a surprise to see you here, Malcolm."

"A pleasant one, no doubt?" His eyes danced merrily as he placed her hand on his arm. Daphne darted a quick look to where Hugh was receiving and saw his attention was engaged by a flamboyant woman spilling out of her dangerously low-cut gold silk gown—as was almost every other person in the room. Nobody was paying attention to Malcolm and Daphne.

"This is hardly the time or place, but I daresay that does not matter to you, Malcolm. You want to discuss something with me?" She glanced around the huge ballroom until she noticed an alcove almost obscured by a potted palm.

"How astute you are." His words were slurred and his voice overly loud. If he wasn't foxed yet, he was almost there. The alcove would not be good enough. Daphne needed to get him away from the ballroom—and the guests.

"You will lose the hold you think you have over me if you start behaving like a fool in public. The library is behind the second door in the main hall. We can get there through the cardroom and you can say what you came to say in private."

"Of course, sweet Daphne—lead on, lead on."

But before they could reach the cardroom, Simon materialized beside her.

"I believe we are promised for the opening set, Daphne." Simon looked quizzically from her to Malcolm.

Daphne hesitated, thinking to put him off, but Malcolm took the decision from her hands.

"By all means, my good man," Malcolm said, practically shoving Daphne into the other man's arms. "Dance with my lovely cousin. I'll step into the cardroom for a few moments." He gave them an oily smile before lurching away.

"Shall we take our places?" Daphne said, before the older man could ask any awkward questions.

The set lasted forever and just when she'd extricated herself from Simon, the Marquess of Abermarle appeared.

Daphne bit back a scream. Instead, she smiled and said, "I'm rather fatigued, my lord. Would you mind terribly if we sat out this set?"

"Not at all, my lady, I shall sit with you."

She ground her teeth. "I am so thirsty. Would you—"

"Of course, perhaps some lemonade?"

"That would be lovely." The instant Abermarle turned his back, she darted toward the cardroom. Her vision was poor, but not so poor she didn't recognize Hugh's towering form coming toward her.

"Blast and damn, blast and damn," she muttered, pushing into the thickest part of the crowd. Guests were cheek by jowl, and the bodies formed a seemingly endless thicket. When a gap appeared on her left, she lunged toward it, bumping into a trio of wallflowers.

"Oh, excuse me. Please, pardon me. I'm terribly sorry," Daphne muttered, treading on slippers and toes to get to the other side. The reward for leaving a swath of destruction was

Malcolm, dead ahead. He was leaning against one of the large columns that flanked each side of the cardroom, as if needing its support to stand. More bodies separated them and Daphne had just pushed her way past a clutch of laughing young bucks when the orchestra struck up music heralding the arrival of a member of the royal family.

One advantage to being so tall was that Daphne could see over most heads: it was Ernest, the Duke of Cumberland. A buzz loud enough to overpower the orchestra swept through the cavernous room. Daphne assumed the duke must have made this public appearance to combat the rumors swirling around the death of his valet—the most scandalous being that Cumberland had murdered the man. Crowds of gawkers surged toward the duke, unable to resist the royal pull. This cleared a space and Daphne bolted toward Malcolm.

"Ah, Daphne," he slurred. "Old Ernest is looking rather hagged, isn't he? It's my opinion he had a rather unsavory—"

"Keep your voice down!" Daphne hissed, swallowing her disgust at touching him and grabbing his elbow. The cardroom had been abandoned, the players gone to see what the commotion was about. She opened the door to the hall and peeked out. It was empty and only a short distance to the library. She opened one of the double doors and peered inside; also empty.

Daphne dropped Malcolm's arm the second she entered the room, moving away from him. Malcolm fumbled with the door and Daphne realized he was locking it—or at least trying to, his hands so shaky he could hardly throw the bolt. He turned and grinned. "There, now we will be undisturbed while we talk."

"What do you want?"

"Shame on you, Daphne! So hasty." He wagged a finger at her. "I would like to conduct our courtship like civilized people, not like some coal miner and his trollop."

Daphne ignored the tired old dig, and Malcolm made a

beeline toward a cluster of decanters. He poured himself a drink, drained it in one swallow, and poured himself another. At this rate he'd be facedown on the floor before he got around to his blackmailing.

He turned, smacking his lips. "Your dead husband's relatives have excellent taste in spirits." He propped his hip against the massive desk behind him. "Now, where were we?"

"You were explaining why you are here."

He shrugged extravagantly. "How else does a betrothed couple spend their evenings, but together?"

"We are not betrothed, nor will we be. Ever."

Something in Daphne's attitude pierced even the thick fog of drink that surrounded him. "Why are you so bold all of a sudden, you saucy piece? Do you think I will hesitate to use the evidence I have if you do not give me what I want? Your pitiful life won't be worth living by the time I'm finished with your reputation—and that of *our* sons."

Daphne let every ounce of loathing she felt show on her face. "You have received the only money I will ever give you. If you are wise, you will be grateful for it and go your own way. But I know you are the farthest thing from wise."

Malcolm narrowed his eyes, his drink forgotten in his hand. "What?" The single word was filled with all the malice Daphne knew he bore her. It was the same look his uncle, Sir Walter, had given her mother every day of their married lives. Both men hated the fact their very existence depended on women so far beneath their station.

Daphne could recall the last time Malcolm's loathing had possessed the power to hurt—the fateful day he'd accosted her in the woods just outside Whitton Park.

"You know what they call girls like you?" he had asked, not waiting for an answer as he backed her up against a tree. "They call them prick-teasers."

Daphne had been more stunned by the vulgar phrase than his menacing behavior. He had taken advantage of her brief hesitation and sprung at her, slamming her head against the tree behind her hard enough to knock her unconscious.

And then he'd raped her.

The knowledge of what he'd done to her had hovered at the edges of her mind for years. It was never far from her conscious thoughts, but she'd kept it muted and tucked away. Until now.

Her body was shaking as if she were violently chilled; but she was hot all over—even her eyes were hot. Steam seemed to roll off her in waves, worsening her already poor vision. She blinked through her white-hot rage at her tormentor and released more than a decade's worth of hatred.

"I have a letter, written, signed, and sworn by the late Lord Davenport before a magistrate. The letter warns that you might try to blackmail me." She gave him a smile of pure loathing. "You may do whatever you want, of course, but you will *never* lay your repulsive hands on another penny of my son's money. He is the Earl of Davenport and there is not a thing in the world you can do to change that."

Daphne didn't tell him that tomorrow morning *she* would change that; that *she* would tell the real Earl of Davenport the truth and render her son plain Lucien Redvers.

He set down his glass but it missed the desk, tumbling to the rug unnoticed.

"You're lying. He never would have done such a thing. Especially not if he learned you tricked him."

Daphne laughed, genuinely amused. "You are even stupider than I believed—which is saying something. The earl knew *exactly* what transpired and he knew *exactly* what manner of filth you are and he knew *exactly* what to do to stop you." She thrilled at the expression of shock on his pale, bloated face. "He knew you would fritter away your wife's money and one day come sniffing around your betters like a dog begging for scraps." Her rage boiled over and she made no attempt to stop it. The fury in his eyes should have warned her, but instead, it stoked her anger.

One moment he was on the other side of the room gawking at her with an open mouth, the next he was slamming her against a bookcase. Her vision exploded in white, searing flashes and she slid to the floor, with Malcolm straddling her body.

"You lying whore," he said between gritted teeth, squeezing her throat hard enough to cut off her air. Daphne bucked and twisted beneath him, striking him with her fists, clawing at his hands, but her vision blurred and her chest burned from lack of air. Her arms became too heavy to lift and the room began to darken—

Suddenly the crushing hands were gone and the punishing weight disappeared from her chest. Daphne rolled onto her side, choking and coughing and gasping for air.

The first thing she saw when she opened her eyes was Hugh, his hands around Malcolm's neck, holding him a foot off the floor against a wall of books.

Her cousin's face was dark purple and his eyes had rolled back into his head. Daphne lurched to her feet, staggering toward Hugh.

"Stop!" she rasped, clawing weakly at hands as hard as grappling hooks. "Stop or you will kill him. Hugh." She pulled on his arms. "Hugh. Hugh!" She struck his forearms repeatedly, but it was like trying to move a coach with no wheels.

She fisted one hand and punched him in the shoulder with all her might. "*Hugh!*"

Pain exploded in her hand and arm.

Hugh turned to her. "You would let this swine live?" The words were like hot sparks from a blacksmith's forge and his pupil was a black pinprick. His hand flexed even tighter around Malcolm's throat.

"I care nothing for *him* but I would not see you hanged!" She pulled with all her strength, but his arm wouldn't budge.

His gaze was still linked with hers when he relinquished his hold. Daphne had not anticipated the movement and would have fallen had Hugh not steadied her while Malcolm's limp body slithered to the floor.

She pulled away from Hugh and dropped to her knees beside Malcolm. His pulse beat strongly, if erratically. *Thank God.* She slumped against the bookshelf and closed her eyes. Arms slipped around her shoulders and Hugh lifted her, cradling her against his chest. He carried her to the settee and laid her down before crouching beside her, taking her hand.

"How do you feel?"

"Short of breath."

His expression was bleak. "You were almost permanently short of breath."

She glanced at the library door. "Malcolm locked it, how were you able to enter?"

He pointed toward a door that looked like it concealed a large cupboard. "It is a secret entrance, built into the house for some long ago nefarious purpose. I used to play here with Simon and John when we were young."

"How did you know we were in here?"

"I saw you—when you turned to avoid me. I followed your progress by watching the crowd." He smiled. "You left quite a trail of destruction in your wake." He ran his finger down her cheek, ending under her chin, which he tilted so that he might see her better. "I seem to be in the habit of interrupting you in the process of chastising Hastings."

"I was not so lucky this time. Without your help I would not be breathing right now."

He glanced at Malcolm's still crumpled form and his face darkened. He stood. "What do you want me to do with him? You could have him before a magistrate. I would gladly stand witness. Or I could take care of him in a less conspicuous fashion."

Daphne shuddered at what his second suggestion must mean. "I do not want the attention a magistrate would draw. Have him taken to wherever he is lodging. I don't think I will have any further problems with him."

"Daphne, I do not—"

"Please, Hugh."

Hugh subjected her to a long, hard look. "This is a mistake."

"It is what I want."

He finally nodded. "Very well, I will do as you say. Come, let's get you tidied up so that we may leave with as little fuss as possible." He took her hand and led her to a large mirror, watching as she set her hair and dress to rights.

"I'm afraid you will have no small amount of bruising." He grimaced at the already vivid marks around her sapphire necklace. "I will fetch your wrap, it should hide most of the marks." He glanced at Malcolm. "Will you be all right if I leave you for a few moments? I must summon my groom and tell my aunt I am taking you home."

"Oh no, Hugh, you cannot leave your own ball so early."

Hugh did not answer. Instead, he led her to a chair, this one facing Malcolm but far across the room. "I will be back directly. If he makes any move at all you may hit him with this." He grabbed a marble statue from the table and handed it to her. He grinned suddenly, the expression causing her heart to beat madly. "Or just hit him if the urge strikes you."

Hugh returned a short time later with his groom, Wilkins, a glum, older man who never smiled. The two looked at Malcolm's prone form and exchanged a few quiet words before Wilkins departed.

Hugh arranged Daphne's wrap about her neck and shoulders and stood back.

"It interferes with your masterpiece of a gown, but your

neck is already several colors so it is best to sacrifice fashion at this point. I told Aunt Letitia you were suffering from a headache." He jerked his chin toward Malcolm's inert form. "Wilkins will take him to wherever he is lodging. Now come, before somebody bumbles in here."

The guests were at supper and they made their way toward the servants' entrance without any interruptions. The Davenport coach awaited them in the mews. It was pitch-dark in the narrow alley and Daphne was unable to see Hugh's face as the carriage rumbled away from Thornehill House.

"Thank you, Hugh."

"Whatever for?" He sounded his usual, teasing self again.

Daphne's remaining strand of self-control snapped. "For saving my life, you idiot." Was the man *never* serious?

His laughter filled the darkness. "That is twice in one night you've called me an idiot. I'm beginning to think you like me. Besides, I don't know why you're thanking me. If I'd kept better watch on you, you wouldn't need to hide your bruises for the next month." After a brief pause he added, "But if you really want to thank me, you can do so later, in a manner of my own choosing."

Daphne doubted he would feel quite so amorous after she'd told him everything.

Chapter Seventeen

Hugh handed his hat and gloves to the footman who'd waited up for them at Davenport House and turned to Daphne.

"Will you join me in the library?"

"I shall be in directly." Daphne needed to see her sons before commencing the task at hand. The boys were fast asleep when she entered the room they shared. A candle had been left burning in a wall sconce beside the door because Lucien was terrified of the dark, although he would never admit it.

Even in sleep they were two very different boys. Lucien had kicked off his blankets and slept with one bare foot hanging off the end of the bed. Richard was lying perfectly aligned in the middle of the bed, his blanket neatly pulled up around him. They would survive whatever happened tomorrow; the three of them together would survive. She kissed them and extinguished the light before making her way to the library.

Hugh turned away from the window when she entered. "All is well with the boys?"

How had he known where she'd gone? "Yes, they are sound sleepers. You could murder them in their beds without waking them." Daphne took a seat on the large leather sofa nearest the fireplace, which he must have lighted. She was glad of the warmth as she felt chilled to the bone.

"Would you like something to drink?"

"Perhaps some sherry."

She took the glass of amber liquid he offered and drank it quickly, the shock of the alcohol making her gasp.

Hugh raised his eyebrows but made no comment as he took the chair opposite her.

She dropped her eyes to his legs, rather than his face.

"Tonight I must disclose something I'd always hoped would stay private."

The muscles under the smooth black satin of his breeches grew taut as he stretched his legs out and crossed his ankles.

"Malcolm Hastings is the father of your sons."

Daphne's head whipped up. "How—Who—?"

"I made the connection myself when I saw him tonight." Daphne gaped.

"He is blackmailing you, I take it?"

She nodded dumbly.

Reproach and pain flickered across his face. "Why did you not tell me, Daphne?"

It was the last thing she expected him to say; the very last thing. "I—I was afraid of what you might think."

"Which was?"

"That I'd deceived Thomas when I married him."

He shook his head. "I hoped you might believe better of me, but I suppose I did little to earn it." Daphne closed her eyes at the disappointment in his voice. She heard him sigh. "Will you tell me what happened?"

When she opened her eyes she saw his expression was patient—the way it was with her sons or Lady Amelia or anyone else who was in need of some gentle handling. How could she ever have thought he would not believe her?

"Malcolm attacked me."

He remained silent but the temperature in the room dropped.

Daphne lowered her gaze to the floor between them, where the intricate, repetitive patterns in the rug were somehow soothing.

"Sir Walter brought Malcolm to live at Whitton Park when it became obvious my mother would not give him a son. I was not much more than a child and he was already a young man, but, even so, we never got along. He did spiteful things, taunted me, insulted my mother—but he never laid hands on me until after his uncle died. He didn't even wait a year before he began throwing house parties—debauches where he and his friends would gamble night and day. Sometimes he even brought in women.

"I did what I could to avoid him and his friends, but it became increasingly difficult. One day I encountered a group of them while out walking. They pressured me to join them firing pistols—just a lark to alleviate their boredom." She laughed bitterly. "What could be more quaint than a girl shooting a pistol? Anyway, I . . . I bested Malcolm and they laughed and taunted him. He found me afterward, alone. He was furious. He said—well, it doesn't matter what he said. I ran and he chased me into the woods, attacked me, and . . . well, to put it bluntly, he raped me." She said the words quickly, before she lost her nerve.

"He struck me hard enough that I lost consciousness. Fortunately, I have no memory of the actual event. Of course the truth of what had happened became unavoidable several weeks later."

A loud noise startled her into looking up. The glass Hugh had been holding lay in shards on the carpet, blood and brandy dripping from his fingers.

Daphne was up in a heartbeat and dropped beside his chair, taking his hand in hers. It was curled into a rigid claw.

His face was carved from granite and bore the same terrifying expression it had earlier. "Hugh?"

He tried to pull away. "It is nothing."

"It is something. Give me your handkerchief." She wished she'd had the sense to wear her spectacles. Instead, she had to find the few shards of glass embedded in his hand by touch. Once she was sure she'd found them all, she wrapped the square of cloth around his cut fingers.

She looked up. "I should get some plasters."

"Later." His face was shockingly pale. Even his lips, usually so full and sensual, were thin and gray. He helped her to her feet and led her back to the sofa, where he sat down beside her.

"My uncle married you when you learned you were to have a child?" His voice was flat and calm.

"Yes. It was a marriage in name only, Hugh. We never lived as man and wife."

He closed his eye briefly and exhaled. "And Hastings didn't suspect anything?"

"My mother, Rowena, and I were very careful to keep the truth from anyone—even Fowler, my maid." She bit her lip. "Although my mother was quite ill, she arranged to speak with Thomas before she died." Her fingers were clasped so tightly her knuckles were white. "I believe what Malcolm did to me hastened her death. Thomas said we must marry immediately—without the usual mourning period. He said our public justification for not waiting would be that it was inappropriate for a girl of seventeen to live with her unwed cousin of twenty-five. Thomas took charge of everything—even bringing me to Lessing Hall before the wedding and ensuring I didn't have to see Malcolm again. And I didn't see him—not until the day you returned to Lessing Hall."

"He was blackmailing you and you attacked him."

"Yes, but I only attacked him after he tried to—" Hugh's face darkened and Daphne hurried on. "He told me he would give me time to prepare myself if I demonstrated my intentions with a payment of one thousand pounds. I dithered and dithered like a fool, hoping for some miracle to come along." Daphne stared up at him. "That is why I delayed telling you for so long. It was *so* important to me. Don't you see, Hugh?" She rushed on. "Little did I know the very thing I hoped for—a way to thwart Malcolm permanently—waited for me in London." She grimaced. "So, I paid him the money."

He stared through her, as if seeing something or someone else.

"Please, Hugh, do not be angry with me."

His gaze sharpened and his eyebrows snapped into a straight line. "Angry? With *you*?"

"Yes, because it is really your money I used."

His brow wrinkled. "What the devil are you talking about, Daphne?"

"The money I used to pay Malcolm—it belongs to the Earl of Davenport—*you*."

"Good Lord, love! What a load of bollocks."

Daphne didn't know which shocked her more—his attitude or hearing the word *bollocks* spoken out loud.

He waved his uninjured hand dismissively. "We shall come back to this in a moment. But first I want to get to the bottom of this business with Hastings. What is this proof you are referring to?"

Daphne told him about her meeting with Sir Marcus and the letters. "Would you like me to fetch them for you?" she asked.

"I can look at them later." He stared into space, shaking his head. "I guess it *was* Hastings who tampered with my saddle—or at least had his servant do so. It seems a foolish thing to do, but then he is a fool. I can only suppose he thought it best to secure Lucien's future just in case I ferreted out the truth, or"—he glanced down at her—"or you finally told me the truth."

Daphne's face heated. "I would have, Hugh. I had decided—"

He laid a big finger across her lips. "Shhh, darling. We'll deal with that in a moment." He smiled and continued. "He must have decided that if he could remove me from the equation, then he could marry you without worrying about any interference."

"But he must have known that I would *never* marry him, no matter what he threatened me with."

"I think you overestimate his intelligence—or at least his awareness."

The dry certainty in his voice made her smile. "Even so, I can't believe he would have been bold enough to attempt murder, and in such an uncertain way."

Hugh shrugged. "I agree, but if not Malcolm, who else might have done it?"

Daphne stared at his damaged hand, which she was cradling in both of hers. "I was terrified you would think it was me—after all, I am the one who would stand to gain."

Hugh snorted. "Don't be daft."

She hid a smile at his conviction "Maybe the person who did it didn't want to kill you, but to give you a lesson."

"A *lesson*?"

"Is it possible—"

"Yes, is what possible?" he prodded.

Daphne knew it was likely her roiling jealousy rather than any true conviction that provoked her to utter the next words, but she could not stop them. "I have dreaded saying this to you, my lord, but I haven't been able to miss the fact that William Standish is angry with you. Very angry." His eyebrows—already raised—went even higher. "You admitted that yourself when you said you thought it was because you sent him back. Is it possible he might be angry for some other reason? Perhaps not on *his* behalf but his sister's?" There. She'd said it.

He blinked. "You believe William severed the girth to avenge his sister?"

It sounded utterly mad when spoken out loud. It also sounded like the statement of a jealous woman, which it was. Daphne wanted the floor to open and swallow her.

"My dearest Daphne." He slipped an arm over her shoulders and caressed the bare skin of her arm with his big, warm hand. "I've realized almost from the first that you possess an impressive intellect, but now I see you have a staggering imagination, as well. This is the second time you've mentioned my amorous adventures in conjunction with people wishing to kill me. I am gratified you think I inspire such passion. I am also pleased by your opinion of my virility. And I am *most* fascinated to learn what acts your imagination has me performing to engender such long-lasting desire for vengeance." He grinned down at her. "But we will speak of such things later." He kissed the tip of her nose. "Right now I will address your suspicions regarding Meg Standish and her brother's quest for vengeance. I believe I mentioned that Meg and William and I grew up like siblings?"

She nodded.

"When Meg learned she was with child, it was to me she turned first. She confessed the father was none other than Blake." He smiled at her gasp of surprise. "She was afraid Will would kill Blake if he ever found out. I happened to agree with her—Will *would* have killed Blake and then hanged for it. This all happened not long before Will and I departed on our fateful journey." His hand, which was still on her shoulder, traced patterns on her skin. "My reputation was already in tatters so I told Meg to claim I was the father." He chuckled at Daphne's expression of disbelief. "I see you are thinking I'm some kind of martyr. But I'm not— it cost me nothing to accept the blame and it meant a great deal to her. It is sad but true that a woman giving birth to an aristocrat's bastard receives far better treatment from her peers than if she gives birth to a butcher's bastard. She accepted my offer and we both went to speak to Will together. Meg lied to Will and told him she'd become pregnant by a man who'd stayed at the local inn. When I told Will what Meg and I planned to do he was furious, but there was no way he could stop me, so I had my way." He smiled, no doubt at the memory of *getting his way*.

"To add weight to the rumors, I had my solicitor draw up a trust for Meg's child before I left. The purpose of the money was twofold: to take care of her and the boy, and to stoke suspicion that he was my son. It certainly seems to have stoked yours," he teased, pulling her tighter against his body. Daphne swallowed, both at his story and at the sensations his touch was stirring.

He became serious. "Do you have any other questions for me on this subject?"

Daphne shook her head, too embarrassed to speak.

"Excellent. Then I'd like to address the topic of Euphemia Marlington. First, I apologize for not explaining myself immediately."

She opened her mouth to tell him she had no right to expect anything from him but, again, he laid a finger across her lips.

"Please allow me to finish?"

She nodded but he did not immediately remove his finger. Instead, his pupil flared and he began to lean forward, his gaze on her mouth. But then he stopped, took a deep breath, and muttered something unintelligible.

"I understand what it may have looked like, but the night you saw us I was offering Mia nothing but comfort. She was terrified about returning home after almost twenty years. I couldn't tell you who she was because it wasn't my secret to tell." He inhaled and then let it out slowly. "I'll admit I was no saint when I was young or during the years I spent away, but since my return I have desired only one woman." He ran his finger lightly up her arm and shoulder before taking her chin in his hand. "You must know who that woman is." He stroked her jaw, the slight roughness of his skin leaving goose bumps. "Even when I believed you'd been my uncle's wife"—he grimaced—"*truly* his wife and the mother of his children, I could not fight my feelings for you. I have never been skilled at denying myself what I want." He dipped his mouth to brush her lips. "And I want you so very, very much, my love."

She became hot, and then cold. "You want to be my . . . lover?" It was painful and mortifying to speak so plainly, but she could no longer abide dealing with uncertainties.

"Among other things."

"Other . . . things?"

"Yes, many other things. Which only seems fair, since I returned because of you."

"Me?"

"Yes, you." He smiled at her obvious confusion. "Will sent me two letters in the last year. One informing me my uncle was on his deathbed, and a second that said he'd received two letters threatening you, not long after my uncle's funeral."

"Me?" Daphne sounded like Hugh's parrot, but less articulate.

"Yes, you and the boys."

Daphne's brain exploded at his words and she sprang to her feet.

"Steady, love," Hugh said, gently pulling her back down. "They are upstairs, safe in their beds. Also, Kemal is sleeping in the small room beside the schoolroom."

"He *is*?"

"Yes, he is. The letters are why I returned—to make sure

you and your sons were safe. I have tried very hard to do so, although I'm not sure there was really any threat."

Daphne heard the words but could make no sense of them. "You came here for a woman you didn't even *know* and for her sons, the eldest of whom had usurped your place?"

Hugh laughed. "For an intelligent woman you can be quite a goose, sometimes. Does it appear to you that I have much interest in what you call *my place*? A position in society, which I abandoned almost two decades ago? Does it appear I lack for wealth and want what belongs to your son?" He shook his head. "No, Daphne. My place has been anywhere *but* here for almost twenty years."

"You are *leaving*?"

"I won't leave England until I determine the source of those letters, even though I'm fairly sure they were about Hastings."

Daphne struggled to marshal her thoughts into some form of order, but all she could manage was, "You are *leaving*."

He hesitated, and then appeared to come to a decision. "I cannot stay in England if you will not have me. I cannot. But know this, whether you will have me or not, I will never challenge Lucien's right to the title—even if such a thing were possible. On the contrary, I would do everything in my power to defend it. On that you have my word."

Daphne couldn't speak, or even think.

He stroked her cheek. "I love your treacherous skin, sweetheart—it is one of the few things that kept me hoping you might care for me when your haughty, cool looks made me lose heart. In answer to your question, yes, I want to be your lover, but I am also asking you to be my wife."

"But . . ."

"The scandal?" He nuzzled her neck.

She nodded.

"It is true," he said, not pausing his nuzzling. "We would

be breaking ecclesiastical law by marrying. Many in the *ton* would cut us and there is a possibility—albeit slight—that someone might challenge our union."

Daphne nodded. She, too, had researched the subject. She felt his lips curve into a smile against the thin skin of her neck.

"But I am richer than Croesus and have a lifetime of experience protecting myself and my own. I do not fear such threats. It is more the social cuts—the death by a thousand cuts as they call it in China—that I fear. Especially for you. You must consider that, Daphne. Is that something you could endure? Something you would *wish* to endure? And what about Lucien and Richard? Could you do this to them—to their future?"

He continued to kiss and confuse her while disturbing words poured from his mouth. The things he said were true, but he said nothing of himself and how he would be affected. Did he truly not care about casting himself beyond the pale? Did she?

He took her earlobe into his mouth and sucked, and her thoughts shattered like glass. She shook her head, as if to clear away the shards.

"I cannot fault you for such a decision," he said, mistaking her gesture as one of rejection. "Your sons should always come first." His voice was hollow and brittle.

Daphne let out a soft huff and leaned against his chest, amazed he could be so foolish. "How can such an intelligent man be such a goose?" she teased. "I've spent my life on the fringes—even when I was married to Thomas. People stared and whispered about the coal miner's granddaughter who had taken advantage of a doddering earl." She shrugged. "And before then—when I lived with Sir Walter and Malcolm? Well, I was an outcast of a different kind, isolated and alone with only my mother and my books to keep me company." She pressed herself against his tense, waiting body. "You realize, don't you, that the boys will be relentless when they learn about us. You will have no peace ever again."

Hugh gripped her shoulders and held her at arm's length, his expression one she'd not seen before: amazement tinged with anxiety. "This is unlike you, Daphne. It is your way to contemplate matters carefully before making a decision—especially one of this magnitude. Are you certain? *Entirely* certain? Scandal aside, you've had very little exposure to the world—to men. Don't you wish to sample the pleasures life has to offer before committing yourself? Especially before committing yourself to a life of certain censure?" His jaw hardened. "I will give you time to consider my offer—as much time as you need."

She took his hand. "My hasty decision is not hasty at all. Do you think you are the only one who has wondered about us and what might be? I have struggled and struggled to look beyond your amiable, teasing manner, to discern whether you held me in any special esteem. And then—" She bit her lip.

"And then there was Mia."

She nodded. "Yes, that was . . . difficult."

He chuckled and pulled her close. "I daresay you wanted to kill me."

"No, only maim you. A little." She pulled away with some difficulty. "I have no need to contemplate any further. I believe any shame my boys and I might face will be far outweighed by the benefit of having you beside us. I would have no other man." Her face was so hot by the end of her forward speech, it was a wonder she didn't faint.

Hugh threw back his head and gave a triumphant howl of laughter before crushing her against his chest.

"I lied when I said I would give you time to consider." He spoke into the top of her head, his words rumbling like rolling boulders. "And I would thrash any man who so much as looked at you. You see what a domineering scoundrel you are agreeing to take to husband? If you hadn't agreed, I was going to carry you to my ship and have my way with you until you complied."

Daphne burrowed into his embrace, inhaling the intoxicating scent of him into her lungs and holding it before reluctantly releasing her breath.

"You could still do that," she mumbled into the hard warmth of his chest.

"Daphne!" he chortled. "How wicked you are—and how much I approve." But he disentangled himself and moved away. "We are not yet finished, I think. You have voiced concerns about my . . . amorous nature more than once." His beautiful lips curved into a smile as he kissed her hand. "You must ask me what you need to know. I would have no secrets between us, at least nothing that would cause you to regret your decision later. Now is your opportunity, my lady. Once you are mine, there will be no going back."

All the moisture left her mouth as she met his possessive stare. She willed herself to be calm—to ask the many questions that had tormented her almost since his arrival.

"You mentioned leaving."

His smile faltered and she sensed a struggle inside him. "Yes, I will need to do so from time to time."

It was not what she'd been hoping to hear. "Would you be gone long?"

He hesitated. "I would try not to be."

"You would always return?"

"I would always return."

"Would you go . . . often?"

He stroked her arm. "I hope not."

The answers were less than she wanted, but she could not ask him to entirely give up his way of life, could she? She would not want to give up hers. It was something they could discuss—at length, later. For now—

"What else?" he murmured.

"You have had many lovers." Her voice broke on the last

word and she gritted her teeth, wishing she could take back the bald statement.

"Yes, that is true."

Her reaction was primal: a fierce, violent surge of jealousy stronger than anything she'd ever experienced— anything except the love she felt for her sons, and now Hugh. She swallowed. Yes, love. Not infatuation, not lust— well, partly lust—but love. She loved him and knew she should leave this painful subject untouched. But the part of her mind that dealt only in reason needed more.

"How can you know I will be enough for you, Hugh? I am not an exciting woman. I like books, not balls."

He squeezed her hands hard enough to hurt. "It is *because* I've experienced so much that I know what I want." There wasn't a trace of humor on his face. "I have known other women—*many* other women—but I have never wanted to spend the rest of my life with one, or raise children with one. Not until now."

Daphne wanted to seize his words out of the air and hold them to her chest, to savor them, over and over. To—

"What about you, Daphne? Could I not ask you the same questions, but in reverse? How can you know that I am what you want? You have had no experience with men or physical love. How can you be certain I will keep you satisfied and happy?"

Daphne was struck by his reasoning. There was as much truth behind his question as there was in hers. There were no guarantees, only faith and trust. And love.

"I am certain. Hugh."

He heaved a sigh. "I am beyond grateful Hastings and his vicious, appalling cruelty has not put you off men for life."

So was Daphne.

His lips tightened and his grateful expression slid away. "Had I known what he did to you earlier this evening, you could not have stopped me from killing him, Daphne. Indeed,

I am nowhere near to being finished with him." The cold intensity in his green eye made her shiver and he was immediately solicitous. "You are chilled?"

"I am not shivering because I am cold. I am shivering for Malcolm and how close this came to being his last day."

"That would have been a great loss to you?" The disbelief in his voice was unmistakable.

"It would be a great loss if you were forced to flee England to avoid a murder charge."

A sly look flashed across his changeable face. "You would miss me, would you?"

She opened her mouth but he chuckled and drew her close, burying his face in her neck and inhaling her as if she were a flower.

"You would," he murmured in between trailing kisses over her pulse, her throat, across her jaw. "You'd miss me terribly. And I would go mad without you."

His words left her light-headed and he wove his fingers into her hair and pulled her head back until their eyes met. "I want to make love to you, Daphne."

She blinked up at him, her body humming with a wildness she'd not felt since the last time he touched her. "Here? Now?"

Chapter Eighteen

It took a moment for Hugh's brain to accept what his ears had heard. He shook his head in wonder. "My God, you are a gift!"

Hooded blue eyes flared with a need that matched his own.

"I have wanted to do this since the moment I saw you this evening, you temptress." He lowered his mouth to the exposed, rounded swell of one breast and she shuddered beneath his lips and pushed closer. He traced the gentle curves with the tip of his tongue, teasing the thin silk barrier that molded to her lithe body. As he'd suspected—a million years ago at the wretched dinner—her nipples were less than an inch below the tissue-thin fabric of her gown.

Daphne shifted and arched as he suckled her through the silk, bringing the tip to tantalizing hardness before moving to the other, working her until the noises coming from deep in her throat were so hungry he had to see her.

He held her at arm's length, staring into her sleepy eyes. "You are so beautiful," he said, his hands moving to the damp, stretched fabric that barely covered her. He pushed his thumbs beneath the silk and eased it down until she was exposed.

"Good God." He stretched the fabric even lower, until it was beneath her breasts, the taut silk forcing them high. He drank in her beauty while spanning her delicate rib cage, his fingers forming a double prison with her corset. Her head fell back, a long sigh escaping her, and her spine arched as she offered herself to him. Hugh lowered his mouth to the area between her breasts and briefly closed his eyes.

His ever fertile imagination flogged him with arousing images: Daphne against a wall of books, her long, slim legs around his hips while he buried himself hilt-deep; Daphne bent over the big library desk, skirts bunched at her waist, his fists tangled in her blond curls, his—

Hugh tugged the now ruined fabric back over the rosy mounds and pulled her to her feet.

"Come."

Sultry blue eyes, dazed and hungry, gazed up at him and, once again, Hugh was tempted to take her over the desk. But she deserved more tenderness for what was essentially her first bedding. The desk would come later.

He scooped her swaying body into his arms.

"*Hugh*. What—"

"Hush," he ordered. "Get the door."

She blinked up at him, but found the handle without looking and flung it open.

"Good girl."

Her eyes narrowed, but she remained unresisting while he strode down the hall and took the stairs two at a time to get to her bedchamber.

He was wheezing like a punctured bellows by the time he reached her door. He lowered her feet to the floor and reached for the handle. And then stopped.

Daphne raised her shapely brows and gave him a look of cool hauteur that made his erect cock throb.

"She's not in there, is she?"

"She?"

"Your maid."

Her lips parted. "I believe you're frightened of her."

"You're bloody right I am." He gave her a gentle push. "You go in first. I shouldn't be surprised if the old gorgon is lying in wait to catch me defiling you."

She gave a low, delighted laugh and shook her head, but opened the door and disappeared inside.

Hugh had to wait only a few seconds before the door swung open.

"Ahoy, Captain Standish! The coast is clear," she said in a stage whisper.

"Ha. How droll you are." Hugh stepped inside and closed and locked the door before turning to her. She wore a smile he'd never seen before: saucy, erotic, teasing.

"And just what do *you* find so amusing, my lady?"

"You."

Hugh yanked her close and held her tight. "Is that so?" he murmured against her temple, burying his nose in her hair and inhaling until he was dizzy.

She made a sound suspiciously like a giggle. "What would the world say if they knew the fearsome One-Eyed Standish was cowed by a lady's maid?"

Hugh nibbled her jaw, which he decided was his new hobby. "I will deny it to my last breath."

Her hands slid around his neck and she pulled him down, pressing her mouth over his. Hugh stood unmoving under her exploration, his body vibrating with want beneath the tentative probing of her tongue, surely the most erotic experience of his life—until she latched on to his tongue and sucked it into her mouth. He groaned; languages didn't seem to be the only thing she learned quickly.

Just when Hugh believed he could not bear another

second of suggestive sucking without throwing her onto the bed and plowing into her—she released his tongue.

But she wasn't finished.

She lightly dragged the very tip over his lips, as if drawing his features, leaving a searing trail of heat as she kissed and licked and nipped her way up his scar, pulling his head lower and feathering the torn, tender skin with the lightest of kisses. Before Hugh knew what she was doing she'd untied the ends of the strap that held the patch over his eye.

He moved to grab it, but she flung it away and then clutched his face in both hands and pulled him lower.

"I want all of you."

He hadn't believed he could become any harder; he'd been wrong.

Her lips were already dropping kisses around the damaged skin around his eye, as if to claim the territory as her own. Air moved over his sightless orb, the sensation making him feel strangely naked and vulnerable. So he closed both eyes and gave himself up to her exploration, which stalled at his temple, where the line disappeared into his hair.

"Mm, you smell so good," she murmured, her nose pressing against his scalp. "I smell mint and something else . . . something sharp and spicy I cannot place."

"It is bergamot in my shaving soap. That old woman Kemal makes it for me, swearing it will protect me from bad spirits," he laughed. "If you like it, I will bathe in it for you." He all but purred as her hands moved from his hair to massage the rigid muscles of his neck while pulling him lower and lower, until he was almost bent double. He gritted his teeth and pulled away before straightening his back. Slowly.

"Hugh?" Her eyes were blue pools rippling with reproach—and lust.

"I'm an old man, darling. You must take care not to break me."

She snorted and he reached behind her, grabbed several cushions, and piled them up.

And just because he knew it would ruffle her feathers, he ordered, "Now lie back like a good girl."

She gave him a dangerous stare but complied.

Hugh took a step back to admire her. Her expression was sulky as she pulled her legs onto the bed, folding them demurely to one side, the silk gown molding to her body. Her eyes glared up at him in a slightly out-of-focus way. Her lips, lush and pink in general, were now deep red and swollen from tormenting him.

He fiercely wished he had two eyes to drink her in. Which made him remember something.

"Where are your spectacles?"

She shrugged. "I can see."

"But you usually wear them." He paused. "In fact, you haven't worn them all evening. Why?"

A frown puckered her brow and she gave him an adorably mulish frown. "What of it?"

"Why aren't you wearing them?"

"Rowena says men find them disfiguring."

"Your maid is a fool. Where are they?" He glanced at her bedside table and reached for the drawer.

Daphne flung herself across the bed after him. "No! Wait!"

But he'd already opened the drawer and looked inside. There were her tiny spectacles—right next to a copy of *Fanny Hill*. Hugh flicked the cover open to the flyleaf and snorted: *his* copy of *Fanny Hill*.

She twisted her hands. "It is not what you think."

"Oh?" he said, raising his brows. "Tell me, what do I think?"

"I didn't steal it—I was going to return it."

Hugh laughed. "Believe me, darling, that is *not* what I was thinking." He shut the book and took out the spectacles.

They were unusual, a horizontal line running across the bottom third. He held them up and saw there were different magnifications in each lens. He suspected she needed them quite badly.

He handed them to her. "Put them on."

She snatched them from his hand, but put them on nonetheless. She probably hoped it would help him forget about the pilfered book. Hugh smiled and stored the information away for later use.

"Are you always this bossy?" she demanded.

"Always. You might as well accustom yourself to obeying me as I shall soon be your lord and master."

"There is still plenty of time for me to change my mind."

Hugh stepped back to admire the intoxicating view of her prim glasses, delicious body, and petulant scowl. "No," he said, well pleased with the picture she made. "There isn't."

She grabbed them off her face and crossed her arms.

He smiled at the small rebellion. "Come, Daphne, put them back on. There is something I want to show you and I should like you to see it. Clearly." He lowered himself into the chair across from the bed and assumed the position of a man prepared to wait as long as it took. She stared for a moment before making a small huffing sound and putting on her glasses.

"Good girl," he said deliberately.

She reached a hand up to the fragile frame as if in challenge. Hugh raised his eyebrows, genuinely curious as to what she would do and quite certain any outcome would afford him entertainment.

With much exaggeration, she lowered her hand and crossed her arms. "Very well, what is it that you were going to show me, my lord?"

Hugh stretched his legs and kicked off his evening shoes, one at a time.

Her chest rose, the action pushing her delectable breasts higher.

He removed his stockings, taking his time while he released and rolled down one, and then the other, all the while watching her. She sat up straighter, craning her neck to watch, her eyes hidden from him by the candlelight glinting off her spectacles.

"I'm going to undress," he said, not caring that his explanation was redundant. "Members of our class typically do so in their separate rooms or in the dark." He smiled as he stood, unbuttoned his coat, and then peeled it off his hot, pounding body. He paused. "I should have asked—would you like to watch me undress or do you prefer I do so in the dark?"

She swallowed hard enough that Hugh could hear it. "I should like to watch you undress."

Hugh could almost hear the blood go thundering to his cock and was mildly surprised there'd been any left elsewhere in his body. He tossed his coat onto the chair he had just vacated but paused in the act of removing his cravat. He first removed the emerald cravat pin and set it on the side table, moving closer to the bed as he untied his neckcloth, pulled it off, and then tossed it onto the chair behind him.

Her eyes followed his fingers as he began unbuttoning his waistcoat and he slowed down to savor her rapt attention. When he finished the last button he shrugged out of the garment, the action pulling open the slit that ran down the center of his shirt.

Her breasts were swelling with quick, shallow breaths and she fastened her hot blue eyes on the deep V of his shirt. Hugh watched until she became aware of his scrutiny. She stared directly at him—*into* him.

He reached over his head and seized his shirt, pulling it off and tossing it to the floor. He expected she'd be looking at his scarred shoulders and chest, but she was looking down, her attention arrested by his distended breeches. She'd gone utterly still.

Hugh smiled. "Breathe, darling."

Her eyes darted up and narrowed.

Hugh had begun this slow stripping because he wasn't sure she'd ever seen a naked male body and hadn't wanted to frighten or repulse her. But now he was thoroughly enjoying the tension that filled the room with each garment he removed.

He brushed a hand across his chest and her eye followed it like a cat tracking its prey. He lowered the hand slowly, sliding it over his abdomen and pushing the tips of his fingers beneath the slick warm satin. He stroked his belly from left to right, drinking in her rapt gaze and harsh breathing. He unhooked the small catches that held his fall in place and paused to shift his pounding organ to one side, reveling in the effect the gesture had on her bodice, even if it did not offer any relief to him.

Hugh worked the six buttons of his fall with the speed of a man who was paid by the hour. By the time he reached the last button, she was leaning so far over she was in danger of toppling off the bed and he was in danger of exploding.

Hugh bent low to push down breeches and small clothes together and then stood.

She was perfectly still, her gaze fastened on his aroused organ, the slight parting of her lips causing his cock to twitch wildly.

She gasped. "Are *you* doing that?"

Hugh considered asking her who else it might be, but dismissed the teasing thought when she reached for him. At which point Hugh's erection took control of his body and yanked the rest of him toward her.

Her smooth, cool hand closed with promising firmness around his girth.

"*Guh*," was all Hugh could manage.

Her brows arched and she wore the same serious look on her face as when she was reading a German philosophy tome. She stroked up and down his shaft, her motions measured and confident; his entire body thrummed.

"Is this nice?"

Hugh found his voice—although not the same one he usually used. "*Nice* would not be my first word of choice."

Her lips curved into a smile he'd only fantasized about seeing on her beautiful face.

"You like this." It was not a question. Her hand tightened and swirled the head of his cock.

"Ah God, Daphne!" He hissed in a breath, every nerve on fire, his body already primed to thrust and thrust and spend. Hugh reached down and gently removed her hand; it was one of the most difficult things he'd ever done.

Her eyebrows rose and he gave her a strained smile.

"It has been some time since my cock has made the, er, acquaintance of a woman."

Daphne blinked at the vulgar word and Hugh reminded himself he was bedding a lady.

He took her other hand and lifted her to her feet. "I should hate to end things so . . . abruptly." She still looked adorably confused. "Besides, it is my turn, Daphne."

"Your turn?"

"Mmm-hmm, my turn. You've seen me." He felt his lips curve. "You've *touched* me. Now I want to see . . . and touch, you. Would you like to strip for me, or shall I undress you?" Hugh found either option deeply arousing.

She hesitated only a moment. "I would like you to undress me."

A choir seemed to be singing somewhere inside his skull as Hugh pulled her close and turned her in his arms, his entire body throbbing as she submitted to his ministrations.

She bent her head to allow him access to her gown and he

lowered his lips over the vulnerable ridge of spine, reveling in her swift intake of breath as he mouthed the curvature of her arched neck, kissing the bruised, scratched skin that had been savaged by Hastings, laving her with languorous strokes. His cock pulsed dangerously and Hugh forced himself to stop.

Savoring her sweet, salty taste, he turned to buttons not made for hands his size. As his fingers brushed her skin, she shivered, leaning into his touch. The smooth silk of her gown rubbed against the hot, sensitive skin of his erection. His inflamed brain encouraged him to rip the dress off but he worked with calm diligence until the last button was open, smiling to himself when the garment slipped but, miraculously, did not fall.

He left the gown for the moment and turned to her hair, removing a remarkable number of pins before he could unbind the heavy rope, raking it with his fingers until a froth of blond curls fell to her waist and tickled the head of his cock.

She stood with her hands clasping the gown to her breasts. Hugh took her unresisting fingers and lifted them, his gaze riveted as the gown slipped from her grasp. She made a small noise in her throat but her chin tilted defiantly as she submitted to his inspection; Hugh allowed himself a long, lingering look. She was slender and fine-boned, her tiny waist flaring out to unexpectedly generous hips and long, long shapely legs. Her chemise and corset were the same shade as her blushes, her stockings held up with garters embroidered with roses.

Hugh reached both arms around her and located the laces. He loosened the first few eyes, but then, instead of releasing her from her bondage, he pulled the laces tighter. She gasped as he tightened the bone-and-cloth prison, the corset forcing her breasts higher.

Hugh wrapped the silken cording around his fist and held

her away from him to inspect his work. Creamy breasts spilled over the corset, her nipples jutting upward, two hard, pink pebbles.

"*Bloody hell.*"

Only when she shuddered did Hugh realize he'd spoken out loud. He felt as if he'd been struck in the head by a boom mast. He bent low and sucked a nipple into his mouth, grazing her with his teeth. She moaned and arched. Encouraged, he suckled her harder, ruthlessly stiffening the already hard peak even more before doing the same thing to her other breast.

She shuddered and Hugh's fingers took matters into their own hands, working in a blind frenzy to loosen the laces enough to push the garment down over her slim hips.

Without being bidden she stepped daintily out of the circle of clothes and stood in her chemise, partly transparent from the moist trail his mouth had made.

"My God." His throat was so thick he could barely speak. She raised her hands instinctively to cover herself from his gaze. Hugh caught them and shook his head emphatically. "Oh no, darling, fair is fair." He gawked like a schoolboy at the beautiful sight before him while his mind raged; his own private parliament engaged in a critical debate: Naked? Not naked? Naked? Not naked—

She turned her head to the side, the taut column of her throat flushed.

"Daphne."

But she wouldn't turn.

He circled her, enjoying the view from all angles. Like every good governing body, his brain reached a compromise: leave her chemise and stockings—an erotic package to unwrap later at his leisure.

He smiled at his decision and buried his nose in her hair and inhaled before asking, "Don't you like me looking at you?"

Receiving no response, he stopped behind her and pressed himself against the whisper-thin muslin of her chemise.

"You can feel how much you excite me, can you not?" he said, nuzzling her thick hair as his hands explored her from throat to hips, all the while stroking his erection against the sweet curve of her back. She didn't speak, but he felt her nod slightly.

His hand moved lower, grazing her mound with his palm while his other arm formed a rigid band around her slim waist. He felt the answering pressure of her buttocks pressed against his thighs, firm and round through the thin muslin.

Hugh laughed softly as she moved against him, provoking his hardness, teasing him until it hurt.

"That is a sweet torture, my love, but you move far too quickly and I like to wait for my pleasure." He scooped her into his arms and laid her out on the bed. His eye roamed her body as he straddled her and pressed his erection into the crease between her thighs, stroking against her silky skin as he bent his head to savage her mouth. She responded with equal ardor, pressing herself against him while her hands explored his body, kneading the muscles of his back on the way to his buttocks, which she caressed and teased over and over with a firm, forceful touch.

A distant part of his mind reminded him that although Daphne had children—and had apparently done a damned fine job of memorizing the racier bits of *Fanny Hill*—she'd never consciously engaged in the sexual act. He was dangerously aroused by the feel of her hands on him and he needed to slow down.

She made a small, disgruntled sound as he moved out of her grasp, her lips clinging to his as he pulled away. He smiled at her irritable moue and gently pushed her back onto the bed, propping himself up on his elbow beside her.

Her lids were heavy and low, her eyes mere crescents of blue. Hugh smiled at what looked very much like sexual frustration. Good. As long as she wanted more, he wouldn't be overwhelming her.

Her chemise had bunched up behind her, the fabric pulled so tight over her chest and hips it fit her sleek form like a rosy second skin. He circled her nipples through the thin fabric, brushing over her again and again with his palm, only gradually allowing his hand to drift from her breasts toward the swell of her stomach, his finger dipping into the dimple of her navel. Daphne made a sound suspiciously like a laugh.

"Ah, you are ticklish here." He tucked away that information for future exploration and took her lobe into his mouth while his hand worked from her breasts to her stomach, stopping only when he felt the soft curls at the apex of her thighs. He circled his hand over her, stroking her pelvis from side to side until her hips pressed against his palm on the next sweep over her sex.

Hugh smiled at the familiar gesture of need and cupped her in his hand before dipping a finger between her swollen lips. She reacted with a convulsive thrust and he probed deeper, working her with a gentle but persistent rhythm, each stroke a little deeper, a little harder. She swelled around him and her hot wetness told him when she could take more. A second finger joined the first and her hips responded eagerly, thrusting in time to the motion of his hand.

"God, you're so wet. So sweet and tight," he whispered, the words causing her body to shake.

Hugh felt as though he'd barely begun when she contracted, her hips bucking hard, as if she couldn't get him deep enough. He watched her face as the first wave of pleasure hit her, her eyes squeezed shut to contain the sensation within herself. She shook her head back and forth as the waves washed over her, her skin sheened with sweat and as luminescent as a pearl.

Hugh gently stroked her quivering stomach in the aftermath and she opened her eyes.

"Hello, Daphne." Her already flushed cheeks darkened. "I need to be inside you before I go mad." He ran a string of kisses down her throat and smiled into her neck when he heard the two words he wanted.

"Yes, please." Her thighs spread wider in silent invitation.

Hugh groaned. "I want to feel your skin beneath me. Lift a little so that I might remove your chemise." Hugh left her stockings on, the sight of them against her flushed, spread thighs almost bringing him to climax as he lowered himself over her.

"Take me in your hand and guide me inside."

Her hand closed around him before he'd even finished speaking. She tightened her grip and then slid her hand up, and then back down.

Hugh shuddered. "Please, darling," he murmured. "You are being cruel."

The witch *chuckled* but guided his slick, pulsing head between her legs, gasping when he breached her.

Hugh fisted the bedding with both hands to hold himself in check, gently rocking back and forth, filling her slowly, easing deeper and deeper. "You fit me just like a glove. A very tight, wet glove." He forced himself to pause. "Are you in any discomfort, love?" he asked shakily, teetering on the brink of no longer caring about anything but his pleasure—his need.

"It feels . . . strange, but very . . . pleasant."

Hugh choked out a laugh and slid into her until he was fully sheathed and then stopped, enjoying the surge of raw possession and the further, almost painful, hardening of his body inside hers.

"Does it still feel good, Daphne?"

She nodded, her eyes wide. "I want you, Hugh. I want to give you the same pleasure you gave me."

Holding her gaze, he withdrew almost all the way and then filled her with a single slick thrust. Her eyelids fluttered and her body tightened around his and a groan tore out of his chest.

"Touch me, Daphne. Stroke me while I stroke you." Again he pulled all the way out and drove himself home, harder this time. Her hands began to roam his body, exploring his torso, his chest, his buttocks. He moved faster and pumped harder, driving into her with powerful, deep thrusts, holding nothing back.

He was nearing the edge of reason when her mouth grazed his nipple. He gasped and then rammed into her hard enough to reach her core. She stiffened, and then deliberately raised her hips to take him deeper. The erotic gesture frayed the last of his control and he let himself go.

She met him stroke for brutal stroke, until his body was about to fly apart. He was afraid he could no longer wait when she contracted around him.

"Yes, Daphne, yes. Come for me." He punctuated his words with one savage thrust after another. She sank her teeth into his chest, her crisis coming fast and hard and triggering his own *petite mort*. Hugh threw back his head and yelled something mindless as he drove himself home and spent deep inside her.

The only sound for some time was that of labored breathing.

"Mm, my darling," Hugh moaned, his arms no longer willing to hold him. He rolled to the side and pulled her close before draping a leg over her slim hips. He brushed the curls from her face and sucked in a sharp breath at the sight of her throat. "Oh, sweetheart—your neck—is it paining you?"

She smiled and it was the lazy, satisfied smile of a well-pleasured woman. Hugh allowed himself a moment of smugness.

"I'd completely forgotten about it. I think it looks more

painful than it is. He did not have me long before you stopped him."

"Too long," he corrected. "I hate to see your beautiful skin with such angry marks."

She ran a hand over the scars on his shoulders and chest, her eyes never leaving his. "I know the feeling."

He dropped a kiss on her nose and steered the subject in another direction. "I hope I was not too rough, and did not use you too hard."

"I feel deliciously well-used, my lord." She gave him a shy smile, which was suddenly distorted by a huge yawn. "I'm sorry, Hugh. I don't know what came over me."

Hugh pulled her close and curled his body around hers. "I came over you, darling." She laughed and snuggled closer. "You'd better get some sleep," he murmured into her hair, "because I'm likely to come over you again before the night is through."

Daphne chuckled, opened her mouth to say something, and fell asleep.

The next time she opened her eyes it was to see Hugh watching her, his eyes drowsy, a faintly arrogant smile on his lips as his hand stroked her softly between her legs.

"I was beginning to wonder if you would ever wake up," he said, dipping a finger into her.

"Mm," Daphne moaned, her hips beginning to rock with the movement of his hand. "What time is it?"

"Time for your next lesson," he murmured, moving away from her. She blinked her eyes and tried to wake herself from her torpid state, rising to her elbows and watching as he backed down the bed until he lay between her legs, pushing them apart before bracing his forearms along the length of each thigh, his face only inches from the place that she knew was already soaked and swollen in anticipation.

"What are you doing?" Her voice was breathy as his forearms inexorably pushed against her inner thighs, spreading them wider until she felt an exquisite tightness in her hips.

"I'm going to do something I've been dreaming of doing for a long time," he said, his attention riveted by what he saw.

Her eyebrows shot up. "You dream about things like this, too?"

He grinned up at her. "You wouldn't believe the things I dream about, Daphne. But trust me, I'll show them all to you, in time." He brushed his lips over the sensitive skin at the top of her thighs, his hot mouth ripping a harsh gasp from her.

"So soft," he murmured, his hands drifting toward her triangle of blond hair with agonizing slowness.

"Mmmm," he hummed, his fingers delving into her curls and parting her, caressing her.

Daphne shuddered and bit her lip to keep from crying out as he lightly flicked her core.

"You are so wet for me," he said in a tone of wonder, stroking her again and again and again, until her hips bucked and twitched with frustration.

"I want you to watch me, Daphne." He cut her a look with his mismatched eyes—one so green and warm and the other forever unknowable—and then he lowered his mouth.

"Oh my," she groaned, her vision becoming even blurrier as his tongue danced, flicked, and tormented that most sensitive part of her, circling and circling until she teetered on the brink of madness.

Until he stopped . . . And then commenced the exquisite torture all over again. And again.

Daphne fisted the blankets beside her until her hands ached and she could stand it no longer.

"Hugh!" She sounded like a woman at the end of her

tether, but she didn't care. Instead, she used the last of her strength to thrust her hips hard, her message clear.

His low, satisfied laugh vibrated through her and sent spirals of pleasure to every part of her body. For a moment she feared he would continue his relentless teasing, but then he relaxed his weight on her thighs, lowered his head, and took her into the hot embrace of his mouth.

Daphne gasped, her gaze riveted to the sight of him between her thighs: a sight that was almost as amazing as what he was doing.

The sculpted muscles of his back and shoulders bunched with controlled power as his blond head moved rhythmically, his skilled tongue and fingers working their magic. Daphne gave herself up to pure pleasure and rode the crest of the wave that had been a long time coming. A wave that built and built until it crashed, taking her with it and pummeling her body over and over, until she was weak, breathless, and limp.

"Hugh," she whispered, her hands slipping from his hair, where they'd somehow become tangled.

He kissed his way back to her breasts, lightly grazing their too sensitive tips before rising to his knees, proof of his arousal jutting from his taut, powerful hips. He looked the very image of some ancient warrior as he towered above her, the scars that marked his glorious body telling a silent tale of battles won and lost.

And when he lifted one hand to push back his damp curls, the muscles that rippled across his chest, shoulders, and arm were enough to make her weep. Daphne knew the proper reaction for a woman who'd just engaged in such a raw activity should be shame—or perhaps entering a convent—but the only thing she felt as she looked up at her beautiful lover was the hunger to have him inside her.

She spread her legs and his lips curved into a smile that was pure sin.

"Good girl," he said, mischief and lust mingling on his

expressive features as he took her thighs in his hands and kneeled between them.

Daphne gave a weak chuckle. "Hugh?" The word was barely a sigh.

"Yes, darling?" he asked as his palms slid beneath her bottom, positioning her.

"I—I want . . ." Daphne had no recollection of what she'd meant to say.

He laughed wickedly. "You want . . . this?" He entered her in one slick, endless thrust, driving her in to the mattress with the force of his action.

Daphne groaned, her head falling back, her eyes closing. It was . . . too much, too intense, too—

And then he began to pound her with merciless, measured thrusts, each invasion deeper than the last.

"Your body is heaven," he gasped, halting his savage thrusting and instead pushing slowly into her, inch by inch by inch. "Take all of me, darling."

She wrapped her legs around him, tilted her pelvis, and tightened.

"My God, Daphne!" He shuddered violently enough to shake the four-poster bed, lifting her higher, his fingers digging into her hips while he drove into her, his body taut and slick with the strength of his need.

Daphne slid her hands from his waist to the bunching muscles of his buttocks, splaying her fingers and pulling him deeper. She was already beginning to unravel when the unmistakable signs of his impending climax gripped his big body. He uttered something unintelligible, stiffened, and then froze, buried deep inside her, pulsing into her, filling her. Completing her. Driving her over the edge and into obliterating pleasure once again.

The familiar lassitude swept over her and she was already drifting toward sleep when he lowered himself to his forearms and then rolled alongside her.

Daphne groaned when their bodies parted, missing him already. "That was . . ."

Hugh chuckled. "Yes, it was."

"I'm so . . ."

"Hmmm?" He stroked her hair and she smiled, pushing and snuggling against him, molding her body to his. She wanted to stay awake but her eyes were so heavy and she was so tired—as if the worries of the previous months and weeks had finally taken their toll.

"I just need to close my eyes for a moment, Hugh," she mumbled.

A featherlight kiss landed on her lips. "Rest, sweetheart, just rest."

Chapter Nineteen

Daphne woke at first light, her eyes bleary and her neck oddly sore. She extended her arms over her head to stretch and realized she was nude. Utterly nude. Memories of last night came hurtling into her half-awake mind with breathtaking clarity. She grabbed the pillow that still bore his imprint and buried her face in it: bergamot.

It hadn't been a dream!

Daphne had finally made love—three times—at the grand old age of twenty-seven, and it had been world-shattering— she yawned hugely—and apparently exhausting. Well, she had nothing to do today. Nothing at all. She cradled the pillow in her arms and drifted back toward sleep—

Only to be shocked bolt upright: she was nude.

Rowena!

Daphne glanced at the clock: ten after eight. She jumped out of bed and grabbed the nightgown Rowena had left laid out the night before and fastened the buttons up to her neck.

Her dress and underclothes from last night—which she'd left on the floor—were now draped over the back of the chair. The same chair where Hugh's clothes had been after he'd stripped for her. Daphne closed her eyes and put her hands to her flaming cheeks. What an evening. What a wanton she'd been. The things she'd done were—

"What happened?"

Daphne's eyes flew open to find Rowena standing in the open doorway.

For a moment, Daphne thought her maid meant what she'd done last night—in her bed, with Hugh—but then she saw that Rowena's horrified gaze was on her throat.

It took Daphne the better part of an hour to convince Rowena she was fine. Even after she'd told her about the late earl's letter and her confession to Hugh, the woman still looked haggard and scared. She only left Daphne's chambers because she needed to fetch something to hide the worst of the bruises.

Once she'd gone, Daphne lowered herself into her bath, hoping she could dress in time to join Hugh at breakfast. Thinking about seeing him made her flush—both with pleasure and embarrassment. She couldn't help looking at her body with an entirely new eye. Her figure, which she'd always thought too tall, angular, and thin, now struck her differently and she saw herself as Hugh had: as a desirable woman.

She watched the water moving over her body, remembering where his hands had roamed so freely the night before. Even though she was alone she blushed at the memory of the things they'd done. The night had been magical in every way.

It was true that all was not perfect; there would be scandal to face and Hugh would still pursue his life at sea—a life that was dangerous and would take him away from her. But those were small concerns compared to what she'd faced only yesterday at this time. Daphne closed her eyes and allowed herself a little time to luxuriate in her happiness.

* * *

When Daphne came into her dressing room she saw one of her new gowns laid out, a yellow walking costume.

"Am I going someplace?" she asked as she sat at her dressing table.

"You promised to take Lucien and Richard to the park. They're mad to try out that contraption Lord Ramsay gave them. They broke one of the schoolroom windows chucking the wretched thing about inside. I thought the yellow would be best as it has such a high collar."

Daphne nodded absently, her mind on Hugh and whether he might join them in the park. He'd found the toy—more of a weapon, it sounded—on one of his journeys, perhaps it had been Australia? She would invite him at breakfast.

She hadn't paid attention to the yellow gown when Rowena had showed it to her, but now she saw how flattering it was. It was trimmed with three rows of ruching around the bottom of the narrow skirt and had a lovely crushed velvet spencer with a keyhole to show the matching ruched panel across the bodice and then buttoned again at the neck. Even Daphne, with her chronic lack of interest in clothing, could not help but admire the gown.

Still, it was all she could do to sit patiently as Rowena fussed with her hair and then clasped pearl earrings in her ears and a five-stranded pearl bracelet on her wrist. Daphne opened her mouth to protest the jewels but then looked at her reflection and realized she looked quite nice. She warmed at the thought of Hugh's reaction and stood.

"My lady?" Rowena held out her hand to relieve Daphne of her spectacles.

"I will wear them, Rowena." She ignored her maid's look of disapproval. Why walk through the world bumping into doorways when the only person whose opinion mattered loved the way she looked wearing spectacles—and nothing else.

Cherishing that thought, Daphne hurried from her room on a rare cloud of bliss.

The breakfast room was empty when she arrived. She was just about to ring and ask if Lord Ramsay had come down when two footmen entered. One bore fresh coffee and the other a letter.

"Lord Ramsay said to wait until you'd come down to breakfast to give you this, my lady."

Daphne forced herself to take a sip from her cup of coffee and order some fresh toast from the remaining footman, waiting until he'd left before tearing open the letter:

My Beautiful Lover,
*   It was wretched work leaving you lying so warm and soft in bed this morning. Only the knowledge that I must secure the means to have you in my bed and arms every night and morning caused me to make indecent haste and leave you. I am off to procure a special license. I will not rest easy until I can call you my own—in law as well as deed (are you blushing at that thought, my beautiful darling?).*

Yours alone,
Hugh

As love letters went, it was not a long one. However, his desire to wed her so speedily told her everything she needed to know about his feelings for her.

Despite her best efforts to move the morning's activities along, it was past noon before Daphne, Rowena, the two boys, and one boomerang set out from Davenport House.

They took the barouche and enjoyed a leisurely if overcast ride to the park.

Since the item Lucien and Richard would be hurling might cause harm to bystanders, Daphne had the coachman set them down in one of the less frequented areas of the park.

She took one of the footmen with her but waved away the other. "We will not be long," she told the coachman. "Return for us in three-quarters of an hour."

They walked a short distance from the carriage path to a clearing that was well shaded. Daphne and Rowena settled themselves on a blanket while the footman led the boys through the trees toward the nearby clearing.

"Do not throw that instrument at one another, and take turns," Daphne called after them.

Rowena took one of the boys' jackets from her large canvas bag and began darning one of the tears or holes they made in every garment they possessed.

Daphne leaned back against a tree and opened Herr Goethe's *Zur Farbenlehre*, which she'd purchased at Hatchards. She read, listening with one ear for any howls of pain or arguments.

She couldn't have said how long they'd been seated thus when an angry shout came from beyond the trees.

Rowena frowned. "Oh, Lord. It sounds as if they might have hit someone." She began to put down her work but Daphne stopped her.

"Don't disturb your labors," she said, getting to her feet, "I am much less profitably employed. I will go see what they have got up to."

The first thing she saw when she emerged from the trees was Richard running toward another small stand of oaks on the far side of the clearing. Lucien was nowhere in sight; neither was the footman.

Daphne cupped her hands around her mouth and called

out, "Richard! Please tell your brother to fetch his toy and come back!" Richard either didn't hear her or didn't heed her as he, too, disappeared into the trees.

"Disobedient little wretches," she muttered beneath her breath, walking faster than was easy in such a form-fitting dress and becoming uncomfortably warm in the process. As she neared the trees she heard the sound of boyish squealing followed by adult voices. Without any thought for her dress she broke into a run, rounding the trees in time to see a burly man grab Richard. A second man was vainly attempting to drag a flailing, kicking, and yelling Lucien toward a large rickety coach. Her footman lay in an unmoving heap.

Daphne's body was already in motion. "Stop! Release him at once!" She lunged at the closer man—the one holding Richard. "Let him go!" she shrieked.

"That's the one—grab her," the other man yelled, and then let out a blood-curdling shriek. Daphne saw Lucien's mouth was attached to the man's arm. His captor drew back his free hand and struck her son hard enough to send him reeling.

"You brute!" she screamed, grabbing Richard's arm with one hand and lunging toward Lucien. She'd taken only a few steps when a hand like a vise grabbed the nape of her neck and stopped her in her tracks.

"Now ear then, missus, you howd on a minnit! We don't reckon to arms the boys or you neever. Jes' calm yerself, luvvy," he crooned in a reasonable tone as he effortlessly drew her toward him, in spite of her struggling and flailing.

Richard struggled and squirmed and kicked, which made it difficult for the man to pin Daphne to his side—obviously his intention. Daphne would be lost if he got her into the crook of his huge arm, so she kicked and fought as hard as her son, punching him over and over. He responded to her abuse by squeezing her neck so hard she thought her spine would snap. A hoarse scream came from the direction of the carriage and they all froze.

Again, it was Lucien's tormentor who'd issued the anguished cry. By the manner in which he was clutching his groin, Daphne thought Lucien must have hit him between the legs with the boomerang, which he held while running toward Daphne and Richard.

It was only because the large man holding them had two arms rather than three that Lucien was able to beat him on the back with the wooden implement. He aimed again for the man's private parts and must have struck home because the huge brute dropped Richard's arm in order to reach behind him to stop his small tormentor.

"*Run, Richard!*" Daphne screamed, her loud screech startling everyone around her. "*Run!*" He ran, but Daphne felt as though he were moving in water. She twisted in her captor's grip and caught a glimpse of Lucien. He was behind them, kicking at the man, who'd somehow gained possession of his boomerang.

"Go, Lucien! Get Rowena!" Her voice dropped to a gasp as the man got his arm around her throat and drew her tight.

Just then Rowena came running around the trees, her mouth and eyes wide at the scene before her. Daphne could no longer scream to order her maid to flee, but the boys kept running, for once obeying their mother.

The man who was still huddled beside the waiting carriage screamed at his partner in an unnaturally high voice. "We needs to get out o' ere, Sidney! Get the mort, e said she's wurf the most dosh."

Her captor dragged Daphne, his arm around her neck.

"*No!*" The sound came from behind them and was accompanied by an enraged scream.

A second later the man holding Daphne staggered and grunted before turning around, his elbow tightening around her neck until her eyes bulged.

"Ow! Give over, luvvy!" He sounded more perplexed than angry.

"Let! Her! Go!" Rowena screamed, punctuating each word with something that sounded like a kick.

"Leave off, ye owd bird!"

He evidently decided Rowena was more of an annoyance than a danger and began moving toward the carriage again. Daphne heard sounds of scuffling but was too busy trying to breathe as the man's grip tightened every time Rowena commenced assaulting him. There was nothing for a long moment and then an enraged scream as Rowena's kicking struck home.

Unfortunately, his yell was followed by a sickening *crunch* and the dull *thud* of something hitting the ground. Daphne could see nothing but sky as she fought for breath, her vision beginning to darken. She'd begun to drift into unconsciousness when something heavy—a wool cloak?—dropped over her head. Arms picked her up and tossed her. She landed on something padded and a door slammed shut. The carriage lurched into motion and she teetered on the edge of the seat before rolling off and landing on her head.

The last sounds she heard as darkness engulfed her were, "*Mama! Mama!*"

Chapter Twenty

Hugh tossed Pasha's reins to his groom. "I shan't need him again today, Wilkins."

Perhaps he would be in luck and Daphne would have no other engagements and they could dine at home this evening. He grinned. If that were the case, they might skip dinner altogether and just go right to dessert. He mounted the steps two at a time, tossing his hat and gloves to the footman as he entered the hall.

"Is Lady Davenport in?" he asked, not breaking his stride.

"No, my lord. She took the young masters to the park and has not yet returned."

"Tell her I am in the library and would see her when she returns."

Once in the privacy of the library, Hugh took out the marriage license and laid it on the desk, thinking about his morning's work.

While he hadn't been looking forward to confronting Lady Letitia after last night, he had to admit the conversation had gone better than he'd expected.

She'd received him in her chambers, far earlier than was usual for her to take callers.

Her hair, bereft of its usual turban, was a soft, white cloud beneath its cap. But her eyes were still as sharp as daggers.

"You have come to explain your wretched decampment last night?"

Hugh took her hand and bowed low over it before seating himself in the spindly gilt chair her maid had placed at the side of the bed.

"Thank you for seeing me at such an uncivilized hour, Aunt. I have indeed come to apologize for last night."

Her mouth twisted. "You lie very prettily. I expect you have really come to tell me you will be marrying Thomas's widow."

Hugh couldn't help laughing. "As usual your directness is superseded only by your acuity."

"Ha! You'd best enjoy my candor, my boy. I suspect there will be many among our acquaintance who will not do you such a courtesy. I know the snubs and cuts won't cause you any heartache, but what of the gel?"

"She is not concerned with the opinions of London society. I believe she has had her fill of life among the *ton* after only a brief time."

"So she says."

"She is an intelligent woman who knows her own mind. I will not second-guess her."

Lady Letitia snorted. "Well, it wouldn't surprise me if it were true. I daresay a decade with my brother broke her of too many expectations in that department." She shook her head in disgust. "Will you protect and care for her and her brats? You abandoned this life twenty years ago. Why do you think you are more suited to it now?"

Hugh refused to rise to the bait. "I have not come seeking your blessing or approval, my lady. I am here merely as a courtesy." He gave her his blandest smile.

This time it was she who laughed. "Ho! Look at Captain High-and-Mighty! Smooth your feathers, boy. You needn't come on your high ropes with me." Her old eyes became sly. "I'll still receive the pair of you, don't you fret about that. After all, what is the point of money and position if you cannot draft your own rules?"

Hugh tried to hide how stunned he was that she was so sanguine about his decision to marry her brother's widow. But he must have failed because she chuckled evilly.

"You'd better close your mouth or something might choose to make a nest in such a great cavern."

Hugh chuckled and began to stand, but she was not finished shocking him yet.

"I knew from the first moment I saw those two brats they did not belong to Thomas. The boys' eyes are the only attractive feature their true great-grandfather, Caleb Hastings, could claim."

"You knew Hastings's grandfather?" Hugh said stupidly.

"Of course I did, dolt! And rather well—too well. Caleb was between Thomas and me in age and I was bosom bows with his first wife. She was a sweet gel and he drove her to kill herself as surely as if he'd done it with his own hands." She scowled. "Her two sons took after their father, I'm afraid. No doubt Daphne and her mother endured more than a decent woman should be forced to bear while under Walter Hastings's roof. I imagine it became far worse when his nephew Malcolm inherited Whitton Hall—there's a rotten apple that did not fall far from the tree. I've always suspected Thomas rescued the poor thing." She glared at Hugh. "Well, that was one of the wisest things my brother ever did. Believe me when I tell you nobody except your cousin John wanted John as the next Earl of Davenport." Waves of anger rolled off her. "Which—thanks to *your* absconding hide— he would have been!"

Hugh's face became hot, but he kept his mouth shut.

"I would have rather seen the title go to an unlettered savage than to John to destroy." Her gray eyes glinted a challenge—

as if Hugh might judge her for condoning her dead brother's deception. "You will let the situation stand."

It was not a question, but Hugh nodded. "Lucien Redvers is the Earl of Davenport. Anyone who says otherwise will have to answer to me."

His words failed to appease her and she raised a hectoring finger.

"You might have my approval for this marriage, boy, but you'll find yourselves under the glass for a time—you can lay a wager on that. If that wretched war weren't dragging on, you could remove to Paris for a few years. Most of the nitwits here can't remember anything beyond more than a few days. But of course that little Corsican monster has made Paris impossible." She fumed and ground her teeth as she considered the gall of the man who dominated a goodly chunk of the Continent.

Hugh laughed. The old lady managed to reduce the war raging across Europe to a personal inconvenience to the Redvers family.

She ignored his levity. "You'd best go about your wedding the correct way. No hole-and-corner nonsense or you'll both live to regret it, you mark my words. I recall that was what happened with that Pendleton chit some time back—she just ran off to Scotland with the old fool." She stopped and looked musingly into space. "Although I believe she was his brother's *widow*, and not his niece?" She shook her head. "It makes no difference. They carried on as if they were in the wrong from the very start. No, it won't serve!" she snapped, as if Hugh had offered any argument—or any words at all, for that matter. "You must do it the right way."

Hugh refused to allow the ferocious old bat to bully him. "I've procured a special license and I—"

"Do you have a pudding between your ears?"

Hugh frowned. "I will—"

"Have you lost your grip of English after living among

savages for so many years?" she demanded. "I just *told* you
the thing would have to be done *correctly*."

"No, I just—"

"Hold your breath to cool your porridge, fool!"

Hugh was stunned to silence, unable to recall when he'd
last endured such a thorough—and effective—bollocking.

"You must invite *everyone* and it must have more pomp
and ceremony than a royal wedding."

"Yes, well I shall leave those decisions to Daphne and—"

"You will not!" She hurled the words at his head like a
club. "Every word that leaves your mouth only proves you
have more hair than wit. The two of you lovelorn dunces
would only make a hash of it. That gel knows as much about
social strictures as I know about that wretched philosophical
claptrap she and Thomas were so fond of boring on about."
She shot Hugh a look of supreme contempt. "*I* shall manage
this and contrive to pass everything off creditably. I daresay
I've dealt with greater challenges in my day than sorting out
the likes of you two." Her face creased into an impish expression that made her resemble a wicked fairy. "You've got
more money than God, boy, and none of our set will be able
to stop themselves from paying court to your wealth. Now,"
she said, her tone businesslike and abrupt, "get out." She
flicked her hands in a shooing motion toward the door. "No
need for you to be lurching around here any longer."

Hugh could only grin in the face of such an onslaught.
"Thank you, Aunt Letitia. As usual, it has taken only a small
dose of your company to put me back in my place."

"Ha!" The old lady almost smiled but narrowly avoided
the unprecedented action thanks to the entrance of her ancient lady's maid, who pointedly showed Hugh the way out
of her mistress's chambers.

After leaving his aunt, Hugh had one more errand: a visit
to Rundell and Bridge.

Hugh already possessed a king's ransom in jewelry and

gems, but he wanted to give Daphne something that was not some corsair's ill-gotten booty.

He pondered the selection for longer than he expected and was on the verge of making a special order when he saw the ring Daphne needed: the biggest star sapphire he'd ever laid eyes on, its cabochon shape surrounded by diamonds. It was the only thing he'd ever seen that came close to being the same beautiful blue as her eyes.

Hugh took out his watch for the umpteenth time. Where the devil was she? She should have been back an hour ago. He was just about to ring for a servant when the door burst open and two disheveled and babbling boys burst into the library with Ponsby directly behind them.

Hugh stood. "What is it, Ponsby?" he asked as the boys launched themselves at him.

"I . . . I'm not quite sure, my lord," Ponsby stammered.

"Where is Lady Davenport?"

"I don't know. I've had Miss Claxton carried upstairs and summoned the doctor. She is unconscious and I can get nothing from the boys other than . . . well, it sounds as if Lady Davenport has been *abducted*, my lord." His face was whiter than parchment. "The footman who was with them, young Charles, was struck on the head and can recall nothing that happened after leaving the house to go to Hyde Park."

The boys' small bodies were racked with sobs.

"Give me a few minutes alone, Ponsby."

The butler left and Hugh carefully disentangled both boys and dropped to his haunches in front of them.

"Lucien, Richard, I need you to attend me." He held each of them by a shoulder. "Come now," he said, giving them a gentle squeeze. "You must tell me what has befallen your mother and Rowena. Richard?" He looked toward the generally more composed of the two boys.

Richard gulped hard several times, knuckling his eyes to rub away his tears. "There were two men," he said in a wobbly voice. "They came upon us as we were throwing the boomerang. Lucien threw it into the trees and when we went to find it the smaller man grabbed him. The other man had just taken me by the arm when Mama found us. She yelled at them to let us go—" He made another loud gulping noise but couldn't hold back a watery sob.

"Steady on, man," Hugh murmured. "You're doing fine."

Richard sniffed loudly a few times before resuming his story. "She tried to take me from the man, but he grabbed her instead. We both struggled but could not get free until we heard a terrible scream, and the man lost his grip on me."

"I hit the man between the legs with the boomerang, sir," Lucien said, emerging from his misery, tearstained but proud. "I ran toward Mama and tried to help her but she yelled at us over and over, sir, telling us to run to Rowena. So we did, we ran—and they took her!" His voice broke and he sobbed.

Hugh hugged both boys to his chest. "You fought bravely, but you could not hold off two grown men, and your mama would not have wanted you to be taken as well. What you can do now is help me find her. You must be calm and think, think hard and fast about anything you can remember. What did the carriage look like? Did the men say anything that you remember? Think, boys, is there anything?"

"The carriage," Lucien said, his words muffled by Hugh's jacket.

Hugh leaned back. "What about the carriage?"

"The man holding me almost put me into a carriage before I bit his hand. It was very old and ugly—the carriage, not his hand. There was only half a crest but I think it was a horse on a field of green." His face scrunched up in thought. "And some red and white checks, maybe."

The Hastings crest. Hugh had seen it many times in his

youth. That bloody bastard! And Hugh had been a *stupid* bastard to release him. Now Daphne and her sons were paying for his stupidity.

"Hugh?" Lucien's frightened voice pulled him back from the brink of rage.

Hugh forced a smile onto his face. "Good work, Lucien. Can you recall anything else? Did they perhaps say where they were taking you?"

"He only said we would be going for a long ride and if I was good I'd get to go on a boat. But that is all, sir. He no longer spoke to me after I bit him," he added.

Richard broke in. "The man Lucien bit called out to the other man to take Mama and that it was she who was wanted, and then he said something I couldn't understand." His pale, tearstained face crumpled. "Rowena is hurt badly, Cousin Hugh. Do you think she will die?"

Hugh had no idea but he could hardly say that. "She is a tough lady. Tell me what happened to her. Was she with you?"

Richard's breathing was still irregular but he'd stopped crying. "Rowena attacked the man and then he hit her so hard she dropped to the ground. He dragged Mama toward the carriage and they were gone before we reached Rowena. I held her head in my lap while Lucien ran to find the barouche. And then Charles woke up and waited with me."

"You've done very well, both of you. Now"—Hugh stood and ushered the twins toward the door—"I'd like to see Rowena."

When Hugh entered the maid's room a few minutes later, he found Daphne's housekeeper tending to the older woman. He gestured her into the woman's small sitting room.

"Is she conscious? Can she speak?"

"Yes, my lord, she woke up only a few minutes ago. I was just going to send for you as she is most agitated about something and wanted to speak to you."

Hugh nodded. "The boys are waiting outside—take them

to the kitchen and get them something to eat while I speak with Miss Claxton. Tell them I will come fetch them when I'm finished." That way he could see if the maid was in any shape to see the boys.

The housekeeper smiled. "Aye, my lord, a spot of tea will do them good."

Hugh closed the door before drawing a chair close to the bed.

"My lord," Rowena said, not waiting for him to begin, "it was Walter Hastings's old carriage. I saw the crest." She winced from the pain of speaking.

"Shhh, do not make yourself ill; take your time. The boys told me about the carriage. They also said something about taking a ride on a boat. Did you hear any part of that?"

Rowena very slightly shook her head and winced even at that small movement. "By the time I got there, one of them had her almost to the carriage, where the other was waiting."

"Do you know if Hastings owns a place by the water? Or perhaps owns a yacht?"

"I cannot recall Sir Malcolm ever mentioning any other property. Nor his uncle, Sir Walter." She shook her head in frustration and then groaned. "I am sorry, but I cannot think of anyplace. I just wished to tell you of the carriage and—" She paused and swallowed hard.

"And?" Hugh prodded, trying to remain patient when all he wanted was to be in motion and doing something—anything— although he knew not what.

"My lord," she said, her voice barely a whisper, "I may not survive and I would not want to go to my grave with this on my soul."

Hugh opened his mouth to reassure her she'd be fine, but could see she badly needed to say something.

"It was I, my lord. It was I who . . . who cut your girth." Her eyes shied away from his.

Hugh could not believe he'd heard her correctly. "I beg your pardon?"

She nodded, her face a mask of misery.

"*You* cut Pasha's girth?" Tears leaked from the corners of her eyes. "But why?" Hugh could hardly have been more shocked if Ponsby or Gates had admitted to doing such a thing.

"I was terrified you meant to take everything away from us and change things. Just like what happened to Daphne's mother when Walter Hastings came and took her." Her face twisted with self-loathing. "I did *nothing* then, even though I knew he was a lying, wicked man who didn't love her." She swallowed. "I was afraid your coming would wreck everything we'd worked so hard for. I was foolish." She clutched at his hand. "I know I was wrong, my lord. Wrong to do it and wrong about what you meant to us. You have protected her against him. I will turn myself in." Tears ran freely down her cheeks.

Hugh shook his head to clear the bizarre revelation from it. "Don't talk rubbish, woman," he said more harshly than he'd intended. "The last thing I want is to cause your mistress any grief. Throwing you in gaol would do just that. Besides, if I'd protected her as I should have, this wouldn't have happened," he said, indulging in a little self-loathing of his own.

"You will find her, my lord." Her scared brown eyes bored into his.

"Yes, I will find her."

The door opened and a man entered. "I am Doctor Compton," a young blond man said, looking toward the small figure in the bed. "And what have we here?" he asked in a calm, friendly tone.

Hugh stood. "Please take good care of her, Doctor. She is very dear to Lady Davenport." He reached down and took

Rowena's hand, giving it a firm squeeze. "I will send news as soon as I have some," he assured her.

Hugh encountered Kemal on his way to the stairs.

"Martín is here, Captain. He has ridden through the night to see you and is dirty and fatigued but insists he speak to you before anything else. I put him in your sitting room."

"I'll join him directly. Will you go to the kitchen and tell the boys they may visit Miss Claxton as soon as the doctor is finished?"

Hugh wasted no time going to his chambers. "Martín," he said, extending his hand and gripping the shorter man's brawny forearm in greeting.

"Captain." For once the younger man did not wear his insolent smile.

"Please, sit." Hugh gestured to the chair the exhausted man had been occupying before his entrance.

"I ride 'ere like the devil, my lord, but 'ope I am not already too late," he confessed as he seated himself beside a small table where Kemal had already set up a pot of coffee and bread and butter for the famished man.

"I 'ave been at Whltton ever since dat pig 'ave leff." He paused in this unkind epithet to stuff a chunk of heavily buttered bread into his mouth and wash it down with a generous mouthful of black coffee.

Hugh almost rolled his eyes—he should have waited to feed the man. Martín's speech was almost impossible to understand even without a mouthful of food. He could not make the sound *th*, and instead pronounced it as a *d*; treated words beginning with an *o* as if they had an *h* in front of them, and vice-versa; and referred to inanimate objects as *he* or *she*.

"I 'ave bedded dat, dat"—here he appeared to search without success for an English word before resorting to the French equivalent—"*salope* until my cock, he is raw, and still she give me nutting. Nutting! And 'oo do I see come in de night? You cannot believe it, Captain. You will never believe 'oo show up."

"Good Lord! *Who*, Martín?"

"Calitain!"

Hugh blinked. "Calitain? Here? You must be mistaken."

Martín gave him a withering look of contempt. "I tink I know if I see Calitain."

"What in the name of God would he be doing at Whitton?" Hugh demanded, his mind reeling.

"Not in God's name—the *Devil's*. And dat is what I find out." Martín's voice was triumphant even through a mouthful of bread. "I make sure ee not see me, but I sneak out and go to the stable, where Blake is waiting, dat . . . dat *tête de chou*!" He shook his head in disgust. "You know Blake?" Martín demanded.

Hugh smothered a smile at Martín's use of the English slang term, *cabbage head*. Clearly he'd been working on his English, although not the level of discourse Hugh had hoped for.

"I've met Blake—he is Hastings's footman or groom or some such." Hugh could no longer stand to wait while the younger man struggled to find the correct English words.

"Tell me the rest in French, Martín."

Martín's shoulders sagged with relief. "Thank you, Captain," he said in his native tongue. "Calitain told Blake that if his master didn't bring him the remainder of the money he owed, he would take the offer to some other Englishman. He also said he would make 'Aystink very sorry.'" Martín stuffed another chunk of bread in his mouth and Hugh waited impatiently while he chewed and swallowed.

"Blake tried to calm Calitain and told him 'Aystink had the money and would meet him at his ship. When Calitain left, I followed him to a shack outside of town—eh, maybe for smuggling. I saw only one other man with him." Martín gulped down a mouthful of coffee before continuing. "After

I left there I went to talk to Delacroix. He said he would do what he could to find Calitain's ship. And after I left him I rode directly here. *En fin!"* He made a chopping motion with his hand to indicate he'd finished his tale.

Hugh sat back in his chair, speechless at the turn of events. Calitain had been running slaves for years. Hugh could think of only one reason the notorious slaver would risk coming onto English soil—where he was a wanted man: to collect money from a delinquent investor.

"If Hastings owes him money it can only be for one thing," Hugh finally said.

"Oui, slaves." Martín's voice was flat. An escaped slave himself, Martín was not well-disposed toward those who dealt in human cargo.

The first time Hugh met Martín, it had been with the blood of his last master still fresh on his hands. Apparently the man had attempted to make use of Martín's body one time too often for the young man's patience. Like many who worked the bordellos of New Orleans, Martín was of mixed blood. The fact that he was what the Americans called *high creole*, owing only a fraction of his heritage to the blood of captured Africans, made no difference to his situation under American law. He'd been born a slave and would have died one if he'd not taken matters into his own hands.

Hugh looked at Martín as he worked on the last pieces of what had been a formidable pile of bread. While he seemed much like any other man his age—obsessed equally with women, money, and fine clothes—there was a strange kind of deadness in his exotic golden eyes.

Hugh had seen the look more than once when he looked in the mirror. It was a deadness that came from having once been another man's possession. Not always as well tended as his master's other livestock—horses or dogs—and constantly awaiting the day when one's value decreased and one would face a humiliating sale, to be passed along to some other master.

"Now that Hastings's plan to marry Lady Davenport has fallen apart, I can only assume he has decided to ransom her." Hugh took a deep breath and forced himself to put into words the sickening thoughts in his head. "It is also possible Hastings has learned of the bad blood between me and Calitain and will offer Daphne to him as payment."

Martín nodded grimly.

"The boys mentioned that the men who tried to abduct them talked about a boat ride. I believe Hastings must be taking her to Calitain, who is obviously somewhere close to Eastbourne."

Martín finished the last of his coffee and exhaled with satisfaction. "You are ready to ride, milor'?" His lips twisted into an impudent grin, making sure Hugh knew that it would take more than one grueling ride to slow down a man of his abilities.

"I am only delayed by the pleasure of watching you gorge yourself," Hugh replied, already on his feet. The door opened and Kemal entered.

"Ah, Kemal, perfect timing. Will you lay out my regular kit, not the town foppery, pack my new pair of pistols, and take another pair for you and Martín. I'll have my sword as well," he said with a grim smile. "Perhaps I'll even find somebody to use it on."

Chapter Twenty-One

Daphne woke in utter darkness, her hands bound together and secured to something over her head. Her arms had gone numb; she must have been in the carriage for some time.

Her eyes were accustomed to the gloom so at least she could confirm she was alone. She almost wept with relief; the men had not gone back for her sons.

If the boys and Rowena had made it to safety, then Hugh would already know what had happened. Malcolm must be desperate indeed to use so recognizable a conveyance to commit the crime of kidnapping a peer.

The coach windows had been blackened over with some substance but she could see light where there were scratches. So, it was still day—she hadn't been gone that long after all. She lifted her arms to relieve some of the pressure on them, breathing deeply and ignoring the terror that clawed at her. Where was Malcolm taking her? He wouldn't go to Whitton, where it would be difficult to keep her presence a secret. And Walter Hastings had sold the only other estate the Hastings family owned years ago. Where else could he take her? And what in God's name did he think to do with her once he got her to his destination? Did he think to force her into marriage? Or perhaps he meant to extort more money from her?

Daphne closed her eyes against the deluge of unanswerable questions.

Why speculate? Instead, she concentrated on calming her pounding heart and husbanding her strength—for when she would really need it.

Hugh was ready to leave Davenport House within the hour. He met Martín coming from the kitchens, where he'd gone to fortify himself with something more filling than bread. Hugh watched as one of the housemaids came running up behind Martín. He stopped and turned to the pretty young woman, who leaned toward him as if her body were magnetically attracted to his. They exchanged a few quiet words before Martín laughed and ran his finger down her cheek.

Hugh shook his head. Martín had only been in the house an hour and had already made a conquest. It would be wise to get him away before brawls and fisticuffs broke out.

The younger man smirked as Hugh approached him, his swagger bursting with arrogance.

"I thought you went to the kitchen for sustenance."

"*Je l'ai fait*," Martín said.

Even as tense as he was, Hugh couldn't help laughing. "In English, Martín."

The three men left without delay. They would go to Lessing Hall and begin their search at Whitton. Hugh believed he would not have to search at all—he suspected Hastings would be contacting him soon. The man couldn't believe Daphne would ever marry him—something she might have done if the boys were also in Hastings's grasp. No, he must be holding her for ransom. Or perhaps as bait. After all, Calitain had come to Whitton looking for Hastings and was waiting for his money. Hugh had only his instinct to go on, but he thought they'd find Daphne wherever Calitain was holed up.

His head ached and became unaccountably hot at the thought of Calitain within leagues of Daphne. He wanted to ride directly to the shack where Martín had seen Calitain, but he knew that was foolish and unsafe—especially for Daphne if she was being held there. Cornering Hastings or Calitain could very well end in disaster.

No, they needed to find out what game Calitain was playing and Hugh needed to stop dwelling on the horror of Daphne in Calitain's grasp. Instead, he should be thinking about whatever it was Hastings might be planning.

But that didn't help his state of mind, either. Hastings had already raped Daphne once—which Hugh could not think about without becoming half mad. If Malcolm Hastings was caught up with men like Calitain, then he'd formed the worst associations a man could make. Hugh had seen the desperation in the other man's eyes when he'd held him by the throat. He should have obeyed his impulses and killed him. He should have known that no good would come of releasing such a venomous reptile back into the world.

"Damnation!" he swore.

Martín must have heard him over the din of the horses' hooves. "*Ne vous inquiétez pas, Capitaine*," he assured him. "We ave time. And Aystink and Calitain? Pfft." He made a dismissive motion with his hand along with the rude noise. "Dey are stupid men! Do not worry, milor', Delacroix will find dat *crotte de nez* and ees cheap."

Hugh shook his head. "It is pronounced *his ship,* Martín, not *ees cheap.* And it is not done to refer to someone as 'dung of the nose' even if it *is* true. We really must work on your English, my friend. But not right now. Now we must ride."

Hugh leaned low and spurred Pasha into a headlong gallop, determined to win the race against time and fear.

* * *

The sudden sunlight was like sharp daggers in her eyes after the solid dark of the coach.

"If you lay a finger on me I'll kill you!" Daphne snarled, staring blindly at the looming figure.

"Hush now, sweet cousin. One more sound out of you and I'll bind your mouth so tightly you'll scarcely be able to draw breath." Malcolm edged himself into the coach sideways and shut the door behind him, plunging the interior of the carriage back into darkness. His arm snaked around her neck and she felt the sharp prick of a knife against her throat. He put his other hand over her mouth, leaving nothing to chance as he settled beside her.

"Nice and quiet, my dear," he soothed, his rank breath on her cheek. "We're changing horses right now and it would be a very bad thing if you called for help. I have this knife—" He skimmed the tip of cold metal down her cheek to punctuate his point. "I should hate to use it on you. I wouldn't want to kill you but I wouldn't mind hurting you just a little." He dropped the blade to her throat. "Now," he said, lowering the hand covering her mouth, "we can finish the conversation Lord Ramsay so rudely interrupted the last time we were together." His lips brushed her temple and he squeezed her thigh. Daphne jerked away, more horrified by his touch than his knife.

"I shall never marry you, Malcolm. You will have to kill me, so you may as well go ahead and do so now."

"I'm sure it won't come to that." He stroked her thigh, a smile in his voice. "Besides, I'm not interested in the rights marriage will grant me over your person. After all, I've had a sample without any of the bother. Don't worry, sweetheart, if I want what you have under that skirt, I'll take it without a license."

Daphne's mind stopped racing and cold clarity took hold.

"This time you'll have to take me after I'm dead," she hissed in his ear. He jerked away from her, but not far. A moment later she heard the striking of tinder and the lantern that hung just inside the door flamed to life. She turned away from the glare but that brought his repellent, bloodshot face into view. He grinned and looked from her face to her bosom and slowly back to her eyes. Daphne shuddered with revulsion.

Malcolm laughed. "Now, now, my dear, I know you are eager, but you must wait for those pleasures," he said, purposely misconstruing her reaction. "Although it seems as if you are not very good at waiting." He pulled a piece of paper from his breast pocket with his free hand and tapped her on the nose with it before holding it up before her face for her to see.

Daphne didn't need to read it; she recognized Hugh's bold handwriting.

"You disgusting, loathsome swine." She could hardly force the words past her fury.

"Tut, tut," he warned, raising the knife once again, pressing it into the hollow of her throat. Daphne stared at Malcolm's slimy smile, the urge to disregard the knife at her throat and slam her forehead into his mocking face almost unbearable. As if reading her mind, he pressed the knife harder. "No, you will not do what you are thinking, because I will not hesitate to begin carving on you, and that might diminish your value with that great buffoon I hope will pay so much for you."

So that was his plan, extorting money from Hugh for her release. Daphne could not help the hope that flared in her breast. Hugh would find her.

Once again Malcolm read her face with ease. "Oh yes, I mean to sell you to the highest bidder." He gave a rude bark of laughter. "Well, the only bidder. But I am not a stupid man, nor am I in a hurry. Maybe I won't turn you over to him so readily. Maybe I'll keep you for a while and see if he is even more generous the second time I make my demand. When he understands how serious I am." He smiled at whatever vile thoughts were in his head before pressing the knife harder. "I should have liked to bring our charming sons along. They look very much like I did at their age. Handsome young fellows, and clever like their father, I'll bet." His smile dissolved as quickly as it came, and for a minute Daphne thought he might press the knife deeper. But he lowered the knife to her thigh, shaking his head.

"I've been watching you for quite some time, my dear, and I have seen Ramsay with the two brats. It would seem he has formed some inexplicable attachment to them. You cannot have told him the truth about his little *cousins*."

"There is nothing you can blackmail me with. He knows the truth."

"My, my! You must have given him a better ride between those sweet thighs than I recall having. Perhaps I will have to revisit your pleasure palace before letting him have you back?" He stroked her thigh and leaned closer, sour alcohol misting her skin.

Daphne jerked back, relieved to the point of fainting when he chuckled and relaxed against the seat.

"Don't worry, pet, there will be plenty of opportunities for me to scratch your itch later. I've not sent Ramsay a list of my demands yet, so we have some time. I need to make sure you're nice and snug before I alert him to my plan."

Daphne almost laughed. The stupid man had forgotten the boys and Rowena would have seen the coach and its crest. She turned to face the blackened window and hid her smile.

It felt as though the journey would never end. After the horse-change—when Malcolm entered the carriage and held her at knife-point—the lumbering coach had stopped to change horses again, but that had been hours ago and Daphne thought the new horses must be half-dead by now. Not that Malcolm let that sort of thing concern him.

Thankfully he'd left her alone in the carriage shortly after their departure from the first posting house and she'd not seen him again. She could not say how far they'd traveled, but she could see the sky was dark through a tiny scratch in the window. At this time of year the sun did not go down completely until well after nine o'clock. By that reckoning they must have been on the road for at least ten hours. It had been shortly after noon that she'd finally herded the boys into the barouche for their trip to the park. Where was he taking her? Whitton Park? If so, it would not be longer than a few more hours. But surely he would need to change horses again or—

The rickety coach shuddered to a halt and Daphne struggled to sit up higher on the seat, biting back a scream at the pain in her arms. She heard the murmur of men's voices and then the sound of the steps being lowered before the door creaked open.

"Hello, darling, still awake?" Malcolm held up a lantern, casting a glow into the carriage as well as illuminating his flushed and excited face. Daphne shied away from the light and buried her face in the side of her arm, not bothering to answer.

"We're here, sweetness." His blunt fingers yanked at her bound wrists and Daphne had to grit her teeth to keep from crying out. He cursed, frustrated when the knot held. "One of you get over here and give me a hand." He was slurring, as if he'd been drinking.

The smaller man scrambled into the coach, studiously keeping his eyes away from her as he cut the rope that held her bound.

Malcolm raised the knife. "Now then, don't try any of your tricks on me, sweet cousin. There would be nowhere for you to run even if you did break free. Behave yourself and perhaps we'll let you have a little private time to take care of your womanly business. No doubt you're busting for a slash." His use of the vulgarism caused hilarity among his two henchmen. Daphne didn't care. It was all she could do to stop from weeping as blood rushed into her limbs.

At least Malcolm looked beaten to an inch and it was her guess all three men would need several hours of sleep and rest before they were fit to make their next move, whatever that might be. She, on the other hand, had already enjoyed several hours of sleep and only needed to ease the screaming pain in her arms to feel normal.

Malcolm took her wrist in a proprietary grasp and pulled her toward a small thatched cottage not far from the coach. It was partly hidden by the scruffy oak trees the locals referred to as "Sussex Weeds." The building itself was a ragged assembly of wooden slats with boards nailed over the spots that once had contained windows. It was a mean hovel, and Daphne would not have thought it occupied but for the light that escaped between the haphazard boards.

The big man pounded his fist against the door.

"It is Hastings," Malcolm shouted. There was a long moment in which nothing but shuffling and murmuring could be heard behind the rude wooden door before it finally swung inward.

Daphne tried to step back but Malcolm's grip tightened like a steel trap around her upper arm, almost as if he were . . . scared.

As well he should be.

The man who stood in the open doorway had one of the most frightening faces Daphne had ever seen. It wasn't that he was deformed or hideous. In fact, his features might actually have been handsome if they'd not been so twisted with contempt. What frightened her—what almost sent her running—was the hatred that boiled off him like steam from a kettle.

He was tall and stocky, his ruddy face and clothing proclaiming him a sailor. His eyes narrowed and he gave her a rude once-over before moving on to Malcolm. Daphne wouldn't have believed it possible, but even more menace filled his gaze when it settled on Malcolm. Her cousin must truly be a fool if he couldn't see this man meant him grievous harm.

"Well, if it isn't little Lord Hastings," the man drawled, his mouth twisting as he misstated Malcolm's title. His English was strange, as if rusty from disuse. He smirked at Malcolm before returning his gaze to Daphne. "What have you brought me? This does not look like money, lordling. Do you think to curry my favor by bringing me a whore?" He gave a rude bark of laughter. "I'm afraid you have mistaken my tastes, my friend." Daphne was staggered at the derision he put into the last two words. It was a depth of loathing that should have put even a stupid man on notice. Not so Malcolm.

"Hallo, old chap," Malcolm exclaimed merrily, as if he were greeting an old school chum. "You wouldn't believe what I've brought for you, Captain, something even better than money."

"Oh?" The single word was pregnant with menace, but the man stepped aside and Malcolm shoved Daphne into the dingy hut.

A second man, who looked bored rather than evil, swept Daphne and Malcolm with a lazy, uninterested gaze, his leg slung carelessly over the arm of a rude wooden chair. He shot an amused glance at the man who'd answered the door. The two of them stared at Malcolm with an expression in their eyes that should have stripped the skin from his ignorant hide.

Instead, Malcolm flung his hand out dramatically. "My

dear friend Captain Calitain—" He yanked Daphne close and forced her down into a curtsy. "Let me present to you One-Eyed Standish's woman!"

Daphne fought the urge to run when both men looked at her with more interest than was probably good for her health.

Calitain strode toward her without taking his eyes from hers. He stopped so close she could smell him. His initial smell wasn't unpleasant—soap mingled with a hint of brandy—but something corrupt and rotten lurked just below the surface.

"Standish's whore, eh?" He raised one eyebrow and gave her bosom a lingering look before turning to Malcolm. "What of it?" The words were like the crack of a whip.

Malcolm faltered, opening his mouth and then closing it again.

"Standish has *many* whores," Calitain sneered, this directed at Daphne. "I have even had a few of them myself. Like that one in New Orleans, eh?" He turned to his silent friend and they both laughed in what could only be described as a very nasty fashion. Still chuckling, he walked around her, giving her rumpled and dirty walking costume an exaggerated inspection as he did so. "My, my, my," he said, not bothering to explain himself, merely glancing again at the other man, who returned his look with one that was oddly . . . significant.

Malcolm found his voice. "You don't understand, Captain, he plans to marry this one." He sounded far less confident, almost whiney.

"Marriage?" His brows drew down like check marks over his tar-black eyes.

"Yes, he wants to marry her, the fool. Even though he's already had her. As have I." Malcolm added a manly laugh, as if to join in the merriment the other two men had just shared.

Calitain ignored him, instead focusing his penetrating

gaze on Daphne. The pause dragged on until she wondered if he expected her to confirm or deny Malcolm's words.

"You have had the big man, have you? Tell me, was he as good as you hoped?" He grinned at his friend. "Jean-Paul would like to know."

Whatever he saw in Daphne's face made him laugh even harder and it took a few minutes for both him and his associate to stop.

He wiped a tear from his eye before turning to Malcolm. "You have done well, little lordling." He patted Malcolm on the head. His eyes were on Daphne, so he missed the venomous look Malcolm shot him. "Yes, you have brought me a nice present." He trailed one finger down the curve of her jaw, toward her chin, and down her neck and lower, lingering on the swells of her breasts, which were visible through the keyhole neckline of the coat. Daphne believed he was on the verge of doing something vile to her right then and there, but in the blink of an eye he was holding Malcolm by the throat, slamming him up against the wall and lifting his feet a couple of inches off the ground. Daphne couldn't help thinking Malcolm found himself in the same position rather frequently.

"I. Want. My. Money." The softness of his voice caused the small hairs on the back of her neck to stand up. "Your man Blake said you had it," he continued, his voice silky smooth as he leaned close to Malcolm, who was choking. "I have to pick up my shipment and I have no time to find another rich English *cochon* to put up the money. If you have made me come here for nothing, I will not be happy. Do you understand this, *lordling*?" He leaned in closer to Malcolm, as if listening. "Eh, what is that you say? I can't understand." He cocked his head to one side with exaggerated concern, looking over at the other man, who laughed silently and shook his head.

Daphne almost felt sorry for Malcolm. Almost.

As suddenly as Calitain had grabbed Malcolm, he let him go and watched in amusement as he fell to his knees and fought to catch his breath.

Calitain lost interest in him while he flailed and turned his attention instead to the two openmouthed men who'd helped kidnap Daphne. He put his hands on his hips and let his mouth fall open, gaping mockingly before laughing. "And who are you two gentlemen, eh?" The word *gentlemen* dripped like poison from an adder's fang.

The bigger man raised his hands in a placating gesture. "'Ere then, we's just paid to do a job, sir. We don't want no trouble," he said in a soothing tone. The smaller man stood motionless beside him, clutching his hat in his white-knuckled hands.

Both were spared whatever Calitain was going to say by the sound of hoarse pleading coming from the floor.

"*She's* the money," Malcolm wheezed, pointing at Daphne. "She's got control of her son's estates—hundreds of thousands of pounds. She's worth even more now that Standish wants her. He'll bring the money for her and think nothing of it as he'll only be expecting me." He collapsed, exhausted by his brief soliloquy.

Calitain looked from Malcolm to her and back again before a bleak smile settled on his lips. He dropped to his haunches in front of Malcolm. "For your sake, little lord, you'd better hope she is worth every penny and more to Standish." When he stood he brought Malcolm up with him, holding him by the hair and dragging him kicking and squealing across the room before thrusting him onto the dirty mattress in the farthest corner. "You will sleep there."

He turned to the other two and pointed to the same corner. Both men scrambled to sit beside their unfortunate employer.

"It is lucky for you that I must wait here in any case. My ship will not come for me and my money until tomorrow night, after it is dark. That means *you* have until tomorrow after dark to get my money. I don't care how you get it. Standish can bring it, little fairies can bring it, or even the bloody king himself. But if I don't have it by then, both you"—he pointed at Malcolm—"and her"—he turned to look at Daphne, his eyes like bottomless black wells—"will die. Is that understood?"

Malcolm nodded, a low whimper coming from his throat while he stared up at his tormentor. "Y-y-yes, it is clear."

Satisfied with Malcolm's response, Calitain grabbed Daphne by the shoulder and propelled her toward a dark doorway. He smiled down at her as his arm snaked around her waist and drew her close.

"You are lucky, my lady. We have a private chamber in which you will spend the night while we men make plans for your rescue." He squeezed her hard before leaning down to whisper in her ear. "You'd better hope the little lordling is smarter than he looks," he hissed before shoving her into the darkness and slamming the door behind her.

The only light in the room came from the cracks around the ill-fitting door. Daphne stayed put until her eyes adjusted enough that she could see the outlines of the room. There was a bed in one corner and a small cabinet opposite the door, and that was all. She felt her way toward the bed and sat on the edge, trying not to think about who else had used it.

Gradually, her pulse slowed and her breathing became less ragged. She could hear Calitain and his associate talking, his voice almost loud enough to distinguish the words, but not quite. She listened without moving for perhaps an hour, when the voices stopped. Not long after there was the sound of boots and the slamming of a door.

Daphne could still hear Calitain's voice and assumed that it had only been the two hirelings who'd left, probably going to do something with the horses. She remained crouched in silence, listening so hard her entire body ached with the tension. She couldn't have said how long she sat waiting for something—anything—to happen. But finally she could bear it no longer. Her shoulders and arms screamed from the punishing carriage ride and it was all she could do to remain upright. So she curled up on her side, wrapping her arms around her knees and hugging herself. At least the night was warm and she would not be forced to use the moldy-smelling blanket.

The last sound she heard before giving up the fight against exhaustion was the pounding of hooves.

Chapter Twenty-Two

It was full dark when the three men rode into the courtyard at Lessing Hall. The sound of their horses on the cobblestones brought a sleepy lad from the stables. He blinked hard at finding three men, two of them already having dismounted while the third stopped only long enough to toss his heavy saddlebag to the ground before wheeling his mount and galloping off in the direction of town.

"Give the horses a triple ration of grain—they've had a brutal ride. And stay awake—Martín will be back here shortly." Hugh was already striding toward the entrance as the last words left his mouth, Kemal struggling to keep pace.

The massive front door opened before Hugh even reached the top step. There was Gates, holding a candlestick and looking normal but for the fact that he was garbed in a rather exotic red silk banyan and embroidered nightcap.

"My lord."

"Sorry to disturb your beauty sleep, Gates." Hugh was unable to suppress a smile at the old man's sartorial elegance.

"Indeed, my lord. Betsy has gone to ready your chambers. Should you like something brought up to your room?"

Gratitude suffused Hugh's tired body at the suggestion and he tossed his dusty hat and gloves onto a table in the entry hall, moving toward the stairs with Gates trailing behind.

"Enough food for three—no, make that four, and a couple of bottles of claret, something old and dusty from the cellars. Have it sent to the library rather than my chambers. Also send a message to Will Standish, telling him to join me immediately. After you've seen to that, you may take yourself off to bed. We shan't need anything else tonight."

"Very good, my lord." Gates bowed stiffly before heading back down the stairs.

Hugh turned to Kemal, who was waiting at his side, laboring under the burden of Hugh's bags, pistols, and enormous Hessian blade.

"I'll take that." Hugh relieved his servant of the sword and whetstone that hung in a small leather pouch off the hilt. "Put the rest in my chambers and join us in the library."

Hugh could sharpen the damn thing while he waited for his men. He wouldn't be good for much else until Martín returned with Delacroix. He entered the library and poured himself a generous brandy, invigorated by the burn that trailed down his throat. He set the half-empty glass aside and untied the leather cord that held his sword in the scabbard. The soft *hiss* of metal against leather filled the air as he pulled the long sword out of its protective cover. He tossed aside the scabbard and held the blade up to inspect it.

It glittered sullenly under the light of a dozen or so candles. It was not a graceful weapon, far too heavy and broad to rival the beauty of those irons used in fencing. Nor did it have the exotic grace of the Eastern blades he'd encountered during his time in the Mediterranean.

No, this sword had been forged for the sole purpose of expeditious killing. In the right hands it was certain death.

The sword had been a gift from one of the men with whom he'd escaped the sultan's clutches; a Hessian named Wüstenfalke—the Barbary Falcon.

Like Hugh and Delacroix, Wüstenfalke had survived the torture instigated by Calitain's betrayal. The big German was with Hugh from the beginning on the *Batavia's Ghost*, fighting beside him during the earliest, and most dangerous, years. It was during a skirmish with Calitain and another corsair ship almost ten years ago that the Hessian fell. The battle had been brief but fierce and the casualties that day were heavy on both sides.

The stomach wound had not taken Wüstenfalke's life immediately. Instead, the Hessian had lingered, growing sicker each day, until he'd become so crazed with pain he'd begged Hugh to end his agony, ordering him to do so with his own sword: *Kralle*, the German word for talon. When Hugh heeded his friend's last wish, it had been one of the worst days of his life.

It was not until six months later that Hugh learned Calitain's failure to recapture the *Batavia's Ghost* that fateful day had been the last straw between the corsair captain and his capricious master, Sultan Babba Hassan. Calitain left the sultan's service and stole a ship in the process, earning the lasting enmity of his former patron. After that, Calitain had kept to the shadows, a wanted man without any allies.

Since then, Hugh had used the blade in a manner that would have made the Hessian proud. The distinctive weapon, almost a two-handed sword for a smaller man, gained a reputation as fearsome as Hugh's own. Hugh was not spiritual, but he could not help feeling Wüstenfalke was sometimes beside him when he wielded the sword.

He wasn't the only one to believe such a thing. He'd heard the tales men told of him. That he was a Norse berserker reborn, a man who became so blind with rage during battle, he entered a trancelike state. Hugh stared at the weapon in his hand, wondering not for the first time if the barely legible runes beneath the sword's guard might be Old Norse.

He spoke enough German to know they were not of that language.

In any case, it was a magnificent weapon and contributed much to the lore surrounding One-Eyed Standish. It was good to have a fearsome reputation when you lived among men who respected nothing *but* fear.

He took out his whetstone and began to sharpen the already sharp blade, moving his hand in slow, steady strokes. He worked quietly for a time, the only sound the soft rasp of stone against metal.

His tired mind wandered to Daphne, but he wrenched it back. He could not afford to have his resolve weakened and gnawed at by pointless worry.

Instead, he fed his always hungry need for vengeance and turned his thoughts to Calitain.

He was astounded the slaver would dare set foot in Britain—a country he despised virulently. In spite of his French name, Calitain had grown up in London but he'd left at a very early age because of an incident involving the death of a peer. Calitain made no secret of his hatred of the aristocracy. Hugh had heard him claim more than once that he was the bastard get of a lord who'd raped Calitain's servant mother. Hugh didn't doubt that. He knew many men of his class saw their servants as nothing more than bed warmers. He'd found the same attitude in America among the men who owned slaves.

To Hugh's way of thinking, rape was as bad as murder, and any man who forced himself on another person deserved a public shaming that ended in killing. And Hugh had no qualms about delivering such a punishment.

He tested his thumb against the edge of the blade he'd just sharpened, pleased at the small cut that resulted from his featherlight touch. He flipped the sword and started on the other side.

It had been years since he'd last seen Calitain, but he

knew the man frequented the West African coastline and made his money running slaves to the Americas. The profit for those willing to traffic in human misery was even greater since the United States had banned the importation of slaves several years earlier.

A light knock on the door interrupted his musings and Will entered, his hair sticking out in all directions and his face creased with sleep.

"I came as fast as I could, my lord."

Hugh put aside his whetstone and sheathed his sword while the other man stared at the massive weapon, suddenly alert and awake.

Hugh gestured to a chair across from his desk. "Have a seat. Would you like a drink?"

"No, thank you, my lord." Curiosity and worry were writ large on his face.

Hugh poured himself another brandy and sat back. "Martín came to London with some rather important information."

"Aye, I saw him ride out."

"Martín's arrival was fortunate, as Hastings has seized Lady Davenport."

Will's pale blue eyes widened and bulged. "Good God! How? When?"

Before Hugh could answer, the door flew open hard enough to hit the wall. Martín and Delacroix entered, dragging a third man between them. It was clear his two men had already enjoyed some interaction with their captive. One of his eyes was swollen shut and his mouth was leaking blood.

Hugh got to his feet. "What have we here?"

Delacroix smiled, the vicious expression sliding over his battered face like oil on water.

"We found him riding away from Lessing Hall. It seems he'd just deposited this." Delacroix held up a small square of paper with his free hand. "Evidently he did not want anyone to know he had done so." He twitched his captive's arm to elicit a response. "Tell His Majesty why you were in such a hurry to leave his lovely house."

Hugh rolled his eyes at Delacroix's mocking form of address. His crew had been very entertained upon learning One-Eyed Standish was actually an English peer. No doubt it was the source of much hilarity on his ship.

"I was jest to drop off the note, yer, eh, Yer Majesty," the man croaked, deeming it prudent to stick with the accepted form of address. Delacroix and Martín exchanged amused looks and Hugh shook his head.

The pathetic creature coughed and sputtered, bringing up a mouthful of blood and mucus, which he spat on the rug.

"Damnation," Hugh yelled, barely moving his foot in time to avoid the gelatinous mass. He glared down at the cowering man. "Do that again and I will remove your head from your neck."

The man gaped and Hugh flicked open the note:

Ramsay,
    We've got your wench. If you don't show up with
£50,000 after dark today, at the old cottage below
the lighthouse, we'll kill her or sell her, whichever is
best for us. We know you have the money. Don't come
late and don't try to come early and sneak up on us,
we have people watching you and your house. Do
what we say or the consequences are on your head.

Hugh looked at their captive. "I suppose *you* were the *people* who were to watch us?"

"Aye, Yer Majesty," the man muttered, staring at the floor.

"You have engaged in the kidnapping and attempted ransom of a peer. Do you realize what that means?" Hugh didn't wait for an answer. "If you help me in this matter, I may decide to be kind. If you are lying to me, I will make the punishments of hanging or transportation seem like tea and crumpets by comparison. Do you understand me?"

"I'm tellin' the trufe, Yer Majesty. The man what paid me an' Jed says I was to deliver the notes and wait. I was to look fer a big bloke wiff only one eye." He glanced nervously up at Hugh as he said this. "If you left, I was to foller you. When you went to meet up tonight I was to foller and then we'd get paid."

"Where is your associate?"

"He went to London, Yer Majesty, to yer house to deliver the same note jest in case."

The man's simple story had the ring of truth. "Are any others watching the house?"

"No, Yer Majesty."

"How many are at the cottage?"

"Jes' the three blokes and the mort." He contorted his face as he tried to open his swollen eye.

Hugh gritted his teeth at the other man's disrespectful mention of Daphne. "Who are the three men?"

"I dunno. We was in the pay of the littler one, but we never know'd his name. The other two was dressed strange and didn't talk like they was from here. Frenchies, maybe. The one said he was waitin' for his ship and would kill the swell and the mort if he didn't get his money before tomorrow night," he added, giving up on opening his swollen eye.

A chill ran down Hugh's spine at his words. He turned to Will and Martín. "You know where the dungeon is, I presume?"

The man's head jerked up at the word *dungeon*.

"Aye." Will's expression was fierce as he glared down at the kneeling man.

"Please take our guest there and make sure he is kept safe and secure."

"With pleasure." Will grabbed one arm while Martín grabbed the other, and they marched their prisoner from the room.

Hugh turned to Delacroix and motioned to the small table laden with cold pies, meat, bread, and cheese. "Eat while you tell me what you found out about Calitain."

Delacroix did not hesitate to load up a plate. "We found the *Scythe* a few hours west, my lord. We'd been looking in the wrong places—searching all the smuggler hideouts and coves. Instead she was anchored not far from Plymouth, just as bold as you please. Calitain must have bought himself some bona fides. I left the *Ghost* just a few miles east with instructions to follow the *Scythe* if she goes anywhere. We're only awaiting your orders." He sank into a chair and commenced to eat.

Hugh tried not to grasp at the faint spark of hope in his breast. He picked up the glass of brandy and swirled it in restless circles while he considered the situation.

"The *Scythe* will have to leave no later than tomorrow afternoon if its crew is to meet Calitain at dark." Delacroix nodded. "You will be waiting for the *Scythe* when she moves."

Delacroix gave him a smile that did not bode well for the crew of the *Golden Scythe*. "Aye. It is long past time we finished with this, Captain."

There was a gentle knock and Kemal entered. He looked at Hugh and then at Delacroix, his eyebrows raised.

"My lord?" he asked, the two words speaking volumes.

Hugh felt his lips pull into a grim smile. "I have the beginnings of a rather lovely plan forming in my head." He poured another brandy and handed it to Kemal, his smile growing the more he thought about the next twenty-four hours. He lifted his glass in a toast.

"Here's to concluding our business with Calitain, once and for all."

Chapter Twenty-Three

Daphne felt an odd tickling sensation against her lips and brushed her hand across her mouth, drowsily annoyed at the disturbance. A deep chuckle shot arrows of terror down her spine and she bolted upright and encountered the solid body of a man. Two strong hands grabbed her shoulders and pushed her back down onto the bed. A pair of bottomless eyes bored into hers, only inches away.

"Now, now, my lady. You needn't be alarmed," Calitain said, gently brushing back the tendrils of hair that floated around her face. His eyes pinned her more firmly than his hands. "I won't hurt you." He stroked her jaw with the back of his fingers. "I came to see if you wanted to break your fast." His eyes lingered on her bodice and then he laughed. "Actually, I came to see if you would *make* us food, but then I recalled you are a fine English lady and do not know how to do such lowly things as feed yourself."

He was right; Daphne had never cooked a meal in her life. Like most women of her class, the extent of her culinary skill was the distribution of tea and biscuits.

"It is no matter," he said, continuing to study her closely while stroking her hair. "Jean-Paul is not a bad cook. Come."

He grabbed her hand and yanked her up. "You are sleeping away your day. And it might be your last, eh? You must enjoy *every* minute of it and tell me how it feels. Not everyone is fortunate enough to know when they are living their last day."

He took both her hands in his and pulled her close, until her body touched his from chest to thighs. "You see," he said, smiling down at her, "I am giving you something most people will never have when they die. You will be able to consider what your life has meant before you go to your higher reward." His gaze was rapturous and Daphne could almost hear his unstable thoughts clattering and clanking around inside his skull.

He was absolutely insane.

He released her as quickly as he'd grabbed her and Daphne followed him without hesitation, not wishing to annoy or upset him in any way. They entered the larger room and she glanced from the small table with three chairs to the mattress where Malcolm's unconscious form lay sprawled.

Calitain followed her gaze. "Ah, you look at the little lordling. Are you concerned for him? Don't be. He is fine, just a little bit the worse for drink. I think the gift of consciousness on his last day is not something he can appreciate at this point. Perhaps later in the day he will come around, eh? But for now, sit. Jean-Paul will make us a breakfast worthy of your last meal."

The other man was bent over a smoky hearth, stirring something in a large metal pot that smelled awful.

Calitain, who must have been very observant indeed, noticed the quivering of her nostrils.

"Oh, for shame!" He grinned at his partner-in-crime. "I fear your humble food is not good enough for my lady, Jean-Paul. Do you not have something else to offer? Perhaps a croissant or a bowl of strawberries and cream?" The two

men laughed unpleasantly and Daphne resolved to do a
better job of hiding her thoughts.

"Don't worry." He was beside her, moving in the disconcertingly quick way he had, standing no more than an inch
away. "Jean-Paul's food is an acquired taste, but I feel sure
you will acquire it soon enough." He tore a chunk of bread
off the large black loaf that sat on the table and slammed it
down in front of her.

"Eat," he said, his voice no longer amused.

Daphne ate. She followed his example, dipping pieces of
bread into what was very strong coffee; the combination was
surprisingly good. She studied the Frenchman surrepti-
tiously while she ate. Like the sailors she'd seen on Hugh's
ship, both Calitain and Jean-Paul were hard-looking, as if
they'd been fired in a kiln. The fine network of scars that
webbed his face and throat made him resemble a broken
piece of pottery that had been rudely reassembled. His excessively muscular forearms rested on the table, the sinews
rippling beneath his tanned skin. His hands were almost as
big as Hugh's and just as calloused from a lifetime of hard
work. He looked as if he could break her in half just as easily
as he tore chunks from the loaf of bread.

Both men moved with a brittle awareness, as if they
were constantly anticipating attack from any quarter.
While Jean-Paul was tense, Calitain looked like a man in
the process of coming undone, unraveling in fits and starts
and cracking along the many seams that riddled him. He was
never still. Even when his body was motionless his eyes
were not. They flickered restlessly about the room, like
wolves circling a kill. Sometimes his lips moved but no
sound came out, as if he were engaged in an endless internal
argument.

All in all, he was the most terrifying person she'd
ever met.

Daphne was concentrating on not doing anything that might annoy the volatile man when an agonized moan came from the corner of the room. She and Calitain turned to see Malcolm hunched against the wall, clutching his head in both hands.

Calitain burst out laughing, the sound heavy with contempt.

"Wha—what was in that bottle?" Malcolm whimpered.

"It was nothing but a little clap of thunder." Calitain's lips twisted into a sneer. "It is one of Jean-Paul's specialties. You don't want to hurt his feelings, do you?" His face lost all traces of humor. Jean-Paul, also, had stopped whatever he was doing to stare at Malcolm's shivering form.

"No! I meant nothing untoward, only that is was rather . . . uh, strong. Devil take it but my head is pounding. Might I have some tea?" he asked piteously.

Daphne could have told her cousin that asking these men for anything, not to mention anything that sounded too English—a country they clearly despised—was a terrible idea.

Calitain was at Malcolm's throat before she could blink.

"*What* did you say?" He shook Malcolm so hard his teeth rattled like dice. He shot a look at Jean-Paul while squeezing Malcolm with one enormous fist. "What did my lord say, Jean-Paul?" he bellowed, spittle flying out of his mouth and showering Malcolm's face.

Jean-Paul shrugged, taking his time before uttering the first words she'd heard him speak. "Ee wants *le thé*." He grinned, mockingly emphasizing the French word for tea.

"That's what I thought he said." Calitain frowned, as if he couldn't decide whether he was pleased or disappointed he'd been correct. He blinked at Malcolm as if he did not recall why he was gripping his neck.

Malcolm gaped up at his captor and Calitain released him just as abruptly as he'd grabbed him, watching without a flicker of emotion as Malcolm slid back to the soiled mattress, gasping for air like a trout on a stringer.

Calitain pointed to the third chair at the small table. "Get up and eat. Jean-Paul will give you some good French coffee, none of *le thé*."

Malcolm scrambled to his feet and flung himself toward the flimsy chair, his face an unrecognizable mask of fear. He yelped and cringed when Jean-Paul came up behind him and thumped a chipped bowl of coffee onto the table.

Calitain watched Malcolm eye the bowl and then look at both his and Daphne's mugs. For an instant Daphne thought Malcolm might be so foolish as to request a proper mug. But then he looked at Calitain and saw something that made him pick up the bowl and slurp noisily.

Calitain turned to Daphne, a malicious gleam in his eyes.

"We are not set up for company, Jean-Paul and me. We did not think to be here so long. In fact, we did not think to be here *at all*, but for his lordship here. It is my fault, I suppose. I took *his lordship's* word that he would have my money. The word of a gentleman, eh, Jean-Paul?"

The other Frenchman gave Malcolm a look that was even more menacing for its complete detachment.

Malcolm prudently studied his bowl of coffee rather than the mentally unhinged pirate with whom he'd made such an unfortunate alliance. Calitain's hand clenched and twitched on the table and Daphne thought he might strike Malcolm, but he just waved his hand, the gesture flamboyant and dismissive.

"I should not complain," he said, leaning close and taking one of Daphne's hands, caressing it lightly as he spoke. "But for the lordling here, I would not soon be reunited with my good friend One-Eyed Standish. I cannot wait to see the complete look of surprise on my old friend's face. Just like the surprise it was for me to learn he is Lord Ramsay, eh? A *baron*, Jean-Paul! Can you believe it?" He looked from Daphne to the laconic Frenchman.

"*La vérité est plus étrange que la fiction*," Jean-Paul said, smiling at Malcolm in a particularly unpleasant way.

Calitain, too, looked at Malcolm, his expression like that of a young boy who was about to pull the wings off a fly.

"*You* know what Jean-Paul means, eh, milor'? You are an educated member of the British aristocracy. No doubt you speak several languages with fluency." Calitain's eyes lit with unholy amusement when Malcolm miserably shook his head. Calitain barked a laugh and turned to Daphne, looking at her with narrowed eyes, as if he were reading something written on her face. "You are a smart lady, not like your ignorant companion, eh? Tell milor' what it means."

"Truth is stranger than fiction," Daphne translated, giving in to the small smile that twitched at the corner of her mouth as she stared across at Malcolm. In spite of the unstable nature of her current position, she was truly enjoying Malcolm's humiliation at the hands of the diabolical lunatic. Calitain saw her smile and laughed; this time the sound was genuine.

"I think the lady does not like you, *my lord*."

Daphne realized the madman was purposely misstating Malcolm's title. He was crazy, not stupid.

His eyes flickered to Malcolm for an instant before returning to her. "Your *amour*, Lord Ramsay, he and I have been—shall we say—not the best of friends these past years. He is a man who holds a grudge, you see." He lifted his hands in a very Gallic gesture and shrugged. "I am not that type of man. To me it is business. You understand?" It seemed he was finally asking her a question that required an answer.

"Yes." Daphne gave him the answer he wanted and kept her face expressionless.

Calitain continued his monologue with a deeply thoughtful look. "For years I've had to deal with Standish and his grudge. He is, as you say here in England, like a bulldog with a pork chop, eh?" He shook his head in disgust. "He should be grateful to me rather than bearing me a grudge." He pounded his fist on the table, his eyes glazed as he relived some memory. "Yes, he should thank me. But for me, he would have been dead while still in the hands of the sultan. *I* am the one who convinced the old man to let him live after he was caught scheming. I made the sultan see that he would get many hours of entertainment from him." Flames danced in his dead black eyes. "But for *me* your baron would have been dead long ago. But does he thank me? No!" He lunged toward her but Daphne kept utterly still as he hung over her, seconds lasting years.

He slumped back. "No, he does not. He harries and torments and tracks me like an animal, until there is almost nowhere I can go where I am not hounded and hunted for the bounty he has placed on my head." Calitain stared through, rather than at, Malcolm, his hands clenching and unclenching. Clenching and unclenching. For a moment, she believed his tenuous grip on sanity might slip enough that he'd put a period to her miserable cousin's life.

But then he deflated, the tension draining from his body like water from a sieve. His hands, which had twitched with menace a mere moment earlier, now lay motionless on the table like two belly-up crabs at low tide.

His face spasmed with an emotion Daphne could not decipher. His eyes locked with hers, an almost pleading expression in them. "It is because of *him* that I am forced to deal in slaves—it is the only thing I can do to make money. And it is his fault I must always stay aware and awake. Always on the move. Always wondering if one of my very own crew will claim the bounty that sits so heavily on my head." His neck bowed, as if the burden were weighing on him at that very minute.

Daphne stared at his shaggy black head and imagined smashing her half-empty mug over it.

He leapt to his feet and his chair skittered backward and collided with the wall behind it. "Now I see that being in this miserable little cottage is nothing but an act of God. The Mohammedans call it kismet—you have heard of this?" he asked Daphne, his conversational tone at odds with the mad joy shining from his eyes.

"Fate."

He hooted and slammed his hand down on the table, making the crockery dance. "I begin to see why Standish is so enamored of you, my lady. I, too, enjoy the company of a well-read lover. Is that not so, Jean-Paul?" He threw the question over his shoulder.

The Frenchman smiled.

Calitain snatched up his fallen chair and dropped into it.

"So, we wait for Standish to come tonight. And then, *mon amour*," he said, gently chucking Daphne under the chin with rough fingers, "I will take the money he has brought and I will kill him and finally put an end to this." His smile was almost beatific. "After tonight, kismet can bugger off to torture some other poor fool."

Once again it was Malcolm who shifted the insane man's attention away from her.

"What about her?" Even with his life hanging by a thread, Malcolm hated her.

Quicker than a bolt of lightning, Calitain swung his arm, his hammer-like fist striking Malcolm's face so hard he spun in a complete circle before toppling to the floor.

"Who are *you* to ask me anything?" Calitain raged. "You are not even necessary to me anymore. If Standish comes or if he does not come, what good are you? I should kill you now. Or maybe I should let *her* do it?" He towered over Malcolm's writhing body.

Daphne's eyebrows shot up at the sudden proposition and she wondered if she would be capable of killing Malcolm.

Calitain moved to the next topic as quickly as he had the last one. "You are a fool and have an inflated sense of your worth, just like the rest of your class. I have known many men like you." He threw back his head and crowed gleefully. "I am *related* to men like you. Ah, that surprises you, eh? Scum like me making such a claim?" He booted Malcolm in the backside, but his heart didn't seem to be in it. He turned back to the table and flung himself into his seat with an irritated grunt. Malcolm crawled across the floor and tucked himself into the dark corner, not even on the mattress now. Daphne believed he might have realized, at last, that staying out of Calitain's reach was the wisest thing he could do.

Jean-Paul approached the table and plunked down two bowls of food with his usual lack of decorum, not bothering to offer any to Malcolm. Daphne picked up her spoon without hesitation and began eating.

Calitain had sunk into a blue study and paid her no mind. He dragged the bowl toward himself and began shoveling food into his mouth, his gaze bent inward.

They ate in silence for what seemed like an eternity before he slammed down his spoon.

"Yes, I know about *noblemen*." His lip curled. "My dear departed mother learned about *noblemen* too, much to her detriment." He dipped black bread into the bowl and stuffed it into his mouth, masticating furiously before he spoke. "She was brought to England by some French aristos who were visiting their English cousins. The son of the house took quite a fancy to my mother, the charming little maid who didn't speak any English."

His black eyes narrowed. "But that suited the little lordling. He was not interested in witty banter with a mere *servant*. After he raped her, my mother went to her mistress, her dress in tatters, tears running down her face, and she told

her what the fancy English lord had done to her." He smiled
bitterly. "Her mistress slapped her face so hard she was
knocked off her feet. She called her a *putain*—you know this
word?" he asked Daphne, not waiting for an answer. "It means
whore. Yes, she called my mother a whore, a lying whore and
then she turned her off, threw her out of the house with nothing
but the clothes on her back. She cut her adrift in a country
whose language she could not speak or understand."

Calitain's fist was curled around the handle of the spoon
as if it were a weapon. "So my mother did the only thing she
could to feed herself. She became a whore, a real whore." He
gave Daphne a chilling smile. "Yes, it is true—you are sitting
next to a man with almost as fine a bloodline as yours. Imagine that! Of course, I was not raised in the family mansion,
but I saw it often as I grew up. From the outside, at least.
Perhaps some of that aristocratic polish rubbed off on me
after all, eh?" His nostrils flared with insane rage and his
black gaze ate through her like acid; Daphne thought she
might die with a spoon in her chest.

But then he closed his eyes and an oddly sensual expression slid over his harsh features. "I saw my dear father again.
You see, he married and had children, my half-brothers and
-sisters. We did not move in the same circles, of course." He
chuckled harshly. "I spoke to my father just one time, but
really that turned out to be enough for the things I wanted to
discuss with him." He gave her a pained look. "You will be
sad to hear he did not welcome me with open arms. In fact,
he denied that I was even his son! That would not have
bothered me so much, but then, if you can believe it, he
called my mother a lying French whore who'd seduced him."
His voice broke on the last word and he stared sightlessly
into space before striking the table so hard she was amazed
it didn't shatter.

His eyes slowly refocused on her. "I couldn't have that,
could I? Would you sit still while *your* mother was being so

wickedly disparaged? And after she had died so young. So worn out by the life he'd inflicted upon her, leaving me to fend for myself at a tender age, forcing me to follow in her footsteps. I told him all of this. I believe I finally convinced him of the truth . . . in the end. Yes, right before he died he said he was sorry for how poorly he'd treated me—his eldest son."

He spread his hands out on the table and studied them as if he'd never seen them before. "I was so saddened by his death I had to leave England." He looked up, his tone confiding. "If I am to be perfectly honest, I must admit that being taken by corsairs shortly into my first journey at sea was the best thing that could have happened to a young and impressionable boy like me. Don't believe everything you hear about how wicked they are, my lady," he said wryly. "They do provide opportunities for advancement—you just need to seize them when they present themselves."

He sighed. "That is something Standish *never* understood. I always wondered why he thought himself so much better than me, and now I find out he is nothing but another spoiled aristo. Wait until I tell him that we might even be related." He grinned, his mad eyes shining at the thought of his reunion with Hugh.

Dear God.

Calitain talked almost nonstop during the course of the day. Daphne's brain was so frayed from the nerve-racking combination of remaining expressionless and listening to Calitain rave, she felt she might begin raving herself. If the man's fighting skills were not up to scratch, he could always talk a person to death.

As dusk approached, Malcolm gathered his nerve and asked the questions Daphne wished she might, but did not dare.

"The men have not returned. It would appear Ramsay has not tried to go to the authorities or plan any kind of ambush. It will be dark soon, what should . . . what should I do?" he asked, his confidence visibly dwindling the longer he had to endure the demented pirate's stare.

Calitain heaved himself up from the table and went to the small alcove behind the hearth. He returned with two weapons, one of which he tossed to Jean-Paul, who caught it handily, although he'd appeared to be dozing in the ragged chair beside Malcolm's mattress.

"I am going to prepare to greet Standish, milor'. And Jean-Paul will prepare to greet whoever he brings along. I hazard he'll bring his boy-whore and whoever else he keeps with him at that big house. If your hired hands have done their job, he should not be bringing the entire crew of the *Batavia's Ghost* with him." Calitain drew a wickedly curved blade from an ornately decorated scabbard and turned to Malcolm wearing an utterly chilling smile. "But really I do not care who he brings or how many. We will be ready no matter what, eh?" He looked at Jean-Paul, who was running a stone along the edge of his blade.

Malcolm, who appeared to have learned nothing about their captor's uncertain temper in the past day, had more questions. "But what if my men have failed to notice and Ramsay sent a message to his ship? What if *all* his men arrive to help him? How can you two possibly fight them all?"

Calitain laughed, punctuating the sound with a long rasp of stone on metal as he sharpened the wicked blade.

"We have you on our side, don't we? That should be worth at least a dozen men, eh?" He and Jean-Paul laughed so hard they had to pause in their sharpening. Once he'd caught his breath he looked up. "Don't you fret, little man, my men will be here; we will not be overmatched." He eyed

Malcolm scornfully before turning his attention back to the dangerous metal in his hands.

Malcolm opened his mouth just as Calitain sprang to his feet.

"Shh!" he hissed, cocking his head and listening.

They sat perfectly still and Daphne heard the low keening of a horn.

Calitain's mouth curved into a triumphant smile and he grabbed his sword belt from the table, strapping it around his waist before sliding the blade into the scabbard.

"What? What is it?" Malcolm demanded.

The pirate ignored him as he and Jean-Paul readied themselves. Calitain lighted the only lantern while Jean-Paul picked up two rough torches from a bundle that lay on the floor and lit them at the hearth. The two men headed toward the door.

"Come," Calitain said, beckoning to Malcolm. "You hold the girl—you can do that much, can you not?" He yanked open the door.

Jean-Paul followed closely behind him, stopping long enough to place a torch in each of the metal rings set in the wood pillars beside the door.

"You arrogant, insolent scum," Malcolm murmured, leveling a look of sulfurous hatred at the backs of the two sailors. "Come on!" He grabbed Daphne's upper arm. "Don't try anything on me, precious, because I'm in the mood to cut your bloody throat without thinking twice." To illustrate his point he held up the small knife he'd menaced her with inside the coach.

Daphne followed him willingly, grateful to leave the confines of the wretched shack. It was immediately clear why the cottage was so dank and damp; a small inlet lay not two hundred feet from the building. The rank smell of rotting vegetation filled her nostrils and told her the little cove was marshy and would be too shallow for any but the smallest of boats.

Daphne saw a flicker of light some distance from the shore and realized a rowboat was approaching. Whoever it was, they carried only a small light, which they flashed briefly before concealing it again, as if to avoid detection.

"Ho there!" Jean-Paul called out. The four of them stood frozen in suspense, waiting for some response; but there was nothing but the faint sound of oars in water. Jean-Paul cupped his hands to his mouth to call again when a familiar voice sounded behind them.

"Ho there!"

Chapter Twenty-Four

Daphne spun around. "Hugh!" Malcolm's arm snaked around her neck and jerked her back, his knife against her throat.

"Move again and I'll cut you," he hissed in her ear, the cold metal scraping her skin.

"Standish!" Calitain's voice pulsed with excitement as Hugh rode into the small circle of light cast by the torches and lantern. "You are early, my friend. You must be eager to see me."

There was Hugh, so impossibly huge on Pasha. Daphne's eyes searched frantically behind him—but there was just one other figure. Only Kemal attended him. Her heart, which had just been leaping for joy, froze. How could two men fight Calitain's entire crew?

"Hugh! It's a trap! There are more men in the—"

Malcolm's arm tightened and cut off her air along with her words. Daphne struggled against him, feeling the point of the knife beside her eye. "You'd better shut your mouth, you slut!"

Calitain turned to look at them, making a *tsk, tsk, tsk.* "Come now, lordling, that is no way to treat a lady. Loosen your grip and lower the knife. We don't want you slipping and perhaps poking out your own eye, do we?" His words were polite but his tone was menacing.

Daphne felt the internal struggle in Malcolm, but he lowered the knife and loosened his arm, allowing Daphne to gasp for air.

Calitain turned back to Hugh. "There, you see? Nothing to worry about now; she is safe."

Daphne raised her eyes to Hugh and he gave her one of those smiles that melted her heart, before gracefully sliding off Pasha. He handed the reins to Kemal and walked toward the two men, keeping his eye on her as he came closer. He moved with a lazy confidence that breathed new life into her. She was no longer alone; she now had somebody to fight beside her—her eyes flickered to Kemal, who smiled reassuringly and nodded—two somebodies.

"You've come far enough," Calitain cautioned him.

Hugh stopped. He was no longer wearing his eye patch and his mismatched eyes were so beautiful it was almost painful. He was dressed in a way she'd never seen before. Everything he wore, from his caped coat, shirt, and gloves to the leather of his thin-soled boots, had been dyed the deepest black and fit his body like a second skin. The only part of his ensemble that wasn't black was the monstrous sword slung over his shoulder. Daphne gaped; it was so big it was like something out of an Arthurian legend.

"That is a very fine horse you have there, Standish," Calitain drawled, his tense stance belying his casual words. "Perhaps I will take him with me after I kill you."

"You can try," Hugh said, the amiable rumble of his voice at odds with the contemptuous look he cut the other man, "but I think he might have other ideas. You see, he has no tolerance for treacherous slaving trash."

Calitain looked amused rather than insulted by Hugh's words. His crazed eyes were the only part of him that betrayed his unease as they jumped nervously between Hugh and the rowboat, which seemed to be creeping toward the shore at a glacial pace.

"I want my money. Where is it?" he asked, no longer bothering to act amused.

"Money?" Hugh chuckled. "Why the devil would I bring you any money?" His laughter filled the night air.

Calitain's hand settled on the hilt of his saber. "I'll not play word games with you, Standish. Give me the money or his lordship here"—he tossed his head toward Malcolm—"will kill the whore."

Daphne met Hugh's gaze. He stared at her, pointedly looked at the ground, and gave a slight nod. The message was clear: she should drop to the ground. Malcolm tightened his arm, but, thanks to Calitain's earlier words, he didn't raise the knife. It was now or never.

Daphne opened her mouth wide and sank her teeth into Malcolm's hand.

Malcolm gave an earsplitting howl and yanked away his arm, shoving her in the back to get away. Daphne stumbled and caught her foot in the hem of her tattered gown. She struggled to free her slipper and Malcolm buffeted her in the head, knocking her to her hands and knees.

"You bitch!" He stared from her to the bloody bite on his hand and drew back a booted leg to kick her. Daphne threw her body sideways as his foot came her way, closing her eyes and wrapping her arms around her head to protect it.

But the blow never came.

She peeked out between her forearms and squinted up at her tormentor. Malcolm still stood over her but his eyes were no longer fixed on her. Instead, he was staring at a sharp point sticking out of his chest, just above his breastbone. He opened his mouth but nothing came out. His wide eyes flickered from the metal point that spitted him to Daphne.

He blinked. "I—"

Blood spilled over his lips and dripped down his chest to

join the stain that was spreading out from the wicked metal point like a vivid sunrise. He plucked at the arrow convulsively as his eyes rolled back in his head and he crumpled like a cow felled by an ax.

Daphne wasn't the only one staring in openmouthed surprise. Calitain and Jean-Paul began to back away. As if waking from a daze, they simultaneously drew their weapons, eyes darting and searching frantically for the source of the arrow.

Daphne pushed herself to her feet and lurched toward the cottage, expecting any moment to feel the cruel bite of an arrow through her own chest. When she collapsed against the wall, still unscathed, she turned to find Kemal crouched beside her, his usually inscrutable face smiling.

"Come, my lady." He slid his arm around her and pulled her toward the safety of the trees, where he'd tethered the two horses.

Hugh had watched her escape and winked at her before turning to the two men, his movements those of a relaxed, leisured man. Calitain and Jean-Paul, on the other hand, were back-to-back, circling and craning their necks toward the men in the boat. The skiff hit the rocky shore and the men who poured out of it threw off their dark cloaks.

Daphne didn't need her spectacles to recognize the giant figure of Two Canoes as he advanced on them, a massive bow in his hands, another arrow nocked and ready to release.

Calitain turned from the men converging on him, a grudging smile on his face. Daphne could only see Hugh's profile; for once, he was not smiling.

"You"—Hugh pointed to Jean-Paul—"throw down your weapon. This is between me and *him*." One of his hands was at the hilt of his sword while the other held the scabbard; a hiss filled the air as he freed the giant weapon and tossed the belt to the side.

Jean-Paul and Calitain looked at one another for a long

moment. Daphne could not see well enough to say what passed between the two men but at the end of that lingering look, Jean-Paul threw down his sword and pulled out three more knives, one from the back of his belt and one from each boot. He threw the knives into the dirt at Two Canoes's feet and swaggered toward the armed group of men with his hands in the air.

Calitain smirked at Hugh. "It has been a long time, eh? Not since I killed the last owner of that fine sword, Wüsten-falke. Tell me, what have you done with my crew?" He sounded curious rather than concerned.

"They have been redistributed." Hugh held his own blade almost negligently.

"And my ship?" Calitain's voice was tight and a violent twitch pulled at his left eye.

"*Your* ship?" Hugh chuckled. "Why it seems to have fallen into the hands of someone better equipped to keep hold of it. You might recall Martín Bouchard? The man who made such a mess of you and your crew the last time he ran across the *Golden Scythe*?" Hugh didn't wait for an answer. "He's been hounding me for some time for a ship of his own. Nag, nag, nag! So when we found the *Scythe* just bobbing about, waiting to be taken—actually *begging* to be taken with that pathetic crew you left in charge—I decided to give in to his infernal nagging. The last I saw of Martín, he was moving his possessions into your cabin." He grinned. "He was complaining the wardrobe was not large enough for his needs."

All day long Daphne had seen Calitain move quickly, but she'd not seen him move with the intent to kill. If she had been standing where Hugh was, she never would have moved in time to block the savage man who launched him-self with such lightning speed.

But Hugh merely smiled and stepped to his blind side as Calitain's blade came down where his head had been only a split second before. When the crazed man turned around to confront his tormentor, Hugh was already pressing down on him, plying the giant sword as if it were an extension of his body. He drove fast and hard with the five feet of steel, and the two weapons met with a harsh *clang*, metal scraping against metal as each man pulled away, circling like tomcats in an alley.

Even with no knowledge of fighting, Daphne could see Calitain was dangerous. Not only was he remarkably strong and fast, but his unpredictable behavior would keep his opponent constantly guessing. He darted and retreated like an angry hornet, driving at Hugh's blind side and pushing him back a step with each thrust. Hugh moved fast for such a big man, but he would always be slower than Calitain. Not only was he slower, but he was handicapped by his blind eye, a disadvantage Calitain was making the most of.

Even so, a six-and-a-half-foot man swinging a five-foot sword was no small threat, and Hugh wielded the lethal blade with fearsome strength. Whenever his sword made contact with Calitain's, the impact reverberated through the smaller man's body like vibrations through a bell. If even one of those blows got inside Calitain's defenses, it would prove fatal.

The disparate weapons meant this fight was unlike anything in a text on swordplay. The movements of both men were abrupt, actions conceived in haste rather than the result of any given style.

The only sound beyond the scrape of metal on metal was the shuffling of feet as the crowd of men moved to accommodate the combatants. The two men were in a world of their own, their breathing increasingly harsh. Their dance was mesmerizing, the vicious beauty of flickering steel lulling Daphne into a trancelike state. But then, in the midst of it all, Calitain broke from the dance and feinted to Hugh's left, the move faster than her eye—or Hugh's—could follow.

Daphne saw the mistake almost before it happened: Hugh's parry was a fraction too wide, meaning he could not draw back in time to block Calitain's sweeping horizontal slash. The wickedly curved scimitar sliced through shirt and skin with equal ease.

Daphne screamed and lunged toward Hugh, but Kemal held her with arms like iron.

She struggled against him. "Stop them!" she yelled at the circle of silent men. "One of you—help him!" But nobody would meet her eyes as she stood helpless in Kemal's unbreakable hold.

The distinctive clang of metal on metal drew her eyes and she gasped. A long gash striped Hugh's exposed torso, bleeding freely and soaking the thin black cloth around it, which gaped open across his chest.

The sight of Hugh's blood seemed to rejuvenate Calitain and he laughed with maniacal glee and thrust his sword over and over, driving Hugh back, pace by pace by pace.

Hugh blocked the flurry of blows, his face grim and set, his single eye struggling to do the work of two. Daphne saw the piece of driftwood just as Hugh's heel struck it, the impact jarring him as he parried a forceful thrust. He stumbled and his balance was temporarily disturbed, making it impossible for him to completely dodge a sweeping cut aimed at his head.

Calitain's blade missed Hugh's blind eye, leaving a long, thin trail of blood across his forehead.

The pirate laughed. "Oh, what memories this brings back, eh?" he said, using precious breath to taunt Hugh, who'd quickly resumed his stance after his brief stumble but was still being driven back. "Perhaps I will do your other eye today—just as I warned the Barbarossa to do so long ago—the day he killed your friends and promoted me." He grinned. "But he said he liked to make you watch the things he did to you. He liked that too much, eh, Standish? But it cost him his head in the end." He thrust, the movement quicker than the flick of an adder's tail. "I won't make the same mistake."

Hugh dropped low and dodged to Calitain's right to avoid the saber, his huge body flowing like water. Daphne was watching his face when it changed. One moment it was the blood and sweat-slicked face of the man she knew and loved, an instant later he was the embodiment of vengeful fury. Someone else looked out of his eyes—both eyes, although she knew that was impossible—and they leaked hate as freely as his body leaked blood.

Rather than retreat, he took a step forward. The action so startled Calitain, he stepped back and hesitated a second too long to make his next thrust. It was all the time Hugh needed to heft his sword and swing the huge blade in a sweeping arc, the heavy steel slicing the air like a giant scythe.

Calitain had to scramble to dodge the massive blade, staggering to one side and overcorrecting in his haste to avoid the savage cut.

He wasn't smiling when he righted himself just in time to block the next blow. Hugh wielded his blade like an ax as he stalked the retreating man, and the clang of metal on metal was deafening as he swung five feet of steel with all the power his enormous frame could summon.

Calitain blenched each time he blocked blows so savage Daphne couldn't believe his blade didn't snap in half.

It ceased to be a swordfight and became a beating. Again and again and again Hugh bashed the stumbling and retreating man. Calitain's sword arm became shakier and his battered body responded sluggishly to his commands, until a stunning blow knocked the sword from his nerveless fingers. He cried out, turned on his heel, and ran for the shack.

But Hugh was like the winged hangman of death on his heels. He flipped the pommel in his hand and swung the blade with the flat side leading, the wide expanse of the sword making a deafening *crack* when it struck Calitain across the shoulders and slammed him to the ground.

Calitain screamed and crawled on hands and knees before rolling over and wedging his back against the wall. He covered his head with his arms.

"Do it! Finish it, you bastard!" he yelled from behind his protective cage, his words coming between ragged gasps for breath. "This is what you've wanted for fifteen bloody years! What are you waiting for?"

Hugh raised the sword over his head, both hands gripping the pommel.

Daphne opened her mouth but her throat was frozen.

Flickering torchlight turned the massive blade into a flaming sword. It hung for what seemed like forever. Nobody spoke, nobody moved, nobody even breathed.

And then his arm began to fall and Daphne closed her eyes.

But the dreaded sound of a man being cut in half never came. She opened her eyes a crack and then a little more.

Hugh stood over his vanquished foe, his sword arm hanging at his side, the blade once again cold, dull steel.

"For fifteen years I was convinced you ruined my life. For fifteen years I lived only to find you and kill you." He shook his head in disgust. "And for fifteen years I've given you control over me, Emile."

Calitain looked up at the sound of his Christian name, his eyes darker than pits in Hell.

Hugh stared down at the other man. "I've been a fool—but no longer. Killing is too good for you and it is no good for me. You've dealt in human misery and have ruined thousands of lives, but mine will not become one of them." He turned away and Daphne closed her eyes to stop the tears, sagging bonelessly against Hugh's giant horse. *Thank God.*

Something warm and velvety brushed her cheek and she opened her eyes to find Pasha watching her. He snorted and gave her a bored look, as if to say this type of thing happened all the time and she'd better become accustomed to it. His jaw resumed its stolid up and down motion as he enjoyed a brief snack, not about to allow human foolishness to get between him and a meal.

Daphne brushed away her tears and rubbed his soft chin. He snorted his approval and stomped a huge hoof in emphasis.

"You are wise to remain calm," she murmured, scratching his chin and causing his eyes to close in equine bliss. She turned toward the clutch of men surrounding the man she loved. "I can see how living with such a man will have taught you that." She planted a kiss on the big beast's nose before going to his master.

The men moved aside as she came near.

Kemal bowed. "The demons are gone now."

Daphne didn't need to ask which demons he meant— she'd seen them with her own eyes.

She touched Hugh's shoulder, almost afraid to look at his face when he turned around. But the first thing she noticed were the bloody cuts that ran across his chest and forehead and she sucked in a noisy breath. "Hugh! Oh, God—"

A big hand gently tilted her head so she was looking at his face, rather than his chest.

"Hello, darling." He stared down at her, his eyes—both of them—warm and smiling.

Daphne's gaze briefly flickered to his blood-smeared forehead. The cut was oozing, but it was nowhere as deep as the one on his torso.

"Hugh, your wounds. You must—"

He wrapped his arms around her, lifted her off the ground, and squeezed her so tightly she couldn't breathe. "Oh my beautiful, beautiful, darling," he rumbled in her ear as he held her close. "How many times do I have to tell you not to get into carriages with strange men?" A chuckle reverberated through his chest as he crushed her body against his.

"Hugh . . . can't . . . breathe."

He lowered her to the ground. "I'm sorry, sweetheart," he murmured, and then covered her mouth with his and kissed her with an urgency that told her more than words ever could. He released her and leaned back to look at her, wincing. "Lord, what a bloody mess I've made of your fetching gown. And I do so love that shade of yellow on you."

Daphne laughed weakly. "I'm afraid you were too late to ruin this one, my lord."

"We'll get you a dozen more in this same design." He ran a big finger around the tattered keyhole neckline, his nostrils flaring as he skimmed her bosom.

She took his hand and pressed it against her cheek. "Don't you ever think about anything else?"

"You mean other than women's fashions?"

Daphne sighed, and Hugh laughed, pulling her close to kiss the top of her head. "Come, let's get you home." He led her toward Pasha.

Daphne stopped and motioned to Malcolm's body. "What about him?" she asked, and then pointed to Calitain and Jean-Paul, who'd been bound and were being led to the rowboat. "And them?"

"Sir Malcolm tragically perished inside his fishing hut when it caught fire. Unfortunately, he'd been drinking and did not smell the smoke." Hugh's grim tone told her how much he regretted her cousin's death.

"As for those two?" They watched the men scrambling into the boat, their hands tied behind them. "I think it is time they had a taste of what they were so willing to inflict on thousands of others. Martín will drop them off with some associates of ours who will make sure Calitain and his crew of slavers don't see freedom for a very long time."

He slid his hands around her waist and lifted her onto

Pasha's back before swinging up behind her only a tad less gracefully than usual. He circled her with one arm and pulled her back against him, his breath hot on her ear. "Shall we go home, my darling wife-to-be so I can get you out of these clothes and into bed?" He gave a wicked chuckle. "Or should we see what is possible on horseback?" His hips pushed suggestively against her back.

"What? You are not up to doing both, my lord?"

His booming laugh echoed through the small clearing and Daphne indulged in a private smile; it seemed she knew how to flirt, after all.

Chapter Twenty-Five

It was well past midnight by the time Hugh came to Daphne's chambers. He wore the same robe she'd seen once before, a luxurious Chinese silk that hugged the contours of his big body. He had a plaster on his temple and a much larger bandage around his chest.

She was sitting at her dressing table, brushing her hair, and their eyes met in the glass. Her entire body tightened at the look on his face as he came toward her.

"Has everything been taken care of?" she asked.

He took the brush from her hand and began to run it through her hair, his gaze fastened to hers. "Malcolm and the fishing shack are now smoldering rubble and Calitain and his crew of slavers are on a long journey." He paused in his brushing and glanced up. "You will be interested to hear it was your prior maid—Fowler, or Mrs. Blake, rather—who was responsible for the anonymous letters Will Standish has been receiving."

Daphne was more than interested—she was stunned. "How did you learn that?"

"Martin went to Whitton Park to find her husband—Blake—to . . . er, question him about his part in your abduction. Instead, he found a very remorseful Mrs. Blake. It seems Blake had absconded and left her to face the consequences." He hesitated. "I'm afraid Mrs. Blake also confessed she was the one who'd disclosed the truth about your sons to Blake to begin with in a moment of weakness. Blake, of course, told Hastings. In any case, she sent the letters, hoping to make up for her actions."

Daphne nodded, too hurt by the woman's betrayal to want to think about it just now. "Well, it sounds as if everything is under control."

"Almost everything." One side of his mouth pulled into a suggestive smile. Naturally, she blushed and, just as naturally, he laughed.

Her heart fluttered under his steady regard. "You are the most appalling tease, Hugh."

"Your hair is glorious," was his answer. He slowly pulled the brush from crown to waist. The sensation of his hands in her hair was nothing compared to watching his powerful arms and hands flexing as he groomed her. And he looked achingly gorgeous in his extravagant robe. Daphne glanced at her own reflection and frowned. She wore the nicest nightgown she possessed, but it was a simple, prim thing, not the lacy confection he was no doubt accustomed to seeing on his women.

She looked up from the high neck of her nightgown and met his eyes. Her breath caught; the planes of his face looked hard and dangerous and his mismatched eyes burned. He put the brush on her dressing table and took her shoulders and drew her back against him, until she could feel the hard ridge of his erection. He flexed his hips against her, stroking his arousal in the hollow between her shoulder blades. He drew in a deep breath and closed his eyes, an expression of bliss on his face.

Daphne stared; could there be anything more erotic than bringing pleasure to one's lover and watching his face? It made her want to give him more, to drive him crazy with sensation, as he had done with her.

Daphne turned around, until she was facing him. When she rested her hands on his thighs, his eyes opened and his lips parted, as if he'd just woken from a trance. She tugged open the sash that held his robe closed. When she parted it, her heart pounded so clamorously she felt sure he must hear it.

She looked at the hard, thick length of him and found it difficult to breath. Her eyes drifted from his arousal to the thin line of hair that ran up his enticingly muscled stomach and up between his ribs before spreading to cover his chest with golden down. He shuddered and leaned in to her touch when she took him in her hand.

"Daphne." The single word sounded as though it had been torn from him: a prayer, a command, a plea.

She stroked the thick shaft from the base to the smooth head, fascinated by everything she held in the palm of her hand. The skin was softer even than a baby's, but it covered a singularly masculine hardness. Moisture formed under her touch. "Tell me how to please you," she said, barely able to tear her eyes away from this fascinating part of him.

He looked at her from beneath heavy lids. "Keep stroking me just as you are. The end is very sensitive, as are my jewels." His green eye glinted with a mixture of amusement and arousal, his voice deeper than usual. She raised her other hand and cupped him, amazed by the fragility of the male body.

"God yes," he groaned, and she smiled at the raw need in his voice, stroking him more confidently while learning the shape of him. She ran her thumb through the moisture he was producing and used it to lubricate her motions. When her hand had developed a rhythm that seemed to please him she leaned in and lapped at his head with her tongue.

"Bloody hell!" The words burst out of him and his feet slid farther apart, bringing him lower and closer to her mouth. She took only the head of him, her other hand continuing its gentle massaging.

"Yes, just so," he praised hoarsely. His hand moved to caress the line of her jaw and then touch the place where her taut lips wrapped around his hard, silky flesh. He made a low animal noise, as if pleased by how he stretched and filled her mouth. "Take me deeper. Ah yes . . . that's it." He wove his fingers into her hair, holding her lightly.

Daphne realized, with no small amount of surprise, that such an activity required a good deal of coordination. Even so, she could tell by his breathing he was struggling to restrain his crisis, so she must be pleasing him.

Encouraged, she moved a hand to hold the base of him and his movements immediately became less controlled, until she felt a tremor ripple through him. He slid his fingers to where her mouth held him and she felt his body stiffen just before he jerked away, holding her firmly with one hand when she tried to follow.

She stared in wide-eyed fascination as he administered a few savage strokes and then spent onto his stomach, his muscles as hard as stone as his body absorbed an explosion of pleasure, and then another, and another.

Daphne had never felt so much power—or such burning physical need.

His eyes opened a crack as he stood swaying in the wake of his climax, his chest heaving. He gave her a languid smile, looking very much like a big cat that had just consumed a bowl of cream.

"You made me come quicker than a boy with his first opera dancer."

Daphne's face heated at his crude words and she dropped her gaze.

He traced her lips with the tip of one finger and chuckled tiredly. "What? Are you shy with me? After that?"

Daphne watched his naked body with growing lust as he

went about the business of cleaning himself. He filled the
basin from a pitcher of water, his back to her, offering an
utterly fascinating view of long, powerful legs, firm, muscular buttocks that flared out to an impossibly broad back
and shoulders. He tossed the soiled cloth to the floor and
turned, catching her gawking, his lips pulling into a wicked,
satisfied smile.

"Come," he said, taking one of her hands and leading her
to her bed, waiting until she climbed in before getting in
beside her and pulling the sheet over them.

He turned on his side, his eye staring into hers as his
fingers worked the buttons of her nightgown, not stopping
until it was open to her navel. His gaze flickered to her exposed
torso and he groaned.

"I'd love nothing better than to slide inside you and ride
you to pleasure." He slipped a warm, strong hand over her
ribs, stroking her sensitive skin with agonizing lightness.
"But your ancient lover needs a little time to rally the troops,
so I'm afraid I'll need to find an alternate way of amusing
us." He reached up to brush back a stray curl, his warm,
slightly roughened hand going from her face to her neck,
before finally stopping at her breast. He circled his palm
over her already hardened nipple and she closed her eyes.

"Did you learn your spectacular new skill from the book
you stole from me?" he whispered, and then took her breast
in his mouth.

Daphne seemed to be having a difficult time finding the
right words.

"Borrowed," she gasped, her voice sounding like somebody else's.

He laughed softly, the sound arrowing from her breast to
her sex. "Do you wish me to take my time or do you want
your pleasure now?"

She kept her eyes closed, trying to give his question the
consideration it deserved. On the one side there was—

His hand slid down her stomach toward the top of her thighs. When he reached his destination he cupped her through the fine cotton, holding her in his grasp, his clever fingers motionless. "Tell me what you want. I'm yours to command— you have enslaved me, Daphne."

She thrilled at his words, her hips shaking with need. "I want my pleasure now." Her voice shook and her face flamed and the last word was a choked whisper.

His lips curved against the thin skin of her temple. "As you wish, my love." He took her earlobe between his teeth, nipping and sucking while his hand inched up the front of her gown with agonizing slowness, until the hem passed over her private curls.

His finger brushed the seam of her tightly clenched thighs. "Open your legs for me, Daphne." The muscles of her thighs jumped and twitched as she spread them. His clever finger grazed her lips from her bud to her entrance, stroking her more firmly with each sweep, until he parted her.

Daphne shivered and clenched her jaws at the moans threatening to escape.

He slid a finger inside her and Daphne bucked against his hand.

His thumb sought the most sensitive spot on her body and began circling while he probed, gently pumping until she could hear the wet sounds of her arousal. He slid a second finger to join the first, his thrusts deeper and less controlled while his relentless thumb worked her until excruciating pleasure overwhelmed all thought and released her from her body.

"That's right, my beautiful darling. Give yourself to me," Hugh whispered as she clenched and convulsed around him, his fingers teasing a second even more acute explosion, the alternating surges of raw sensation robbing her of all thought.

Daphne was vaguely aware of Hugh settling beside her and covering her cooling, sweat-slicked body. She struggled to open her eyes but they were weighted by pleasure and all she could do was make a low noise of contentment.

He slid an arm around her and stroked her, his rhythmic motions hypnotic. Daphne burrowed into him, careful of the bandage across his chest and lowered her mouth over his heart, strong and steady, beating for her.

"I love you, Hugh." The words were simple and yet the most complex any human could ever say to another.

"Mmmm, sweetheart, how I have waited to hear those words from your sweet lips." His voice was husky. "I love you, Daphne."

Daphne slid her arms around the muscular column of his neck. "I was so afraid for you tonight, Hugh. I died a thousand times watching you—fearing for your life." She bit her lip, her eyes blurring with tears. "I know I agreed in London that I could live with you taking voyages on the *Ghost*, doing what you love, but—"

"Daphne." Hugh rolled onto his back and pulled her with him, positioning her on his hips and looking up at her, smiling tenderly. "I promise, my love, no more sword fighting."

She blinked away her tears. "No?"

"No. As for voyages on the *Ghost*? I find suddenly that I'm no longer interested in going out to sea and looking for trouble."

Daphne was dizzy with relief. "Do you mean it? Are you quite certain? I don't wish to force such a decision on you. I wouldn't like it if—"

"Shhh, sweetheart. You aren't making me do anything I don't wish to do." He tucked a strand of hair behind her ear and kissed the palm of her hand. "I'm terribly sorry you had to become a part of my sordid past. You must have been terrified to find yourself in Calitain's hands."

"I was terrified at first, but as the day dragged on I was too exhausted to be scared." She shook her head. "That man is three-quarters insane. He did not hurt me; he saved that for Malcolm. He ranted and raved endlessly. How do you think he met Malcolm?"

Hugh shrugged. "Many Englishmen see no harm in profiting from smuggling, and that leads some to engage in the slave trade, which is more lucrative than any other contraband. I wouldn't be surprised if Malcolm knew somebody who'd done business with Calitain in the past and couldn't resist the return such a venture promised."

"I'm so sorry, Hugh."

He narrowed his eyes. "Sorry? Why? What have you done?

"I believe it was Malcolm who tampered with your saddle, or caused it to be done. I think he was mad enough to think I would marry him and feared you might somehow interfere. If I had told you about his blackmailing, perhaps none of this ever would have happened. It is because of *me* that your life has been threatened at least twice."

As usual, Hugh surprised her. He laughed.

"What could you possibly find amusing in *that*?"

He set his hands on her hips, and his eyes flickered over her as he smiled, the look softening the hard planes of his face. "I'm sorry, I should not laugh. But one of the things you must know about your husband-to-be is that he has a very odd sense of humor."

She crossed her arms. "I've noticed."

"I laughed because I learned the saddle vandal is none other than your cranky servant Rowena."

Daphne's jaw dropped. "*What?*"

"The poor woman believed I had come to disrupt your life the same way Hastings had. She was only trying to protect you. I've told her she is to forget both the unfortunate incident as well as any thoughts of trying such a thing again. I can forgive her for it once; twice would be more difficult."

Daphne's mind raced, recalling all the times Rowena had

railed against Hugh, detailing what an evil man he was. She shook her head, but that did nothing to dispel the thoughts.

"She must be unbalanced."

"She sounded sane when she confessed. I think she was just doing the best she could to protect you and the boys. She feels nothing but remorse."

Daphne had no idea what to say. None.

Hugh pulled her down until he could bite her lightly on the chin. "Have you lost your voice, my dear? Do I need to find some way to help you locate it again?" He raised his eyebrows suggestively, his other hand moving to the apex of her thighs, his hips flexing beneath her. Only now did Daphne realize what she was straddling.

"How can you jest about such a thing?" Daphne demanded. She gasped when his fingers slid into her curls.

"Oh, I'm very serious about *this*, I assure you."

Daphne gritted her teeth at the bolt of intense pleasure his finger incited and gathered every bit of strength in her body to put her hand on his forearm. "Hugh."

"Hmm?"

"Will you look at me, please? My face," she amended when he continued to stare at the place between her thighs.

He looked up, a dreamy smile on his face. "Yes, darling?"

"You are very good at distracting me."

"I intend to practice and get better." She frowned and he pulled back his hand, his expression instantly—but not convincingly—meek. "But I can see that now is not the time—you have something you'd like to say, my dear?"

"Will you tell me what happened to your eye?" She steeled herself for the look of cold menace he'd worn the last time they'd spoken of his eye.

But he just smiled. "Of course I will tell you, darling. I did not mean that it should be a subject of mystery between us." He reached back and stuffed a pillow beneath his head and then lay back, his hand absently stroking her knee.

"The maiming itself was unpleasant but the circumstances surrounding it were worse." His eyes flickered to hers. "I'll have to tell you a bit of a story so it will make sense."

Daphne nodded.

"Several months into my captivity I devised a plan of escape. I included in my scheme several other prisoners with whom I'd formed a type of brotherhood." He paused, his expression pensive. "The experience of slavery is difficult to explain to one who has not known it firsthand. Suffice it to say the sensation of being owned and having no power is so engulfing it is often easy to forget you are anything other than a possession. The effect over time is debilitating and some men lose the battle against their transformation to chattel." He gave her a grim look. "It was the look in those men's eyes that scared me. I swore I would wage war to avoid becoming one of those men.

"The first skirmish in that war was to make the association of like-minded men who would support each other when the despair descended, which it often did." A muscle jumped in his temple and Daphne felt a pang of guilt for opening this door. But it was too late to close it now.

"There were ten of us, a group small enough in number to avoid too much notice but large enough that we could temporarily crew a ship if we were lucky enough to escape. It took several months of painstaking work to develop our plan. We were very close to making our move when, without any warning, nine of us were seized and dragged to the sultan's dungeon.

"One of our number was not present—a half-English, half-French sailor named Emile Calitain."

Daphne felt a chill.

"Calitain had been a slave for perhaps a year longer than I. When he did not appear with the rest of us, I believed he'd fought against our captors and been killed. Unfortunately that was not the case."

Hugh's face was once again a mask of fury but at least he displayed none of the killing rage he'd displayed while choking the life out of Malcolm or fighting Calitain. His anger now seemed less . . . consuming.

"As luck would have it—bad luck—Faisal Barbarossa, the same man who'd captured me, was in port. Barbarossa was a cousin of the sultan, and when he learned about the escape plan and my part in it, he was more than happy to use his considerable skills to get the truth from us."

Daphne didn't want to ask, but if she didn't, this history would continue to stand between them. "Skills?"

Hugh stared up at her, arrested by the word. He swallowed several times, hard enough that she could hear it.

Daphne laid a hand gently on his chest, which was rising and falling faster. "We do not need to speak of this."

"Yes." He inhaled deeply and expelled the breath. "We do. I don't wish to keep things from you, my love, but neither do I wish to sully your mind with the depths to which men will sink—not that you haven't already experienced the worst of it, yourself." His jaw was so tight it hurt just looking at him. "They wanted to know who was involved and who was helping on the outside. I had shared the plan with our group, but the guard whose family was helping us—well, only me, Delacroix, and a very old Portuguese man named Alto knew the guard's name."

Daphne realized his forehead and neck had become sheened with sweat.

"They tortured us all together, forcing the others to watch." He gave a bitter laugh. "It was an incentive and it would eventually pay off." His hand tightened until it hurt and his eyes blazed with hate, fury, pain. "The things they did to us—" His gaze flickered to Daphne. "You know better than most what some men will do when they exercise utter dominion over another human being."

Daphne cocked her head and squinted, for a moment

unsure of what he meant. And then the truth came like an avalanche, crushing the air from her chest, the thoughts from her head, until she was pinioned, the horror of what he'd endured as heavy as a mountain of stone.

As Daphne stared into his cold, hard face, she understood his earlier fury at what Malcolm had done to her. It had been the outrage and anger any decent man would exhibit at such news—but it had also been the murderous wrath of a fellow victim.

Oh, Hugh.

"I don't know how many days it lasted. I lost consciousness more than once during the ordeal. It was after a particularly gruesome interlude with our torturers, an episode which four of our number did not survive, that Calitain entered our chamber of horrors." His lips twisted. "No, he was not dragged in bleeding and in chains. His fat, rosy face was, in fact, the very picture of health and his new clothing proclaimed him to be a sailor, rather than a slave—a member of the Barbarossa's crew, to be precise. It seemed one man's decline—or nine men in this case—was another man's means of ascension. Calitain bought his way out of slavery using his friends as currency." His expression was both stricken and confused, as if he still couldn't believe the betrayal. His eyes became glassy. "This man had been like a brother to me, Daphne. *Like a brother!*"

Daphne squeezed his hand and he gave her the corpse of a smile. "Even in my reduced condition, the sight of his well-fed face incited me into a lamentably animalistic state. By the time they pried me off him, he was minus an earlobe." He shrugged. "It was better than nothing, but it wasn't nearly enough to make up for the loss of my friends."

Tears ran down her face; hot, tiny rivers Daphne wished could carry away his pain.

"Barbarossa took my eye and told the others he would continue taking eyes until those of us who were left were blind. I was not surprised when Alto broke down." He shrugged. "I couldn't blame the old man, he'd suffered the punishments of the damned. The Barbarossa killed him anyhow." He exhaled a long, slow stream of air from between pursed lips.

"The three of us who remained—me, Delacroix, and a Hessian named Wüstenfalke—were thrown back into the cells. Without their help I would have lost more than an eye. Delacroix stitched me up as best as he could and saw me through a fever that would have taken my life. While Delacroix doctored me, Wüstenfalke did most of my work because the sultan expected us to keep working, no matter that we were half-dead." Hugh snorted. "Babba Hassan had a palanquin bring him out to the pits especially to watch me work."

Daphne shook her head. "Why? Why did he hate you so much?" It was a question she'd wanted to ask ever since he'd told her about the ransom and how the sultan had lied.

"I brought it on myself, of course. You see, I was foolish when I was captured, and fought—taking any opportunity to resist. During one of those fights I killed two men—one happened to be a younger brother of the sultan." He gave a humorless laugh. "The sultan never forgave me. Not because he cared about the man—in fact, Babba Hassan had been systematically killing off his male relatives for years, just in case they might challenge him. No, he punished me because I was a slave who'd had the audacity to attack one of his masters." He shoved his hand through his hair and Daphne saw it was shaking. "That kind of defiance set a bad precedent. He could never reward me by letting me go free—no matter how much ransom money my uncle's agent offered."

Daphne's mind reeled at the sheer violence the man before her had undergone.

Hugh stared up at her, his expression oddly taut. "Have I frightened you away?"

She took his face in her hands. "You silly man. You could

never frighten me away. I'm afraid you are stuck with me forever." She kissed his mouth. "I adore you, Hugh. I can't wait to fetch the boys home and begin our life together." She kissed the tip of his nose. "I'll be happy if I don't see London or a society invitation for a decade." She kissed his chin. "I can't wait to be your wife."

Hugh cleared his throat almost nervously. "Uh, I'm glad to hear that."

Daphne pulled back and stared at him. "What is it? Why are you looking like that?"

He opened his mouth. And then closed it.

Daphne frowned. "Hugh, you are worrying me. What is it?"

He laid his hands over hers and squeezed gently. "Oh, it's nothing to be worried about. Or, at least, not very much. It's, er, about the wedding."

"The wedding?"

"Mm-hmm."

"Our wedding?"

He gave her a smile that was more of a grimace. "Yes, that would be the one."

"What aren't you telling me?"

"Well, it appears my Aunt Letitia is in charge of organizing it."

Daphne dropped her hands and sat back. "Oh?" She shrugged. "Well, that is probably best as I have neither the interest nor skill to organize even a small wedding."

"Ah, that's the thing."

"What thing?"

"It isn't going to be a small wedding."

"It isn't?"

He shook his head.

Daphne had a sinking sensation in her stomach. "How big?"

"Big."

"Oh, Hugh, why? It will take ages and ages and will be absolutely agonizing, even worse than a ball."

He wrapped her in his arms. "I know, I know. It's wretched, but Aunt Letitia says it is what must happen if we are to salvage matters."

"But it will mean more time in London." Her words were muffled against his chest. "How long?"

Hugh kissed the top of her head. "I don't know, I told Aunt Letitia that was her decision." He paused. "It's not for us, Daphne. It's for the boys."

She pulled back and pushed her hair from her face, which was coloring.

"Why are you blushing, sweetheart?"

"Because I'm ashamed."

"But why?"

"Because I'm so selfish—I was only thinking of myself and not the boys. Or you."

He grinned up at her. "You should be ashamed, darling. I have an excellent idea of how you can make it up to me."

Daphne choked on a laugh. "You are so wicked."

He nodded, his eyelids drooping low. "Why don't you come down here and let me show you just how wicked I can be?"

And so she did.

Epilogue

London, sometime later . . .

Hugh leaned back in the carriage as it pulled away from Thornehill House, sighing with contentment as he wrapped his arm around Daphne and pulled her close.

"Well, thank God that is done." He glanced down at his wife. "I had no idea Aunt Letitia would pull a bishop out of her hat to marry us. Did you?"

She smiled tightly. "Yes, I knew about the bishop *and* the three hundred and fifty guests we just left behind at our wedding breakfast. I knew about *all* of it and more. Have you forgotten that *I* was forced to discuss nothing but gowns and lace and menus and—"

Hugh kissed her. "Are you trying to say that you've missed me, my dear?"

Daphne growled and Hugh knew she still hadn't forgiven him for allowing his domineering aunt to have her way with their wedding.

Lady Letitia had been more serious about the scope, scale, and grandeur of the wedding than Hugh had believed. She'd actually appeared at Lessing Hall in person the day after Hugh's encounter with Calitain. She'd given Daphne a mere afternoon to pack and had spirited her away to London, where they would collect the boys and then head to Lady Letitia's country estate, leaving Hugh all alone at Lessing Hall. She had then refused to allow the two of them to spend even a night under the same roof until they were properly leg-shackled, as she termed it.

Hugh lifted Daphne's chin toward him, feeling the tightening in his groin that occurred every time he looked into her hooded blue eyes. Or at any other part of her.

"Did the boys enjoy getting to know all their cousins and aunts and uncles?" He bit back a grin at her narrowing eyes. "Did *you* enjoy your holiday, my dear?"

She made an unladylike noise. "Months spent planning a wedding at your Aunt Letitia's country house was not as harrowing as watching you engage in deadly swordplay, but it is a close second." She cut him an arch look. "But we have all the time in the world to discuss how you managed to escape such torture."

Hugh winced.

Her stern expression melted slowly into one of her serious smiles. "But not on our wedding day." She sighed. "I am very glad it is behind us. I will be even happier when we can return to Lessing Hall. I've had quite enough of my first Season."

"What?" Hugh demanded in mock surprise. "How can you wish to leave the scene of your greatest triumph? Haven't you read the papers, my love? You managed to snap up the King's Privateer, by God! The man every matchmaking mamma called the Catch of the Season. No, wait—" He paused and pensively stroked his chin. "I believe I was actually called the Catch of the *Decade* in several newspapers."

"Yes, I read that article—it was right beneath the one about a man from Newington Butts who claims to have created a perpetual motion machine."

Hugh paused, arrested. "And did he?"

Daphne rolled her eyes.

Hugh continued, undaunted. "You can't wish to leave London so soon. Don't you want to flaunt me before all your competitors and gloat while they gnash their teeth in frustrated anguish?"

She stifled a giant yawn with one white-gloved hand.

Hugh threw back his head and laughed. "You are demolishing my self-esteem," he accused, pulling her onto his lap and attempting to peer down the bodice of her pretty blue gown. "Why is it that I have the strongest urge to wreck another of your garments, Lady Ramsay?" He leaned low to lick the top of one breast. He could not seem to get close enough to her; the urge to be wrapped around her body and inside her was all consuming. She giggled at his nuzzling and Hugh pulled back in shock.

"Did my scholarly wife just *giggle*?" He held her at arm's length and stared in stunned surprise.

"Absolutely not." She tipped her chin so he could continue his kissing of her neck. "I've never giggled in my life."

"I should hope not," he murmured, dragging his tongue across the hollow at the base of her throat before pausing at her collarbone, molding his lips over the delicate skin. "If there is to be any giggling done in this family, I believe I should be the one to do it. You have no experience in that area, while my giggling is legendary." He slid a finger beneath her bodice and pulled it down so he could more easily explore with his tongue.

Daphne moaned and wiggled deeper into his lap.

"Good God!" he muttered as she ground against his aching organ. "I feel like I've already waited a lifetime. I fear I cannot wait until we get home," Hugh confessed, reaching for the hem of her gown and running his hand up one leg as he pushed her bodice down further.

"We are less than two minutes from home," she murmured, her words utterly lacking in conviction.

"Too long."

"Mmm," she breathed, her hand moving down his chest to his tight breeches, feeling the truth of what he said for herself. "I should say just long enough."

"*Lady Ramsay!*"

Daphne gave a low chuckle. "I have not made love in a carriage before, my lord." She traced the length of him while her other hand unfastened the buttons of his breeches.

"I know how much you enjoy research," Hugh said hoarsely. He rapped on the roof and when the vent opened he shouted, "Once around the park!" He lowered his mouth to her rumpled bodice to resume his exploration. "Now, where was I?"

"Only *once* around the park, my lord?" Daphne nibbled at his earlobe and slid her hand around him.

"Twice around the park!" he bellowed, his voice cracking as her hand began to move.

This time he was positive he heard her giggle.

AUTHOR'S NOTE

Hugh and Daphne's marriage would have been forbidden by the 1560 Table of Kindred and Affinity.

Laws of consanguinity were ecclesiastical laws, not English Common Law, that were created to prevent marriage among blood relations. The definition of a blood relationship was much stricter in 1811 and marriage was believed to create an actual blood-relationship in the eyes of the church. So a woman who married a man's brother became that man's sister in blood under ecclesiastical law.

If a person decided to thumb their nose at ecclesiastical law (as Charles Austen, Jane's brother, did when he married his deceased wife's sister in 1820), their marriage wasn't illegal or void, but it was voidable. A voidable marriage could always be challenged by anyone who could prove they were an interested legal party, meaning that, in theory, the marriage would always be vulnerable.

Interestingly, the marriage of first cousins was not forbidden by the Table of Kindred and Affinity.

Read on for an excerpt from SCANDALOUS,

the third novel in the Outcasts series,

coming soon!

1815

Martín drummed his fingers on the gleaming wooden railing and stared at the Dutch ship. The vessel was upwind and too far away to smell the stench, but Martín could imagine it. The pitiful cries of the slaves were another matter. Those he could hear even from this distance.

The dirty business of slaving was more lucrative than ever since the British and Americans had banned the importation of slaves several years back. The American South paid well for smuggled slaves as it could not function without slave labor, a fact Martín knew all too well.

He turned to his first mate. "How many crew, Beauville?" he asked in English, rather than his native French. He'd made an effort to speak English more often several years earlier, after the British granted him his Letter of Marque and Reprisal, the document that made his life as a privateer possible.

Beauville lowered his spyglass. "No more than forty, Captain, and most of those appear to be either drunk or incompetent."

Martín laughed at the man's dry assessment and strode to where his second mate held the wheel. "Ready the men, Daniels, and then prepare to make the offer."

Although the Dutch ship had suffered some damage to its mast, it appeared to be a well-maintained ship and far cleaner than the usual run of slavers. Martín's own ship, the *Golden Scythe*, had been a slave ship before he'd captured her, but she'd cleaned up nicely. He regarded the immaculate deck with pride. With a crew of seventy men and fourteen cannon, the *Scythe* greatly outmatched the Dutch brig and was a force to be reckoned with.

Still, it was never wise to be too cocky. If the *Blue Bird* carried to capacity—five hundred souls—the money involved was great. Things would become ugly if the ship's captain was determined to fight for his cargo. Martín was confident he would triumph in such a struggle, but he knew it would not be without cost.

A flurry of activity broke out as he watched the other ship, the crew flapping about like a flock of frightened hens. A dozen men stood near the main mast and gestured wildly to one another—a few with machetes. Martín shook his head; something odd was going on.

Daniels appeared beside him. "Everything is prepared, Captain, and we await your command."

Martín turned to Jenkins, his man of all work, who held out two pistols for his inspection. He checked the guns carefully before inserting them into a holster that kept them resting on his right hip while his rapier lay on his left. The holster was of Martín's design and allowed him to draw any of the three weapons quickly.

He glanced into the large mirror Jenkins held up before him and flicked an imaginary piece of lint from his immaculate coat. He took his time and made a minute adjustment to his cravat, careful to keep his movements languid and his expression bored. His crew was watching, their battered faces amused, yet proud. Martín knew they drew strength from his reputation as a cold, hard killer who was more concerned with his cravat than his life.

To be honest, Martín's stomach churned just as much, if not more, than that of any other man on the ship. If anyone died today, he would be to blame. While that might not bother his conscience—a hardened, shriveled thing—his pride was fat and healthy, and he could not bear to have poor decisions attributed to him.

Martín flicked his hand and Jenkins took away the mirror. Daniels's mouth was pursed with disapproval. The younger man still found his behavior shocking, even though he'd been Martín's second mate for over a year. Martín found his irritation amusing. "Make the offer, Mr. Daniels."

"Aye, Captain!" Daniels turned and gave the midshipman a hand signal and a second later a loud crack issued from one of the *Scythe*'s cannons.

Mere seconds passed and the smoke had barely cleared when a black flag crept up the Dutch ship's pole.

Martín exhaled, weak with relief; they would parley.

"Excellent shot, gentlemen, and very persuasive. Beauville, please escort their captain to the wardroom when he arrives." Martín unhooked his weapon belt and handed it to Jenkins. "Don't unload these just yet," he advised before going below deck.

Once inside his cabin, he cast his hat onto the desk and collapsed in a high-backed chair, careful not to crush the tails of his coat.

His excessive concern for his appearance was only partly feigned: he loved fine clothing. As a young slave in New Orleans, he'd envied the wealthy, well-dressed men who'd frequented Madam Chantel's establishment, vowing he would dress even better one day, when he had the means. Now he was rich enough to dress however he pleased, and what pleased him was the best.

He idly studied his reflection in the glass that hung over his desk, frowning at the man who looked back. Nobody would ever mistake him for a European, no matter how light his eyes, and hair. Even though his skin was paler than anyone imprisoned on the Dutch ship, Martín could be bought and sold just as readily were he to set foot on American soil. Actually, he would face death if he returned home, death being the punishment for a runaway slave.